CW01021731

First edition June 2021
© Cherry Publishing
71-75 Shelton Street, Covent Garden,
London WC2H 9JQ, UK

ISBN 9781801161022

Love You Wild

Becka Mack

Cherry Publishing

Subscribe to our Newsletter and receive a free ebook! You'll also receive the latest updates on all of our upcoming publications!

You can subscribe according to the country you're from:

You are from...

US:
https://mailchi.mp/b78947827e5e/get-your-free-ebook

UK:
https://mailchi.mp/cherry-publishing/get-your-free-uk-copy

Dedication:
To my husband,
Thank you for believing in me.

PROLOGUE

"I've already watched you go. Made plans. Prepared my heart. I know how to deal with the leaving; it's the staying I'm not ready for."
— L. E. Bowman

Here's what I've learned:

True love finds you when you stop looking.

When you're not expecting it.

When the timing is so horribly wrong and you can't even imagine putting yourself out there, can't imagine opening your heart to someone who has the potential to destroy it, destroy *you*.

Sometimes, when it's the last thing you want.

You stumble upon it, or rather, it stumbles upon you, leaving you with no choice but to accept it, take it in, every single bit of it.

It knows your struggles. It sees your challenges, the barriers you've set up to deter anybody who dares to travel the dark, wooded path to your heart.

And it doesn't care.

It stands before you in all its glory, telling you the time is here and now. Reach out and grab it before it's too late.

Because when you find someone who makes your heart stutter in your chest, when you find someone who makes your face light up every single time your eyes fall upon them, that smile of yours splitting your face right in half, you take the risk. You dive right in.

Forget about the timing, the expectations, the fear.

Back the hell up, get a running start, and then

dive

right

in.

CHAPTER ONE

Claire

"You can't be fucking serious, Claire. Come on!"

I'm very fucking serious, and I mean, really, the fact that he thinks I'm anything but is highly comical at this point. The way Aaron's tugging at his stupid hair and rubbing his stubbly jaw tells me that he might actually be starting to believe me, despite his insistence that he doesn't. He keeps dragging his sweaty hands down his pants, pacing back and forth in our apartment.

My apartment.

Poor guy looks stressed. It's entertaining, to say the least. Quite a stark contrast from his normally thoughtless attitude.

"I've never been more serious about anything in my life," I toss out with indifference, as if I couldn't possibly care any less. Because, seriously, I couldn't. I arch a dangerous brow in his direction, pinning my arms across my chest, daring him to test me.

When he reels on me, his red face is painfully twisted. It looks like there's some potential for tears. I wouldn't mind at all. Lord knows I've wasted my fair share on this man.

"Claire, be reasonable, babe. It was a mistake. Don't act like you're so perfect."

"I'm far from perfect, but I would also never do what you did. Now get the fuck out of my apartment." By some luck of the draw, my finger doesn't shake when I point to the door, all his shit piled in front of it. I took the liberty to pack for him while he was at work. He still hasn't thanked me.

"Where the fuck do you expect me to go?" He's drained, exasperated, pretty blue eyes wild. I used to love those eyes. Now I want to jab my fork into them.

1

"I don't know. Dave's. John's. Any of the girls you've been fucking behind my back." All great suggestions, in my opinion. "Quite frankly, I don't give a shit where you go." I grace him with a patronizing smile and lift one shoulder, letting it drop. Not my monkey, not my circus. Not anymore, at least.

Rolling his eyes, he crosses over to me with two long strides. I rip my hands from his slimy grasp the second his fingers curl around mine, instead turning away. I can't look at him right now. I don't want to see him, not now, not ever.

"It was one fucking time, Claire!"

"*Bullshit*!" It's as close to a growl as one can possibly get. The anger is rolling off me in palpable waves. I feel ridiculously like an X-Man right now, like if I concentrate just hard enough, my rage might be enough to send him flying right through the door. Wishful thinking, right? "Do you know how many stories I've heard in the last twenty-four hours?"

Too many. Clearly, I should have taken heed the first time rumors flew around about him getting down and dirty with someone else. But I was naive.

No, naive isn't even the right word. Just stupid. I was stupid. And blind.

"And you're believing them over me?"

My jaw drops. He cannot be serious. "That's exactly what I'm doing."

"I love you," Aaron pleads, eyes begging.

I scoff. It's fitting. This whole scene right here is ridiculous. "Doubt it, but either way, you probably should have thought about that before you fucked somebody that wasn't me." Striding to the door, I kick his things out of the way with maybe a little more force than necessary, swinging the door open. I sweep my hand out in front of me with a quiet sigh. "Get out, Aaron."

His mouth gapes. I want to punch it. "You're serious."

I give him a clipped nod, trying like hell to keep my voice steady. "I'm serious. Take your shit and go."

His shoulders drop and he makes a noise, halfway between a sigh and snarl. Muttering something I couldn't give two shits, he picks his bags up off the floor. Pausing in the doorway, one finger tapping on the frame, he looks back at me.

"Could you at least take a few days, think about it? We can't just be over, Claire. Please."

I hesitate, staring into the handsome face of the man I've loved for the last three years, give or take. Aaron studies me, considers the fact that it looks like I might be wavering, and his lips start to curve up into that smug, jerky smile that I fucking *loathe*.

And that's all it takes. With the roll of my eyes, I slam the door in his face, flipping the lock behind him.

"*Claire!*"

"Bye asshole," I whisper, grabbing a bottle of wine off the counter and stalking into my bedroom.

I flop down on my bed, the bottle rolling into my side as I stare at the ceiling.

"Fuck," I mutter, dragging my palms down my face. My eyes are stinging, my nose crinkling, that familiar tell-tale sign that lets me know I'm about to ugly-sob.

"Don't you dare, Claire," I tell myself. "Don't waste your time."

I've already wasted three years; I'm sure as hell not giving him anything more.

Unfortunately, my brain, body, and heart are rarely ever on the same page. One lone tear sneaks out the corner of my eye and trails a hot path down my cheek, curving around my neck. I squeeze my eyes shut as if that's going to stop the rest of them from coming.

It doesn't.

I'm snotting all over myself—it's not attractive—when my phone starts vibrating in my back pocket. I'm tempted to chuck it across the room, stomp on it, flush it down the toilet, but there's a tiny part of my brain that hasn't been screwed by my entire world being turned upside down, and that part still has some logic left in it. So instead, I breathe a sigh of relief when my best friend's beautiful face lights up my screen.

"Charlee?" I drag the back of my hand across my face, wiping at something wet and slimy. I'm a sight to be seen right now, I'm sure of it.

"Hey gorgeous," she says softly.

Here's the thing about Charlee: she's amazing and kind and generous with the people she loves. But she's also hard as hell. She tells it like it is and gives it to me good when she thinks I need it, which is sometimes often. Which was definitely this morning. She keeps me in check. So, when she's ultra-soft with me, when she's treading water instead of drowning me in it, that's when you know whatever happened was bad enough that she's truly worried about sending me off the deep end.

I don't say anything, just choke on a sob.

"Be there in fifteen," is all she says before the line goes dead.

And like clockwork, she strolls through my door with her spare key fifteen minutes later, arms full of groceries. She drops them on the counter and starts pulling things out like it's a treasure chest. Treasure chest of treats—the very best kind.

"I got everything. Chips, ice cream, cookie dough to eat and cookie dough to bake, licorice, sour watermelon slices, annnd…" She pulls out one last thing and the corner of her mouth lifts. "Crunchwrap Supremes."

A bubble of laughter creeps up my throat and bursts past my lips as I lunge for Charlee, wrapping my arms around her and collapsing into a fresh set of choking sobs. "You know how much I love those."

"They're terrible for you." Her hand is buried in my hair while she whispers to me, rocking me gently back and forth. She'll make a great momma one day.

"They shouldn't make something so terrible taste so delicious," I sniffle.

Charlee and I wind up drunk in my bed, watching episode after episode of trash TV, covered in junk food. I lick the dripping ice cream from the cookie sandwich I made and try to send her an angry glare with my glossy eyes. It doesn't work; she just snorts a laugh and pats my head.

"You yelled at me this morning." I pout up at her, pushing my bottom lip out as far as it'll go in my current state.

"Yeah, well, you needed it." Her arched brow dares me to argue with her. I won't; she's right. "That piece of shit has been in your life way longer than you should have ever allowed him to stay."

"Why do girls do this to themselves? Why do we get so far up our own asses that we refuse to see what's right in front of us? Do you think I'm that desperate? That I wanted to be in a relationship so bad that I refused to acknowledge the pile of garbage that my life turned into?"

Charlee tosses the bag of licorice she's holding, watching as it goes sliding across the bed, dropping to the floor. Her eyes shift my way. "Oops."

She sits up and turns to me, grabbing my wrists in her hands. I still have my ice cream cookie sandwich in my hand, so this is an issue. I drop my head toward my lap, trying to eat my cookie. Priorities.

"You're ridiculous," she laughs out. But then she sighs and reaches forward, brushing a loose wave off my face, tucking it behind my ear. "You weren't desperate to be somebody's girlfriend, Claire. You were desperately trying to hold onto the man you thought he was and the relationship you had in the beginning. And there's no shame in that. You were hoping for the best, but at a certain point, you gotta stop giving people like Aaron second chances."

"Why do people change?" Aaron had been perfect in the beginning. He'd reeled me in in literally one night. I was hooked on a couple charming lines, a few touches, and a sweet goodnight kiss. By the end of the week, we'd been on three dates and I was officially his girlfriend. It'd been that easy. But the last year-and-a-half had been anything but easy.

"Sometimes people change for the better, Claire." Leaning back against the pillows, she stretches her legs out in front of her, fingers lacing behind her head. Her tone changes to match her relaxed posed. "And sometimes they mold themselves into giant pieces of steaming dog shit, like Aaron."

Barking out a laugh, I pull myself from the bed, dusting the crumbs off my sweater. "Okay, I need to put this crap away. I feel so sick and the last thing I wanna do is let myself gain twenty pounds because he couldn't keep his dick in his pants."

Charlee lifts one perfect brow. "Did you literally just get up and dust yourself off? What a great euphemism. I like it." She grins when my eyes roll. "You're gonna be okay, Claire, I know it. You're strong. Don't let him ruin you."

"He's not ruining me." No. I refuse. Still, I tack on a quick, "Just maybe for men."

"But he's not a man; he's a child. You need to get laid by a real man who's gonna toss you around and show you how to feel good."

The tip of my finger absently traces the shape of my lips. That'd be good, to be honest. The sex was often enough with Aaron, but less than stellar. Same position and always over in three minutes, start to finish. Like, including foreplay. Which didn't really exist. Which means I barely ever got off.

Thank God for little plastic toys that vibrate.

"We had to use lube," I blurt out.

Charlee blinks up at me. "What's wrong with using lube? I use it sometimes. You can get those tingly ones, or the flavored ones, or—"

6

"No, like, we *had* to use it." I stare at her, eyes wide. "I never got wet for him. Not for the last while, at least."

Charlee deadpans for a solid minute. Then she collapses backwards on the bed, clutching her stomach, howling with laughter. "Oh my God, Claire, c'mon! How? *How!*" She grabs my shoulders, giving me a violent shake. "How did you go so long like that?"

"I took care of it myself," I say with a shrug.

She gives me a wicked smile. "I bet you did, dirty girl. Okay, you gotta get *properly* laid."

"I literally *just* broke up with my cheating boyfriend. Don't think I'm ready for that yet."

"Why not? This is the best part of a break-up! Now you go out and let all the guys tell you how gorgeous you are and how much they wanna get between those luscious thighs of yours. Then you let them do it, and you feel really fucking good."

"It's tempting." I stumble my way to the kitchen with my arms full. Charlee slides in after me, slamming into me from behind. "But I'm not in the right space for that. I don't do casual well. I'd probably just wind up crying all over them."

"Can we at least go out next weekend and drink our sorrows away? Dance? Grind up on some guys? You don't have to go home with them. Just let them whisper dirty nothings into your ear."

"Isn't it sweet nothings?"

Charlee makes an unimpressed face. "You don't need sweet, Claire. You need dirty. Trust me. It's thrilling to have a guy tell you he wants to bend you over his car and fuck you until you scream his name."

"My God, Charlee, what the hell have you been up to?"

She hits me with a sly wink. "Wouldn't you like to know."

"Literally, yes. It sounds infinitely more exciting than my lackluster sex life."

Leaning over the countertop, she looks me over, all squinty-eyed. "You know, I bet Dex would totally be all over this with you. You guys could be fuck buddies until you get your groove back and you're ready to move on. He'd go for it. He'll make you feel good."

A shudder rolls down my spine at the thought of Dex and I, naked, together. Again. "Can we maybe not talk about me and your brother having sex?"

"Why not? You've done it before." She pops a Dorito out of the bag, wags her perfectly shaped brows, and shoves it in her mouth.

"Once. We've done it once. We both agreed it was weird; he's like my brother."

"I'm just putting it out there. You already know you can do it and still be friends after."

"He's my boss."

"He was your boss when you fucked the first time, too."

I throw my hands in the air and walk away from Charlee. She's relentless when she wants to be, and relentless about me and her brother is not really what I want to deal with right now.

The sex was great though, I'll give him that. Dex is a giver. And oddly enough, Dex and I have insane chemistry. We always have, which is probably why we hooked up the first night I moved to Toronto to work with him. But in the end, we both knew it was a mistake. Unfortunately, I met Aaron three weeks later.

"I'm totally going into work tomorrow hungover. Might even throw up at the office." I've done it before. Not my proudest moment. But then again, I've been in the staff bathroom holding Charlee's hair back while she's done the same. "Think he'll let me take a nap?"

Charlee snorts and taps my nose. "I think Dex will let you get away with anything, just like he always does."

I'm sure she's right, considering Dex is the one who caught Aaron cheating, the one who came over and broke the news to me yesterday, the one who held me and let me snot all over him.

Forgoing my nightly routine because I'm riding the hot mess express tonight, Charlee and I collapse into bed. She pulls the covers over us and snuggles into me.

"I've so missed spooning with you," she says with a quiet sigh.

I grab her hand in mine. "I love you."

"Love you too, Claire Bear. I'm sorry you got your heart broken, but I'm not sorry to see Aaron tossed out on his ass. When you're ready, you'll find someone who treats you so good you won't even know what to do with yourself."

The exhale I blow out is sad, laced with a whole lot of self-pity, because I'm just not sure I see it happening anymore. "I don't know how long it'll take before I'm ready. Hopefully before I'm forty and living with seventeen cats."

"Well, you're only twenty-five and you have zero cats right now, so you're off to a pretty good start. Look at you—you're killing it!"

I drift to sleep in my best friend's arms, dreaming about cats, ice cream sandwiches, and punching Aaron in the face.

Or his dick. His small, useless dick.

CHAPTER TWO

Claire

"Ladies, what can I get ya?"

The man behind the bar winks, tongue peeking out to lick the corner of his mouth. He's hot, but I'm trying not to think with that aching spot between my legs tonight. It's hard, because I'd been drinking for the last two hours at Charlee's apartment, and I'm definitely half in the bag by now. We just walked in here and I'm already giggling my face off. There's a glaring sign in my head with the word *danger* on it, flashing incessantly. Giggles are never a good sign.

"Do you have Strawberry Grove? From Cherry Lane Brewing?" My sentences are still whole and making sense, so that's positive. I've got room for more alcohol and I'm gonna drink until I don't. It's probably not ideal, but I've managed to get through the entire week without doing any major structural damage at home or work, I haven't cried again, and I've ignored every single attempt at communication from Aaron. So, that calls for a celebration, which I'm doing. Clearly.

The bartender gives me an approving once-over. "A sour hop? I'm impressed. A girl after my own heart."

Charlee's chin hits my shoulder. "Claire works at Cherry Lane. She's, like, in charge. Well, second in charge."

"Is that right, Claire?" He says my name slowly, like he's testing it out, seeing how it rolls off his tongue. It rolls well. He fills a pint glass and leans over the bar, propped up on his elbows. He's a little close. I'm not sure if I mind or not. He smells good and he's got great hair and nice forearms. They're all flex-y and partially covered in ink.

His eyes travel slowly down my body and my cheeks flush with heat. Fuck, I don't remember how to flirt. I think that's clear, because I haven't given him a single word yet, aside from my beer order, and he's still smiling at me.

"What are you ladies celebrating tonight?" he asks. He slides my beer into my hands and closes my fingers over my money, pushing it back to me.

"Claire dumped her piece of shit boyfriend!" Charlee yells in my ear and wraps her arms around me from behind. She's drunker than me. It's going to be a disaster of a night.

I drag a palm down my face and groan. This isn't the first guy she's told tonight that I'm newly single, and we've been here all of ten minutes.

"Atta girl, Claire! Single just in time for summer!" His eyes sparkle as he leans closer. "You're gorgeous, so he must have really fucked up to let you go. That, or you just realized you were way too good for him."

My mouth curves up on one side. This guy's good. Maybe I can do this casual sex thing. Just once. I mean, Aaron did it while we were together, so why can't I do it now? Ugh, but my stomach does this weird little flip thing, like it's warning me that I'm not cut out for this.

"You don't say much, do you?" the bartender remarks.

"Just observing," I respond slowly, drumming my fingers on my glass. I make a point of letting my eyes roam the bar before settling my gaze back on his. "Is that okay?"

Grinning, he flattens his hands on the bar. "More than okay." He tips his chin toward the dancefloor. "You gonna be out there tonight?"

"Oh, absolutely. Just gotta get this into me first." I raise my glass to my lips and take a long drink, tongue dragging across my top lip to lick up the drops of beer. "You'll have to watch me and let me know how I do." Okay, maybe I do remember how to flirt.

His light eyes storm over, flickering. "Trust me, gorgeous, I'll be watching."

"Thanks for the beer," I murmur as Charlee leads me across the floor. I throw a glance over my shoulder at the bartender who's still staring after me, a delicious smile on his face.

But he's not the only one staring at me.

The bar is rammed, packed with people hanging over all three sides of the sparkly black marble. And there, tucked around the edge of one corner, is a pair of impossibly dark brown eyes, which just so happen to be glued to me.

I thought the bartender had nice hair, but man—*this guy*. Cropped shorter on the sides, his thick, dark waves are a tousled mess up top. It looks like he spent thirty minutes styling it to look like he just rolled out of bed, or just had sex, but something tells me that it's entirely natural. I have an urge to plow my fingers through those ruffled waves. His mouth tilts with a deliriously sexy smirk and he raises his glass to me before lifting it to his perfect, full lips.

Sweet Lord, he's one fine specimen.

Charlee tugs me hard and I fly forward, crashing into her. She giggles and spins me, stuffing me into a booth. When I raise my gaze, the dark-haired man is laughing. He quirks one brow at me before turning back to his friends.

What was that Charlee said a few days ago about letting someone bend me over their car and fuck me until I scream? Looking at this man has me seriously considering it. My eyes drift over his broad chest, his thick arms. He looks like he could do me well.

I mean, *it* well. I mean, I guess that's the same thing, isn't it?

Charlee's rambling on about something I'm definitely not hearing. I'm not paying a bit of attention. I can't look away from this guy, and it's *so* bad. He's listening to his friends talk and swirling his glass. His gaze lifts once more to me, an unmistakably mischievous glint hiding in plain sight, and I watch as his tongue flicks over his top lip, licking up a drop of liquid. His mouth is perfect and I think he knows it.

A swift slap to my shoulder has my gazes swinging, glaring at Charlee. "Ow! What was that for?" I rub my shoulder before reaching forward and hitting her back.

"You weren't paying attention to me! I was talking about the bartender. You should hook up with him tonight. Just have some fun, Claire. One night."

Totally forgot about the bartender. I glance up to find him watching me from behind the bar. He smiles and throws me a wink, but I can't even consider hooking up with him now.

And my eyes slide back to the reason why.

Charlee's chins lands on my shoulder, lips against my ear. "Unless you've found someone you like better."

I watch the dark-haired man's eyes flicker between me and Charlee and for a fleeting moment, I'm jealous of my best friend. She's got the kind of legs that go straight to heaven, and these amazing dirty blond locks, all soft and fluffy, paired with enormous brown eyes. It's maybe not all that fleeting of a moment, because rather than watch him realize that Charlee's incredible to look at, I decide to look away.

"He looks like he likes you too," she whispers. "Can't take his eyes off you."

Swallowing the thickness that creeps into my throat and reminds me that I'm not enough, I press my thumb to my pint glass, watching the frost melt away from the heat of my skin. "Doubt it. Can't keep my boyfriend interested, wouldn't be able to keep a guy that looks like that interested."

Charlee pulls away with a fierce scowl. "What did you just say about my best friend?" She lifts my glass to my lips, jerking my head backwards with a fistful of my hair. She's forceful and a whole lot scary, but she's always been this way, so I'm used to it.

"Drink this, and then drink four more. I'm not sitting here and listening to you put yourself down. What happened with Aaron has absolutely nothing to do with you. Drink until you remember all the things you love about yourself, which, by the way, should be everything because you're un-fucking-real, Claire."

She shakes her head and takes a sip of her own drink before staring at me, her eyes going all soft. "I seriously hate that he made you question that."

I do too, but how do you climb out of a hole you've already started descending at rapid speed? Regardless, I need to snap out of this mopey mood for at least a few hours, so I guzzle my beer down and grin when the rest of our girlfriends make their way to our table. It's both a blessing and a curse that they sit across from me, blocking my view of that gorgeous man.

Two beers later, Charlee returns from the bar, arms full of brown shots.

"I'm not drinking that," I say pointedly, crossing my arms over my chest.

"You are, actually, and you're gonna like it."

"I'm gonna hate it and you know it." But I raise it to my nose anyway and give it a sniff. A shudder rolls down my spine and I squeeze my eyes shut. "It smells like gasoline, Charlee."

Her grin is calculating. "You have two men asking about you."

"Pardon?"

She points to the shot in my hands. "Drink and I'll tell you."

I roll my eyes but comply, because I'm riding that fine line and I know this shot is going to take me right to the edge, be the thing that keeps me dancing the rest of the night away.

"Good girl. So, Mr. Bartender—*Chris*—wants to know if you're ready to move on."

That's a big *n-o* for me.

"And Mr...Hmm, I donno. Mr. Tall, Dark, and Sexy? That seems fitting." She shrugs, gaze sliding across the bar. I know

14

where she's looking. That's why I keep my eyes trained on my fingernails, pretending they're super interesting. They're not, of course. I haven't had them painted in half a year, but they are looking nice and healthy right now. Longer than they've been in ages.

Distraction works wonders for me.

"Anyway, he had lots of questions about you."

My head snaps up at that. "What? You talked to him?"

"Oh, yeah." Her head bobs as she waves her hand around. "I told him he'd have to find out about you himself. He seemed to like that. Got this secret, sexy smile and promised he would."

She slides me a second shot and holds hers up, waiting for me to clink my glass to hers. When I do, we throw them back and I let her drag me out to the dancefloor.

The music is exactly what I need to forget about everything—Aaron's wandering dick, the sexy man with the dark hair, and the fact that I normally care about what I look like when dancing in public. Under the strobing lights, music pulsing in my ears, I drown everything else out until all I can feel is the alcohol coursing through my veins, making my hips move and my hands run a sinuous path over my own body.

Charlee's hands land on my hips and she spins me around, crushing my back against her as we move together. With our friends dancing around us, a group of men descend, trying to cut in. When one reaches for me, I'm about to let him spin me around.

Until my eyes settle on those deep brown, black-as-night eyes over his shoulder, the ones fixed on me.

My heart thumps against my ribcage as I watch him stand. He starts crossing the dancefloor to…to me? No, he can't be. I throw a slightly frightened glance back at Charlee and she grins, yanking on the hands of the man who's just grabbed for my waist. He doesn't object, and the two of them disappear into the swarm of people on the dancefloor. I'm left gaping as this huge man makes his way over to me like an animal on the prowl, all fluid and silk, slipping effortlessly through the crowd, eyes locked on his prey.

My brain searches for one word to describe him, but I come up empty. Sexy is good, but not nearly enough. It doesn't dictate the need I feel coursing through me with the way he's looking at me. And handsome? Sure, but also no. It's too composed, and one look at this man tells me he's the farthest thing from composed. He's absolutely feral.

He's perfection if I've ever seen it, dark fitted jeans on his thick, mile-long legs, a light blue button up stretching across his broad chest, hugging his lean waist. I'm not even ashamed when a moan ripples in the back of my throat as I watch those tendons flex below his rolled sleeves.

The air is sucked from the room as this burly man comes to a stop in front of me. He's unnaturally large, but in the best kind of way. The kind where he'd likely absolutely destroy me if only I'd let him.

Spoiler alert: I would.

My heart thrums so wildly that it draws my fingers to my chest, pressing the tips there in an attempt to still it. It doesn't work, and his penetrating gaze follows the movement. A tiny smirk curls his lips, alluring in just the right way, making me lean closer.

"Don't stop dancing on my account."

Ah, shit. A voice to match the body, all dark and husky. Big surprise. I think my knees might actually buckle, because his hand—giant too, just like the rest of him—shoots out, gripping my waist, steadying me.

"You haven't had too much to drink, have you? I counted three beers and two shots, but you are a tiny little thing, so I suppose that could be enough to tip you right over the edge."

Like crushed velvet, his voice is smooth and rich. Desperate to feel it against my skin, instinct draws me closer. I realize I'm still not talking when his grin just keeps growing, all crooked and broad. He knows exactly what he's doing to me.

"Unless you've been drinking for much longer than you've been here. I've had my eyes on you all night; I know I didn't miss a single one of those drinks."

I blink up at him, and when those dark brows quirk up above those piercing eyes of his, waiting for me to either confirm or deny his suspicions, I feel a smile start to spread across my face, pulling those dimples of mine into my cheeks. "Might have had a few drinks before I came."

His eyes glisten with mirth as they drift over my body. "How many more before you come again?"

I don't even attempt to bite back my smile when realization hits, the innuendo in his words clear. I do, however, swat his shoulder. "That was good."

"I know," he says with a devilish wink.

The liquid courage warming my body from the tips of my toes to the blush in my cheeks has me stepping into him, pulling my bottom lip between my teeth. "Did you come over here to dance with me?"

Closing the remaining distance between us, his warm fingers grip my hips. "I'd love to dance with you." Flipping me around, his body molds to mine as we start moving together. "Love to do more than just dance with you."

The wobble in my knees is back, as is the gentle throb of the space between my thighs. The voice in my head is chanting, reminding me of why I came here tonight: to have a good time with my girlfriends and go home alone, possibly with a pitstop at the McDonald's drive-thru for a late-night McFlurry.

But his body feels amazing on mine. He's hard but soft somehow, warm hands sliding over my hips, my belly, my arms, leaving a blazing trail in their wake. My body is tingling everywhere and I'm pretty sure he knows it.

"I know you didn't come here with anyone but your girls," he whispers in my ear, "but do you have someone waiting for you at home?"

"No." Just the aforementioned ice cream.

His hand glides along my jaw, turning my face to his. "No? I find that incredibly difficult to believe."

"I just broke up with my boyfriend," I accidentally blurt. Don't know why I'm telling him this. I blame the shots, which means I blame Charlee.

"Hmm. Pity."

"Is it?" I ask with a cheeky smile. "Because the look on your face says otherwise."

His lips part on a breathy chuckle. "Caught me. Who broke up with who?"

"I did." He's so close. All I can focus on are his full lips, and I'm dying for a taste.

"And why's that?"

Honestly? I don't know how to answer this. Admitting to someone other than my family and closest friends that my boyfriend cheated on me makes me feel inferior, and I hate that. It makes me feel worthless and weak, and I can't deny that I've spent the last week wondering what it was that made me not good enough.

I drop my gaze, looking for a lie, but I've never been good at lying or thinking on my feet. Somehow, I think this man holding me suspects that, because his thumb sweeps across my cheekbone, drawing my eyes back to his. And something there has me opening my mouth and spilling the truth.

"He cheated on me," I admit in a whisper.

The grip on my hip tightens and those smooth chocolate eyes peering down at me flicker. "Somebody cheated on you?"

When all I can do is nod, he releases my face, his gaze softening. I think this is when he's going to lose interest, validate my feelings of inferiority, so I start to pull away. But his hands slip over my stomach, keeping me tight against him as we dance. The music is fast but he moves slowly, guiding my hips along his, my entire body buzzing under his touch.

"Fuck him. You're better off."

I snort a laugh, enjoying the odd sense of ease that rolls over me, bringing a calmness to my storm. "I'm inclined to agree with you," I tell him, wrapping my palm around the curve of his neck. He laughs along with me and before I know what's happening, his lips touch my shoulder, and my mouth opens with a sharp inhale. My body screams *yes* while my brain tells me to run for cover. "Look, I…I'm really not looking for anything right now. I mean…it was only last weekend."

"Mhmm," he murmurs against my shoulder. "We're not doing anything wrong. Just having a little fun. I am, at least. Aren't you?"

Hell yes I am, but I don't know how to have fun like this. I don't know how to do this without emotions. I've never had a one-night stand before.

He must sense my apprehension because his traveling hands still. "Do you want me to stop?"

I should, I think. I'm so confused. Whatever's inside my head is just swirling around. But *no* is the answer that leaves my mouth.

He winds my hair around one fist and tosses it over my shoulder. His lips press to the back of my neck and I tip my head backwards at the feel of his mouth on me. I want it everywhere and my stomach tingles with anticipation.

"Come with me," he whispers, fingers tangling with mine.

My heart jumps to my throat. "What? Where? I-I…I can't."

His lips press to the spot beneath my ear that makes me want to drop my panties right here, right now. "You can."

Heat pools in my cheeks when he kisses me there, and then walks away, just like that.

Halfway across the dancefloor, he stops, glancing back at me. He smirks and cocks his head, and I hear the unspoken question: *Are you coming?*

My gaze darts nervously around the dancefloor, my stomach doing gymnastic moves I don't know the names of and most definitely could never do even if my life depended on it.

But then, hesitantly, as if I'm walking along the edge of a mountainous cliff, I take one step. And then another. And one more. When I'm close enough, his smile explodes off his face and he reaches for my hand. My skin ignites when his fingers lace through mine.

He drags me across the dancefloor and out the patio door, into the cool, late spring night.

The patio is empty aside from a couple smoking on one end, and—hell, I don't even know his name—this *man* leads me around the corner of the building. It's dark and quiet, only the soft glow of the twinkling lights on the railing lighting the small space.

He presses me up against the wall and closes in on me, his chest rising and falling, his breath hot and heavy as it washes over me.

I don't know what I want.

No, that's not true. I know what I want. I want this man. This man I don't even know, not even his name.

But I can't. I can't do this, can I?

I'm not ready for this. This isn't me. Casual? One-night stands? I don't do this. I don't know how. Even if I accept this for what it is, for what it could be, I'll still want to see him again. And obviously he won't. I mean, what kind of man just walks up to a woman and five minutes later has her flat against a wall, alone in the dark?

A man who knows what he's doing. A man who does this all the time. A man who's not interested in more. Not the man for me. I'm not built for casual, for meaningless. I feel too much, too deeply.

"Stop thinking so much," he growls, his fingers wrapping around my hips. "I can see it all over your face. You're terrified." The laugh lines in his cheeks and around his eyes disappear, and he backs up a half step. "Are you scared of me?"

Yes. "No." This feels like the kind of thing that winds up getting my face splashed on a milk carton. But that's not what's really scaring me. "I'm scared of…this." I gesture between the two of us, trying to control my rapid breath.

"How do you mean?" He reaches forward and brushes my hair off my neck, tucking it behind my ear.

"I don't do this," I tell him honestly. "I don't hook up with people I just met. I don't know you." But God, I want to.

I don't know how it happens, but my hands reach out and my fingers curl around the collar of his shirt. I tug him into me and he comes willingly, his body flush against mine. His hands run a blazing path up and down my sides until his fingers settle on the hem of my dress, dusting along my thighs. His face dips, the tip of his nose tracing along mine.

"You're fucking gorgeous. But I won't make you do anything you don't want to." He pulls back and grins, all cheeky and arrogant. "Even though I really fucking want to."

I'm so distracted by that damn chiseled jaw, the tiny dimple in his chin, the laugh lines in his hollow cheeks. It's infuriating how sexy this man is.

"How often do you do this?"

"Do what?" He looks like he wants to devour me, and I kinda wanna let him.

"This. This thing we're doing right now."

The corner of his mouth pulls up and his eyes squint as he studies my face, likely weighing the benefits of honesty *vs* little white lies. "A bit."

Hmm. Honesty. At least partial honesty. He's not telling me he never does it. He's not promising me I'm the first and only.

21

Still, his answer doesn't sit well with me. I may not be ready to date, or even for this, but I know I want to feel special when I'm with someone, not like every other girl. That's what I am to this man though, just the flavor of the week, the one he's given the honors of pressing up against the wall outside for a quickie.

"It's different though. You're different."

Oh, Christ. Here we go. I'm different. I'm different, everybody! Claire Thompson is different! My eyes do a major roll and I lift one unamused brow, pinning my arms across my chest.

He chuckles. "Did you just roll your eyes at me?"

"Uh huh. 'Cause I'm about to get the *you're different* speech." Straightening off the wall, I step into him. There's a little fire brewing inside me, part anger, part lust. I sweep my hands out between us with a little extra flourish. "Well, let's hear it. What makes me so different?"

The smirk that dons that handsome face of his is so damn sexy. And intoxicating. And irritating. "Aside from the fact that you aren't just falling into my lap and you're calling me out on my shit right now?"

I bite back a smile, but I'm not sure it's working. He just laughs.

"I'm not really sure," he finally answers. "Haven't figured it out yet." He plows his fingers through his waves, my suspicions from earlier confirmed—there's not a single drop of product in there. It's all natural. He lifts a shoulder and lets it fall. "I can just tell. Felt it as soon as you walked through the door. Saw it when you were trying to figure out how to flirt with the bartender. When you looked at me and looked away, like you didn't really wanna be noticed. When you yelled at your friend for bringing shots, but then did them all anyway." He takes a step toward me and his fingers brush along the edge of my bare shoulders. "Forgive me for being interested in such a breathtaking woman."

Leaning against the wall, I drink in the long, lean lines of his ridiculously glorious body. "This normally works for you, doesn't it?"

His eyes glitter with amusement. "Every time."

There's the reminder I was looking for: I'm *not* different, not special. I try not to let it bother me, because this—whatever this is—means nothing.

Dragging my teeth across my bottom lip, I reach forward, boldly fingering the button on his shirt, right below his collarbone. Our eyes lock. "Are you frustrated that it's not working right now?"

"Very," he snarls, pinning me to the wall with his hips. I gasp at the feel of the very noticeable bulge in his pants pressing against the hot spot between my legs. His fingers slide along my jaw and into my hair. "But I think it is working, little strawberry."

"Pardon?" *Little strawberry?* What in the actual—

"Mmm. This fucking hair." He twists a lock of my auburn hair around one long finger.

Oh no. I can't do this. My knees start to go all wibbly-wobbly. He's right. It *is* working.

My breath catches in my throat and his eyes flit to mine, dark and demanding.

Ohhh no, no, no. Come on, Claire! Be strong.

But he's so sexy. Just one…one what? One kiss? One night? Fuck. Fuck, fuck, fuck.

"I don't even know your name," I justify, then quickly realize I don't care. Because if I'm going to do this, and if what I'm worried about is wanting to see him again, falling for him…

"My name is A—"

I slap my hand over his mouth. His forehead creases and his eyes crinkle. "No! I don't wanna know. Okay?"

He nods once before his teeth nip the flesh of my palm.

"Ow!" Ripping my hand away, I cradle it against my chest. I hit him with my best angry eyes. I give good angry eyes. Ask Aaron.

23

"Why don't you want to know my name?"

A slow smile spreads across my face, decision made. I don't know who made it, or rather, what body part. It sure as hell wasn't my brain.

"Because if I know your name, it'll be a lot harder for me to do this."

"Do what?"

I don't answer him. Not with words, anyway.

Instead, I yank him into me, wrapping myself around his body, fusing our mouths together.

Yes. I can do this. Just once. No names, no commitments.

How hard can it be?

CHAPTER THREE

Avery

I'll be damned. This girl's as fiery as her luscious ginger waves.

Which are currently tickling my cheeks and forearms.

Because she's wrapped around my body, crushing herself to me. Her fingers are tangled in my hair, her legs an anchor around my waist, holding me tight. I back her into the wall so I can press myself right into her, feel the lick of every flame pouring off her skin, igniting mine.

Her succulent lips move hungrily against mine, and when my teeth find her bottom lip, she rips her mouth away and tips her head back against the brick, panting.

"Stop fucking biting me," she growls.

"I think you like it." I nip her again, because I'm an asshole, and I enjoy the way she grinds her hips into mine, like she can't get enough.

Tugging her face up to mine, I devour her mouth, my tongue sweeping inside, fighting for control, something she's not willing to relinquish easily. She tastes amazing, like citrus fruit and beer, but there's a hint of bite on her plump lips, like mint.

"You put up a good fight," I breathe into her mouth. I can't stop kissing her, can't pull away. One minute of kissing and I've never been so wrapped up in a girl. "All ten minutes of it."

Her teeth tug at my lower lip. "Stop talking. Use your mouth for the only thing it's good for."

I chuckle darkly and drag my mouth off hers, nipping along the edge of her jaw while she writhes and groans beneath me. When I find her ear, my tongue flicks out, tasting the soft spot just beneath it. "My mouth is good for so much more than just kissing that pretty pink pout of yours."

I'm insatiable, trailing hot, wet kisses down her neck, along her collarbone. She's fucking delectable.

She's wearing this amazing dress, all dark green silk that matches perfectly with those lush forest eyes of hers. I follow the dip of the plunging neckline down to her cleavage and press my teeth into the swell of her breast. I want her naked, but that can't happen here.

"Come home with me," I murmur against her creamy skin. She smells like strawberries, just like her hair. "Please."

She lets out a load moan when my hands slide along her thighs and slip underneath her dress. I grip her hips, feeling the lace that hugs her there. I want to see it, and then I want to peel it off her.

"No." The breathless way she says it isn't convincing. I've already won her over once; I can definitely do it again.

"I want you. I wanna bury myself inside you and fucking *feel you.*"

"No." I'll give it to her, the word is firmer this time around. But the way she grinds herself against my cock, which is now fully erect, begging to be set free from the confines of my jeans, tells a different story.

My head dips with a deep belly groan. "*Please*," I beg. I'm absolutely not above begging, not for this girl. Who I hardly know. Shit.

I'm not bothered that I'm about to fuck a beautiful girl I don't know. I do that often enough. I'm bothered that I'm *begging* for a girl I don't even know. What the hell is that about?

But still, I keep going.

"Let me show you what it feels like to be fucked by a real man." Capturing her mouth, my tongue dives inside, massaging hers. "'Cause that piece of shit ex was just a boy."

My stomach lurches when she whimpers into my mouth, the voice in my head telling me she likely doesn't need the reminder. I can only guess what the kind of deception she's had forced upon her does to a person.

My best guess is that she's feeling a little less than, which is bullshit, because she's not. She's perfect; fuck any guy that's ever made her feel any other way.

But she still hasn't answered me.

Pulling back, I drink her in. Her eyes are hooded with lust, flawless lips glistening and swollen. She knows the question I'm about to ask because she licks her lips and shakes her head.

A growl rips through me as I flip her over, taking her hands and slapping them onto the brick. If she won't let me take her home, I'm going to give her whatever she'll let me, until she tells me to stop.

Gripping her hips, I jerk her ass into me, draping myself over her back. "You feel what you do to me, don't you?" I sweep her silky waves over her shoulder and brush my lips down her neck. "I want to touch you…everywhere. I want to feel every inch of you."

A shudder shakes her spine and she makes a noise deep in her throat. I smile against her neck, because this isn't one-sided. She wants me as much as I want her, which is a fuck-ton.

"Is that a yes? Can I touch you?"

The way she trembles in my hold tells me how honest she was being when she said she never does this. I'm also thinking she hasn't had a proper fucking from her ex in a long time, if ever.

"Come on, baby. Let me make you feel good. It doesn't have to mean anything other than pleasure, pure and simple."

Her fingers dig into the wall as I stroke her thigh, and she drops her head. "Okay." It's timid and quiet, unsure maybe, or just nervous as all hell. I won't do this without her unwavering permission, though.

"Say it again, gorgeous."

Throwing her head back over my shoulder, she levels me with a look that tells me not to push her. She's so fired up, and biting back my laugh is becoming near impossible. "*I said okay!*"

"Mmm, good girl."

My mouth clamps over the hot skin on her neck, sucking, and she yelps out, jamming her ass back into my cock. I drag the silk of her dress up her thighs and over her hips, letting it pool around her waist.

I have to take a minute to step back and just appreciate this sight before me, because she's an absolute vision, hands pressed to the wall, back bowed, her perfect, heart-shaped ass covered in black lace and on display for me to admire. I scrub a hand over my mouth, feeling like I might actually drool.

She throws me a less than impressed, highly impatient scowl over her shoulder. "What are you doing? Touch me now before I change my mind!"

Her feistiness just eggs me on. "Just admiring you, baby." I step back to her and grab her chin, kissing her hard. "Ask me nicely this time."

"Fuck you."

"You're a feisty little thing."

She rolls her hips, hitting me with an adorably cocky smirk. "You know you want me."

"I do," I agree with a light chuckle. "Very much so. Just waiting for you to tell me you want me too."

"You already know I do."

"Wanna hear those words, little strawberry." My fingers dance up her torso and I palm one perfect, full tit through her bra. "Say it."

She makes this sound, half sigh, half snarl. "I want you. Touch me."

"Please?"

"*Please*," she grits out through clenched teeth.

"Sure thing, baby. Whatever you want." My fingers dig their way under her bra and I pinch one nipple.

She moans and throws her head back, peering up at me from beneath her long lashes, lips parted. "More please." It's all soft and breathy.

I laugh at her sudden change in demeanor, her newfound manners, her pleading. "Are you begging, beautiful?"

Her throat works with a swallow as she nods, and the corner of my mouth curves. She's sweet, and despite her fiery attitude, I can tell she's pretty innocent. I gather all the other stuff is just a front to guard her heart after the cheating asshole.

I think that's why I drop a tender, slow kiss to her lips. "Where do you want me to touch you?"

Her trembling hand creeps up her dress and settles on mine. She drags my fingers down her flat belly and pauses when they pass over her panties. I can feel the heat blazing beneath them. Pressing my fingers against the lace, I groan when I find it drenched.

"Shit," I breathe. "You're soaking."

Those emeralds are absolutely massive as she peers up at me, riddled with shock, like she didn't think this was possible. "I'm wet…"

My brows pinch with confusion, but the feeling is fleeting, because my fingers find her swollen nub and she gasps, bucking against me. I push her panties aside and run one finger up her slick slit.

"*Ohhh*," she moans as I stroke her center.

My thumb starts rubbing light circles around her clit, teasing, enticing every little whimper right out of her. My mouth closes over her neck and I start sucking, licking, nipping. She's whimpering, shaking, chanting *yes, yes, yes* over and over again.

"Come home with me," I plead softly. "I don't wanna stop, not with you."

Her head rolls back, brows furrowed as she studies me. She looks so small and innocent, I almost feel bad about what I'm doing right now. Her breath comes in short, heavy bursts, washing over my lips as I move in to kiss her again.

The patio door around the corner slams open and footsteps spill out over the wooden deck boards.

"She's not here either," a voice whines. "I've lost her. I've fucking lost her. Great."

The girl in my arms yelps into my mouth and shoves against my chest, sending me backwards.

"What?" I ask, reaching for her.

Her eyes are frantic as she pulls her dress down, trying to straighten herself out as the footsteps get louder, closer. We both turn our heads as a blonde appears.

I recognize her immediately as Ginger's best friend. I know because they've been inseparable until I swooped in, and also because I approached her at the bar and asked her about her friend.

She's my best friend, she told me at the time. *And she's fantastic. But you'll have to find that out for yourself.* Then she winked at me and stalked off, arms full of shots.

With a hand over her heart, she breathes out a dramatic sigh, sagging. "There you are! I've been looking everywhere for you!" Her gaze bounces curiously between us, followed by the devious curl of her lips. "What were you two doing?"

"Nothing," Ginger insists a little too forcefully. The glare she pins me with dares me to say differently. I don't need to. Her friend's not stupid, and her tousled hair, flushed cheeks, and swollen, pouty lips say everything words don't need to.

So I just hold my hands up in innocent surrender, smiling at both of them.

Her friend doesn't buy it, like I said. She raises her brows and then rolls her eyes, waving her hand dismissively. "Whatever." She turns to...fuck, why don't I know her name? This is ridiculous. She turns to her friend, the girl I wish I still had my hands on. "Aaron's here."

Aaron? Who's Aaron?

Ginger's green eyes go wide. "I don't want to see him."

Ah. Must be Mr. Douchebag.

"I know. But he saw you…" The blonde's eyes slide to me. They dart down and widen. I follow her gaze.

Yep. Fuck. I've got a goddamn torpedo in my pants. I clear my throat and turn around, adjusting myself. It's painful; he doesn't want to play along. Actually, that's not right. Playing along is *exactly* what he wants to do.

The blonde continues, amusement dancing on her face when I turn back to them. "He saw you two dancing before you disappeared. He's pissed off."

Little Miss Strawberry clenches her jaw and pins her arms over her chest. "He has no right to be. I can dance with whoever I want to."

"Fuck yeah you can," I say enthusiastically. I hold up a hand, hoping for a high-five, but she only peeks up at me, a smile tugging up one side of her face. A sweet dimple pops in her cheek, but she quickly shakes her head before looking away.

"Can you please come tell him to go fuck himself? I've been dying to knee him in the balls too." The blonde holds her hands up in prayer. "He won't leave until he talks to you. He's been going wild in there."

Well, that doesn't make me feel very good. Is he dangerous? I look to my favorite redhead and hope my expression conveys how serious I am. "If he's that pissed off, you probably shouldn't talk to him right now. It might not be safe."

She considers me carefully for a minute before straightening off the wall. "I appreciate your concern, but I can take care of myself."

Her friend throws me a sympathetic smile. "She can. Don't worry."

I nod, but the discomfort lingers. I might play the field like it's my job, but I'm not cool with guys who treat girls like shit. It's never okay.

"Well…" Strawberry sucks her bottom lip into her mouth and looks up at me. When she releases it, I wanna lick that glisten right off of it. "See ya around."

Grabbing her elbow, I drag her right on back. Because *hell no*.

"You can't be serious," I say to her surprised face. "You're just gonna disappear on me?"

Her small hands press to my chest. "Look, I'm sorry. I told you, I'm not built for this. And I'm definitely not ready for something like this. This was a mistake."

I shake my head. "I don't think so. I don't think this was a mistake." When she only averts her gaze, I sigh. She's not gonna budge, not right now anyway. I'll have to give it another shot in a couple days. I dig my phone out of my pocket and hold it out to her. "Can I grab your number?"

She gnaws on her bottom lip before giving her head a slow shake.

For fuck's sake. "I don't suppose you're gonna give me your name either, are you?"

"I don't think that's a good idea," she whispers.

"Why not? This could be fun. We could have fun together. I *am* having fun with you. You're going to let that guy ruin shit for you?" Shit, I'm really jacked up about this. Maybe because I'm not used to being turned down. All I know is I don't wanna watch her walk away without knowing I'm going to see her again. "You're stronger than that."

She looks at her toes. "Not sure that I am, actually." Then she stands up as tall as she can muster, pushing her shoulders back, eyes fierce with determination. "Thanks for…whatever that was."

She jerks me down to her for a hungry kiss, her tongue lapping at mine. I wind an arm around her back and bury a hand in her soft hair. She pulls away, leaving us both breathless, wanting more.

And then she leaves me standing there like a jackass, staring after the curve of her hips as they swing from side-to-side, her slender shoulders, that beautiful mess of hair tumbling down her back.

And I don't have a single clue why I'm letting her walk away.

CHAPTER FOUR

Avery

It's everything I can do to drag myself back into the bar after I allow myself a couple minutes to cool down.

I slump into my seat next to my friends, and my best friend Wyatt arches one brow as he swirls his glass of scotch. "Struck out with your fiery redhead, didn't ya?"

Ignoring him, I reach forward, grabbing his drink right out of his hand and tossing it down my throat. It's smooth and delicious, warming me on its way down.

Wyatt leans back in his chair, lacing his fingers behind his head. "Well, shit. That doesn't happen often, does it? What happened, big boy? Losing your charm?"

Doubtful. Pretty sure I almost had her there, right at the end. She was crumbling like a sandcastle.

"Just broke up with her boyfriend and apparently he showed up, saw us dancing, and got pissed off." I wave a dismissive hand through the air. "Whatever. I'll find someone else." I start looking around the bar like I'm trying to figure out who that someone else is, rather than what I'm really doing, which is searching for her.

Wyatt snorts. "Yeah, okay. You had your eyes glued to her for two hours."

"And? Did you not see her?"

He lifts a shoulder and lets it fall. "I did. Gorgeous little thing, ain't she?" Gorgeous is an understatement. "But you've fucked lots of bombshells and never given them more than five, ten minutes of your attention."

"I fail to see your point." I catch one of the bartender's eyes and hold up the empty glass in my hand. He nods and pulls out a bottle of scotch.

34

"I don't think you do, but tell yourself whatever you want to hear."

In an attempt to forget about the girl who just walked away from me, I insert myself in the conversation the rest of our table is having. Something about investments and computers, so it's hard to participate. I don't give a shit about work at the moment, and the whole technology thing anyway is more Wyatt's expertise.

I'm halfway through my next drink when I notice the blonde pushing through the crowd. When her eyes lock on mine, she races over, gripping my forearm.

"Have you seen Claire?" she asks, panicked.

"Claire?"

Her nostrils flare at my confusion. "Yes, *Claire*. You know, the girl whose throat you had your tongue down. Maybe you remember her: beautiful little thing, copper hair, perfect tits, and a smile to match." She rolls her eyes and throws her fists on her hourglass hips.

I put my hand on her shoulder to try and get her to tone back the bitch just a little. "Calm down. She wouldn't tell me her name." But *Claire* suits her perfectly, and her friend's description of her is spot-on.

Those creases marring her forehead smooth out, and she takes a deep breath. "Sorry. Aaron and her were talking. I left for a minute—*a minute*! When I came back, they were gone." She shifts on her feet. "I'm worried. He's an asshole."

My jaw tics. "I thought you said she could take care of herself."

"She can, normally. It's just…" She scratches at her hair, averting her gaze for a moment. "He's drunk and really angry. It's not a good combo."

I scrub my jaw on an exhale. This is exactly why I said she shouldn't talk to him right now.

Wyatt's watching the entire interaction with curiosity and maybe a bit of smug amusement. It doesn't take much to guess that he thinks I care about Claire a little more than I normally would.

Tossing back my drink, I set the glass down and stand. "Alright. Let's find our girl."

She smiles up at me with big brown eyes. "Thank you so much. I'm Charlee, by the way."

"Nice to meet you, Charlee. I'm Avery."

I hold out my hand, but she surprises the hell out of me by wrapping her arms around my neck and pulling me in for a hug. My eyes must be huge because Wyatt snickers behind Charlee.

She tugs on my hand, pulling me through the crowd. "I looked everywhere. I went in the girl's bathroom and the boy's bathroom." At the face I make, she giggles. "I've been through every inch of this bar. I asked the bartender because he's had his eyes on her all night." Another giggle, this time at the small growl that rumbles involuntarily in my chest. "But he said he hadn't seen her since she disappeared off the dancefloor with you. I don't know where else they could be."

"Did you check outside?"

She smacks her palm off her forehead. "Oh! Duh! That's where I found you two! God, I'm not thinking."

I chuckle. "It's fine; you're just stressing. How about I check out back and you check out front, and we'll meet back here in five minutes?"

She nods. "Thank you, Avery." She squeezes my hand before heading for the front door.

Outside, the air is colder than it was twenty minutes ago, or maybe it's just the lack of heat from Claire's body against mine. But it's dark and quiet. She's not out here.

I take a moment to lean on the railing, wondering if maybe she went home, or if she left with him. I hope she didn't. He doesn't deserve to ever touch her again, and I hope she respects herself more than that.

And that's when I hear it. It's faint, off in the distance, but I hear it.

"I'm not blind, Claire! Who the fuck is he?"

"How about you go screw yourself and leave me the hell alone?" Well, she sure doesn't sound like she needs anyone's help.

I can't see much of anything aside from a dim glow pouring out an alley. I move toward it.

"He was touching you!" Sure was, and I'd do it again in a heartbeat.

"So what?"

"We broke up five fucking days ago!"

I hear her laugh. It's dark and threatening and if he knows what's good for him, he should probably back the hell away. But he cheated on her, so I doubt he knows the first thing about what's good for him.

"So, let me get this straight. You're upset because you saw me dancing with a man that wasn't you, even though we're no longer together. But it was perfectly acceptable for you to fuck other girls while we were together?"

"Fuck, Claire, it was an accident! How many times do you want me to apologize?"

"An accident happens once. The second time, it's a conscious decision. You made that decision multiple times. I still wouldn't be able to forgive you, Aaron, even if it'd only been the once. But it's not all your fault." The quiet murmur of her voice tugs at my heart, which is kinda weird. "I just wish I hadn't been stupid enough to believe you the first few times."

Ah, fuck. I can't do this. He cheated multiple times and *she* thinks *she's* stupid? Nah, she needs a pep talk, and I'm ready to give it to her.

"I don't trust you anymore," Claire whispers. "And I certainly don't like you."

"But you love me," he urges. "You love me still, right, Claire?"

Her silence lasts only a brief moment. "No. I don't think I have for a while. Goodbye Aaron."

The quick click of heels on the pavement starts, only to come to a sudden halt with her gasp. "Get your hands off me," she growls.

Rounding the corner of the dark alley, anger licks at the base of my spine.

"Don't be so uptight. Loosen up a little. I told you, it won't happen again. I was drunk."

I'm livid, watching her struggle against his chest when he pulls her into him.

"And I told *you* to get your fucking hands off me."

"You're not throwing three years down the drain."

"*Me*? Are you fucking with me right now?"

"No, but I want to be." He can't be serious right now.

"Screw you! I'm not the one who stuck their dick in somebody who wasn't their partner. Wasn't that what we were supposed to be, Aaron? Partners? You single-handedly ruined this one, buddy. I'm done."

Claire tears herself from his grasp, stumbling away from him, but he lunges after her, grabbing her around the waist and pushing her up against the wall.

The dim light overhead shimmers off the tears that start rolling down her cheeks and my fists flex at my sides. Her eyes flicker up to me when I come into the light and relief washes over her features.

As soon as Aaron's within reach, I grip the back of his shirt, ripping him off Claire. "Claire asked you to take your hands off her."

His eyes shine with rage when they settle on me. "You've got to be kidding me," he says with a sinister chuckle. "Who the fuck is this guy? Have you been fucking him this whole time?"

I step in front of Claire when he tries to advance, sweeping my arm out behind me, my hand settling on her hip. Her fingers curl around my forearm, gripping me tight. "She said she was done. Best you leave before this gets any uglier. Now."

It's been a while since I've been in a fistfight. I'd like to think I'm beyond that, but with this guy, I just might be due.

Aaron sizes me up, likely trying to decide if he can take me, but when I step into him, when I tower over him by an easy four inches, his mouth opens and closes, and he falters backwards a half-step. He swipes a hand haphazardly through the air. "Fuck, whatever. She's not worth it." I doubt that, but I'm not going to argue the point with him. He needs to go. Now.

Aaron brushes past me, sauntering down the alley and disappearing around the corner.

Twisting in Claire's direction, I find her shaking against the wall, fingernails biting into the flesh of my arm. "Alright?" I ask her.

Her glossy eyes meet mine. She swallows. All she gives me is the tiniest bob of her head.

I hold my hand out to her, shaking my arm, and watch as her hand glides over the muscles flexing in my arm before her palm slips into mine.

"Thank you," she breathes out, tucking a tendril behind her ear while we wander hand-in-hand back toward the bar.

"Not a problem." I give her hand a squeeze. It feels nice in mine, small and warm. "He's a persistent little shit, isn't he?"

She snorts, swiping her free hand over her cheeks, brushing tears away. "You could say that."

"You going back in?" I tip my chin toward the patio door as we approach the building.

She shakes her head softly, offering me a weak smile. "I think I'm going to head home. Enough excitement for one night."

I flag down a cab, helping her into the backseat. "Bye Claire," I murmur, squeezing her hand once more, simply because I want to.

She looks up at me, a slow, small smile gracing her face, little dimples pulling in her cheeks. "Bye…"

"Avery," I tell her.

That smile turns into a bright grin, warming my insides. "Bye Avery."

I watch the cab until I can't see it anymore, and then head back inside, hands in my pockets. I have to find Charlee to tell her what happened and that Claire's gone home. I also need some info. Phone number, last name, where Claire works, anything that'll help me see her again. I don't know why, but I want to. I have to.

"She's gone," Wyatt says as I approach the table, my head craning around the bar, looking for the pretty blonde.

"Huh?"

"Charlee? You just missed her. Left just a minute ago." His blue eyes draw up and down my body, likely noticing the tension it feels like I'm carrying in every single muscle. "She was waiting here for you but then she got a text from Claire. Said she was in a cab on her way home. Ran out of here but asked me to tell you. You find your girl before she took off?"

"I'm the one that put her in that cab."

His brows jump. "You let her go?"

My head bobs with a nod.

"You get her number?"

I sigh. "No." And now I won't, because Charlee's gone.

There's over six million people in this city. How the hell am I going to find just one?

CHAPTER FIVE

Claire

I'm in the worst mood. I don't know why I'm being so cynical, but I can't help it. The weekend was long and overwhelming, emotionally and physically exhausting.

When I woke up Saturday morning, it was with a splitting headache, an empty stomach, and alcohol accounting for at least fifty percent of my water weight. Now it's Monday, and my headache has decided it likes me too much to leave and wants to be friends.

I'm still not over Avery.

I mean, Friday night. Shit.

Well, that tells me where my head's at this morning. It sounds about right, I guess. I mean, I couldn't get that man out my brain all weekend. His memory set up shop, kicked back and relaxed with a cold beer and an all-too-endearing smirk.

Avery made me feel sexy, and that right there is about the scariest feeling. How could a man I knew absolutely nothing about make me feel something I hadn't felt in years? Hellbent on spiraling down a deep and dark hole of *I'll never be good enough*, a perfect stranger gave me his hand and pulled me right out, if only for a night.

So, I don't feel sexy.

But I did with Avery.

And in comes the man who makes me feel anything but sexy, the reason for all my self-doubt. I should have never let Aaron drag me out of the bar, but that's how we got to that alley—he literally *dragged me* by my elbow.

I hate that I let him get to me, let him see the way he wrecked me.

And then Avery was there, pulling Aaron off me, demanding that he leave.

There was none of that cocky, self-absorbed air left about him then. He was just kind. Quiet. Gentle. Walked me to a cab and put me in it. For a brief moment I'd thought about asking him to come with me.

But then I'd used my brain.

Groaning, I drop my face to my desk, smacking my head off the dark walnut three times for good measure.

"Knock, knock, little strawberry!"

Charlee's too-chipper Monday morning voice makes my groan louder, deeper. Now I sound like a man. I should have never told her about the *little strawberry* nickname that Avery coined.

"Oh, snap out of it, Claire Bear."

She slams something down on my desk and I let my head flop to the side, spying that giant iced coffee. I reach greedily for it, like a fiend about to get their fix.

"I love you, I love you, I love you." It's a moan if I've ever heard one.

"Love you too, babe." She sinks to the couch by the window and slings one leg over the other, bouncing one strappy, heeled foot in the air.

"I was talking about my drink." I slurp on the straw, letting my eyes roll into my head.

"Then you can forget about the muffin I got you."

With my best pout, I tell her, "But I love you more than my iced coffee."

Chuckling, she tosses a paper bag on my desk. "How you feeling this morning? Aaron still delusional and hoping for a reunion?"

I lean back in my chair, swiveling side to side. "I honestly don't know what he's thinking but the only thing calling me a slut is going to get him is a swift kick in the balls."

42

All weekend. Name-calling followed by an apology and an *I love you*. He either doesn't have a brain cell left in his head, or he's incredibly naive. I'm leaning toward the lack of brain cells.

"I personally think you should have fucked Avery."

I've been thinking about that too for the last forty-eight hours, in a constant battle of *Should I have? No, I shouldn't have. Yes, I fucked up. I totally should've. No Claire, you did great. Good for you, gal!* I feel like I have multiple personalities and every single one of them is just fucking exhausted.

But I know I made the right decision. I'm not ready for that. Our chemistry was unreal, I'll give him that. But, for me, it never ends at one night. The last thing I want is to be someone's cling-on because I get attached too quickly, too easily. When I'm in, I'm in. Until I'm out. I'm out now, with Aaron. And never again will that man be *in*.

"We're not the same type of people," I tell Charlee.

"I don't get it. You just got out of a relationship and you don't want to get into another one right now, so what would be the big deal if you just had some fun with a nice man with an even nicer face? Plus, *that body*." She tips her head back and lets out an exaggerated shudder, paired with a loud moan. Charlee is nothing if not dramatic.

"It's a moot point, because I'll never see him again." I wave a flailing hand in front of my face and turn to my computer, booting it up. It's about time; I've been at work for forty-five minutes and haven't done a damn thing. It also distracts from the fact that I'll never see Avery again, which makes me sadder than it reasonably should.

Charlee sighs and runs her fingers through her blond hair, uncrossing her legs. She blows on the hot drink in her hand and stares up at me with her soft chocolate eyes. "Still can't believe you didn't get his number. You could have just kept it in your back pocket or something, used it down the road when you were looking for a fun night. Or, you know, given it to your best gal pal," she adds with a wink.

My eyes narrow. "If I can't hook up with him, neither can you." That jealous pit in my stomach reels it's angry head already, even though I: A) don't even know Avery; B) have no claim to him; and C) didn't even really hook up with him. This is *exactly* why I don't and can't do casual, and a prime example of why I need to chill the hell out on the man front for, like, a year.

Charlee sticks her tongue out at me, and I show her mine right back.

"Do you two ever do any work around here?"

My head snaps to the door of my office and I grin up at Dex, my boss and Charlee's older brother. "Morning, Dex."

Dex is the best. He started Cherry Lane Brewing Company nearly five years ago in Jordan Valley, our little hometown in the middle of wine country in Southern Ontario. It was tiny when it started as a little backyard brewery but took off so quickly that he moved the whole operation to Toronto after only a year-and-a-half. When I finished my business degree, he begged me to come join him at the brewery.

I have no official job title, but he always calls me his second in command. If he isn't around, I'm the go-to. I delegate jobs downstairs in the tasting room, oversee some of the production in the beer house, and manage most of the office staff. The only person who knows more about Cherry Lane is Dex himself.

Dex rounds my desk and pulls me out of my chair for a hug like he does every morning. He's one of my favorite huggers, all big and cuddly, soft and warm like a bear.

And because Charlee is Charlee and she's forever making things awkward, she says in the most nonchalant manner, "I told Claire you and her should be fuck buddies until she's ready to move on."

Dex freezes in my arms and I shove him off me, smoothing my dress down my hips and fixing my hair which is still perfectly in place. Then I hit Charlee with a scowl.

"Can you just not? Can you not make things awkward for once in your life?" I glance at Dex who looks straight-up frightened, hands shoved in his pockets, looking anywhere but at me. "Don't worry, Dex. I've kicked her off this horse a thousand times. She's nuts. How'd you turn out so normal?"

That earns me a chuckle and a smile. His warm hazel eyes dance around my face. God, he really is handsome with those windswept blond locks and big muscles. Sometimes I hate that we have this type of relationship, because if he wasn't such a brother to me, he'd be perfect. I just can't get over what we already have though.

I tried once. It didn't work. Yeah, it hadn't ruined our relationship, but it'd taken me a solid two weeks before I could make eye contact with him, which isn't exactly how you want things to go at your new job. I kept dashing out of the room as soon as meetings were done, until he finally cornered me in the stairwell and demanded that we just forget it ever happened. So that's what we did. Me and him, not Charlee. Charlee never forgot it happened, and I don't think she ever will.

She's constantly suggesting that she should get to hook up with my brother to make it even. I wouldn't put it past either of them to try. Frankly, it's a miracle it hasn't happened yet, but I think it's just because my poor brother has had the weight of the world thrust onto his shoulders in recent years. Hook-ups haven't been on his radar for a while now.

Dex flops down beside his sister on the couch and steals a chunk of her muffin. She slaps him away. He shoves his hand in her face, pushing her backwards.

"Claire," he mumbles with his mouth full. "You ready for the meeting?"

Ah, shoot. Meeting. I glance at my phone. "What time is it at again?"

"Twenty minutes."

"Right, right, right." I drum my fingers on the desk and let my head bounce, trying to ignore the renewed thudding this sets off inside my skull.

He laughs, his head shaking. "You don't have to do anything today, just show your pretty face. Might need you to help me field some questions. But if this goes well, and I can't see why it wouldn't, you'll be their number one contact."

"Yes, of course. And you're right, it'll go well. Didn't you say they're friends of yours? Uh, Jones & Beck, right?" God, I hope I've at least got the name of the investment firm right or this is going to look really bad. I'm so unprepared today. At least I've got my trusty binder. I whip open my filing cabinet and pull it out, running the tip of my finger along the color-coded tabs. My shoulders sag with the relief that floods my system at the one part of my life I keep mostly organized.

Minus this whole forgetting-about-the-meeting debacle.

Dex nods and swipes Charlee's coffee, sipping it. He makes a funky face. "What the fuck is this?"

"Cinnamon chai latte," she replies with a shrug.

"Gross." He crosses the room to my desk and grabs my iced coffee, sucking hungrily through the straw. "Mmm, so much better." He slams it down and heads for the door. "Yeah, we were friends in college. They're good guys. Excited about this. They don't usually bother with investments this small but, like I said, they're good guys. Happy to help me out." His eyes linger on me a moment before he raps his knuckles on the doorframe. "See ya in a few." He points at Charlee. "Go sell my beer."

With a groan, Charlee pulls herself off the couch, making a face at the back of Dex's head as he exits. "Yes, boss," she hisses and mock salutes the spot where he used to be standing. "I hate working for him."

"No you don't. You love it. He's the best boss there is."

Charlee does all of the marketing for Cherry Lane. She visits the liquor stores, beer stores, grocery stores, bars, and restaurants, and convinces them to stock Cherry Lane. It's not particularly difficult. Cherry Lane is so popular in Ontario and it's spreading through a lot of the other provinces now too, even some states just over the border. Its craft speaks for itself and people love to shop and buy local in this day and age, so that certainly helps. Regardless, Charlee is absolutely fantastic at what she does. She could sell underwear to a nudist.

She also plans all of our events, usually with me although I'm definitely unneeded, because *goddamn*, that woman knows how to throw a party. But after eighteen years by her side, I don't need to work on her party planning committee to know that.

Charlee wraps her arms around me from behind, resting her chin on my shoulder. "Go be a pretty face at the meeting," she whispers.

I'm secretly glad I don't have to do anything at the meeting. I'm too tired, maybe a bit hungover still, and just pure lazy this Monday morning. It's not my usual style, so I can get away with it once in a while. I almost wore my PJs to work today, but thought better of it, because it's not an ideal way to start a workweek. Also, not professional and would make being productive difficult.

Avery's brown eyes and those ridiculous waves drift through my head, telling me I wouldn't have paid attention anyway because my mind is elsewhere today. I try to shoo them away. Literally, I wave my hand in front of my face like I'm swatting at a fly.

Charlee swings around to hit me with two raised brows. "You okay there, Clarice?"

I shudder at the name and the way she says it, like she's coaxing me out of a hiding spot in a pitch-black house with the empty promise not to hurt me. "Can you not call me that? All I think about is cannibals and that damn movie." My body shakes with another shudder, entirely unholy images clouding my mind. "Oh God, that's literally all I'm thinking about now! Charlee!"

Laughing like the evil witch she is, she drums her fingers together in front of her mouth.

"That's not even my name!" I shout as she backs out my office. Her cackle echoes off the walls in the hallway.

Good, she's gone. Now back to those piercing brown eyes. And oh God, those hands. Those big, warm hands, dipping under my—

"Hey Claire. You wanna head over to the meeting together?"

I'm not proud of the high-pitched shriek that escapes my mouth as I rocket out of my chair.

Grant, one of the accountants, arches a brow at me from my doorway. "Sorry. Didn't mean to scare you. Little jumpy this morning?"

Trying to swallow down the lump of pure lust lodged in my chest, I dust off my dress, because it's…dusty? God, I'm a wreck. I clear my throat. "Just a bit. I'd love to walk down with you, but I need to make a pit stop first."

I consider calling it a day and heading home, but it's not even 10am yet, so that seems like a no-go. Instead, I head to the bathroom.

To dry my panties.

I already said I was a wreck, right?

CHAPTER SIX

Avery

"Isn't it a little early for scotch?" I lift an amused brow, watching Wyatt pour himself a glass in the back of the car. He swirls it once and tosses the whole thing back. "It's ten in the morning."

He shrugs and pours himself another. "If we were girls and we were at bunch, it'd be perfectly acceptable for us to have mimosas."

Well, shit. He's got me there. "Touché, my friend."

He shakes the bottle. "Want some?"

"Ah, fuck it. Just a finger." It'll settle my nerves before the meeting. Not that I have nerves before any meeting, ever. My stomach is made of steel and always has been. I don't question it.

I watch him pour me three fingers, but I don't complain. I take the drink and let the smooth liquid coat my mouth like velvet before it travels down to my stomach, warming me on the way. The only problem is I haven't had a drop of scotch since Friday night, and now all I'm thinking about is a certain fiery redhead. I shake her face from my head and swallow it down, enjoying the way it toasts my insides.

We stop in front of a charming three-story brick building in the old distillery district of Toronto. The south side of the building has great views of the Toronto Harbour, making it a great spot for what this place has planned. They're already pulling in a huge revenue that'll easily triple by the time we're done with it.

Stepping out of the car, I fix the button on my suit jacket.

"Avery?"

My head lifts at my name, and I spot a beautiful blonde. Her gaping mouth tells me she's as stunned to see me here as I am to see her.

"Charlee?"

Grinning, she steps up to me, brown eyes drifting down my body. The half-smile on her face tells me she likes what she sees. I can't blame her—this suit was made for me. Literally. "Hey handsome. What are you doing here?"

"Got a meeting in…" I glance down at my watch. "Ten minutes."

"Oh my God." She pulls her lips into her mouth and slaps a hand over it. She starts giggling like a thirteen-year-old girl at a Backstreet Boys concert in 1998.

"Something funny?"

She shakes her head and pretends to button her mouth. "Nope. Nothing at all." Another giggle slips out. It's kind of got this evil way about it that makes me a little nervous, but mostly intrigued. "You're gonna have so much fun in there. See ya!" She turns on her heel and heads for a car that's just pulled up behind us.

"Charlee, wait! I wanted to ask—"

"Gotta go, Avery! Sorry!" She wiggles her fingers in way of a wave and climbs into the backseat, slamming the door behind her. She sticks her head out the window. "All will be revealed inside," she says, drumming her fingers together. Shit, she's kinda scary. I like her.

But still, she just rode away, leaving me here with no answers. So that's why I groan, dragging my hand down my face. "Fuck."

Wyatt claps me on the back. "Shit, eh? That was Ginger's friend? Shoulda got her number."

Thank you, Captain Obvious. "Yes, Wyatt, I'm aware. That's why I said *fuck* when she drove away."

Chuckling, he shoves his hands in his pants pockets, walking ahead of me through the glass doors.

We pause in the entryway, taking in the space. I feel like shit. The owner is an old friend of ours. We went to school together here in Toronto, but lost touch pretty quickly when he moved back to his hometown afterwards. He's been back in Toronto for a few

50

years now, returning when he expanded this brewery of his, and though we'd met up for a couple drinks here and there, Wyatt and I hadn't been down to check out the place before today.

"We're shit friends," I say quietly.

Wyatt sighs, scratching a hand through his hair. "Was just thinking the same."

I do a slow spin, taking in all the details, the touches that make this place unique. "It's gorgeous."

Wyatt hums his agreement. "Might not be a huge investment for us, but I think it's a good one."

My head bobs. "It's got that charm people love. It'll turn a big profit for him." And by fault, for us too.

The whole thing is brick walls, exposed ceilings, dark wooden beams, black metal, and Edison bulbs. That perfect mix of old and new, modern and industrial.

I stroll over to the big U-shaped bar. The wall behind it is a giant chalkboard with all their drink options and a couple appetizers written in various intricate fonts. It looks like someone spent a lot of time on it. The bar top is amazing, dark walnut with a red river that runs through the center. I rap my knuckles on it. I like it. I want it.

A rough voice booms from my right. "Who the hell let you two in here?"

I grin when I see Dex, the owner, jogging down a set of wooden stairs in one corner of the big space. I take his hand before pulling him in for a hug.

"Shit, dude." I look him over. "I don't remember you being so big."

He laughs, embracing Wyatt. "Been hitting the gym a bit harder than I used to. Gotta pack on the muscles to keep up with you two."

Dex has always been a big guy, tall like me, with broad shoulders. But it looks like he's put on a solid twenty pounds of muscle since I've seen him last, which was…

"How long's it been this time?" I scrub my jaw, searching through my memories.

"Too long," he chuckles, clapping my back.

"Can't believe we haven't been here before," Wyatt says, guilt draping his features. "We should have been here a thousand times over. The space is amazing, man."

Dex waves a dismissive hand and smiles. "Ah, don't worry about it. Life gets in the way. You're here now." He points to the staircase. "We're up on the third floor. Shall we?"

The third floor is just as charming as the first with all the same touches. Dex introduces us to the secretary and I notice she's got a desk that matches the bar downstairs.

"I think you're gonna love the staff here," he tells us as we follow him into a large conference room. "It's casual here. We're not too serious."

Wyatt swipes a hunk of cheese off the table. "You never were too serious."

Dex only shrugs. "Not a way to live life." Laughter rings with the voices that start floating down the hallway, and he looks up, grinning.

"Here's the gang now."

I watch his employees start to filter in, noting that they're all male. Dex starts with introductions, but when I hear a soft, pretty laugh drift into the room, my head swivels.

And there she is, ladies and gentlemen.

The reason Charlee said I was going to have so much fun in my meeting today.

CHAPTER SEVEN

Avery

My heart stutters as I take Claire in. Her copper hair is swept back into a long ponytail that waves down her back, a few loose tendrils framing her face. She's wearing a simple white t-shirt tucked into a long red skirt with little white flowers that hugs the curve of her hips and flows down her legs, sweeping open in the front with each step she takes. It's tied together with a little bow on the front of one hip, and the finishing touch is the strappy, white heels, little pink toes peeping out.

I swear, she's utter perfection.

What's even more perfect is that she doesn't notice me. Yet.

An elbow jabs me hard in the ribs. "Stop fucking staring."

I see that stupid smirk on Wyatt's face, and my matching one slips up, because I can't help it. He chuckles and shakes his head, his eyes flitting to Claire as he gives her the old once-over. And then twice-over. And then three times over.

I flick his ear. "Back off."

"What? She turned you down." His brows quirk with smug amusement. "Fair game."

I give him a half playful growl, but my gaze slides back to Claire. Her arms are full. She's balancing a cellphone, pencil case, notebook, binder, drink, and a muffin, all on top of a laptop. Everything wobbles when she takes a step. Her eyes go wide with fear, making the corner of my mouth lift. I have an urge to dart over there and help her.

But someone else gets there first.

"Here, Claire," the sandy-haired man says to her, grinning down at her. He takes her drink and muffin off her laptop. "Let me help you with that."

She beams up at him, setting the rest of her things down at the far end of the table, except for her pen, which she twirls between her fingers. "Thanks so much, Grant. You're the best."

"Only for you." He winks at her. He fucking *winks* at her.

Wyatt leans in, his voice dropping low. "You've got competition."

"Fuck off," I mutter, shoving him with my shoulder.

Laughing, he wanders over to her, tapping her shoulder, making her spin. Her forehead creases for a moment like she's trying to place him, but then she just shakes his hand, gives him a breathtaking smile, and tells him how nice it is to meet him.

"You've gotta meet my partner," Wyatt tells her, placing a hand on her lower back as he ushers her my way. "I think you'll really like him."

It bothers me more than it should that Claire gets stopped every couple of steps for hugs that last too long, tugs on the tip of her ponytail. I resist the urge to go over there and slap all their hands away. I have no inclination to share, even if she's still hesitant about sharing with me.

Her pen slips from her grasp and tumbles to the ground just a moment before our gazes should meet. "Whoops," she breathes out with an airy giggle, bending to pick it up.

But I get there first.

She watches my fingers wrap around her black pen and her eyes travel slowly up my body, starting at my feet, as she follows the line of my body up, up, until our gazes finally lock. Her jaw unhinges with the broad grin I flash her, cheeks flooding with pink, and that's the first time I notice the light smattering of freckles that dot down her nose and across her cheekbones.

"Hey there." My voice is husky; I don't mean it to be. But when I notice the way her chest starts rapidly rising and falling, when each exhale is raspier then the last, my dick stands at attention, urging me to keep going.

Claire opens her mouth. She closes her mouth. She opens it again. Looks like I've rendered her speechless. I'm feeling a bit smug and the irritation clouding her lovely features tells me it shows.

A heavy hand claps me on the back as Dex steps up to us. "Ah, Avery. I see you've met our Miss Thompson."

Thompson. Claire Thompson.

Claire comes to life suddenly, planting a smile on her face. It's huge and fake as hell. Her deep green eyes are throwing daggers at me.

"Claire Thompson," she says when I slip my hand into hers. It's tiny and warm and a whole lot clammy. She's nervous. "Nice to meet you, Mr…?"

My grin grows until I'm sure my cheeks are going to split wide open. She's gonna play this game, is she? "Beck. Avery Beck."

"Right. Nice to meet you, Mr. Beck." She tries to pull her hand back, but I'm holding on for dear life. Her gaze falls to the connection before lifting back up to mine, expression frantic like she's terrified I'm going to set her skin ablaze.

When she gives her hand a good tug, I make the reluctant decision to let her go. It's my second choice. My first is to toss her over my shoulder, cart her off to a closet, and fuck her brains out.

"Claire's my second-in-command," Dex tells me, seemingly oblivious to whatever the hell is going on between us. "I'm lucky to have her. She'll be your number one contact if things proceed. I know she'll be a great asset to you."

Great asset. Yeah, that sounds about right.

"I have no doubt," I murmur, not able to wipe that smirk off my face. "Well Claire, I look forward to working with you." *And fucking you.* "I can't wait for you to show me the ropes." *And your bedroom.* "I'm sure we'll make a great team." *I make you come; you scream my name. Partnership at its finest.*

Claire's nostrils flare, lips smashing together and cheeks blazing like she's just read my mind. Kinda hope she has.

I quirk one suggestive brow at her. She turns on her heel to walk away. More like storm. She *storms* away, fists curled tight at her sides.

"Uh, Claire?" She swivels back, that strawberry ponytail spinning out in one wild wave. I don't miss the way she sucks in a breath that I'm sure is meant to steel her nerves. I hold up her pen. "Forgot something."

Her shoulders sag on a heavy exhale. "Right. Thanks." She plucks it out of my hand, careful not to touch me in any way, shape, or form, and stalks off to the far end of the table. She sinks into her chair and opens her laptop, disappearing behind the screen.

The spot to her right is open and she glances up at me at the exact moment my eyes land on it. Her emerald gaze darts to it, then back to me. Her mouth drops. She looks, quite literally, ready to throw herself over the damn chair.

I make it there in three long strides, plopping down next to her. Tilting my head over my shoulder, I flash her my best grin. Her cheeks burn bright and she averts her gaze to her keyboard, flexing her fingers over it.

Dex leans over, whispering something in her ear. She smiles up at him and nods. His answering grin is huge, and his eyes stay on her face a little longer than I'd like.

He glances around the room and claps his hands. "Alright boys and lady." He looks pointedly at Claire, and that's when I realize she's the only female in the room. "Are we ready to get started?" he asks before swiping Claire's iced coffee off the table, guzzling down a long sip. What the fuck is going on there?

Moving to the front of the room, Dex keys up his laptop, turning on the projector screen behind him. He waves a hand through the air. "Drinks are coming around. Have whatever you like."

As if on cue, a pretty, leggy brunette appears in the room, towing in a cart of bottles and tall cans. Her eyes meet mine and linger, coy smile playing on her scarlet lips. Claire's eyes dart between us and her knee starts bouncing beneath the table. I slip my hand under it and rest it on her knee. It stills immediately as she swallows, fixing her gaze on the pen in her hands.

The woman with the beer winks at Claire. "I know what you want."

Claire laughs softly. "Am I that predictable?"

"Nope, you just know what you like, and so do the rest of us." She opens a tall red can and pours the beer into a wide, round glass with a short stem, handing it to Claire. It's an interesting shade of amber, almost pink, or coral, maybe. The woman looks back to me, fluttering her lashes. "What can I get for you, handsome?"

I gesture to Claire's drink. "I'll have whatever she's having."

Claire blinks at me. "You don't even know what I'm drinking. What if you don't like it?"

Ah, there's that sass. I swipe her glass and take a sip before she can stop me. Her fingers tighten around her pen. With a loud smacking noise, I swallow the fruity, mildly sour beer. "I like it. I'll have what she's having."

Wyatt chuckles beside me, Dex watching the curiosity. The woman makes her way around the table, twisting caps off, popping tabs, pouring beers for everyone.

I grab a piece of cheese and a grape off the spread that's set up down the middle of the table. That's when I notice that the table matches the secretary's desk in the main office and the bar top downstairs, the same dark walnut, the cherry red epoxy river that runs in waves down the center of it.

"I love these," I admire out loud, rapping my knuckles on the wood.

"Claire's dad and brother made them," Dex pipes up. "She can hook you up."

Beside me, Claire groans and sinks lower into her chair, muttering something I can't hear. I throw her a look. She's really doing her damnedest to pretend I'm not here. So, to remind her, I slip one finger underneath the front hem of her skirt, which was fallen off the side of her legs, and trail a slow path up her silky thigh.

A sharp gasp bursts past her lips and her hand shoots under the table, gripping mine, forcing it to a stop. She doesn't look at me, just clenches her jaw and shoves my hand back to my own lap. I smother a chuckle, because this is fun. Does she forget how well-acquainted my hands got with her body on Friday?

Dex launches into the meeting at full force, talking about his plans to turn the second floor into a restaurant, building a second-deck patio, and expanding on the one downstairs. It's a good plan, one Wyatt and I have reviewed multiple times. We've already decided we're going to back the investment at our firm, so the meeting is really a formality, but Dex insisted he wanted to do it the right way, which I can appreciate. It puts some of our accountants at ease because they can't understand why we'd be interested in something so small.

If it wasn't Dex, we'd probably pass on it. Not because we don't think it'll succeed—it will—but because it really is so far off from our normal investments. We'd suggest a smaller firm, maybe one just starting out. It'd be a great project for a starter company and would turn them a decent profit, get them valuable experience and their foot in the door. But Dex is our friend and we know what type of businessman he is, so we agreed to take him on in a heartbeat.

That's why I let my mind wander to the beautiful redhead beside me. That's what I tell myself, at least. The way she's staring at her laptop leads me to believe it's the most riveting thing in the world, so I look over her shoulder to see what she's doing. Her breath catches in her throat. I can smell her shampoo, juicy citrus, and I want to devour her.

She's also doing absolutely nothing on her laptop.

She turns her head just a fraction of an inch to glare at me.

"Working hard?" I whisper with a cheeky smile.

"No harder than you," she retorts.

"Hmm." I drop my palm to her knee and shift back in my chair, rocking in it. "Hey Dex? What about selling merchandise?" I point to the Cherry Lane tee one of the guys is wearing. "Bet people would love those. Tees, hoodies, drinkware…" I shrug. "Simple, easy, and could bring in a pretty penny." I stand and stroll to the wall of windows that overlooks a beautiful stone patio, surrounded by a garden that's just recently started to come to life in the middle of May. "And big events. Weddings, engagement parties, work functions…People love doing that shit at wineries. Breweries are the new wineries."

Dex's smile is instantaneous and huge when I turn back to the room. "This is why I called you."

"That's what we're here for," I reply graciously, sweeping my hands out in front of me and reclaiming my seat beside Claire. She looks mildly annoyed that I'm not only paying attention, but also making fantastic suggestions.

She starts picking apart her muffin as a conversation about merchandise and event-planning picks up steam. Red jam oozes from the middle and I'm absolutely engrossed as she shoves a piece in her mouth, her tongue sweeping across her bottom lip to swipe at a drop of jam.

I reach over and break off a chunk, throwing it in my mouth. *Strawberry*. Why am I not surprised?

Claire leans into me, all squinty-eyed. "You know no boundaries, do you?"

"Aren't we past boundaries, little Miss Strawberry?"

Her cheeks flush with heat. "Oh my God," she breathes angrily. "You're infuriating." Picking up her pen, she starts turning it in her fingers, as if she needs anything to do to distract from the fact that I'm sitting here beside her, annoying the hell out of her.

So I take that too, plucking it right from her grasp, sliding the top of it between my teeth and leaning back in my chair to smile at her. I might wag my eyebrows too. She looks like she's either going to blow a gasket or back me up against a wall and shove her tongue down my throat. Teasing her is entirely too easy and way too much fun.

Huffing, she pins her arms over her chest—which looks absolutely fantastic in that skin-tight tee, by the way. "You're ruining my Monday morning."

"Really? 'Cause you're making mine a hundred times better."

The corner of her mouth twitches. She's doing a piss-poor job of hiding that smile.

"I've been thinking about you all weekend," I tell her in a hushed voice, twisting closer to her in my chair.

Her eyes shift to sideways to meet mine. "You have not."

"I have, I promise you." Leaning in obnoxiously close, I flip through the pages in her journal, pretending like we're talking about something to do with the brewery. It's filled with notes and a lot of doodles. It makes me smile. Absently, I scroll my name across a page. Then hers. Might add a plus sign in between the two and circle it with a heart. "Been thinking about how delicious you taste, how you feel under my fingers…Are you telling me you haven't thought about me once since you rode away from me on Friday night?"

Her breath stutters, heat radiating off her face like a furnace. Her lashes flutter and her lips part. She uncrosses and crosses her legs. She's an open book, terrible at hiding her feelings. "I…Avery…"

"Yes, Claire?"

A sudden and swift kick to my shin sends me folding forward over the table, my hand clutching tightly at Claire's. I flip Wyatt the bird, because he's the obvious culprit.

"Would you two shut the hell up or take this outside and screw already?" he seethes quietly, jerking his head toward the front of the room where Dex's gaze flickers between the three of us.

Claire rips her hand out from under mine, burying her red face in her hands. She's adorable.

"Rein yourself in, Beck," Wyatt begs. "Like, ten more minutes, that's all I'm asking. Then you two can go back to whatever the hell this is." He circles a hand around our general vicinity.

"What it is, is *nothing*," Claire insists on a hiss.

Wyatt snorts. "Yeah, okay. We may have just met, beautiful Claire, but I'm not blind."

"Right?" I whisper-yell. "Thanks, man."

"*Seriously*? I'm gonna punch both of you in the face!" She jabs an angry finger into my shoulder and shoots Wyatt a fierce scowl. Quiet, angry Claire is the best Claire. She stands abruptly and gives Dex a tight-lipped smile. "I'm so sorry, Dex. I'll be right back. Just need to use the bathroom."

I watch her leave, those hips of hers bouncing back and forth, and as soon as the thought starts rolling through my head, Wyatt speaks it and shuts it right down.

"Don't even think about it. You're not following her."

I grumble to myself but then spy her cell sitting next to her laptop, and—would you look at that—it's not password protected. Typical. So I do the only logical thing: add my contact and then call myself from her phone so that I have her number too. Tucking it back beside her laptop, I give Claire a smile as she slips back into the room, and then do as Wyatt requested: I rein myself in.

For the next twenty minutes, I listen and participate actively in the discussion and pretend that the most fascinating girl I've ever met isn't sitting beside me. I like when Claire talks, because it gives me a reason to be absolutely enthralled with her without getting my ass handed to me by Wyatt or any weird looks from Dex. She flips through a color-coded binder, offering up tidbits of information about the contractors she's been in touch with so far.

But when the meeting is over, she's the first out of the room, scooping up her belongings and dashing down the hallway like the room is on fire and we're all going down.

Dex takes Wyatt and I on a tour of the facility and we get a firsthand look at the space on the second floor for the proposed restaurant. One wall is floor-to-ceiling window views of the Toronto Harbour.

"It's going to be amazing," I tell him honestly, tucking my hands in my pockets as we head back up to the third floor and disappear into his office. "You're going to absolutely explode here when this takes off. You ready for that?" I sink into an oversized leather couch under one of the many windows.

Dex nods, wringing his hands together. "Think so. I'm really excited about this."

I meet Wyatt's gaze and he gestures for me to continue. "Well, we're in."

Dex's mouth drops as he slides his palms over the desk. "Seriously?"

"Dude, we told you before that we were in," Wyatt reminds him with a chuckle.

"Well, I know, but…I don't know. I guess I just…I can't believe this is really happening. This is incredible." He rounds the desk, taking a turn to pull us both in for one of those man hugs, clapping us on the back. "I can't thank you enough."

"Ah, shit." Wyatt tugs his ringing phone out of his pocket and glances up at us. "Sorry, guys. Gotta take this." He sighs as he walks out the door. "Hi Mom."

Dex leans on his desk, staring down at me, pensive. I know that look.

I sweep my hands out in front of me. "Go ahead, Dex. What's on your mind?" I'm ninety-nine percent sure I already know.

He grins, skimming his jaw with his fingers. "You know Claire." It's not a question.

"I do."

"How?"

"Met her Friday night. She was out with some friends."

"Did you two…" His eyebrows climb his forehead in question.

"Nah." I kick my feet out in front of me. "I won't lie—I wanted to. She's…" Gorgeous? Sexy as sin? Sassy? It's impossible to choose just one.

"I know," he says on an exhale. Clearly, he doesn't need me to finish my sentence.

I eye him curiously. There's an odd dynamic between those two. "You two ever hook up?"

Chuckling, he plops down in the chair behind his desk, lacing his fingers behind his head. "Once. Three years ago."

I have to admit, I'm a little bit jealous. I'm also wondering how the hell someone manages just once with Claire. I mean, I haven't had sex with her, but if our brief encounter is any indication, the sex would be wild. "Only once? Not worth a second trip around the block?" Even I feel like an asshole asking that question.

"The sex was fantastic if that's what you're asking. I mean, you've met her. She's…"

"Feisty?"

He laughs. "Yeah."

"Mmm. So why only once then?"

He sighs, scratching at the gold scruff lining his jaw. "I've known Claire since she was eight. She's like my little sister. And she *is* my little sister's best friend."

My brows shoot up. "Charlee?"

He nods. "You know her?"

"Met her Friday. And again out front this morning."

"Yeah, she runs marketing here. And party planning," he adds with an eyeroll. "Claire moved out here to work for me, and I took her out her first night to celebrate. We had way too much to drink and acted on impulse. She regretted it immediately, said we never should have crossed that line."

"Did you?" I ask. "Regret it?"

His lips curl with a secret smile. "Does she look like the type of girl anyone would ever regret?"

Nope. Definitely not. And I'm still jealous.

"Is it going to be a problem? You two working together? I mean, you'll be together a lot."

Just perfect. "Nope," I assure him. "Not a problem, man. Don't worry."

"Okay." He looks like he's not done. "I just…I mean, I hate to say it this way, but don't be a dick, Avery." I bark out a laugh but he shakes his head, pointing a threatening finger at me. "No, I'm not joking. She just got out of a relationship with a real piece of shit. I know Claire's got a big attitude, but she's sensitive. She also hasn't had a particularly easy life these past six years or so. I'm just warning you—she's not made for your world."

"What do you mean?" I'm mildly hooked on what his definition of *my world* is, but mostly curious about what's happened to her in the last six years.

"You know what I mean. Look, I know you're up-front about your playboy lifestyle, girls know what they're getting themselves into, all that bullshit, but that's not Claire. She's not a casual sex kinda girl. She's the kinda girl you wanna marry. Don't fuck around with her unless you have plans to actually get serious."

I nod thoughtfully, chewing the inside of my cheek. I'm not a serious kinda guy. Dex hit the nail on the head with the playboy lifestyle comment.

Claire's already made a point of telling me this several times. It doesn't take a genius to take a look at her and know she's the marrying kind. But I'm not the marrying kind. Maybe in a couple years, but who the hell knows. One day, I always assumed. When I'm ready.

"Note taken, though you act like I'm incapable of dating, my friend," I say with a smile as I stand up, smoothing my hand down my tie.

He snorts. "I'm not sure if I've ever known you to have a girlfriend."

"I've had…a few."

"Right, and how long have they lasted?"

"The most recent one? Three weeks." I couldn't handle her level of crazy cling-on, and honestly, it wasn't even recent. I'm actually not even sure I'd call her a girlfriend, but I did stop sleeping with anyone but her for those three weeks, so there's that.

Laughing, Dex shakes his head. "Exactly." He rounds his desk, gripping my hand. "Guess we'll be seeing a lot of each other."

"Sure will. I'll touch base with you and Claire in a couple days and we'll get started right away. How's that sound?"

"Perfect, Beck. Perfect. Hey, I appreciate it. Again, man. Can't tell you enough." He pauses at his door, his fingers drumming against the frame. "Please remember what I said. Be careful…with Claire. She means a lot to me."

"Gotcha." I lift two fingers to my forehead in mock salute. Then I smile genuinely. "Nah, it's all good, man. I'll be careful."

But then I catch sight of Claire, bent over the secretary's desk. She stands up, shakes her ponytail down her back, throws her head back in laughter, and locks eyes with me.

Those green eyes pop and her smile melts right off her face before she turns on her heel, darting down the hallway much faster than I would have ever dreamed possible for those little legs of hers.

And just like that, all my good intentions fly right out the window.

CHAPTER EIGHT

Claire

I've never been more annoyed at the length of my legs in my entire life. I'm cursing them every step of the way as I dash down the hallway like the time my brother stole the tarantula out of the science lab and chased me through the entire high school.

I throw one last glance over my shoulder to see Avery fucking Beck absolutely devouring the distance between us with his mile-long legs and that unquestionably infuriating, self-righteous smirk glued to his stupidly sexy face.

Nope, not happening. Not today, Satan.

Flinging myself through the door, I stumble into my office, spinning wildly to slam the door before Avery—see sexy Satan—can trap me inside.

Except that an arm shoots out and shoves the door open, sending me flying backwards, because obviously that's how this day is gonna go.

Avery steps into my office, shutting the door behind him. He flips the lock, sending my heart into overdrive. "Shit, Claire, almost thought you had me beat there for a second." He wipes nonexistent sweat off his dark brow and grins at me.

I want to shove my tongue down his throat. Fuck.

My arm is way too shaky when I point at the door. "Out! Get out!"

Could the man honestly look any more arrogant than he does right now? And also, so highly fuckable in that perfectly tailored suit, hugging his lean waistline, his broad shoulders. Oh dear Lord, this is bad. This is so, *so* bad.

"Now, Claire," he says proudly, not bothering to attempt to hide the smug amusement lingering on his tongue. He holds his palms up in a bullshit show of innocence and takes a step toward me. I mirror it with my own step backwards.

He takes another forward. I take another back.

He bites back his smile. "I love this little cat and mouse game you and I have going on."

"There's no game. You and I have nothing going on." Except how badly I wanna climb him. The back of my knees hit my couch. "Stop walking toward me!"

"Why? Nowhere to go?"

He chuckles at my horrified expression. Because if this man lays a finger on me, I'm going to melt into a puddle, and I think I've suffered enough humiliation for one day.

Isn't it enough that I had to literally escape the meeting to wipe the hot spot between my legs? My panties are still uncomfortably damp an hour later and now I'm going to be squeezing my thighs together the rest of the day. It's embarrassing, and I can't understand for the life of me why this man is having this effect on me, other than just being insanely nice to look at.

"I'm just trying to be cordial, Claire. We're going to be working together, you and I. Spending a lot of time together. Getting close. It's best to be friendly, isn't it?"

I snort. "Why do I think your definition of 'friendly' is a fuckload different than the one in the dictionary?"

"You think so?"

I pin my arms across my chest, effectively closing myself off. "I know so, Mr. Beck."

"Well then, why don't we have a look?"

Blinking up at him, I drop my arms. "What?"

He sweeps one hand—one large, magical hand—out toward my computer. "Let's look it up. *Friendly*."

"Is that really necessary?"

An amused smile dons his flawlessly chiseled face and he tucks his hands in his pant pockets, rocking back on his heels. It should be illegal for someone to look this ridiculously good in a suit. It's like it was made for him.

I mean, it probably was. For some reason, that just irritates me further.

"Afraid I'm right?" Avery teases, luring me in.

"Pfft. No." Back go my arms across my chest, hip popping.

I stalk over to my computer and let him pull my chair out for me. He slides me into my desk, and I watch his long fingers glide slowly across the walnut.

"I really like these desks," he murmurs, almost to himself. He grips the edge of the wood and leans overtop of me.

"Must you stand so close?"

Avery drops forward until I feel his chest pressing against my back, his breath tickling my ear. "Stop stalling, lovely Claire."

My teeth clack together keep from screaming. My hand takes way longer than it should to find my mouse, considering it's only three inches to the right. I move the cursor around the screen when it wakes up, but apparently, I'm not moving fast enough for Mr. Beck. His hand closes over mine on the mouse and he jerks it, minimizing my email and clicking for the Safari tab.

Ignoring the way his hand feels on mine, like I just stuck my fingers in a live socket, I turn and glare at him. It's a mistake, because our lips are like, a half inch apart. I can taste his breath, the sweet acidity of the Strawberry Grove beer he drank during the meeting sweeping into my mouth, caressing my tongue. I yelp and turn back to the screen while he chuckles into my hair.

"I can do it," I insist harshly, throwing his hand off mine and jabbing an elbow back into his thigh. I just narrowly miss the impressive package lurking between his legs. Damn.

Clicking on the search bar, I flex my fingers over the keys, but all I can feel is *him*. Behind me, beside me, *on* me. He smells so good, like cedar and citrus. It's intoxicating and maddening. I feel like banging my head off the keyboard.

"F…R…"

"Oh my God!" Swiveling, I shove him. Hard. He doesn't even budge. "I know how to spell, you ass!"

The way his eyes twinkle when he laughs, deep lines forming around his cheeks, makes my face soften for a moment. I feel the corner of my mouth twitch.

"Holy shit," Avery breathes, dipping his head to look at me. His dark chocolate eyes widen.

"What?" I swipe at my chin, hoping I don't have strawberry jam on it from my muffin.

He taps the corner of my mouth. "Is that a smile? Are you smiling at me?"

"Oh, shut up." I slap his hand away and turn back to the computer. But now my smile is full-grown. How the hell did this happen? I shake my head and type *friendly definition* into the Google search bar. I click on the first link.

"Kind and pleasant," I read aloud. This is stupid. Why did I let him con me into this?

"Check and check," Avery says proudly.

My eyes roll and his grin only broadens. It's all cute and lopsided, that little dimple in his chin popping. I just wanna touch it.

I hum as I skim over the weird stuff about friendly soccer matches, because—what the hell?

"Oh, look." Avery snatches the mouse away. He circles the cursor near the bottom of the screen. "On affectionate terms." He drops his cheek to mine, chin resting on my shoulder. "I think you'll remember that I can be *very* affectionate." He turns, ever so slightly, and brushes his lips across my cheekbone.

I go completely rigid, every single part of me—except for that thing in the center of my chest, which happens to be pumping on overdrive right now, slamming wildly against my sternum. I feel like my chest cavity is cracking wide-open.

Avery keeps reading, and I wish he wouldn't. "Favorable or serviceable. Hmm..." His hands settle on my shoulders and he drags them slowly down my arms. I watch as goosebumps dot my traitorous skin. "What do you think, Claire?" he whispers in my ear. A shiver rocks my body and I feel him smile against my neck. "Would you consider me serviceable? I mean, I know we didn't have much time together on Friday, but you seemed very *favorable* of my *services*." He jerks my chair out from the desk and spins me toward him. "I can show you just how serviceable I can be, sweet little strawberry."

I gasp as his long fingers grip my knees, uncrossing my legs, my wrap skirt falling to the side, exposing me in a way I'm not entirely comfortable with in broad daylight with only one beer pumping through me. Still, I send a silent prayer up to whoever reminded me to shave my legs this morning. "What are you doing?"

He slides his palms over my knees and up my thighs, leaving my skin tingling in the wake of his touch. I'm gripping the arms of my leather chair so hard my knuckles are turning white. His fingers curve over the side of my legs and he reaches up, grabbing my hips under my skirt as he tugs me to the edge of my chair.

"Avery," I breathe, my eyes wildly searching his. He drops to his knees between my legs, his gaze too intense, too penetrating, but I can't look away. It's like a bad car wreck, except it's wonderful. But also awful.

"I've been thinking about you, Claire," Avery's husky voices rasps. His soft lips skim the inside of my knee. "For the last three days. Can't get you out of my head." He runs a finger along the waistband of my satin panties. "Don't even know why. It's infuriating, to tell you the truth."

There's a voice somewhere in the back of my head telling me I should shut this shit down, but it's like it's disconnected from the rest of me.

"Do you remember how my fingers felt? When I touched you…here?" His thumb grazes over my aching nub through my panties and he arches a pleased brow. "You're wet, Claire."

I've never worked so hard to suppress a groan. "No shit," I say with as much bite as I can spit out. But I can't deny it—I'm pretty shocked about it. I can't honestly remember the last time Aaron made me wet. This man has made me wet three times in the three days that I've known him, and that's not including the four times I got myself all hyped up just thinking about him over the weekend. I took care of myself those times.

He chuckles and shakes his head, pressing his thumb against my clit. I gasp, my head lolling to the side. I wanna yell at him to stop. I wanna lift my knee right into his face. I wanna rip his hands off me and run away from him. I wanna drop my panties and have him bend me right over this desk.

To put it bluntly, the man's undoing all of my well-laid plans. I want to fuck him, and that just can't happen. I'm on a man-fast, and it needs to stay that way.

But he keeps pressing, circling, his mocha eyes gazing curiously into mine, like he's trying to figure me out. It's kind of alarming, and I feel oddly exposed. And I don't mean because my legs are wide open, on display for him, and he's touching me. In my office.

"Oh my God!" I clamp my legs shut and push him off me. "I'm at work!" I shout, as if I'm just realizing this. I spring from my chair and back way the hell up, hands wringing nervously in front of my chest.

"So what?" He closes the distance between us in three quick strides. "I locked the door." His hand slides along my jaw, curving over my neck.

I nearly forgot how damn tall this man is. He absolutely towers over me, even in my three-inch heels, making me feel tiny. Before I can stop myself, my hands glide over his thick arms in his navy

71

suit jacket, sweeping over his broad shoulders. Honestly, the man is huge.

Bet he could really throw me around.

"I can, Claire," Avery chuckles, pulling me closer. "Want me to show you?"

I blink. Twice. "What?"

Bending his neck, his mouth skims along the edge of my jaw. My head tilts and a groan rumbles deep in my throat. "Throw you around," he murmurs when he stops at my ear.

My body freezes, my hands squeezing his shoulders so tightly he actually flinches a bit. "I said that out loud?" I shake my head, mortified, my cheeks flooding with heat. "No." God, *no*. Could I possibly humiliate myself any further?

I take a step back but his hand catches mine, towing me back.

"You only spoke my thoughts, Miss Thompson. Don't be shy." His chocolate eyes darken and his lids hood, tongue dragging across his lower lip. "I'm going to kiss you now."

Oh, shit. No. No, I shouldn't. I shouldn't, right?

His lips descend in slow motion and I have every single intention of saying no, stepping aside, but when his full lips part, my tongue darts out to sweep across mine, wetting them in anticipation of what I know is going to be one hell of a kiss.

But that's when I hear it. A shrill giggle and a scream, followed by the gentle slam of a little body into the outside of my door. I startle with a jump and Avery's head snaps up, his forehead creasing with confusion. The handle jiggles.

"Daddyyy!" a tiny voice shrieks. "Help! Open! Puh-*lease!*"

Saved, saved, saved! No bad decisions for Claire Thompson today!

I shove away from a very perplexed Avery and make a mad dash for the door, whipping it open after hitting the lock. A tiny copper-haired beauty comes stumbling in on her chunky, roly-poly little legs. She shrieks when she sees me, her bright green eyes and wide

72

smile lighting up her entire face and mine, because sweet Lord, I love this little chick.

I scoop her up in my arms and spin her around, showering her face in loud, smacking kisses. "My baby," I cry, never letting up on those kisses. She bubbles over with laughter, her pudgy hands pressing against my cheeks as she tips her head backwards in an attempt to escape me, even though I know she doesn't really want to go anywhere.

My eyes land on a terrified Avery, cowering in the corner. I fight the urge to bark out a laugh. He doesn't do kids, clearly, and this whole scene before him is frightening. So now I kinda wanna mess with him.

I tip Vivi back up to me and smile, rubbing the tip of my nose across hers before I plant a soft kiss on her pink pout. "I missed you."

"Oh, fuck—I mean, shit. I mean, fuck." My brother—my very exhausted looking brother—pauses in the doorway, his shoulders sagging with a dramatic huff when he sees Vivi. "Fuck it, I can't think of another word." His eyes bounce between Vivi and me. "She won't remember, right?"

And because Vivi is Vivi and she's related to us, she looks her dad square in the face and says, "Oh, fuck, Daddy!"

We explode with laughter, even Avery's quiet chuckle filling the room. I look up to find him still looking a little uncertain, but also slightly amused. He's also no longer cowering in the corner. There's a major crease marring that forehead as his eyes bounce between me and Vivi, likely noting the similarities. Part of me wants to see how long I can drag this out for. If he thinks I have a kid, I bet it would send him running for the hills and this whole teasing gig would be over quick.

Casey pushes the stroller through the door and slings the bag off his shoulder and into the seat. He wraps his arms around me and his daughter, planting a kiss on my cheek. "Thanks so much for doing this so last minute, Claire."

He pulls away and drags his curious gaze over Avery. I shift a little awkwardly on my feet as I watch the two of them size each other up.

Casey thumbs at Avery. "Who's that?"

Ugh, I guess the charade is up.

"Casey, this is Avery," I tell him, tipping my head toward Avery. To my surprise, Avery steps forward, hand outstretched. "Avery, Casey." Avery's eyes flit back and forth between me and Casey and I fight the urge to roll my eyes, because I know what he's wondering. "My brother."

I don't miss the way his entire expression softens, and I think he even breathes a sigh of relief, all his suspicions firmly squashed.

I watch the two of them exchange a firm handshake before Casey slaps Avery on the back. "Sorry about my swearing daughter. I guess it's unavoidable between me and Claire."

Avery chuckles, twinkling eyes set on me. "Yeah, your sister swears like a trucker."

Casey grins and winks, placing a palm over his proud chest. "Learned from the best." He turns back to me and plants another kiss on my cheek. "Hey, I really gotta go, sorry." He takes his daughter out of my arms and throws her in the air before pulling her shirt up and blowing on her belly. "Bye, baby. Be good for Auntie Claire. I'll pick you up tomorrow, 'kay?"

Vivi always does this adorable thing where she scrunches her nose up and pretends she's a pig. She chooses this moment to do that, oinking so hard I worry she might choke. Avery's face lights up and my heart does this weird flippy thing that I hate.

Casey tickles Vivi's belly. "Love you, little Miss Piggy." He plops her back in my arms and runs a hand through his messy hair. "Oh, hey, is Charlee around?"

My eyes narrow. "Thought you really had to go."

He hits me with a guilty grin. "Just wanted to say hi; fucking shoot me." He glances at Vivi and covers her ears.

"Casey, it doesn't work when you cover her ears *after* you fucking swear."

Avery's hearty laugh coaxes my gaze to his. "And chastising your brother for swearing by swearing back at him doesn't really work either, Claire."

"Yeah, *Claire*," Casey teases, tugging on the tip of my pony. He shakes Avery's hand again and I'm annoyed by how chummy they already are. "Nice to meet you, Avery. I'm sure I'll be seeing you again."

My nostrils flare at his assumption.

My brother gives me a look, one that says he wants to know what's going on there, one brow quirked high on his forehead. I roll my eyes and shove him out the door with my foot. He closes it behind him, but I wish he hadn't.

"Fwend?" Vivi asks me, squishing my cheeks together. She looks at Avery.

"Yes, baby. That's my friend." He's not, but how do you explain that to your two-and-a-half-year-old niece? I need to be a good role model, because I'd prefer that she doesn't wind up like me one day. "His name is Avery." I look at the man in question who's now slowly approaching, hands in his pockets, wide grin planted on his face. It's adorable. Where's the scared man from a few minutes ago? "Avery, this is my niece, Vivi."

"Hi Vivi," he says softly. "Nice to meet you."

"You Care Bear fwend," she says, reaching out to poke him in the chest. She picks up his silky black tie and rubs it against her chubby cheek. "Wight, A'wy?" Her toddler-speak is adorable and heart-melting, no matter how regularly I hear it, making me melt into her, cuddling her closer.

Avery gives me a quizzical smile. "Care Bear?"

My chest sags with a groan. "My brother and Charlee have called me Claire Bear my whole life. Vivi couldn't pronounce her L's at first, so it was Care Bear to her. She can say my name just fine now, but…"

"But now you're Care Bear?"

I smile and nod. "I'm Care Bear."

"I luh Care Bear," Vivi tells Avery. "You luh Care Bear?"

Avery's head rolls on his shoulders. "Oh, I *love* Care Bear."

My squinty-eyed glare only has him winking.

Vivi giggles and squirms in my arms, trying to crawl down my body. "I hug A'wy."

"Honey," I start softly, tapping her nose. "Remember, you can't just hug people. Some people don't like to be hugged. You have to ask permission first."

Because she's got my sass, she scowls in my direction before turning her sweet, irresistible pout on Avery. I hope he likes hugs, 'cause little Miss Thang doesn't take no for an answer. "I hug you, A'wy?"

He presses a hand over his heart. "I would *love* a hug, Miss Vivi."

Vivi squeals with delight and I drop her carefully to her feet. She hops like a bunny to Avery, who bends and scoops her up, making a big deal of it with a loud grunt.

"Oh my God," he cries out. "You're so heavy!" He wraps his arms around her and cuddles her close while she buries her little face in his neck.

Ah, shit. They're adorable. Like, panty-melting adorable. My ovaries are bursting. Avery's eyes dart up to mine at the exact moment I realize I just moaned out loud. I grin sheepishly and clear my throat, looking to the window while I twirl the tip of my ponytail around my fingers.

But I drag my eyes back, because how can I not? Vivi's got one hand on his cheek while she babbles on about something, and her other hand is playing with the dark waves on top of Avery's head. I can't take it—my uterus officially goes into overdrive.

Avery's eyes crinkle when he laughs at something Vivi says, and then he tells her, "You know, Care Bear never gives me hugs." His eyes glisten playfully and his brows twitch up when he meets my narrowed, irritated gaze, because I know what game he's playing at.

Vivi gasps, outraged. Her head swivels and she beckons me over with her hand. "Come," she tells me. *Yes ma'am.*

I swallow my groan and walk over to them. Avery holds one arm out and I hesitantly step into his side. He wraps me up in their hug while I stand there with my arms pinned to my sides.

"Claire, you have to put your arms around us," he instructs as if I were the toddler.

Grumbling, I slip one arm around Vivi and the other around his waist. "You think you're so smooth," I hiss in his ear.

"I don't think, Care Bear. I know." His palm slides down my side, settling on my hip.

I want to swat his hand away. I want to tell him he's an egomaniacal jerk. But I can't. I hate to admit it, but he feels damn good. Too good. It's scary.

Vivi sighs happily, snuggling into us. "Best hug," she murmurs.

Avery chuckles softly, deep gaze set on me. His face is different, all cute and gentle, a tender smile tugging at his lips. My breath catches in my throat and I feel myself melting into his hard body.

The door opens with vigor, rebounding off the wall.

"I'm back, babe! Bumped into Casey downstairs. Lookin' hot, as per usual. Wanna go grab some lun—Oh, holy mother of dragons! What the shit is going on here?"

I shove away from Avery and push my hair off my hot cheeks, fluffing up my skirt, you know, in case it needs…fluffing.

Vivi shrieks. "Cha-Cha!" She wiggles in Avery's hold until he puts her down, running at full speed toward Charlee who catches her and squeals just as excitedly.

"Baby girl!" Charlee coos, spinning her around. She hugs her close and smirks at me and Avery. "I see you two found each other."

"Shut up," I mutter, turning on my heel and stalking off toward my desk. "Yes, let's get lunch. We just have to bring Viv."

"Not a problem. Just us gals." She looks sideways at Avery. "Sorry 'bout your luck, dude."

Holding his palms up, he shakes his head. "I'd hate to interrupt girl time." He turns and saunters over to me while I stuff my phone in my purse. "Well, I know your first and last name, I know where you work, and I've already met your best friend, your brother, and your niece. Think I can get your phone number now?"

"Nope."

"No?" He leans over my desk, covering my hand with his. I stare at it. "Come on, Claire."

"I already told you, I'm not fucking you," I whisper-yell.

"So? We don't have to fuck. Right away," he adds with a cheeky grin and a wink. "Let's go for dinner. Or lunch. Or dessert." I think dessert is code for fucking, but I'm not going to ask, because if it's not, it's just going to give him ideas.

So I just smile up at him and sling my purse over my shoulder. "Gotta go. See ya around."

I don't make it two steps before his hand wraps around my wrist and tugs me back to him. I stare up at him with huge eyes. It's incredible—*incredibly annoying*—how this man can turn me from strong, independent woman, to weak-in-the-knees schoolgirl in a split-second.

The way Avery's eyes cloud over makes me utterly confused, to say the least. My breathing kicks up, matching his rhythm, the rise and fall of his chest. He drops his face, the tip of his nose grazing across mine. "Bye Claire," he whispers.

He brushes the softest, lightest, almost-not-even-there kiss against my lips, and then strolls out of the office, but not before planting a quick cheek-peck on both Vivi and Charlee.

Charlee's jaw hangs as we stare at each other.

Vivi snickers, covering her mouth with her chubby little hands. "A'wy and Care Bear kiss."

Thirty minutes later, I'm sitting on a patio with my two favorite ladies, enjoying the warm afternoon, but mostly enjoying watching Vivi blow bubbles in her chocolate milk. It makes her so damn happy. She keeps squealing and clapping her hands. I miss when happiness was that simple. I'd blow the shit out of some chocolate milk to be even half as happy as she is right now.

"Still no word from her m-o-m?" Charlee asks, her gaze flipping to Vivi as she pretends her pizza is a dinosaur eating a french fry.

"Nope." And I hope it stays that way.

Charlee purses her lips to the side. "That's sad."

"Not really." I lay the menu down on the table. "She's better off without that awful bitch—I mean, *not nice lady*—in her life."

That woman doesn't deserve someone as beautiful and pure as Vivi. She didn't want her. She fought tooth and nail to get rid of her, right up until the last minute. She signed over all her parental rights—all too gladly—and got the hell out of Dodge. Her only regret was that Casey didn't go with her.

"Yeah," Charlee says on a heavy exhale. "You're probably right. Plus, she's got you."

I smile and squeeze her hand. "And you." Charlee's been an amazing help to Casey, and another auntie to Vivi. They love each other unconditionally and it makes me so incredibly happy. I never fail to realize how lucky I am to have Charlee in my life.

79

I watch the two of them gab back and forth. My phone dings in my purse and I dig it out. I've been waiting to hear back from a contractor about some prices on the kitchen expansion. Fingers crossed it's him, because he's been taking his sweet-ass time.

I blanch at the name rolling across my screen with its text message.

Avery: *How's lunch with the girls?*

My fingers fly over the keys at a furious speed.

Me: *How the hell did you get my number? And how is your contact in my phone???*

His response is instantaneous.

Avery: *We exchanged numbers in your office. Don't you remember?*

Oh. My. God.

Me: *No. Nope. Nuh uh. I specifically remember NOT giving you my number.*

Avery: *Huh. Weird.*

Avery: *Musta been when you ran off to the bathroom during the meeting then.*

I click through my call logs and, sure enough, there's an outgoing call to Avery Beck that I sure as hell didn't make, right smack dab in the middle of our meeting. I'm stuck somewhere between utterly outraged and a whole lot flattered that he wanted my number that badly. Also, kind of impressed that he already knows me well enough to know I was going to say no when he asked again. Nevertheless, I click through my settings and reinstate the passcode on my phone.

A tiny smile tilts my mouth at the kissing lips emoji and strawberry next to his name.

Me: *You are absolutely unbelievable.*

"Claire?" I hear Charlee's voice but I'm too engrossed to look up. "What's got you so worked up that you're smashing away at your phone?"

Holding my phone up to her, I huff, watching her eyes trail over the screen, her lips moving as she reads.

"Ha!" She grins settling back in her chair. "That's hilarious. I like him."

"It's *not* hilarious," I whine. My phone dings again.

Avery: *Don't forget friendly. Unbelievable AND friendly.*

Avery: *Friday. 6:30pm.*

Is this guy for real? Seriously, is he real life?

Me: *I'm not fucking you.*

Me: *And I'm not having dinner with you either.*

Avery: *Nope. You're coming to my office and we're working. This is a professional relationship, Claire. Get your mind out of the gutter. Bring your floorspace plans and any info/quotes you've gotten from contractors already.*

A tingle of embarrassment tickles my cheeks, because of course that's what this is about. We have to work together, and closely at that. Like Dex said, I'm the contact person for this job. He's not messaging me for *me*.

Avery: *You might want to dress in comfy clothes. There's no telling how long we'll be holed up together. I plan on working you hard all night long.*

Okay, screw this shit.

CHAPTER NINE

Avery

"Here you go, handsome." A tall red can slides across the marble table in front of me and a frosty pint glass drops beside it. "Anything else I can get for you?"

I look up at the waitress. Tall-ish, blond hair, bright blue eyes, sexy red smirk, and a nice set of tits, invariably swelling out from a low-cut top. We've been flirting relentlessly during lunch every Friday for the last two months. Gwen is her name. I only remember because of her nametag.

Today, I avert my gaze to my beer, popping the tab. "Nah, I'm good."

I catch her pout from the corner of my eye before she turns and saunters off, adding a little too much sway in her hips.

Wyatt snorts beside me. "Ouch, Beck, what was that?"

I ignore him, instead focusing on pouring the pinkish amber liquid into my glass, watching it froth.

"And also, what the fuck? That's the fourth day in a row you've had beer at lunch."

"And that's a problem because…?"

His brows lift. "Because you drink scotch." Examining the can, he asks, "Is this the same one Claire was drinking at the meeting?"

I pick up the empty can and turn it in my hands, pretending to read the label. I don't. I already know what it says. *Cherry Lane Brewing Company. Strawberry Grove. Sour Ale.* Like Wyatt said, I've been drinking a lot of these this week. I've become a little too familiar with the label truth be told. "Hmm. So it is."

He barks out a laugh. "You got it bad, buddy. Is that why you just blew off the waitress?"

"No I don't." I might. "And I didn't blow her off." Totally did.

"Yeah, okay, Beck. Ginger's getting under your skin."

"Nope. Girls don't get under my skin."

Yet the second my phone vibrates in my pocket, I whip it out, eager to see what Claire has to say in response to my most recent message. Lucky me, I've been graced with not one, but two replies from the fiery redhead.

Me: *Can I trust you to keep it professional tonight? I know it's difficult for you to keep your hands and eyes to yourself, Care Bear.*

Claire Bear: *Are you kidding me right now?!?!*

Claire Bear: *I want to punch you in that pretty little face of yours.*

I huff out a laugh and start typing back.

Me: *Already not off to a good start on the professionalism front. Swearing, compliments on my looks, and physical threats aren't very professional. Maybe I should have a word with your boss.*

My phone lights up with a picture of Claire's middle finger, pretty pale blush polish donning her nail. I send her back a picture of my hand, wrapped around my glass of beer, the can sitting beside it.

Me: *Are we sending pictures of our hands? Remember when I put these fingers between your luscious legs and touched your little strawberry?*

Claire Bear: *OMG! Now who's being unprofessional?! And why are you drinking my beer? And don't call my vagina a strawberry!*

Me: *Bet you taste just as fruity.*

I can't *not* do it. It's just too easy. I love getting her all riled up, flirting, teasing. Keeping my hands off her tonight is going to be impossible.

Which is why I have no plans of doing that.

"Are you texting her right now?" Wyatt asks, leaning over the table.

"No." I tug my phone into my chest. It's a stupid fucking move because Wyatt stands up, reaches over, and rips my phone right out of my hands. "Give it back, fucker."

I watch his face morph into one of pure amusement as he reads over our message thread. He shoves my phone back into my hands and sits down, shaking his head with a shit-eating grin. "You've met your match, Avery."

"Mmm," I murmur, maybe in agreement, maybe not, as I look down at my phone.

Claire Bear: *Maybe I do, but you'll never know. Too bad, so sad.*

Game on, Claire Thompson. Game on.

The waitress slams my lunch down in front of me before stalking off.

"Well, I think I've ruined any chance I ever had there," I say with a chuckle as I lift my beer to my lips.

"Like you give two shits," Wyatt retorts.

Nope, not a single one.

I check the clock on my computer for the fifth time, drumming my pen on my desk.

6:43pm. Claire's late.

Now I'm worried she's not going to show, and that irritates me beyond belief. Did I take it too far with the texts today? I don't think so. We've had this thing going all week, and she could easily ignore me, but she never fails to text me back. I think she secretly enjoys our banter.

I open my phone to ask her where she is but stop myself before I can hit send. Leaning back in my chair, I peel off the dark-rimmed glasses I wear when I'm staring at my computer for a long time. I pinch the bridge of my nose and rub my eyes because—*what the fuck?*

Wyatt's right. Claire's getting under my skin. She *is* under my skin. I have no idea how she got there, but she wormed her way in

84

without even trying. In fact, I fucking put her there. She tried the distance thing. It's like she's got a leg out, foot kicking at me at all times, trying to keep me at bay, but I just keep swatting her leg away and grabbing for her, dragging her right back.

I can't help it, and it's screwing with my brain.

Wyatt pops his head in. "You look wrecked, dude."

I clear my throat and sit up, fixing my glasses back in place and resting my elbows on my desk. "Little bit. Just tired, end of the work week and all that."

He checks his watch. "You sure she's coming?"

Not sure about anything right now. "She'll be here."

His lips purse, head bobbing. A door opens somewhere in the outer office and Wyatt leans out to see who it is. His face splits in two. "Well, well, well. We were just talking about you, little Miss Sunshine."

"Well, stop it," I hear Claire say, all sassy with a hint of humor.

She appears in the doorway, keeping her eyes off me. Wyatt wraps her in a hug and they kiss each other on the cheek. When the hell did they get so chummy?

"You look ravishing as always," he tells her with the slow sweep of his gaze, letting it linger on her hips.

I can't blame him. She's wearing the tightest pair of jeans I've ever seen with slits at the knees and frayed hems. Literally, these things may as well be painted over her delicious curves. A pair of white Chuck's decorate her feet and a simple, gray Cherry Lane T-shirt stretches across her chest, the tiniest bit of skin peeking out above the waistline of her jeans.

"Your compliments are so much nicer than his," Claire says, jerking her thumb toward me.

"Because I don't talk about your strawberry-flavored vagina?" Wyatt flashes her a devilish grin.

Claire falters for a solid ten seconds, mouth gaping, before she smacks him in the shoulder.

85

Wyatt feigns hurt, rubbing the spot and pouting at her. "Feisty."

"You're both little piglets." She hits him with my favorite squinty eyes.

"The best of us are, darling." He hits her with a wink. "Alright, I'm off. Have a good night and try not to kill each other."

"You're leaving?" The words tumble frantically from Claire's mouth.

He nods. "Avery's taking the lead on Cherry Lane. I'm just here to be a pretty face, and when he needs my extra brain cells." He taps his temple with two fingers.

I roll my eyes but Claire's smile tugs up her face, pulling in those dimples. I love her smile.

"I like you better than him," she whispers cheekily. I want to throw her over my shoulder.

Wyatt leans forward and brushes a lock of hair off her neck. "As you should. And I'd treat you much better, too."

I crumple up a piece of paper and send it flying across the room, hitting him in the side of his blond head. "Get the fuck outta here."

His laughter bounces off the walls, following him down the hall until I hear the ding of the elevator.

Claire strolls the rest of the way into my office and throws her bag to the floor, sinking onto my cognac leather couch. She crosses one leg over the other and pretends to be interested in her fingernails. I really don't think she gives a shit about her nails. "'Kay. Let's get on with this."

"Places to be?"

"Yes, actually. Anywhere but he—" She stops when she looks up at me, finally. The tips of her ears redden and I think her bottom lip trembles a bit. "Uh, you have…glasses…on."

I smile at her. "Glad to see your eyes work just fine. Yes, Claire, I do have glasses on. They keep me from getting headaches when I stare at the computer screen. Although I have to say, somehow

I've managed to get one anyway in the last fifteen minutes."
Because you're late.

She rips her gaze off me. "They look good," she murmurs.

"Pardon?"

"I said they look good!" Fuck, the woman could yell at me all damn day, I wouldn't care.

"A compliment from Miss Thompson? Such a rarity. I suppose I should count myself lucky. Or blessed. Maybe both."

She ignores me, looking around my office. I follow everywhere her gaze goes, and I can tell by the way her mouth opens and closes a few times that she's secretly impressed.

Jones & Beck Investments is located on the forty-first floor of a high-end high-rise, smack dab in the heart of downtown Toronto. The outer office is all white and gray marble floors, chandeliers and there's even a fishpond, but my personal office is completely different, and much more similar to what she's got going on at Cherry Lane.

Dark gray wooden plank flooring, a brick accent wall, a wall of windows into the hallway, though they're covered, a dark walnut console that's built into the wall behind my desk, and floor-to-ceiling windows on the final wall, looking out over the city skyline. The sun's still up, but my space is lit up with the soft glow of floor lamps. It's the way I like it, all warm and cozy, instead of blinding and sterile.

"You're late," I finally say.

Her gaze shifts to me. "Fashionably."

"You could have texted."

The corner of her mouth twitches and her eyes dance. "Are you upset with me, Mr. Beck?"

I shrug and lean back in my chair, twirling my pen in my fingers. "It's just common courtesy to be on time, or to at least inform the other party if you're going to be late."

Her eyes narrow and her lips purse. She looks like she's about to chew my head off. But then she lets out an exhale and relaxes, the tension she's been holding in her shoulders slipping. She has the good sense to look remorseful. "I'm sorry. I didn't actually work today. I had to take my dad to an appointment. Traffic was brutal getting back to Toronto."

I feel my face soften. I can, on occasion, be a bit of an ass. "Why didn't you tell me you weren't working? We didn't have to do this today."

She lifts a shoulder and lets it fall. "Not a big deal."

"You're from Jordan Valley too, right?" I remember visiting Dex's start-up brewery there once, way back when. "That's a far drive to make there and back today. I'm sorry. I would have rescheduled had I known."

Toronto traffic, or any traffic coming into or out of the city within a fifty-kilometer radius, is a shit show any day of the week. Jordan Valley is an hour-and-a-half drive on a good day. She probably spent nearly five hours stuck in traffic today.

Claire just stares at me, barely blinking.

"What?" I ask.

"I don't know. Stop being nice." She moves her hand around the general vicinity of my face. "It's weirding me out."

Chuckling, I tap my pen on my desk. "You make me smile, Claire Bear, I'll give you that."

She's still staring, this sweet smile dancing on her full lips, but then her eyes widen and her cheeks blaze. She drops her gaze, clearing her throat and tucking a loose wave behind her ear. "Uh, I brought, um…" She pulls a binder out of her bag and shakes it at me. "I brought everything I've got so far. Proposed plans, spaces, ideas, some quotes from a few contractors."

I stand, rolling my sleeves up. Her eyes track the movement. "Great. Are you hungry?"

"Uh…"

I pull out a bag of microwave popcorn from a drawer in my desk, ripping the plastic casing off. She's got this amused half-grin her face.

"I love popcorn," I tell her. "Gonna go pop it, 'kay?"

She nods and I disappear down the hallway and into the lunchroom. I grab a couple bottles of sparkling water and two beers from the fridge while the buttery, salty aroma fills the air. Wyatt hates when I microwave popcorn. He says it makes the whole office smell. It does. It makes it smell amazing.

I dump it into a bowl and when I return to my office, Claire's got her shoes kicked off and she's sitting cross-legged on the floor in front of the coffee table, papers spread out around her. She's pulled her hair up into a messy top knot, several loose tendrils spilling down her neck and around her face while she rolls her pen between her teeth, and I'm struck by how effortlessly gorgeous she is.

I drop down across from her. "Is that the same pen I had in my mouth on Monday?"

She pulls the black pen out of her mouth and stares at the bite marks on it. "Ugh, yuck."

My brows lift in question. "You've had my tongue down your throat."

She taps a finger against her cute little chin, pretending to be perplexed. "Nope, definitely don't remember that. Must be thinking of someone else."

"Trust me, Claire, I'm not. Yours is the only mouth my tongue has been in for a week." Two, actually, since the last time I hooked up with someone was the weekend before we met.

"Ha! Doubt it." She shoves her hand into the bowl, tossing some buttery kernels into her mouth. I'd like to be in there myself.

"It's true."

Laughing, she shakes her head. "You know, you say that as if you deserve an award for somehow managing to only mouth fuck one girl in the past eight days. But when I look at you, I realize it's probably a huge accomplishment. So," she sweeps her hands out in front of her, "how commendable of you, Mr. Beck."

My mouth quirks up. "You're so saucy."

She flashes me a grin that matches her tone. "It's all part of my charm."

"It sure is. So is your brutal honesty."

"You mean because I just called you out on being a huge player?" She twists the top off a beer and takes a long swig. "You asked me to fuck and we'd known each other all of ten minutes. We didn't even know each other's names."

"You wouldn't let me give you my name," I remind her.

"Yeah. 'Cause you're a huge player."

My blood starts to tingle on its own accord, coursing through my veins with a little more vigor than I'm used to. "I'm not a player."

"Do you go on dates?"

"Sometimes." I think for a moment. "But not often," I admit.

"And do you sleep with a lot of women?"

My eyes narrow. "A player would imply that I lead women on, make them think I'm after one thing when I'm really after another. I'm upfront and honest about what I want. If it doesn't suit the woman, it ends there. Hence why I told you I wanted to fuck you." I shrug casually. "I was being honest with you. I don't think there's anything wrong with either of those things."

Claire looks away, focusing on her hands resting on top of her pile of papers. "Right," she says softly. I don't know where her sass went. She clears her throat and pops the binder tabs open, pulling a few sheets out and passing them to me. "I think the kitchen is probably the most important place to start, because we can't really proceed with anything else if we don't have the kitchen to do the work. These are the plans, though they're not set in stone." She points to a blueprint and then shoves another set of papers in my hands. "These are the quotes I've gotten so far. They seem a little high, but I don't really know the first thing about building a restaurant-style kitchen."

My gaze drifts over the quotes. They're definitely high. Higher than high. I only know this because we've invested in a few high-end restaurants in the past. "These are way too high," I murmur, glancing at her. "I know a guy. I'll reach out to him. See if he can come by next week and look at the place."

"That would be great." She's still not looking at me and her voice is crazy quiet.

"What did I say?"

Her eyes land on mine. "Hmm?"

"What did I say that's got you upset?"

Her nose scrunches. It's cute. "I'm not upset."

"You lost your sass, you're all quiet, and you're barely looking at me. You're upset."

I lean forward on my elbows, studying her face. There's a tiny crease between her eyebrows and she pulls her bottom lip into her mouth, chewing on it. She looks away. Again.

"Can we just focus on this?" She gestures to the papers in front of us.

"Sure." I toss a handful of popcorn into my mouth. "When you tell me what I said that hurt your feelings."

"My feelings aren't hurt." She crosses her arms over her chest and that tiny crease between her brows becomes a deep line in her forehead. "I was already well aware that you only think of me as somewhere to stick your dick."

Oh. *Oh.*

I open my mouth to tell her that's not at all how I regard her, but she's not done.

She pins me with a patronizing smile. "Don't worry, Avery. I'm used to guys wanting nothing but sex and not giving a crap about the person behind the body. I have no expectations of you, or any

91

other man for that matter." Her eyes flicker, hurt or pain slashing her features before she stands. "Excuse me. I need to use the bathroom."

I'm fucking lost, but also not, and that alone makes no sense. My brain is swimming. Her braindead ex was a moron and a cheater, so her distrust of men, the perceived lack of self-worth she feels, it's all justified. It makes sense.

What doesn't make sense is why she's upset with me. Sure, I'm into her body. I mean, just look at her. But it's more than that. It's the way she laughs, the way she talks, the way she doesn't take my shit and challenges me. It's her bright as hell smile that makes my own shine. She may not think so, but she's strong.

I think about Dex's words from Monday, the mention of her ultra-sensitive side, buried beneath her big attitude. The way she scooped up her niece and showered her in kisses while the two of them giggled. The way she melted into my side when I conned her into a group hug with me and Vivi. I remember how surprisingly good it all felt, how I hadn't wanted it to end so quickly.

My request for a date had come right after that, completely unplanned. The words flew from my mouth before I could stop them. And that's the thing: I don't date much. Sometimes a dinner here and there as a formality, wine and dine before the fun, but I'd told Claire we didn't have to have sex and I'd actually meant it. *That* is something I don't do.

Something else I don't do is casually text girls, and especially not for days at a time.

So of course now Claire thinks I'm playing her, reeling her in.

Am I though? What's my plan here? I sigh and tug at my hair. I honestly don't even know. She intrigues me and I like being around her, talking to her. I *want* to talk to her, spend time with her. I mean, shit, here I am on a Friday night, with her, in my office, when I could be anywhere else with any other woman who wouldn't be giving me anywhere near the amount of trouble she is.

When she returns, Claire settles on the couch, further away from me than before. She tucks her feet underneath her butt and pops her pen back in her mouth, flipping through her journal.

I don't know what to say. This is not going at all the way I thought it would. Not that I thought we'd fuck, and I definitely expected to bicker, but what I hadn't planned for was an upset Claire and a confused Avery and the yanking feeling in my stomach that's making me feel like a bit of an asshole.

"The company we use to make our staff shirts and signage has agreed to do all our merchandise. They can even do glass etching, which is cool, so we can use them exclusively," she says, as if nothing had happened. "It's a small company and they've never handled orders this big, so I know it's a bit of a risk, but I like the idea of keeping it local. Also, it's a couple of girls who do it to pay their way through school, which I feel good about."

I nod thoughtfully. "I agree. That's a good idea."

"Yeah. They're really excited about it. Cost is good too, since they don't have any overhead."

Claire trails off and I go back to looking through the kitchen plans she's put together, sensing she needs some space.

Twenty minutes later, I can't stand the silence anymore. I look up to find her twirling a loose copper wave around her finger, sea green eyes trained on me. Her face flushes when our gazes meet, and she looks back down to her paper.

"You okay?" I ask her. I don't know why. It's a stupid question. She's not okay, but she's not going to be honest with me.

A slow, mischievous smirk takes over her face. "Are you?" This woman is a conundrum.

I lean back on my hands. "Depends on how you answer the question, Claire."

With a sigh, she waves a hand around. "I'm fine. Don't worry about me."

"'Kay. But I do."

"Why?"

"I'm not sure," I murmur truthfully.

"Am I turning you soft?" she teases playfully, stretching out on the couch. She kicks her legs up on the back of the couch and wiggles her toes, which match her blushing fingernails, and her shirt rides up her stomach.

My brows inch up. "Do you have a belly ring, little Miss Strawberry?" How the hell did I miss that last Friday? I had my hands all up in that dress of hers.

She looks down at the jewel in her navel and blushes, tugging her shirt down. She gives me a cheeky little smile. "I asked my mom to get my belly button pierced when I was thirteen. She said no." Claire laughs. "Actually, she said, *Hell no, Claire!* So, naturally, Charlee and I snuck out one Friday night, went to the shadiest place we could find that didn't care that you were supposed to have parental consent before the age of sixteen, and got our belly buttons pierced."

I chuckle. *"Naturally.* How long until your mom found out?"

"Seventeen hours." She pushes her hands against the armrest and slides down the length of the couch. "Fuck, I thought she was gonna kill me. She was so angry with me." She shakes her head. "No, she was 'disappointed.'" Her air quotes make me smile, and she gives me a stern mom face I know all too well. *"I'm not mad, Claire, I'm just disappointed. Why would you ruin your body like that?"*

"Well, if it's any consolation, you definitely did *not* ruin your body," I say with a sly wink.

"Still not fucking you." The pointed yet amused glare she sends my way tells me she's at least considering it.

I look at her belly ring that's peeking out of her shirt again, and the two holes decorating each earlobe. "So you've got a couple piercings. What about tattoos? Got any of those?"

"Just one."

I check out her arms, her bare feet, but come up empty. "Can I see it?"

The smile on her face falters as she considers my request. There's still a hint of it, just there in the corner, but it makes me wonder how personal it is.

Claire pulls herself off the couch, her hesitant hands fumbling at her chest while she stares at me, like she's waiting for me. When I join her, those timid fingers find the hem of her top. My breath catches in my throat as she starts tugging it up, dragging it slowly over her creamy skin. Each inch reveals more of her stomach, the soft curve of her killer hips, the dip in her waist. I'm so distracted I almost forget what I'm supposed to be looking for.

She stops right below the swell of her breasts, showing off the edge of a lacy black bra where I spy the tiniest bit of black ink peeking out from underneath it on the side of her ribcage. I reach for it and then stop, lifting my gaze to hers.

"Can I?" I ask softly.

She sucks in her bottom lip and nods. Then she squints and bites out, "Don't touch my boobs!"

With a chuckle, I assure her, "I won't touch your perfect tits, Claire, don't worry."

My thumb skims the edge of her bra and I watch her abdomen clench. Her reaction to my touch makes me smile. Slowly, I lift the lace, pushing it up until it reveals the handwritten words etched into her skin. The tip of my finger traces over every letter as a single tear drips down Claire's beautiful face.

I'm with you always.
XOX
Mom

CHAPTER TEN

Avery

My gaze lifts, meeting Claire's. Those beautiful jade orbs are guarded, a little red-rimmed, her smile small and sad. I swipe a tender thumb across her cheek, catching a lone tear.

"My mom was diagnosed with ovarian cancer about six years ago, right before my twentieth birthday. It came out of nowhere. She actually thought she was pregnant." Claire looks away, pressing her teeth into her trembling lip. "She died eight months later."

I don't know what to say. *I'm sorry* never seems like enough, and it doesn't fix anything.

So I sweep my thumb across the ink, lean forward, and press the softest kiss to it. Then I pull her shirt down. Before she can say anything, I wrap her in my arms. She's stiff as a board for a moment before her hands move slowly up my back and she melts against me with a quiet sigh.

"Thank you," she whispers.

Claire tilts her head back and peers up at me, and when our eyes meet, something happens inside me. I don't know what it is, but my stomach tightens. I think she feels it too because her eyes grow wide and she suddenly pushes away from me, putting a shitload of distance between us.

She steps up to the window, watching the sun dip low into the Toronto skyline. The CN Tower is lit up blue and white tonight because the Blue Jays are playing.

"Wow," she murmurs in amazement, fingers pressing against the glass. "You have an incredible view."

I step up beside her, admiring the way the blue sky turns pink and orange. "If you think this is nice, you should see the view from

96

my condo." She gives me side-eye and I laugh. "I didn't mean it like that."

"Mhmm. Sure, Mr. Beck."

"You can see the sunset and the sunrise." I wink at her, because I can't help it. "Come home with me and I can show you both."

Her eyes roll and she makes an exaggerated, exasperated sound, part sigh, part groan. "You're relentless."

"I'll win you over yet, Claire Bear." I hope so, at least.

"Only time will tell." The way she smiles tells me I might be winning her over already.

"Wanna get dinner?" *What the hell, man? Two dinner invites in one week? Get your shit together, Beck.* Whatever. I'm gonna roll with it.

Body still, Claire blinks up at me. "What?"

"Dinner. You know, that thing you eat after lunch and before you go to bed."

"No," she replies quickly.

"Why not?"

"I'm…not hungry." Her darty-eyed expression is suspect.

"There's no way you ate already. You've been on the road all day. And all we ate tonight was popcorn. Come on, let me feed you, Claire."

"I'm fine, Avery. I'll eat at home."

"I thought you said you weren't hungry?"

"Ugh, shut up." She shoves a finger in my chest. "You fight me on everything."

"I think you mean *you* fight *me* on everything." I cross my arms over my chest and quirk a suggestive brow, challenging her to fight me on this, too.

She takes the bait, her flaily arms making an appearance. "I do not! You won't leave me alone!"

"You like it, Claire."

She stomps one foot, wild arms still in the air. "You're so annoying!"

"Not as annoying as you."

Her nostrils flare, hands curling into tight fists at her sides. "I don't like you!" *Lies.*

"I don't like you either." *More lies.*

"Ugh!" She's so angry she's shaking. "I just wanna…I just wanna…"

"What, Claire? What do you wanna do?" Because I wanna kiss her.

I step closer. She licks her full lips, chest lifting on a sharp inhale. My gaze lifts to the messy topknot on her head. I reach over and pull on her elastic, watching those thick copper waves tumble down around her shoulders.

Shoulders back, standing tall, Claire lifts her face to look me dead in the eyes. "You're so fucking arrogant."

"You're so fucking beautiful."

She steps toward me. "You think every woman wants you."

"But I only want you."

Her eyes flick to my lips. "Liar."

"Nah. Not lying."

It all happens at once. I reach for her face and she lunges at me, jumping into my arms. The second our lips collide it's like a mad dash to the finish line. Her tongue shoves past my lips and her fingers slide through my hair, tugging, grasping for dear life.

I slam her against the wall and she gasps when my hips press into hers. She wiggles against me and her legs tighten around my waist, the heels of her bare feet digging into my ass.

"Ready to admit you want me?"

"Never," she rasps, nipping my lip.

"Are we biting again?" I grab a fistful of her hair and jerk her head to the side, clamping my mouth over her neck, teeth pressing into warm skin. She groans, nails digging into my shoulders.

"Asshole," she puffs out.

"You bring out this side of me, baby."

I flick my tongue over the red spot and drag my lips down her neck, kissing, licking, sucking. Claire tips her head backwards and it lands against the brick wall. I slip my hand behind her, cupping the back of her head to keep it protected, and then continue my assault.

"Shit, Claire, you feel so fucking good," I tell her, rolling my hips. She moans and bucks beneath me. "You gonna let me fuck you?" I'm ninety-nine percent sure I already know the answer.

"No," she says on a heavy exhale.

I drop her to the ground and flip her around, slapping her hands against the wall. "'Kay. I'm good with hands only." I drop my voice an octave and brush my lips below her ear. "Unless you wanna feel my tongue, too."

Her answer is a shuddering groan and her head drops back, rolling over my shoulder. She looks up at me with the roundest eyes and I grip her jaw, kissing her fiercely, my tongue plunging, taking. My other hand slips up her shirt, rubbing over her belly, feeling the jewel that's nestled into her navel.

When her ass grinds against my growing erection, my fingers find the button of her jeans, tugging it free and yanking on her zipper. The second my hand slips down the front of her jeans and I find her soaked, hot and ready for me, she gasps.

"No! Shit! No, no, no." She pulls my hand out and spins away from me, slipping under my arms. She stares at me and then down at her opened pants like she doesn't know how that happened.

"What's wrong?" I take a step toward her, wiping my wet mouth on my arm, chest heaving.

She holds up a shaky hand, stopping me. "Stop, please. I can't do this. I shouldn't do this."

"Do you not want to?" Shit, I'm so confused. The sexual tension between us is so palpable I could cut that shit with a knife.

"I *do* want to. That's the problem." She does up her pants and scrambles to pick up the papers scattered over the coffee table. "I gotta go. Sorry, Avery."

"Hey, what's wrong?" Reaching for her hips, I frown when she spins away from me. "Did I do something?" I'm pretty sure that kiss was both of us.

"No, I'm sorry. You didn't do anything. I just…I told you. I'm not good at casual."

"Right, so let's go get something to eat."

"Eating before fucking doesn't make it not casual."

"Let's go on *a date*, Claire," I clarify, for her sake or mine, I'm not really sure, because I have no idea what I'm doing right now. A date? Like a real date? The look on her face tells me she's just as shocked and confused as I am.

She snaps out of her momentary fog and shakes her head. "I gotta go home."

I sigh, because I know we aren't going to get anywhere tonight, and I don't mean sexually. She's not going to talk to me about this. I pull out my phone and text my driver while Claire goes back to frantically gathering her paperwork. She promptly drops it all over the floor.

"Shit." She falls to her knees and starts reaching for it, but her hands shake chaotically.

I crouch down beside her. "Will you relax? My driver will be here in ten minutes, okay? I'll take you home. Let me get this stuff."

She doesn't look at me. "That's not necessary. I can get an Uber."

"You could, but I've kept you here all night, and I have a car coming to get me anyway."

"But I—"

"*Claire.*" My tone is unyielding, and she finally meets my gaze. "Just accept the damn ride." I rip the papers out of her clutch and grab a bottle of sparkling water off the coffee table, shoving it into her hands. "Go sit on the couch and drink some water."

She blinks up at a me several times before she slumps down to the floor, resting her back on the couch. She twists the top off the bottle and sips it. "I'm sorry, Avery," she murmurs before rubbing her eyes.

"It's all good."

I think about her ex while I gather up the papers, clipping them back into her binder. Everything is color-coded, but I already knew that. I like that. But I don't like what he did to her.

I'm not mad that I'm not getting laid, that I'm not even getting *any*. I'm mad that he fucked with her brain enough that she can't allow herself to let loose, give herself permission to feel pleasure, and that she's so closed off to the idea of spending time with someone she obviously has a shit-ton of chemistry with.

Because we do. It's good chemistry. It's hot and it's passionate. But more, it's fun. She makes me laugh and I actually enjoy being with her. Despite the way she's acting right now, like I set her fucking pants on fire or something, I think she likes being with me too.

I gather my bag and Claire's, slinging them both over my shoulder, and hold my hand out to her. She takes it timidly, and I shut the lights off as we make our way to the elevator.

"Night, Mr. Beck," the security guard downstairs says with a nod as he holds the door open for us. He smiles at Claire and tips his head. "Miss."

"Have a good weekend, Kirk," I say while Claire offers him a genuine, albeit shaky, smile.

My driver steps out of the car and I wave him off, opening the door for Claire and ushering her inside. I slide in beside her. "Where do you live, Claire?"

"Eighty-nine Church Street," she tells me quietly.

My body stills before it starts vibrating. I bite down on my lip. *No fucking shit.*

Claire narrows her eyes. I give up on trying to hold back my laughter. She pins her arms across her chest. "Why are you laughing?"

I shake my head and clap her knee, taking a deep breath and getting a handle on myself. "No reason." *You'll see.*

The streets are busy after the baseball game, so it takes us nearly twenty minutes to drive home. We could have walked in as much time and enjoyed the warm night air. When we pull up out front of the condo, I hold my hand out for Claire to take as she climbs out.

"Thank you for the ride, Avery." She gives me one last lingering look before turning and starting for the door.

"No problem at all." I tap on the passenger window and wait for it to roll down. "Night, Jacob. Enjoy your weekend." His response is a wink and a grin.

I follow Claire through the front doors and nod at the concierge when he lets us both in.

Claire turns around when she realizes I'm still with her. "What are you doing?"

I smile at her and stop in front of the bank of elevators. Pressing the call button, I watch the floor numbers above light up as one moves down to us.

"*Avery*," she seethes, voice dangerously low. "I told you, I'm not fucking you." Her eyes shift nervously around, as if she's worried somebody in the very empty lobby might hear her.

"I'm aware, Claire. You've said it a few times now."

"Well then what are you doing? Isn't this a little presumptuous of you? I don't want to hook up. I don't—"

"Do casual, I know. Do you think I've forgotten?" It's only been plaguing my dreams for the last week.

"I…well…no. I'm just…confused." She stares at the elevator when the doors open and then slices her gaze back to me. She plants two irritated fists on hips I want to grab. "Seriously, what are you doing?"

"Going upstairs." With a gentle hand on her back, I guide her through the doors and follow her in. "Floor?"

"*Avery!*" She stomps her foot for the second time tonight, like a toddler having a temper tantrum. I wonder if I'm the only person who gets her this worked up.

I can't hold it in anymore. My head dips, my body trembling with laughter.

"Why are you laughing?" she demands. "What is happening?" She presses a floor button and turns back to me. "You're pissing me off!" She reaches forward and shoves me.

My fingers close over her wrists and I pull her into me. "Oh, sweet, beautiful Claire. I live here."

She makes an amused, disbelieving sound. "No you don't."

I stroke her cheek once, smile glued to my lips. "I do."

Her jaw drops. "But *I* live here."

I snort. "Apparently."

I see the exact moment she realizes I'm telling the truth. She shuts her mouth, her teeth clattering as she does, and drops her arms. Her brows pinch in confusion and then soften. "How long have you lived here?"

"Two years."

"But I…you…how have I never seen you before?"

I shake my head, because I don't fucking know, and I've been asking myself that question the entire car ride over. "I'm wondering the same thing. How could I have missed *you*?"

She keeps blinking. "What floor are you on?"

I reach forward and tap on forty-seven. It's located below all the other buttons and requires a special code, so I punch it in.

"*Forty-seven*? But that's the top floor! That's a pent…house…" She trails off, staring up at me with mortified wonder.

103

I smirk and touch her chin, closing her mouth. Guess she didn't realize how much a highly successful investment banker in the city of Toronto makes, one that owns his own firm and has dealings across North America.

For the next eight seconds, she does her best to keep from meeting my gaze in the mirrored elevator walls. She fails. Our eyes meet three times.

The elevator dings and the doors open on the twenty-sixth floor. She makes no move to get out.

Finally, she turns her glare on me. "You know, you have a completely private elevator so you don't have to ride with us *peasants.*"

In truth, this is the first time I've taken one of the public elevators. "And miss irritating you a minute longer? Nuh-uh." I smile down at her and kiss her cheek, then give her a gentle push out into the hall. "Goodnight Claire."

She slinks slowly down the hallway, glancing back at me every couple of steps, shock still pouring over her features. I wait 'til she stops at her door so I can see which apartment is hers, and then I disappear back into the elevator.

Two minutes later, I'm greeted by two giant paws on my torso when I step through my door.

"Hey Sully," I whisper, planting a kiss on my dog's black nose. "How's my handsome guy?" He drops to his side and rolls over, tongue lolling out of his mouth as I rub his belly.

"Daddy made a new friend. I think you'd like her. I know I do."

CHAPTER ELEVEN

Claire

"You need some make up tonight." Charlee prods the bags under my eyes and frowns. "You look like crap."

"Gee, thanks, Charlee." I throw her a cynical, tight-lipped smile. "You're so sweet."

"I'm just saying. You're fucking purple under there! Did you sleep at all last night?"

"Barely." I was too busy thinking about the long limbs and stupidly sexy dark brown waves sleeping twenty-one floors above me.

The man has given me nothing but sleepless nights since I met him. Every night this week I had laid in bed and re-read whatever messages he'd sent me that day, flirting with me in one way or another. Then I'd think about his irritating smirk, his perfect hair, his fingers on me, his lips…

Ugh. I can't stand it.

And now? Now that I know he's in the same building? How can I sleep now? I left the condo once today, looking a whole lot like I was sneaking out of Tiffany's with a five million dollar diamond hidden in my back pocket the way my wild eyes darted anxiously around every corner before I made a mad dash across the front foyer, glancing over my shoulder seventeen thousand times for any sign of Avery.

I don't know how I managed to go two years without seeing him once, or at least without noticing him. I mean, no. If we'd ever been in the same elevator or in the foyer at the same time, I would have noticed him. There's no way somebody simply *doesn't notice* that man. For fuck's sake, he's all long limbs, knotted muscles, and chiseled jaw, and looks like he just stepped off a freaking runway.

His mere presence is overpowering, like he dominates every space he's in.

"You gonna tell me how your night with Mr. Handsome went?" Charlee wags her brows and nudges me in the ribs.

My eyes shift to my brother, who's sprawled across my living room couch, watching Vivi put on a dance performance for the fifteenth time in the last half hour.

"Later," I whisper to Charlee. Then I clear my throat and speak louder. "So, we're doing dinner and drinks?"

Charlee gets the hint and winks. She pulls two beers out of the fridge and I reach for one, but she gives me a dirty look and walks over to the couch.

"Shove a bum," she tells Casey, who happily sits up and makes room for her. She hands him one of the beers. Traitor. "Yep," she says then, answering my earlier question. "We're going to The George for dinner. Dex mentioned going down the street afterwards. There's this new bar with ping pong tables and shit like that."

Casey looks longingly at Charlee. "That sounds fun."

"It's just Dex and us?" I ask, because it seems like a lot for just the three of us.

Charlee's eyes flit to me. "And a couple of the other guys from work." She smacks Casey's knee. "You should come, Case."

"I would, but..." He gestures to the dancing, bouncing, crazy ball of energy that's half him.

"I bet my mom can come to your place and watch her. You know she loves Vivi."

Casey considers her offer. "You don't think it's too late of notice?" He checks his watch. "What time you guys going?"

"Reservations aren't 'til eight."

"Shit," he breathes, looking mildly excited. He drums his long fingers on his beer bottle. "I can't remember the last time I went out and got drunk."

That's my brother. He used to be a huge party animal back in the day, and while he scaled it back a bit when he hit his mid-twenties, Vivi had sobered his nights up instantly. As a single father, he's utterly devoted to her and hates spending unnecessary time away from her. At twenty-nine years old, the man has been pretty much without a social life for the last two-and-a-half years, especially since most of his friends disappeared when Vivi came along, which is total bullshit.

"Done!" Charlee slaps her phone down on the table and grins at Casey. "Mom will be at your place for six-thirty."

"Fuck yeah! Thanks Charlee." He presses a kiss to her cheek and her face goes crimson.

Charlee starts twirling a lock of blond around her finger, gaze bouncing between Casey and a spot on the wall. "Is there a special girl you want to invite before I get Dex to add to the reservations?" I smother a laugh. Special girl. Real subtle, Charlee.

"Nope." He pops the *P* sound and slings an arm over Charlee's shoulders. "All my special ladies are right here in this room."

"You're such a cheeseball," I tell him as I drop to the ground. Vivi comes running over to me, crashing into my chest and tackling me backwards.

"Dance wif me!"

"Uggghhh," I groan, wrapping my arms around her. But then, like the good auntie I am, I drag my tired ass off the floor, and we re-start Let It Go for the hundredth time.

Casey leaves a half hour later with the promise to be back for seven-thirty so the three of us can head to the restaurant together. But five minutes after he walks out my door, he texts me to say he's going to meet us there instead, because he's going to have a drink with 'the guys' beforehand, whatever the hell that means. I guess him and Dex are pre-drinking for dinner, and I guess Casey's taking his first night out since forever pretty damn seriously, and rightfully so.

"Oh my God." Charlee's big brown eyes twinkle as we stroll down the street toward the restaurant. "I can't believe it. What the hell are the chances of that? In a city this big?"

Exactly what I've been thinking. "So, you can see why I couldn't sleep last night."

"Just think of all the sex you could have. Any night of the week, any time you want. *Hey Avery, wanna fuck? Sure babe, just come up to my penthouse.*"

I'm mildly irritated that she thinks this is humorous in any way, shape, or form, but I have to laugh at her high-pitched squeal of an impression of my voice, and her deep baritone Avery. "I don't sound like that, and I'm sorry, but Avery's voice is *way* sexier."

"That was incredibly sexy."

"Sorry, didn't get my panties wet."

She stops on the sidewalk, gripping my arm. "Please tell me you actually get wet when he talks to you."

I flush with heat and yank my arm back, walking ahead of her. "Sometimes. You know, when he's all in my ear, whispering and shit." I shiver just thinking about it. He's got a dirty mouth and says whatever the hell he's thinking. Pair that with his low, husky drawl and I'm good to go.

"Okay, wait, wait, wait, wait, *wait.* Does he actually make you wet?"

"*Yes*, Charlee, Christ." My eyes dart around the foot traffic surrounding us at the corner while we wait for the stoplight to change. "Can we not talk about this here?" I beg.

"I mean, it's kinda big. Two weeks ago you told me Aaron couldn't get you wet and you *had to* use lube. You clearly don't have that problem with Avery."

"Clearly," I grumble, because I don't need the reminder that the man makes me feel like a leaky faucet. "Though the man is sex on legs, so that's probably why."

"Uh huh, that's why." She looks sidelong at me, her blond curls flying behind her with each long stride. "Why won't you just admit you like him?"

"I *don't* like him," I insist, a little too firmly and a lot too quickly.

"You *do* like him."

"Do not."

"Do too."

"Shut up."

"Thought so." Her smug smirk tells me she's satisfied that she's won this round. I'm just too tired to argue with her. I need beer. And lots of it.

When we stroll through the restaurant doors five minutes later, my ears immediately pinpoint Casey's boisterous laugh. It makes me smile. I'm glad he's getting a fun night out.

My gaze floats over the room before landing on my brother. Our gazes meet and he calls out to me, waving. "Claire Bear! Over here!"

My cheeks blaze. *Must* he *yell* that name in public?

We slip across the floor and I stop dead in my tracks when I spy the rest of our group.

I turn, so fucking slowly, to glare and shoot daggers at my best friend.

Charlee gives me a gritty, guilty-as-sin grin, and giggles. "He-he-he…" Then she scoffs at my expression and rolls her pretty brown eyes, swatting my shoulder. "Oops. Did I forget to leave out who our dinner guests were?"

"You evil, conniving, little bitch." I pinch her in the arm while she squeals with a bout of mischievious laughter.

"I love you, Claire Bear!" She grabs my hand and dances over to the table, dragging me behind her.

I can't tear my eyes off the table as much as I want to. All four men are sitting at a huge, u-shaped booth tucked into a secluded corner of the restaurant. Casey, Dex, and…Wyatt and Avery.

I clench my teeth a bit, but mostly my thighs. Juices are flowing when they definitely shouldn't be.

This can't and won't be good.

CHAPTER TWELVE

Claire

Avery's wearing that ridiculously pompous smirk of his as he watches us approach the booth. The man is drop-dead sexy and he knows it. I only tear my eyes away when Dex steps out of the booth to wrap both Charlee and I in a hug. Charlee slides in between him and an incredibly happy Casey, who kisses her on the cheek. That's the second time today he's done that.

Wyatt steps out and gives me a hug and peck. "Lovely as always, Miss Claire." He gestures for me to climb in between Avery and him. I'd rather not, but I do, because I'm a glutton for punishment, clearly.

Avery slips his arm around my waist and tugs me into his side, pressing his lips to my cheek. There's a hell of a lot of cheek-kissing going on in this booth tonight.

"Well hello, gorgeous. Fancy seeing you here," he purrs in my ear.

"Mhmm." It's less a murmur and more a hiss. "Imagine my surprise to see you tonight."

He arches a brow. "You didn't know you were having dinner with us tonight? I've known for three days. And here I thought you were wearing this little number all for me." He fingers the strap of my dress, ghosting over my shoulder. I shudder and shake off his touch.

"Nice of you to mention it last night." I pick up a menu so I can look anywhere but at Avery.

"I would have but someone's tongue was down my throat."

I drop the menu and glare at him. "*Oh my God*!" I whisper-yell. "For, like, five minutes!"

He lifts one shoulder and lets it fall again. "Five *glorious* minutes."

"You're sitting next to my brother," I remind him with a clenched jaw.

He winks and leans back, speaking up. "I got to see little Miss Vivi this afternoon."

Casey shoots forward, pointing at me. "Oh yeah! You didn't tell me Avery lives with you."

"He doesn't live with me," I gape stupidly before I can stop myself. Obviously *with me* is not what Casey meant.

Casey rolls his eyes. "In the same building. You know what I mean. I ran into him in the front lobby on my way out, and when I told him I was going out with you guys tonight, he invited me to come back to his place for drinks. Fuck, his place is *amazing*. You been in it, Claire?"

"I have not." But super glad my brother has. I glare at Avery. What's his endgame here? Befriending my brother and all. It's dangerous. I don't like it. I try to convey that to him with the daggers I'm throwing his way.

"Vivi loves him," Casey continues with a chuckle. "She was crawling all over him. Asked him to come over so she could show him her dance routine." He sighs. "She's fucking nuts."

There's a huge part of me that's seriously considering dragging Avery off to the bathroom. I don't know why how much Vivi likes him makes me want to jump his bones even more. Maybe it's because she wasn't a superfan of Aaron, which is fine, because he wasn't a fan of her either. And what the fuck is with that? Who isn't a fan of that little chipmunk?

Avery laughs, waving Casey off. "She's adorable is what she is. And funny as hell."

Damnit, it's like an icepick is chipping away at my heart. Meeting his eyes, I decide to see if he can read my mind: *Stop it.*

Stop being so cute. Stop talking about my niece like that. Stop befriending everyone I love. Stop, stop, stop.

He just smiles at me. "Something you wanna say, Claire?"

Yep, he can read my mind. "Nope."

"'Kay." He leans sideways, his lips grazing the shell of my ear. His breath is warm and spicy like the scotch he's sipping on. "We're having dinner. Together. Side by side. Does this count as our first date?" He drops a hand to my knee and starts trailing his fingers up my bare leg.

Oh, for fuck's sake, why did I wear a dress? Oh, I know. Because I didn't know I'd be testing my self-control all night. If I'd known Avery was going to be here, I would've worn a turtleneck and a pair of sweats.

"Oddly enough, when I think about our first date, I don't imagine my brother being here. Or any of these other people, really."

Avery's brows tweak with amusement. "So you've been thinking about what our first date will look like?"

"What? No. I—"

"You guys are dating?" Casey asks, looking curiously—but oddly, not surprised—between the two of us. "That's cool. I mean, I'm kinda surprised you're getting involved again so soon, but Aaron was a douche, so I'm glad you're moving on, Claire. Avery's a good guy." He claps him on the back in a show of friendship. I hate it.

I'm not sure if there's a name for the sound that's coming out of my throat right now. It's kind of growly, a little hissy, and a lot huffy. Avery's grinning proudly like a narcissistic idiot beside me. Wyatt's trying to cover up his laughter with a fresh bout of fake coughing on my other side. Charlee's snickering beside Casey. And Dex is...well, Dex looks pretty shell-shocked, his jaw just kinda hanging there in midair.

"We are *not* dating," I insist through gritted teeth.

"We're still in the getting-to-know-each-other phase," Avery tacks on, as if we've practiced this speech before. We haven't, and this is not what I would have said. "But things are going pretty well, wouldn't you say?" He skims my shoulder with two electrifying fingers and then tucks a strand of hair behind my ear. Oh crap, it sends a chill right through me.

"I'll fucking say," Wyatt pipes up beside me. "They bicker like an old married couple, and Avery spends all day grinning at his phone like a girl."

Avery chokes on his scotch, slapping a huge hand to his chest. I turn my head slowly to peer at him.

"Is that so?" I murmur slowly, lifting my glass to my lips to hide my smirk.

Avery's espresso eyes flicker as he looks down at me and then sends Wyatt the dirtiest look over my shoulder, his cute little cheeks turning a cute little shade of pink.

"My, my, Mr. Beck," I whisper, batting my lashes up at him for full effect. I trail the tip of my finger over his high cheekbone, feeling the warm skin there. "You're not blushing, are you?"

And because he's Avery Beck, cocky son of a bitch, his gaze narrows for only a second before his coy smile slides right back into place. He dips his face until his lips just barely brush mine. "You don't wanna play this game with me, Miss Thompson. I'll win."

Oh, but I think I do want to play.

"Alright!" Wyatt exclaims, clapping his hands and, thankfully, breaking up this very private but somehow public moment. He picks up a glass of champagne and inclines his head toward the one sitting in front of me. "Shall we raise a toast? To old friends, new friends, and exciting business ventures that are going to make some of us here very, very rich." He smirks at that last statement, and we all raise our glasses, toasting each other with big grins and matched excitement.

Avery holds my gaze while we tip our drinks back, the bubbles in the champagne giving me the feels right in the pit of my stomach and, unfortunately, in an irritating spot in my chest which should definitely *not* be feeling a single thing right now.

Dinner goes off without a hitch, and I don't know if I'm happy or disappointed to say that I'm having a really freaking great time by the time our food arrives an hour later. I contemplated the menu for an entire fifteen minutes, humming and hawing between filet mignon and the lobster trio. I decided on the steak, but when the waiter drops the lobster trio in front of Avery and one of them is wrapped in spicy soppressata, I feel like I've made a huge mistake.

"Stop eyeing my food," Avery murmurs while he dips a piece of lobster in an intoxicating aroma of garlicky-lemony melted butter. I lift my eyes to his mouth and watch him chew, mesmerized by the way his tongue flicks out to drag along those generous lips, licking up the glossy sheen from the butter. He moans, eyes falling shut. "So good."

When he opens his eyes to wink at me, my face splits into a grin. I reach forward and pinch his side. "You're doing that to make me jealous."

He chuckles softly and the next thing I know, he's shoving half of his meal onto my plate and cutting my steak, lifting one half to his plate.

"What are you doing?"

"Sharing." He checks out the inside of my steak and groans in approval. "A rare beef girl, eh? After my own heart." He cuts a chunk off and pops it in his mouth, humming.

I smile to myself and shake my head. I don't know about this guy. It's a shame he doesn't date; I'm starting to think he'd actually make a good boyfriend. For someone else. Not for me. *Obviously.*

He sets the melted butter between our plates. I swirl the lobster tail in it and toss it in my mouth. It dissolves against my tongue, my mouth erupting with flavor so intense and delicious it makes my head spin. I moan and tip sideways, leaning my head on his shoulder.

"Sweet mother of God."

Avery looks down at me with a wide smile and bright eyes that dance in the glow of the dim lights. "Amazing, right?"

"It looks like they're dating," I hear Casey say.

"Agreed. But your sister is stubborn as *hell*," Charlee responds.

My cheeks flame and I back up, away from Avery. He shakes his head and pours me another glass of champagne, shoving it into my hands.

"Drink this and stop giving a shit about what people say. You're having a good time. Just let it happen."

When I hesitate, Avery lifts the glass to my lips, and when that bubbly liquid slips down my throat, tingling on its way down into my belly, I decide to take his advice and stop putting so much weight into everything. I'm with my friends, I'm eating a fabulous meal and drinking expensive champagne, and I'm enjoying myself. I'm going to keep enjoying myself, because—why the hell not? I've been in a sheltered, miserable relationship for far too long.

So when Avery stands opposite me at a ping pong table an hour-and-a-half later, rolling his sleeves up to his elbows, eyes narrowed playfully at me, the trash talk just rolls so damn naturally off my tongue.

"Ready to get spanked by a girl?"

"Baby, if you're the girl, I'll let you spank me all night long."

I don't even care that my brother is at the next table and can clearly hear us. He doesn't look like he's listening anyway. That or he doesn't care. He's too wrapped up in everything that is Charlee Williams. They're teasing each other relentlessly while they smash the ping pong ball back and forth.

"Can't take your eyes off me, can you, little Miss Strawberry?" Avery asks smugly, watching the way I'm biting my lip, my brow quirking at his flexing muscles as he spins the paddle in his hand. "I hope I'm not too much of a distraction for you."

"Just looking at the man I'm about to put in the ground." I settle in and throw a glance at Dex and Wyatt who are watching us, looking rightfully entertained. Dex knows which way this is going to go. He's spent many years on the opposite end of a table much like this, wearing a sorry expression. "Get your popcorn ready, gentlemen. I'm about to make a show of Mr. Beck."

They laugh, and so does Avery. He actually has to stop mid-serve to drop his head and compose himself before he looks back up at me. It makes me smile so hard.

"Quit being so arrogant," he says, sending the ball over the table. I smack it back quickly. "I'm not arrogant. I'm good."

"We'll see about that." He returns it effortlessly. He's good, but I'm better; I'm sure of it.

"How much did you have to drink?" I ask when I'm up by six points.

"Why?" Avery's brown eyes flit up to mine and the split second that he takes to drink me in is the perfect opportunity for me to send the ball slamming onto his side of the table. He doesn't even see it coming until it's rolling on the floor. He blinks at me, mouth halfway open.

"'Cause it's like you're not even mentally here. This is fun."

I pick up my beer and take a long sip while Wyatt claps my hand in a high five, and then my ass. I'd be mortified, but it reminds me of guys on a sports team, like he's just cheering me on, and I feel all comradery with him. Avery's gaze narrows though, zeroing in on Wyatt's hand and then his face, wearing a scrumptious scowl.

"Fucking right, Claire," Wyatt booms with a laugh. "This is way too much fun to watch." He clinks his glass to mine and leans in close. "Take him down, baby."

Avery huffs and serves the ball over to me. "Stop fucking bragging."

"It's not bragging if you can back it up." I wink at my drowning opponent.

He starts getting a little cocky when he wins back three points in a row, but when I send my eleventh point over and win the game, Avery lets out a long-suffering groan and drops his palms to the table, hanging his head and looking just as defeated as he actually is.

I flip my paddle in the air and it lands with a *thud* on the table while I throw my hands up and walk away. Okay, it might be a saunter. I'm sauntering.

"Game over." I stop in front of Avery to give him a patronizing pat on his hard, sculpted chest. "There, there, little buddy. You know what they say, don't you?"

His dark gaze slants, fingers closing around my hips, pulling me in. "Enlighten me, oh mighty one."

"You have to learn to lose before you can truly appreciate winning." I lean up and press my lips to the corner of his mouth and dance away before he can say or do anything. I smile when I hear him growling and everyone else laughing.

Nearly three hours later, he's pushing my still-bragging and incredibly intoxicated ass into the elevator at the condo.

"Not gonna take your private elevator, Richie Rich?" I ask him when he presses for my floor and then punches in the code for his. "Gonna grace us common folk with your presence?" I sweep my arms out in an exaggerated flourish at the otherwise empty elevator. His eyes glitter. He thinks I'm funny.

"Someone's gotta make sure you make it all the way to your door, you lush."

"I am not a lush." Pouting from across the elevator, I lean back on the railing to study him through hooded eyes. God, he's so hot. "You're just mad because I beat you. Three times."

"You cheated. Three times."

I gasp and press a hand to my heart. "How dare you!"

He smirks. "Your brother told me you guys had a ping pong table growing up and you played every night."

I wave him off, enjoying the way his gaze drags over me, his teeth skimming his bottom lip. "That's not cheating."

"No," he agrees softly. "Not cheating. Just withholding information and using it to your advantage."

He steps toward the doors as the elevator climbs closer and closer to my floor. I follow him. I'm not sure why. Maybe because I'm getting off in thirty seconds? It's definitely not because I feel any type of magnetic pull toward him whatsoever. Nope. Nuh-uh.

His eyes shift sideways to me. "It's not nice to trick people, Claire."

I fold my arms over my chest. "What are you gonna do about it?"

A wicked grin slides into place as he turns his body to me, getting right up in my space. It's electrifying, and the air between us sizzles. I have an urge to cower away from him, but my feet are cemented in place.

"I thought you'd never ask."

CHAPTER THIRTEEN

Claire

Before I can even begin to comprehend what's happening, Avery slams his fist against the emergency stop button and the elevator jerks to a halt just as he pushes me up against the wall, his hips pinning me in place, hands grasping my face, my hair. Our lips collide in a frenzy and our tongues dance together. It's wild and panicked and we're bouncing around the elevator like we're in a pinball machine, spinning from one wall to the next, hands everywhere.

He tugs my dress up to my hips and he grabs my ass, lifting me to him. When we roll by the panel with the floor numbers, I hammer my hand against the emergency stop button and the elevator springs back to life.

For a split second, before Avery slams it again.

"Someone might come in here," I say with as much determination as I can muster, which isn't much, because this is kinda fun, and I'm totally drunk.

"Then stop fucking touching it," he snarls in my ear before he nips my lobe between his teeth. He rolls me away from the panel before I can reach for it again and pins me against the back corner of the elevator. "Unless you wanna take this to your apartment," he says against my neck, dropping wet kisses down it. "Or mine."

I groan and dip my head back, pushing his shoulders down, because I want more. He feels so damn good. "I'm not...fucking...you." I'm not even telling him at this point. I'm saying it for me. Like, *Hey girl, remember that promise you made to yourself? Yeah, don't forget it.*

He jerks the plunging neckline of my dress to the side and bites down on the swell of my breast. "I know. But I'm going to lick you, right—" one hand pushes between us and right into my already wet panties, "—here." His finger plunges deep inside me and I gasp, smacking my head off the elevator wall.

My gaze bounces around wildly until my eyes connect with my own in the mirrored elevator. My face is flushed, my lips swollen and red, my hair a wild mess. The skin on my shoulders, neck, and chest is blotchy from Avery's possessive touch. His hand is moving between my legs, rubbing, pumping, driving me absolutely insane.

"Please, Claire," Avery begs gruffly, kissing a fiery path up my chest, over my throat, finally capturing my lips with his. "Let me taste you."

He gives me approximately two seconds to voice my objection, and when I don't, the next thing I know, Avery's on his knees and my panties are in his back pocket. I'm not even really sure how it all happened.

He lifts one of my legs and rests it on his shoulder as he peers up at me. His gaze is dark, hooded, penetrating, and it's killing me. He licks his lips and his eyes drop to the apex of my thighs. I've never been so openly on display for a man before. Part of me wants to feel vulnerable, wants to snap my legs closed and cover up, but…I don't. I know this man wants me, and he makes me feel sexy as hell.

"Perfect fucking pussy," he mutters, I think to himself.

His gaze lifts to mine as his face dips between my legs. The second his tongue washes over my soaking folds, I'm boneless. I slump against the wall and sink. He catches me, grabbing my other leg and throwing that one over his shoulder, too. I don't know how he's doing it, holding me up like this and ravishing me like I've never been ravished before, but *my fucking God* he's doing it.

He curls his arms over my thighs, one hand pressing against my stomach while the other disappears up my dress, palming one breast. He tweaks my nipple through my thin lace bra, and I moan, clutching a fistful of his dark waves. His mouth closes over my clit, sucking, pulling, teasing, and I'm thrusting, grinding myself into his face.

I don't know where to look. This is absolutely incredible. I can look down and watch him work his magic—and that's exactly what it is, unearthly magic—or I can watch in the mirrored walls, from the side, from behind him. All views are unreal, perfect, and seeing it like this pushes me to an edge I've never stumbled to before. I'm not going to last.

The hand on my breast disappears and I whimper at the loss. Until one long finger sinks into my heat from below.

"*Avery*," I cry, fingers curling tightly around his silky waves. He pumps slowly while his tongue flicks and teases my aching nub. "M-more," I beg. "Please."

His eyes when I beg, when I ask for more, when I call out his name…they go wild. Where they were all milk chocolate before, painted with little green and gold flecks, bright and playful, now they're black, dark and daunting like a violent storm cloud inching in on the horizon.

With another finger plunging without warning inside me, he fucks me hard and fast while I moan and cry out for him, begging him not to stop. I keel forward, gripping his shoulders, fingernails digging in, my hair curtaining us.

"*Avery*! I'm gonna, g-gonna—"

Static crackles through the elevator and Avery pushes me up, reaching with one arm to clamp a hand over my screaming mouth as my orgasm starts ripping through my trembling body.

"Hello?" a voice asks from a speaker. "Is everything okay in there? I have a notification that the elevator's been stopped for a few minutes."

Avery smirks up at me as he pulls his mouth off my pussy, fingers still pumping, his lips glistening with my arousal. His tongue flicks out to lick his lips before he speaks. "Everything's fine, just a little hiccup. I'm starting the elevator back up now." He punctuates his sentence with a ferocious pump of his fingers and sucking kiss straight to my clit.

How the hell can he talk so calmly at a time like this? I'm squirming, writhing, my eyes rolling up, and when the static finally disappears and Avery pulls his fingers from me, he catches me as I collapse on top of him.

He presses a kiss to my sweaty temple, holding me in his arms. "Delicious," he purrs in my ear.

My answer is a grunt. I can't move. I'm done. And I didn't even do anything.

"Can you move?" he asks quietly, smoothing his palm over my hair.

I make a noise. I hope he gets it.

He chuckles. "Is that a no?"

"Noodles," I wheeze.

"Noodles? Tell me you're thinking about spaghetti right now."

I burst with laughter, shaking against him. "My legs are noodles," I manage. But spaghetti doesn't sound too bad right now.

"Ah. Well, that makes more sense."

My eyes are closed so I can't see what he's doing when I feel him moving beneath me, but he must have pressed the emergency stop button again, because the elevator whirrs to life. It dings and stops five seconds later, a sign that I've finally reached my destination after all this time. Now I just need to remember how to walk.

But I don't have to. In one swift sweep, Avery's on his feet with me in his arms like I weigh nothing. Stupid, infuriating, strong, muscly man.

I crack one sleepy, spent eyelid. "What you doin'?" My voice is all heavy and lazy, thick and drowsy with the most insane orgasm I've ever had.

His smile is boyishly cute, all sweet and gentle. Or maybe I'm just too out of my mind right now. He presses the softest kiss to my

123

lips and I moan at the taste of me on him, still lingering there. "Taking you to bed, noodle legs."

"That's Miss Noodle Legs to you," I whisper-sigh, shoving my finger into his chest. It's weak, and I wind up wrapping my arm around his neck, burying my face in his warmth. "No sexing."

"I knooow," he groans, digging my keys out of my purse.

I expect Avery to set me down in the doorway, but he doesn't. He flips one light on and heads down the only hallway, finding my bedroom in no time at all. I can imagine that my measly six-hundred-and-fifty square foot condo is embarrassingly tiny compared to his top floor penthouse suite. I don't even want to know the difference in square footage.

He pulls back the covers and drops me gently on the bed. Holding the sheet up and blocking me from his view, he orders, "Dress—off."

It's not easy, but I comply, wiggling out of my dress with a lot more grunts and groans than should ever be necessary when simply pulling a garment over your head.

"You just tongue-fucked me straight to heaven in the elevator and now you're being a gentleman?" I toss my dress across the room and he lowers the covers, tucking me in. God, he's cute. Why is he being so cute?

"I'll put in the work to see this flawless body totally naked, Claire."

I'm having too much of an out-of-body experience right now to process that comment and wonder why he doesn't just move on to the next girl who's willing to give it up.

I turn over on my stomach, arms sliding under my pillow as I snuggle into the cool sheets. "'Kay. I'm going back to hating you in the morning," I say, all hush-hush.

Avery chuckles and brushes my hair off my cheek, pushing it over my back. His fingers trail along my shoulder blades and down my spine, making me quiver. "You don't hate me," he murmurs.

"No." I breathe out the biggest sigh. "Not even close."

And then I'm out. Like a light.

I don't wake up until lunchtime on Sunday, and when I do, there's a melted but still cool iced coffee sitting on my kitchen island, along with my key, two Advil, and a note telling me to call Avery if my noodle legs still don't want to work.

Nothing is clear to me, except for the notion that I am absolutely done for.

CHAPTER FOURTEEN

Avery

I meant to leave right away last night, or rather, in the small hours this morning. I meant to just make sure she got inside her door alright. But Claire was so tired, so I carried her to bed.

And then I'd really meant to leave, just as soon as she was tucked in.

But she passed out in ten seconds flat after admitting how much she *didn't* hate me, and the way the moonlight streamed through her window, casting a soft glow on her face and across her milky skin, the curve of her spine...I just had to stop and stare for a minute or two longer.

Then I meant to slip her key under the crack in her door after locking it on my way out. But it was tight. It wouldn't fit, not easily, at least. So I tucked her key into my pocket with the silent promise to knock on her door in the morning and hand it back to her.

Sully and I went for a walk later in the morning and stopped for coffees on the way home. With my dog by my side, I knocked on Claire's door, hoping to not only see her, but maybe spend some time with her, but there was no answer.

I unlocked her door and popped my head in, and Sully sniffed his way straight to her bedroom, where she was still passed out face first in her pillow. I nearly checked to make sure she was breathing, but then she let out a moan and curled into herself, her bare legs kicking out from the light gray sheets. Sully's tongue went straight for her feet, so I had to get the hell out of there, leaving her iced coffee, key, and a quick note on her counter.

Now here I am three hours later, sitting in my parents' backyard, drinking a beer, listening to my mom go on and on about how me and my sister need to get our shit together and find significant others to settle down with so we can give her and my dad the grandbabies she's been dreaming of, all while smiling like an idiot at the text message that just rolled across my screen.

Claire Bear: *Thanks for the iced coffee. And for putting me to bed. My limp noodle legs are in recovery mode today.*

Me: *Aren't you forgetting something?*

Claire Bear: *Nope. Don't think so.*

Me: *I feel like you're forgetting an important thank you.*

Claire Bear: *Oh! Thank you for not crying like a baby when I kicked your ass in ping pong last night. That would have been embarrassing. For you, not me.*

I fight the urge to roll my eyes at that one. Kick my ass she did. It was awful and sexy as hell. She was so incredibly cocky when she did it, spewing trash talk, line after line. Claire let loose last night and it was a sight to see.

Me: *...And?*

Claire Bear: *I think I remember something in the elevator. Not sure.*

Me: *You think? Shit, guess I'll need to try harder next time.*

No I won't. The girl was wild for me in that elevator. Her body loved every second of it, and I loved the way she reacted to me, the way her back arched off the wall, the way her fingers raked through my hair, her nails biting into the flesh of my shoulders. I loved every moan, every whimper, every plea, and watching her watch us, staring down at me with wide eyes, her gaze darting from one mirrored wall to the other.

Claire Bear: *No next time. Stop getting in my head. And my pants.*

Me: *It was a dress.*

Claire Bear: *And where's my underwear?*

At home in my laundry basket, but I'm not about to tell her that. I stuffed her panties in my back pocket when I peeled them off of her last night. I don't know why; I just did.

"Avery Austin Beck, stop ignoring your mother!" A swift slap to my shoulder catches my attention. A glance up has me meeting my scowling mom's narrowed gaze. "Did you hear what I said?"

"Yeah, Avery," my sister Harper teases, jamming her toes into my knee. "Listen to your mother and stop smiling like a jackass at your phone."

Mom shoots Harper a look, the kind that can still make both of us—and Dad—cower. "You too, Harper! It's time for you to meet a man! Or a woman, if that's what you're into."

I chuckle and Harper groans, throwing her head back over her patio chair, her dark hair spilling behind it. "I'm not a lesbian, Mom! Just because I haven't met...Ugh, I'm not having this conversation with you! I'm twenty-five! I've got tons of time!"

Mom points an angry finger at me. "Don't you laugh, mister! You're turning thirty next year! Time is running out!" She slaps the back of her hand in her palm three times for dramatic effect.

I stand up and pat her head like I would Sully. "Okay, crazy lady." I join my dad at the smoker, watching him check the ribs and sausages he's been tending to all afternoon. "Stop leaving me alone with them."

He shakes his head, eyes wide, maybe a little scared. "Ave— you gotta help me out here, buddy. Your mom's on my case about this baby shit every week. *I wanna be a grandma. I wanna spoil my grandbabies.* That woman needs a baby in her life, and I'm afraid if one of you don't give it to her, she's going to suggest we try for a third." Turns out his terrified expression is justified.

"Right, well, I'm not ready to be a dad anytime soon."

"Maybe you could just get a girlfriend," Dad suggests. "Bet that would get your mom off your back for a while. And mine. God, I need a break." He sighs, dragging both hands down his face.

"Retirement getting to you already, old man?"

He throws me a sideways glance and snorts. "You have no idea." But then he meets my mom's gaze across the yard and winks

128

at her, his smile exploding across his face, because no matter how crazy she drives him, she's the love of his life.

I love my family, but an entire day with them can be entirely too exhausting. I think that's why I collapse onto the couch when I get home. My phone vibrates on the coffee table and I feel a surge of excitement thinking it might be Claire.

The disappointment that follows when I realize that it's not Claire, but Sam, a gorgeous, leggy blonde who I hook up with whenever she blows through the city, is confusing, to say the least.

Samantha: *Hey handsome. Just got into town. Here for the week. I can be over in an hour?*

A picture accompanies her words—her bare legs, crossed and a perfect shade of shimmering bronze, a pair of strappy black heels on her feet, fire engine red toenails peeking out.

I check the time. It's only just after eight and the sky is still light. I haven't had sex since the weekend before I met Claire, and I'd be lying if I said I wasn't itching to bury myself in something hot and wet. But the very thought of Claire has my fingers hesitating over my phone and I'm not sure why.

Me: *Sorry Sam. Busy.*

Samantha: *Boo. Tomorrow?*

Me: *Can't. Maybe next time.*

Samantha: *:(*

Shit, what is wrong with me? Sam is hell on wheels, sexy as sin, and up for anything. I honestly can't remember the last time I've gone this long without sex.

Trying to focus on something other than the sex I just turned down and how much my brain hurts from how baffled I am by it, I sift through my work email, noting one from a contractor I reached out to Saturday morning about the kitchen reno at Cherry Lane. His email tells me he can come by tomorrow to take a look, otherwise he's busy for the next three weeks.

I shoot Claire another text.

Me: *Contractor for quote for kitchen coming tomorrow @ 10. See you then. Have your binder ready, noodle legs.*

Claire Bear: *K. Thanks. Will do. Noodle legs are soaking in a bath right now.*

The mental image of Claire in a bath is such a lovely one that I have an urge to ride the elevator down and slip through her door.

And it looks like I might get that chance, because ten minutes later, my phone vibrates where it rests on my thigh. It's Claire, and she's calling me.

"Want me to come dry you off? Or do you wanna get wetter?"

Claire grumbles a string of curses into the phone at my greeting. "How are you with spiders?"

I blink. "Spiders?"

"Spiders. You know, those eight-legged freaks of nature." Her agitation that she needs to waste any time clarifying this to me only makes me want to drag this on, and a slow smile sweeps over my face.

"Do you need me to come downstairs and save you from a spider, Claire Bear?"

Her groan vibrates in my ear. "If you're going to make fun of me, just forget it. But if that's the case, start looking for a new place to live, 'cause I will burn this place to the ground."

My laughter is interrupted by her shrill shrieking. "*Please*, Avery! Oh my God! Oh my God, *stop*! Stop moving!"

There's a shitload of clanging and banging happening on the other end of the phone, and my entire body vibrates with laughter as I push up off the couch. "Be there in two."

When I creep through Claire's unlocked door, her apartment is eerily quiet. The sun finished setting in the two minutes it took me to get down here, and the only illumination comes from the dim glow of the twinkly lights around Claire's balcony door, and the hood above the stove.

"Claire?"

A whimper from my left has my head swiveling, and I almost die when I spot my favorite redhead, perched atop of a high-top stool, balancing on one foot and wielding a frying pan—for what purpose, I'm not sure. She's got a light blue towel wrapped around her head, a baggy Tragically Hip tee hangs off one shoulder and pools around her hips, and—*oh dear God*—she's donning only a pair of pale purple panties with little daisies on her lower half.

Fuck me.

"Well, hey there, crazy." I sidle up next to her, peering up at the gorgeous girl who's been occupying every inch of my brain for the last ten days. I'm tall, so I come face-to-face with her purple cotton-covered pussy. Or I guess face-to-pussy would be the correct term. "Whatcha doin' up there?"

Sage eyes drift down to me, Claire's body quivering. She squeezes her eyes shut.

I wrap my fingers around her ankles, running my hands over her calves. "And why are you half-naked? You know what that's doing to me, right?" Her nipples pebble in her threadbare shirt, letting me know she damn well knows what she's doing to me, and that she also doesn't mind my hands on her, even though she bites out her next words.

"You." She aims the frying pan at my head and then swings it toward the far wall of windows. "Spider. Now." She slices the pan through the air. "Kill."

Jesus, this woman. I lean on the kitchen island with my elbow, propping my chin up in my hand. "What were you planning to do with the frying pan? Smash your wall in? Or catch the little guy and fry him up for dinner?"

With a gagging sound, her shoulders curl forward. "*Avery*. This is no time for games."

"But I like playing with you." I trail a finger up the inside of her thigh, enjoying the way a shudder rolls through her body and her breath puffs past her lips. "Tell me something," I say, glancing over my shoulder to where a tiny black dot is scurrying across the wall. "If the spider is way over there, why are you over here, standing on a stool? You seem pretty safe to me."

"Are you kidding me?" The pan nearly takes my head off when Claire swings it to point at the wall. "Look how fast that monster is! He started in the hallway. *The hallway, Avery*! He was *chasing* me!" Her eyes flip down to me. "Spiders can smell fear, you know."

I'm pretty sure that's not a real thing, but I'm not going to argue with her while she's got a makeshift weapon in her hands and she's teetering on the edge of crazy.

She shifts her weight, kicking one leg out to the side, trying to grab onto a piece of paper towel with her toes.

"Fuck's sake," I say with a groan, dragging a hand down my face. "Can you not? You're going to fall and break your legs. I absolutely cannot have that before I have them wrapped around my waist while I'm buried nine inches deep inside of you." I grab her non-pan wielding hand and steady her on the stool, then move around her and rip off a sheet of paper towel.

"Nine in—" Her head swivels down to me, eyes huge. "*Nine inches*?" Now she's shrieking about something other than the spider who's infiltrated her apartment. Distraction is good.

I move across the room in three long strides and plant my hands on my hips, studying the little spider. It stops, almost as if engaging me in a good old-fashioned stare-down. This thing's tiny, the whole circumference of it—legs and all—the size of my thumbnail.

I throw Claire a glance over my shoulder. She's got the frying pan raised above her shoulder, grip so tight her knuckles are turning white. I stifle the urge to laugh. "So you're scared of spiders, huh?"

"Terrified." It comes out as a burst of air.

"Well then, you won't like this news." I turn back to the spider overhead.

"What? What, Avery? Oh my God, what?" She's freaking out. I love it.

"Looks like big momma here just laid some eggs." I'm so mean. I've earned many a smack upside the head from my sister for shit just like this.

"*What*? No! No!" A soft cry pushes past her lips and I smile at the spider. If it could understand me—which it can't—it'd be laughing too. "Oh, God. I'm gonna be sick."

I can't help it. My shoulders shake and my head drops as the laughter I've been holding back since I walked in here ripples through my body, rumbling out my chest.

"Oh my God! You asshole! I'm gonna kill you, Avery Beck!" Claire shouts at me. I look back at her, watching as she slices the pan through the air. The towel around her head unwinds and tumbles down to the floor, wet hair cascading down around her shoulders. "When I get my hands on you—"

"You're gonna love me for saving your life."

Her mouth twists with rage and her eyes narrow past the point of dangerous. I throw her a wink before turning back to the spider.

"Alright, little guy. You've overstayed your welcome. Let's get you out of here before Claire fries you up and eats you for dinner."

I expect the eight-legged furball to scurry off when I reach for him, but he must be just as terrified of the frying pan-wielding crazy lady as I am, because he stays put, letting me scoop him right off the wall with the paper towel. I step out onto the balcony and deposit him on the railing, and he just sits there for a moment before taking off like he's Usain Bolt.

I find the garbage under the kitchen sink, throw out the napkin, wash my hands, and lean back on the counter. "You good?"

"Y-yes." Claire's shoulders sag as her trembling body slowly stills, arms dropping to her side, the frying pan with along it. Her gaze shifts to mine and she sighs.

I pry the pan out of her fingers. They're cold and clammy, a telltale sign of a real fear. Once the pan is safely stowed away, my hands glide up her legs, over her hips, settling in the dip of her waist. I hoist her off the stool, depositing her in front of me on the floor.

"What do I get as a thank you?"

Without hesitation, she steps forward, wrapping her arms around my waist and hugging me tight, her cheek pressed to my chest. The hesitation comes a moment later when her body goes rigid against mine. It might be because I've apparently frozen solid. I wasn't expecting this, and for some reason, it feels...intimate. Something I'm not all that used to with women. Not in this way, at least.

Slowly, my arms come up, winding around her petite frame as I hold her close, breathing her in. She smells so good, fresh and fruity, a hint of coconut. But she feels even better.

She clears her throat and pushes off me, tucking a damp wave behind her ear. Her gaze lands on the floor. "Thank you," Claire whispers. Then she perks up, speaking with life for the first time since I got here. "My brother used to catch the spiders for me, but then he'd chase me around the house with them. He was such an asshole growing up. Once he accidentally dropped one on my head, and I ran into a wall because I was blinded by tears and rage." She smiles up at me, her nose twitching. "So, thanks for not doing that."

Chuckling, I tweak her nose, 'cause it's kinda cute. I guess. Whatever. "I like to tease you, but I can't imagine doing that to you. That's just plain mean." Harper would have gouged my eyes out with a fork if I pulled that shit on her.

"Oh, I know. Casey never meant to drop it, but I think that's why my fear is so bad now. I honestly thought I was going to have to shave my entire head. He felt so bad he did all my chores for a month and gave me a piggyback to and from school for a week."

"You want me to piggyback you to and from work for pretending there was a bunch of spider eggs somewhere in your apartment?"

She shakes her head, copper hair swishing around her face, stirring up that sweet, fruity fragrance. "I want you to do all my chores."

I step toward her, pulling her into me by her hips. "Sure. I'll come by for bath time tomorrow and help you wash up."

Claire laughs, swatting at my shoulder. "Sounds like the only one around here dirty enough for a bath is you." Turning her back on me, she makes it two steps before I grip her hips again and slam her back into my chest.

I curl over her, lips grazing her ear. "Seriously, why the fuck are you not wearing pants?" My hands skim over the side of her breasts, the dip of her tiny waist. "Or a bra."

I feel her cheek heat against mine as she squirms. "I was getting ready for bed," she manages. It's an unconvincingly convenient excuse, piss-poor even. "I wasn't expecting to find a spider in the hallway or having to call you down here."

I release her with a smile and clap a palm to her ass. "Go put on some pants before I get any wrong ideas."

She snorts, stalking off down the hall. "As if you don't already have them."

Growling, I lunge forward and grab her wrist, spinning her back to me. "You're right. I've already got them." I haul her over to the couch, throwing her down with a bounce and a yelp. "No pants for you."

She scurries backwards but doesn't hesitate to reach for the neck of my shirt as soon as my knee touches down between her legs.

And then I'm on top of her, my tongue sweeping through her mouth, her hands buried in my hair as her hips thrust up, grinding against my thigh. I can't help smiling against her mouth, because as much as she tries to resist this, Claire wants me. There's something here between us, and it's not one-sided.

But as much as I want to see how far I can take this tonight, I kinda wanna leave her wanting more, wanna put her in the shoes I've been wearing these last few days.

So, for a moment, I kiss her harder. It's teeth clashing, lip biting, hair pulling, leg grinding.

And then I pull back.

The two of us are breathless, Claire's green eyes wide, her face flushed, lips swollen and glistening. And her panties…*fuck*.

I bite my knuckles, looking at the dark, damp spot between her legs. I can smell her. She smells…ready. So fucking ready.

"What are you doing?" she rasps out, struggling to sit up as her chest heaves.

I dip my head between her legs, press my lips to her wet panties, feel the heat seeping out of them, and then stand, adjusting my cock, which is happily standing at full attention. The corner of my mouth lifts at the way Claire's gaping at me right now.

"Gotta go, beautiful." I drop my lips to her surprised pout and stalk off toward the door. "See you in the morning."

Except I'm not inside my condo for more than ten seconds before I'm hitting send on that text before I even know what I'm writing.

Me: *Dinner?*

Claire Bear: *???*

Me: *With me. Tomorrow.*

Shit. I think I've got a crush.

CHAPTER FIFTEEN

Avery

I've got a giant grin plastered on my face as I step out of the car and onto the curb in front of the brewery, the late May sunshine warming my back. It's hot already and it's only quarter to nine in the morning. I'm way early for our meeting with the contractor, but I figure I can chat with Dex and annoy Claire.

But the current reason for my smile is a feisty little ginger with bright green eyes, and not the one whose skin I plan on crawling under when I get upstairs.

Casey: *Sorry man, Vivi insisted I send this to you. She pulled my hair.*

I open the attached video and find Vivi doing several wobbly leaps in the air and spinning around in circles, all while scream-singing the words to a song about snow and ice queens. Then she runs to the camera, smashes her face right up against it, and says, "Hi A'wy! You like ma dancin'?"

"Whatcha watchin'?"

I glance over my shoulder just as Charlee drops her chin to it. Her big brown eyes find my screen and her face lights up.

"Isn't she the cutest thing you've ever seen?"

"She seriously is," I murmur my agreement, letting her watch video with me as I replay it.

When it gets to the end and Vivi speaks into the camera to me, Charlee clutches at her chest, giving me this dopey, doe-eyed look. I click my phone off and tuck it into my pocket, taking in her appearance. She's stunning, but she looks tired as hell.

"Still recovering from Saturday?"

She grips my shoulder and groans. "You have *no* idea. Me and Claire spent all afternoon yesterday eating Taco Bell and ice cream." She cringes. "It's not my proudest moment."

I make a face. "Taco Bell?"

"Oh, yeah. Claire's guilty pleasure is a Crunchwrap Supreme." She winks and pats my chest. "Keep that in your back pocket in case you ever need it."

I tuck that little tidbit of information into a corner of my brain and pull the door open for Charlee, sweeping my arm out in front of me. "How long have you and Casey been a thing?"

She stumbles over her own feet and I catch her by the elbow. "What?"

"You and Casey. You're dating, right? Or hooking up?"

She starts fumbling with the dainty silver chain around her neck, cheeks flooding with color. "No. No we're not. Why would you think that?"

I lift one brow. Her guilty expression is suspect. "Because you two were all over each other on Saturday night?"

The night had started off innocently enough, close talking and leaning into each other at the restaurant. But by the time we got to the bar, things had ramped up to a whole new level. They were hanging off each other the whole night, holding hands, dancing, kissing each other's cheeks.

"I was just drunk," Charlee tells me unconvincingly. "And so was Case. He hasn't had a night out like that since before Viv. Plus, he's, like, my brother." She waves her hand around like she's trying to swat away a fly. "He'd never think of me as anything other than his little sister's best friend. And his best friend's little sister," she adds with a huff and a less than enthusiastic eye roll.

"Hmm," I murmur, leading her up the stairs as she loops her arm through mine.

"Hmm? What does that mean? What are you hmm-ing at, Avery?"

138

With a sneaky smile, I shrug. "Nothing. Plus, didn't Claire and your brother hook up? Why are you so quick to assume Casey wouldn't see you as something more?" I'm good at girl talk. My sister and I have always been close. She comes to me with her problems. Like the good brother I am, I always listen, even if my eyebrows are halfway up my forehead the entire time.

But I realize my mistake at the way Charlee gapes up at me, face pale. The Claire and Dex thing maybe isn't supposed to be out in the open.

Gripping my arm, she yanks me into her. "How do you know that? Did Dex tell you?"

"Yes?" It's a question, because I shouldn't have spoken in the first place and now I'm just treading water. "But I asked."

"Oh, crap. Don't tell Claire you know."

"Secret stuff; got it." I scratch a hand through my hair and gesture at nothing in particular. "Do you, uh…think there's still something going on with them?" It's probably a stupid question. We flirted all night Saturday, right in front of Dex. But Dex is hard to read. I can't tell if he's still into her or if he's just protective of her.

Charlee snorts and waves me off. "Nah. Claire's really adamantly against that whole thing. I think Dex liked her for a while, but I think now it's more that he wants to take care of her, make sure she doesn't get hurt, that kinda thing. Especially after everything with Aaron."

I grunt my agreement, kinda happy about her answer. Except… "She's really adamantly against a lot of things, isn't she?"

Charlee's mouth tilts with a half-smile. "You mean casual sex?"

I shake my head, because that's not what I meant. "I've asked her out three times. She refuses every time."

A broad grin detonates her face. "You like her."

I roll my eyes and start back up the stairs. "Eh, whatever. Let's go."

"You mean let's go see your woman?" She dances ahead of me. "C'mon, Mr. Beck!"

I love listening to Claire talk business. It's sexy as hell. She knows every inch of this place, right down to the location of every single electrical socket. She struts around the brewery with her head held high and her binder in her arms.

Actually, no. Her binder is in *my* arms because she was having trouble talking with her expressive hands, so she shoved it into my chest and now just keeps leaning up beside me and flipping through to the pages she needs. Like I said, sexy.

Andre, the contractor I brought in and an old friend of mine, is enthralled with her. He's captivated, watching her with a big smile on his face as she gestures wildly around her when she talks, and I catch him sneaking a peek at her backside more than once. It looks fantastic, so I can't blame him, but that doesn't stop me from wanting to knock his eyes elsewhere.

Claire's teasing me with her outfit today; I just know it. She's wearing skin-tight black pants with thin white stripes that hug every curve of her hips and ass. The black shirt tucked into the waist of her pants also appears to be painted on. It's long-sleeved and a fucking mock turtleneck, of all things. She's not letting me see an inch of that glorious, creamy skin, and the smirk that's etched on her face every time she catches me staring tells me she's getting immense pleasure from it.

She's not even wearing heels. She's got on these little pointed slip-on flats, so all I can see is her ankles. I don't even know what color her toenail polish is today. That bothers me more than it should.

Still, she looks fucking magnificent, skin or no skin.

"So." I clap my hands together. "What's the verdict, Andre?" I lean against the wooden counter and we both watch Claire as she hops on top and starts swinging her legs.

Andre smiles, his gaze lingering on her a moment too long, and then turns to me, eyes twinkling. He clears his throat and raps his knuckles on the counter. "I can definitely beat the other quotes. Gimme a couple days to get a proposal together for you." He turns back to Claire and leans next to her. "That okay with you, sweetheart?"

My jaw snaps together as I swallow my groan.

Claire beams up at him. "That's perfect! Thank you so much, Andre." She squeezes his arm for good measure. I glare at her. She glares right back. I wonder if it's punishment for leaving her high and dry last night, even though she wasn't dry. High and wet? Nah, doesn't sound right.

Her phone starts vibrating on her binder, which I'm still holding like a sucker. I hand it to her and watch her tug on her bottom lip while she reads the message.

"I'm sorry," she apologizes, hopping down from the counter. "I've gotta run." She tilts her head toward the window, drawing our attention to a large truck pulling around the side of the L-shaped building. "We've got a delivery coming in and I need to speak to the driver." She turns to Andre and touches his shoulder. "I look forward to hearing from you." Then she looks at me and smirks, inclining her chin ever so slightly. "Mr. Beck."

She turns on her heel and walks away from us, hips sashaying side-to-side as she goes. Goddamn woman has me in a trance.

Andre lets out a low whistle. "Shit, she's fine."

"Back off," I growl at my old friend.

His brows raise and an amused smile tugs at the corner of his lips. "Yours?"

"No."

"Then I don't see why I would need to back off." His eyes challenge me, just like his tone.

"Because I told you to, that's why."

141

He considers me carefully before a shit-eating grin splits his face in half. "You like her."

Well, I've had enough of that. I straighten off the counter and amble out of the kitchen. Andre follows as I guide him toward the door.

"I'll be waiting on that quote, my friend."

"Uh huh." He gives me one last look, still grinning like an asshole, before he shakes his head and strolls through the door, his next words floating out behind him.

"Avery Beck, the man who never settles for any woman, has feelings. Who woulda thought?"

CHAPTER SIXTEEN

Claire

I'm freaking out this morning. On the inside, at least. On the outside, I look cool, calm, and collected. I also probably look hot as hell. I mean, literally roasting, because this outfit is *not* made for this weather.

I tug on the collar of my mock turtleneck with annoyed frustration. The things I'll do to get a rise out of this freaking man.

Anyway, back to what I was saying before. On the outside, I'm fine. On the inside, I feel like someone's throwing rocks at all my major organs. Or that time I got drunk and thought it was reasonable to eat *five* Crunchwrap Supremes. In theory, it sounded like a great night. It was not.

The brewery turns five on Thursday and we're throwing a party here. At first, it was meant to be small. Family and friends of the staff and the vendors we deal with. But as word got out, the small party slowly turned into a smashing soiree, apparently, and according to Charlee.

We all know whose fault this is. Charlee's. She's a party-loving machine, and she'd been begging Dex to open it up to the public, for us to sell tickets to the event, for at least the last six months. Dex refused, so Charlee did what she always did—took things into her own perfectly manicured hands.

She started slowly dropping the word around to other breweries, restaurants, and bars, and before we knew it, we had a guest list of almost two hundred and fifty people. Now we have to open up the second floor and bring in a temporary bar for up there, too. We're no longer making up our menu of appetizers but hiring a catering company to take care of it for us, because frankly, we don't have the staff to accommodate a party of this size.

I'm irritated because the party's in three days and now we're scrambling to change everything at the last minute and I don't handle change all that well. But I have to admit, it's probably the right move. With the expansion of the brewery into a restaurant and adding big events to our repertoire, this is just the type of publicity we need, and a chance to show everyone how great their events could be if they held them at Cherry Lane.

Strolling through the scorching sunshine, I tug at the collar of my tight top, cursing myself for the thousandth time this morning for wanting to cover up for Avery. I'm convinced we skipped spring completely and headed right into summer and it's not even June yet.

But at least I got one thing sorted. I glance over my shoulder, shielding my eyes from the bright sun as I watch the delivery man start to unload cocktail tables and barstools from his truck for the party. I just accosted him, begging him to deliver two more loads by Wednesday so people would have places to sit and put their drinks on Thursday. Thankfully, a quick call to his warehouse determined that they had more than enough for us to rent for the party.

"Miss Thompson."

I smile when my gaze locks with the owner of the low, husky drawl. Andre, the contractor Avery brought in this morning, is attractive. More than attractive, really, all big muscles and tanned skin, soft brown eyes that match his hair.

"All done?" I stop in front of him and watch as he looks me over for the tenth time this morning. It makes me blush. I wish Avery were here to see it—again. The surge of pride I got from watching him scowl at Andre while he flirted with me in the kitchen was fantastic.

Andre stuffs his hands in his pockets. "Mhmm, that I am." His gaze slides over my shoulder. "New furniture for the restaurant?"

I shake my head. "It's our birthday on Thursday."

He cocks an intrigued brow, making me chuckle.

"Cherry Lane turns five on Thursday. We're having a big event here to celebrate. It was supposed to be small but quickly spiraled out of control," I add with an eyeroll. "He's dropping off some rentals for us."

"Ah. Sounds like it'll be fun."

"It will be, if not incredibly exhausting." I drum my fingers on my phone and then lift my hand, swatting him on the shoulder. "Hey, you should come by if you're not busy. I can email you a couple passes."

His eyes drag down my body. Again. "Can I consider it a date?"

I'm unimpressed with the way I fluster, my fingers fluttering to my neck as I teeter back on the heels of my feet. What is it with these men and being so damn straightforward?

"I, um…I'm not really…available." I don't know what else to say. I'm having enough trouble keeping Avery at bay and out of my pants. I don't need to add another man to the mix. It's too bad, really, because if it wasn't for my cheating ex and also being totally blinded by Avery—a fact I'm still denying to everybody else and kinda myself—then Andre would be the type of man I'd jump at a date with.

He clicks his tongue and gives his head one barely-there shake. "Ah. Of course. Avery."

I blink. Avery? Avery what? "Pardon?"

Andre simply winks. "No worries." He checks his watch. "I've got another consult in Markham, so I've gotta get going. But it was nice to meet you, Claire. I'll be in touch." He looks down at me, a small smile curving his lips. "And hopefully so will you."

With his hands in his pockets, he turns and strolls through the parking lot, climbing into a blue truck and leaving me feeling a little stunned.

Charlee sneaks up behind me. "Who was *that*? He was smokin'!"

"The new contractor for the kitchen," I reply slowly. "I think, at least." If the price is right.

She pulls on my hand, leading me back inside. "Shit gal, you've got men falling all over you."

My brows pull down with my frown. "I do not. They all just wanna fuck."

Charlee folds her lips into her mouth to keep from smiling. "Avery likes you."

"As I said, they all just wanna fuck. Avery is no exception. He doesn't *like* me."

Still, the thought has my pulse kicking it up to a solid trot, a feeling I need to nix in the bud. I can't have Avery. I can't have sex with him because I'll get too attached and he's not the type of guy I can get attached to. I might have been utterly disappointed when he left my apartment last night, but that fleeting feeling lasted only as long as it took to remind myself why it would be a terrible idea.

"Suit yourself. But that's not what he said this morning." Charlee dances ahead of me and I jerk her arm back.

"I'm sorry, but what? And when did you talk to Avery?"

"This morning. We walked in together and had a little chat."

I fold my arms over my chest, hip popping. "About?"

"Did you know him and Casey are on a texting basis?" She twirls her blond hair. "Isn't that cute?"

"Pardon?"

"Yeah, Case sent him a video of Vivi this morning. She wanted to show Avery her dance moves."

"Oh my God." I bury my face in my hands. Poor guy just wants a simple, easy lay, and he winds up getting my entire family, sans the sex.

"Oh, don't be like that. Avery loved it. I watched him watch it three times with the dopiest grin on his face. He thinks Viv is adorable. And him and Casey seemed to get along great on Saturday."

Squinting, I give her a coy smile. "Really? And how would you know, Miss Williams, when the two of you were too busy feeling each other up all night?"

I watch Charlee's cheeks darken, something which doesn't happen too easily, but seems to be happening quite often around my brother lately.

"Uh, I gotta…we should…" She trails off, jerking a thumb toward the door. Inside, she wastes no time changing the subject. "Wanna get smoothie bowls for lunch?"

"I guess I should probably do something healthy to counter all the Crunchwraps from yesterday, huh?"

"And the ice cream."

Yeah, definitely the ice cream. We each ate an entire pint of Ben & Jerry's. I'm trying not to feel too bad about it; we took a break halfway. Also, I think the whole spider shitfest later that night worked off all those extra calories.

"What time?" Charlee asks as I crack my office door and take a half-step inside.

"Hmm. Half hour or so? I'm already hungry." I pat my belly. I forgot my breakfast wrap on the kitchen counter this morning and remembered when I was halfway out the front lobby of the condo. I turned around to head back upstairs but stopped in my tracks when the penthouse elevator opened, revealing a hot as hell Avery Beck in a charcoal suit that hugged every perfect line of his perfect freaking body. His head was down so before he could lift it and notice me, I decided to forget the breakfast wrap and dashed out the front door.

"'Kay, babe. See ya soon." She gives my butt a little swat as I push my door further open. "By the way, your ass is looking absolutely smashing in these."

Laughter rumbles in my belly. "Thanks, Charlee."

"Did you wear this outfit just to fuck with Avery today?"

"You know it," I say with a wink before disappearing into my office and closing the door.

"Mmm, I figured you did," a husky voice drawls from deep inside my office. "But it's nice to get confirmation either way."

Ah, crap.

CHAPTER SEVENTEEN

Claire

My hand flies to my throat with a yelp and a jump as my heart spirals straight down to my stomach at the sight before me: Avery, sitting behind my desk and wearing an unbelievably smug smile, twirling my pen between his teeth while he leans back in my chair. He's so self-assured and smooth it makes my blood boil.

"I mean, really, Claire, a turtleneck? It's seventy-seven degrees outside."

He pushes away from the desk and stands, slowly making his way over to me, hands in his pockets. His suit jacket is thrown over the back of my chair and the sleeves of his crisp white button-up are folded to his elbows. Ugh. Folded sleeves and forearms like *that*. I can't. I resist the urge to fan myself.

"Although I can't deny it," Avery continues, thumb dragging over his lower lip, "I love the thought of you naked in your bedroom, trying to decide what to wear just for me."

I gulp. Oh, sweet baby Jesus, *I gulp*.

Remembering that I'm a strong, independent woman—thank you Destiny's Child for that smash hit—I push my shoulders back and stand tall, chin jutting out. "I wore this outfit so you couldn't stare at me the entire meeting."

"Hate to break it to you, sweetheart, but it's not working. I want to put my hands *all* over you." Avery stops in front of me, his needy gaze drinking me in. "This—" he trails his hand over the dip of my waist, the curve of my hip, "—just accentuates every. Fucking. Curve." He punctuates the first word with the sweep of his tongue over his top lip. The second word with his teeth pressing into his bottom lip. The final word with the flip of his eyes up to mine. "I want to tear it off."

I *really* wish I didn't squeak, but I do, and when Avery smirks at my reaction, I push by him and head toward my desk.

"What are you doing in here? Why am I walking into my office and finding you looking all Dr. Evil up in my chair? All you need is a bald cat to pet."

He laughs and the corner of my own mouth tugs up. I yell at my brain to make it stop. I hate that I like making him laugh. I hate that he makes me smile. I hate that he was my hero last night when he rescued me from the spider that was clearly jacked up on performance-enhancing drugs.

I glance up at the sound of a soft click to find Avery locking the door. Panicked exhilaration races up my spine. "What are you doing? Unlock that!" But also maybe don't.

He saunters over to me, ignoring my demand. "I just wanted to remind you about our date tonight. What time should I pick you up?"

"Pick me up? We live in the same—" I stop mid-sentence, shoving my finger into his hard chest, because he almost had me there. "We are *not* going on a date!"

"We are."

"I thought we decided it was a bad idea." I cross my arms and raise my brows, jutting my hip out to the side. Avery's eyes land there for a moment.

"*We* decided no such thing, Claire. *You* said that, and *I* said it was a *fabulous* idea." His fingers find my waist, heating my skin right through the thin fabric of my shirt.

"No. We can't. I can't. I'm busy tonight. I've got dinner with Casey and Vivi," I lie.

His gaze narrows. He doesn't believe me, and I wish I didn't use somebody whose phone number he has as an excuse. He could have my lie confirmed in two seconds flat with a simple text. "Fine. Another night this week."

150

"Avery, no." I wave my arms in front of me and step back. "No dates. We're not going on a date."

"Why do you keep rejecting me?"

I hate the twang of guilt that jerks in my stomach. He may be smiling like a fool still, but the hurt sure sounds genuine.

The truth is, I'd love to say yes. I'd love to have dinner with him, spend the evening together. I'd love to kiss him without having to pretend like I don't want it, like I don't want *him*.

But I can't. I can't because he doesn't actually want to date me. He's just pacifying me so that it doesn't feel like casual sex or a one-night stand when the inevitable hook-up eventually happens.

I can't because Aaron wrecked my self-image, my self-worth. There's no part of me that feels like I'm enough, not only to keep someone like Avery interested, but enough for myself.

How do I handle being tossed aside after I fall? Because that's what's going to happen. It's not a far stretch, because I already *am* falling. It's ridiculous and stupid and maddening and I want to slap myself out of it.

If we go on a date, it'll feel real. I'll fall. I'll get comfortable. I'll let my guard down.

And then I'll break all over again when my inferiority comes to light.

It's like Avery sees the internal battle going on in my head, because his eyes soften and his smirky smirk becomes a small, sincere smile. "You've got a lot of rules for yourself, don't you?"

"Yeah," I whisper, swallowing the tightness in my throat as I stare out the window. "I do."

"Why don't you let yourself indulge in the people you like, in the things that make you feel good? You did on Saturday, and you had a wicked night. And I'm not even talking about the elevator," he adds with a wink.

"I…well, I…" My fingers reach for my lips but instead of pulling on them, twisting them like I sometimes do when I'm nervous, I stop myself. I let my fists ball up under my chin instead. Not sure it's any better.

"Don't know?" Avery finishes softly.

I do know, but honestly, how do I explain it to him? He's right. I did it on Saturday. I let go. I had fun. I felt free. But I wound up naked with Avery putting me to bed, even though he didn't see me naked and was perfectly respectable, which I'm still surprised about two days later. One look and I would've jerked him down on top of me and ripped his clothes off.

Gently, he spins me around, pressing my hands to the desk as he steps up behind me, his warm breath on my neck. "I think you're scared. What do you think?"

"N-no." I don't bother hiding my sigh at my horrible lie.

"No?" Avery's fingers trail up my arms, and the regret I feel for wearing long sleeves is instantaneous. I'm desperate to feel the way his touch ignites my skin like it always does. "So, you're not scared that you might actually *like me* if we went on a date? That I might treat you right? That things might get…serious?"

What in the world is happening right now? Yes, I am afraid of all those things. Why does he care? Why is he asking? Men like Avery don't talk about this with girls they want to bed. Is this turning into that big of a chase for him?

"I agree, by the way," he continues. "Your ass *does* look absolutely smashing in these pants. Did you wear them so I wouldn't have easy access?"

I roll my eyes to disguise the fact that I'm glad he's back to teasing. Having real conversations with him about feelings is entirely too confusing. "You have *no* access."

"Really? Is that a challenge?"

"A challenge you can't win, because I'm not taking my pants— *oh!*"

Yeah. One swift pull, and my pants are around my ankles.

"What was that you were saying?" His breath tickles my ear, strong hands sliding all over my body, under my shirt, flexing on my stomach, curving over my hips, my ass. "Sorry Claire, but I have to touch you. I got my first real taste on Saturday, and I don't think I'll ever get enough."

I…I don't know what to say. *Stop? No? I don't want this? I'm at work* would be an obvious one. But for some reason, nothing comes out. In fact, my ass juts backwards and I shudder-moan when I feel his bulge press against me.

Avery's palms smooth down my legs as he drops to the floor, helping me step out of my pants and my flats, which I do all too willingly. He lowers himself to my chair and guides me to his lap, propping my bare feet up on the edge of my desk. Wrapping my hair around his fist, he tosses it over one shoulder.

"This fucking turtleneck," he growls playfully, exposing one side of my neck to him when he yanks the material to the side. His lips descend, moving slowly, leaving a wet trail on my heated skin. I'm in heaven. Or hell. I don't know. "Are you wet for me, Claire?"

A noise rumbles in my throat while he continues assaulting my neck, hands palming my breasts.

"Check, baby."

I don't need to. I already know I am. I can feel damp heat pooling between my legs, and a quick peek shows that my pale pink panties have a wet spot. But still, I comply, because he has some sort of weird power over me.

I push the satin fabric to the side and swipe two fingers up my drenched lips, hissing at how sensitive I already am. It's ridiculous how easily this man has my body begging for release.

"Let me see," he whispers against my neck.

Avery vibrates with a groan when I raise my shaky fingers. He grips my wrist and yanks it backwards. When his lips close over my fingers, when his tongue swirls around me, tasting my arousal, I nearly faint in his lap.

His hands slide under my ass and lift my hips, dragging my underwear down to my ankles. He nudges my knees apart, opening my legs wide. My head tips backwards onto his chest and I peer up at him from beneath my lashes. I hate how breathy I am right now, how quickly my chest is moving.

"What are you doing?" It's a stupid question. I know what he's doing. I also know I'm not going to stop him.

Avery's answer is a tender smile, so sweet and handsome it makes my stomach flip. One hand slides along my jaw, tipping my chin up, and his lips meet mine. His free hand runs up the length of my thigh and back down, teasing, and my skin dots with goosebumps. He swallows my whimper when his fingers dust across the juncture of my thigh.

"Please, Avery."

"You'll have to be quiet," he murmurs. "Think you can handle that?"

I don't think I can handle *any* of this, but I'm sure going to try, because the way his fingers keep ghosting over me is luring me right to the edge. He skims my clit, just barely touching it, and I jerk my hips.

"Go on a date with me," he whispers in my ear, rubbing slow, torturous circles around my nub while it aches with need.

"I…Avery…no." My back arches, toes curling.

"Why not?"

I groan, half irritation, half pleasure. "Can't we just…do this and be done with it?"

"No, Claire. I can't be done with you. I want to take you to dinner."

I'm not sure I'd answer if I could. All I can focus on is the way his fingers dip further down, gathering my wetness and spreading it over my clit. He's moving excruciatingly slow and one of my hands reaches back and slides into his hair, scratching at this scalp, while my other hand grips his forearm so tightly my fingernails leave angry, red bite marks.

"Do you like this?" Avery asks.

His free hand comes forward and he plunges his middle finger inside me. My mouth opens on a sharp inhale and my hips start rolling, meeting his hands, begging for pressure, for friction, for harder, faster.

"Tell me you like it or I'll stop," he breathes against my ear.

"No you won't," I manage. It's wheezy as hell.

It's also a mistake, because he pulls both hands away, leaving me feeling empty and anything but sated.

With an embarrassingly strangled noise, I grab his hand, trying to drag it back to the apex of my thighs, where my body is begging for him.

He nips my ear and kisses my jaw. "Tell me you want me, Claire."

No. I can't. Why is he doing this to me? Why is he sending me to the edge, making me beg? I can't need him like this; doesn't he understand that?

I keep trying to push his hand in between my legs, but his fingers just lace through mine.

"Yes, okay? Yes! I want you." Heat creeps up my neck, seeping into my cheeks, the tips of my ears. I realize the irony in this admission being so difficult, considering I'm sitting spread-eagle on his lap, completely open to him. But the simple words have meaning, and I'm not ready to let Avery in, to grant him any control over my mind, or the broken bits of my heart.

Avery relents, just a bit. He returns one broad fingertip to my clit, pressing with feather-light touches until it's cramping with need and I'm aching for release. I'm a withering, whimpering mess, flailing around in his lap. I can feel his erection grinding on my ass, and I'm about two seconds from turning around, pulling out his cock, and sinking down onto it. I want to ride him, right here, right now.

"More, Avery, please," I beg, trying to coax a finger inside me.

"You want to come?" His nose skims my cheekbone, a silent plea to look at him. When I do, he kisses me, his tongue caressing mine, sweeping into my mouth. Fuck, he's such an amazing kisser. I can't remember the last time I enjoyed kissing so much.

"Have dinner with me, Claire."

I make a noise and shake my head. The movement is barely perceptible, and I'm kinda hoping he doesn't even catch it, but he does. His fingers halt.

"'Kay," he says softly. His chest lifts and falls with a heavy sigh. His fingers splay out on my thighs and slide down to my hips. He grabs me and tilts us both forward as if he's going to get up.

"What are you doing?" He can't seriously intend to leave me like this, can he? I whip my head around and grip the arms of my chair, refusing to move. "You-you—" My head shakes back and forth. "You can't,"

"Yeah baby," Avery says on a sigh. "If you won't agree to go out with me, I'm not gonna let you come."

"Avery!" I loop my arms through the armrests, latching on. I'm not going anywhere until this man makes me come. I refuse. He got me here; he needs to take me the rest of the way.

Light dances in his sparkling brown eyes. "You wanna come?"

"Yes, you asshole! I wanna come!" I resist the urge to drive an elbow into his ribs. I don't imagine it helping my case.

With a quiet chuckle and his hands still gripping my hips, he starts moving me, grinding me over his bulge. If he's not careful, I'm going to leave a mess all over his fancy pants.

"Then you know what you need to say. Say you'll go out with me."

"Avery," I whine. I'm on the verge of a temper tantrum. "You don't...you don't want to go on a date with me. You just wanna fuck me."

There's no hesitation when he answers me with his own question. "Why can't I want to do both?" Then, because he's an arrogant little tease, he swipes two fingers through my folds, soaking his fingers, and presses once on my clit. It nearly sends my vision tunneling. "You know what you need to do," he murmurs.

My chin falls to my chest in defeat. "Fine."

"Hmm?"

"I said fine, Avery! I'll go out with you!" Stupid jerk and his stupid jerky smirk. The harder I glare, the harder he smirks.

His lips brush against mine. "There, now, was that so hard?"

His fingers plow through my entrance as I shoot forward, gasping for air. One strong arm wraps around my chest, holding me against him while his thumb finds my clit, rubbing hard and fast.

"Fuck, Claire," Avery rasps. "You've got the most amazing pussy. I love how you feel around me. I can't wait to feel you come around my cock one day."

There's a lot going on in my mind right now. For example: No, you will never feel your cock inside me. Yes, let's do it right now. Fuck me hard, fuck me senseless. Also, I'm never going on a date with you. But also, I'd love to. Finally, you should consider getting your fingers insured, because these things are un-fucking-believable.

"You gonna come for me, baby?" he asks as my walls start tightening around his fingers.

My lids flutter closed as pleasure courses through my body until I'm dangerously close to short-circuiting, my fingernails biting into his arms as my lips part.

The doorhandle jiggles, stealing my gaze. My brain tells me to shriek, to get off this man, but I can't. He feels like heaven and I

157

think he's killing me slowly. Avery doesn't even falter at the sound, though I know he hears it, too.

"Claire?" Charlee's voice calls out from behind the door.

I groan and smack the back of my head off Avery's chest, but my hips keep moving, jerking, riding his palm, his fingers. "B-busy," I stutter. It accidentally comes out as a squeal. I just need two more minutes. That's it. "We're busy!"

There's a pause, and I think she's left.

Until she slowly questions, "We?"

"Fuuuck." I clap a hand over my mouth, because please don't let me talk anymore.

Avery chuckles, his lips pressed to the spot below my ear, making me quiver. "You gotta lie better than that, gorgeous."

"T-two minutes!" I call. "I'll be done in two minutes!"

"You'll be done in thirty seconds, sweetheart." Avery's smile brushes my cheek.

He pumps harder, faster, pressing and rolling my swollen bud. When his fingers curl, hitting that spot that makes me wild, my teeth clamp down on my bottom lip. He growls and tugs it away with his own teeth, sucking my lip into his mouth. He's an animal, and I love the way he ravages me.

"Fuck, even your feet are perfect," he says as my pale blue toes curl in front of us.

With his fingers still curled inside me, his thumb rubs furious circles around my clit, and I come undone. I unravel at the seams, his free hand slapping across my mouth when it opens and starts crying out his name.

My orgasm rocks my entire body, from the tips of my toes to the hair on my head, and I collapse against him, heaving and sweaty. Stupid fucking turtleneck.

Avery pulls his hand from between my trembling legs and winds his arms around me. I hate how easy it is for me to sink back into his chest, how comfortable I feel there, wrapped up in his embrace, like I could stay forever.

His lips linger on my temple and the sweet gesture tugs at my already weak heart.

With one last shudder, I pull myself off him. It's hard, because—noodle legs.

"You okay there, noodle legs?"

I'm unsurprised that he can read my mind. The way he chuckles tells me he knows.

With my pants fixed on my hips and my feet slipping into my shoes, I've finally come back down to earth. I shake the last of the fog from my brain and gaze at Avery. It's the last thing I want to say, but I say it anyway. "That can't happen again."

He cleans his hands with a tissue before standing, smoothing his palms down his rumpled shirt and rearranging the obvious bulge in his charcoal slacks that I'd love to catch a glimpse of. Shit, he's sexy. He also looks completely unbothered by my words. I think he even checks his fingernails.

"Well, we'll see how you feel after our date." He picks his suit jacket up off my chair, slinging it over his arm. Grabbing my chin, he jerks my face to his for a kiss that rocks me to my core. "Friday. I'll pick you up at eight."

He starts for the door with all the swagger of a man who thinks he's won this round.

"Oh," I say softly, twirling a wave around my finger. "Can't. I'm busy."

His hand pauses on the handle, his head swiveling my way. "Busy doing what?"

I pretend to think, tapping my finger on my chin, squinting those green eyes of mine. "Um…"

A knowing smirk spreads across his face. Secretly, I'm glad he's not too mad. "You tricked me."

"Yes." I flutter my eyelashes and flash him my best saucy grin.

"Why?" His jaw ticks just a bit, barely perceptible.

"Isn't it obvious?"

His long legs eat the distance between us as he holds my gaze, that evil glint in his big brown eyes, looking wonderfully hazel today with flecks of green and gold. "You're devious," he whispers, looming over me, the tip of his finger tracing over my jaw. "Anything to get off, hmm? Well, no matter. I guess I'll see you on Thursday night, anyway."

He drops his hand at the same time my mouth falls open.

"Thursday night? What? No. We're having our birthday par…ty…."

There's that smirk again, sliding right into place on his face while I connect the dots. Of course Avery and Wyatt are coming to the party on Thursday. They're working with us now, after all. How could I have been so daft as to not even think of that? I mentally move my name up a couple slots on the stupid list.

Avery glances down at my desk and raps his knuckles on it before lifting his gaze back to mine. "Wear something I can bend you over this desk in." He leans down and touches his lips to mine. "Bye, Claire."

Avery leaves me gaping in my spot as he heads for the door. He twists the lock and Charlee comes tumbling forward into his arms, like she had her ear pressed to the door.

Her wild eyes bounce between us, and so does her finger. "Aha! Caught ya! I knew it! I fucking knew it!"

Avery grins. "Bye Charlee. Make sure Claire gets enough liquids at lunch. Little Miss Strawberry needs to replenish her electrolytes."

He disappears without so much as a second glance in my direction, and Charlee nearly tackles me to the ground.

"You little sex kitten!" Charlee crosses her arms over her chest and shakes her head, wide smile growing by the second. "You are so fucking screwed, Claire."

So. Fucking. Screwed.

CHAPTER EIGHTEEN

Avery

My eyes peel over the proposal in front of me that Andre sent over first thing this morning. Like always, it's impressive. Andre's work is amazing, but he's good to me. He always charges my clients a fair price. This one is no different.

"It's a good proposal," Wyatt murmurs beside me, flipping through his printed copy.

"It is," I mutter my agreement. Maybe even a little too good. Andre's shaven off almost a third of the price from the competing quotes that Claire already received. He likes her. He wants to make sure he gets this contract.

Wyatt tosses his copy on the coffee table and leans back on my couch, stretching out his long legs and lacing his fingers behind his head. "You talk to Claire about it yet?"

"Not yet. I'm gonna call her after you leave." I know she's seen it though. She texted me an hour ago. There were no words, just a series of emojis.

A smirk tugs up the corner of Wyatt's mouth. "Why not call her now? What if I wanna talk to her, too? Or do you not want to share?"

I ignore him and click through my email on my computer, shifting my reading glasses up my nose. I've got a lunch meeting in forty minutes with a client, and I can't for the life of me remember where he wanted to meet. It's been happening all week. My brain feels fried every time I think about Claire.

Fringe. I type the restaurant into my phone now in case I forget after talking to Claire on the phone after this. It doesn't seem far-fetched.

"You heading out early today?" Wyatt asks.

Glancing at him, I nod. "Gotta lunch meeting with Galvin Pharmaceuticals and a couple check-ins, so I won't be back."

"I still can't believe you finally convinced GP to go public with their stocks. This is huge." He runs a hand through his hair, shaking his head. "You're gonna make a pretty penny off this one."

"You too, Wyatt."

"Ah, shit, man. You know I feel bad when it's a deal this huge and one you've worked on so long. We don't have to split."

"We do. We're partners, so that's kinda how this goes." I lean back in my chair, twisting side-to-side. "Plus, you know I could never get this shit done without you."

He touches a hand to his heart. "You know I love it when you get all sappy with me."

I send my pen flying through the air and he swats it away, chuckling.

Wyatt and I started our investment firm with nothing more than a little help from my dad, who generously let us rent a single office in his own firm for us to work from, all while directing small clients our way. We were only there for eight months before we had enough money and steady business to rent an office of our own, and three years later, we moved into the space we're in now, where we've been for the past three years.

Wyatt's my partner and my best friend, and we split everything straight down the middle, no matter who works what deal. He's my second set of eyes when I can't see straight and my voice of reason when I can't find mine. Without him, my big deals like this wouldn't be possible.

"Alright, get the fuck out of here." I dismiss him with the wave of my hand. "I've got a call to make to a sassy redhead."

Wyatt stands, stretching his arms over his head. "When you gonna bite the bullet and ask her out? And don't feed me that *I don't date* bullshit. I know you like her."

"I already have," I utter under my breath, tugging on my tie.

He blinks. "Pardon?"

"I said I already have. Like, three times. Maybe four. I'm losing count at this point. She keeps saying no," I add with a grumble, avoiding his gaze, because he's got a stupid fucking smile creeping up his face.

"Ha!" He slaps a palm to my desk. "Fuck, I like her."

Yeah. Me too.

"See ya at the party tonight?"

I nod, picking up my phone. "Come by for a drink first and we'll ride together."

He salutes me with two fingers to his forehead and disappears while I dial the brewery rather than Claire's cell. I like surprising her.

"Cherry Lane Brewing Company, how can I help you today?" the receptionist answers.

"Can I have Claire Thompson, please?" I rock back in my chair and slip the end of a new pen into my mouth while I wait.

"Claire Thompson."

My mouth splits into a grin at her voice. "Listen to you, my sassy businesswoman."

Claire hesitates for a moment before she asks, "What can I help you with, Mr. Beck?" I don't miss the smile in her voice; I can hear it, loud and clear.

"Your greeting is such a stark contrast to the series of emojis I received from you this morning. I understood the others, but care to explain the meaning behind the ghost?"

She giggles, all light and airy. I love that sound. "I just thought he looked cute, so I threw him in there. His tongue was sticking out. What kind of a ghost sticks his tongue out?"

I can't help but chuckle. "I take it you had a chance to read through Andre's proposal?"

"I did."

"And?" I urge. "Did you like what you saw?"

164

"I loved it. I can't believe the price difference. And his ideas are fabulous."

"Mmm, they are. He does good work for a fair price. Do I get a thank you?"

She huffs a breath. "Thank you, Avery."

"Don't roll your eyes at me." I can see those green eyes rolling, her mouth turned up in the corner. I just know it.

"You can't prove anything," she teases with that hint of fire I love so much. "And don't tell me what to do."

"Right, I'll save that for tonight when I bend you over your desk. What are you wearing?"

"Did you call me to talk business or to figure out your plan of action for getting into my panties tonight?"

"I consider both to be business, Miss Thompson, and I am *in the business* of getting into your lovely panties and between those luscious thighs of yours."

The line goes dead, save for Claire's heavy breathing. It almost sounds like she's panting. I won't tease her, because I wouldn't put it past her to slap me upside the head the next time she sees me, which will be in approximately eight-and-a-half hours.

"I'm keeping my distance from you tonight," she finally says, and I can practically see her sitting up straighter, shifting her shoulders back and jutting that stubborn chin of hers out.

"No you aren't."

"Yes I am."

"'Kay. Like to see you try."

"Well, you *will* see me try."

"And I'll see you fail."

"I'll see *you* fail!" she nearly shouts.

I laugh out loud, my chin hitting my chest. "What does that even mean?"

Her sweet laughter rings in my ear. "I don't know. I just like to argue with you."

"No shit." I chuckle, rubbing my jaw. My cheeks hurt from all the smiling I've been doing in the two weeks I've known this little firecracker. "So you wanna take on Andre? Is Dex good with it?"

"Yeah, he's good. Actually, he didn't really even look at it, just waved his hand and told me to sign it. Apparently he knew your contractor would be better than the ones I picked out."

"I've got connections."

"I bet you do," she murmurs.

I pull my phone away from ear as it vibrates. A text from Troy Galvin rolls through, letting me know he's on his way to the restaurant. "I gotta go, Claire. Got a meeting. I'll see you tonight."

"Yeah, okay. See you tonight. From across the room. Where I'll be. Keeping my distance from you."

"I don't see how that's going to be possible. I don't plan on taking my hands off you all night."

She mumbles something about how I never listen to her and I laugh.

"See you tonight, pretty little strawberry."

"Bye Avery," she says softly before she hangs up.

"Shit, this place is bumpin' tonight." Wyatt climbs out of the limo and fixes the button on his gray suit jacket, surveying the scene before us.

Despite the fact that the event only started fifteen minutes ago, there's a huge line on the sidewalk surrounding Cherry Lane, and music is pouring out the doors and onto the bustling street and the patio. The weather is perfect tonight and, by the looks of the crowd, they're going to need the extra patio space we're about to pay for.

"Wyatt! Avery!"

We turn to see Charlee scurrying over to us. She beams and throws her arms around both our necks at the same time, pulling us together until we bump heads.

166

"Come with me," she coaxes like it's a secret, dancing toward the patio and beckoning us with her hand to follow. Wyatt checks out her ass, and I drive my elbow into his side.

The patio is quiet still but looks incredible, strung up with twinkling lights and a few fires going even though the sun hasn't quite finished its descent yet. Charlee leads us through the patio door, helping us effectively skip the long line out front.

I spot Claire instantly.

"Fuck." The word tumbles aimlessly from my mouth as my gaze floats up and down her stellar, picturesque body. If I could say more than *fuck* I would, but my brain can't seem to formulate a single thought as I stare at her.

Claire's extravagant emerald dress hugs every inch of her body, showcasing her slim waist, the killer dip of her curves. The straps above her shoulders tie together in loopy bows, and when she spins around, I see that it's backless, a silky ribbon lacing over her fair skin, knotting just above the swell of her perfect ass. The material molds tightly around her hips until a scalloped lace hem wisps out halfway down her thighs, draping around her knees.

My cock twitches in my pants, and when she turns again, laughter lighting her face, auburn hair rolling in big waves over her shoulders, my heart squeezes in a way I'm not all that familiar, nor comfortable, with. She catches my eye and I watch as a deep crimson color creeps up her delicate throat, painting her cheeks. She glances down before her lifting her gaze again, trying like hell to bite back that coy smile of hers.

Like hell I'm letting her keep her distance from me tonight, or any night for that matter. And when I start strutting toward her, parting the crowd like I'm parting the Red fucking Sea, we both realize at the same time that her feet seem to be cemented in place. I'm quite fine with that, and she looks like she might be, too.

I ignore Dex, and I even ignore Casey. Claire is all I see when I stop in front of her.

My hands find her waist and slide over her hips, pulling her gently against me, dropping my lips to the shell of her ear. "How are you this perfect?" I whisper, smiling at the way she trembles, her neck pebbling with goosebumps. I brush my lips across her warm cheekbone and pull back.

She clears her throat, eyes dancing, teeth biting into that plump pout. Her hands sweep over my chest, fingers playing with the knot of my tie. "You don't look half bad yourself, Mr. Beck."

Wyatt pushes me aside and sweeps Claire into his arms, telling her how good she looks and how she's way too good for me while I step up to greet Casey and Dex.

"It's nuts in here," I observe.

There are a few journalists walking around snapping pictures, and there's a small booth set up in the corner where they're giving away free Cherry Lane merch as a party favor. The bar is packed and the servers are already swamped, even though half the party hasn't walked through the front doors yet.

I hum in approval. "You guys are gonna kill it tonight. Perfect publicity."

A proud, albeit wobbly, grin flashes across Dex's face and he smooths his hand over his tie, surveying the room. "I'm nervous as fuck."

"Don't be. It's gonna be great. Already is."

"Charlee and Claire did all the planning," he says, jerking his head toward the two of them as they examine the chalkboard menu behind the bar.

"Just leave it, Claire Bear," Charlee urges. "It's fine."

"Now that I know it's there, it's gonna bother me all night." Claire inches forward until she's leaning over the counter, nose nearly touching the blackboard. With one finger, she rubs at some of the fancy white writing and she sighs. "I'm gonna fix it."

Charlee huffs out a long-suffering sigh, rolling her eyes as Claire rifles through a drawer. "You're such a perfectionist sometimes. No one's gonna notice it tonight."

Claire ignores her as she hoists herself up on the countertop, balancing on her knees, all while shaking a white marker. She thrusts her hand behind her, curling her fingers. "Cloth, please."

Charlee wets a paper towel and hands it to Claire and I watch her wipe an entire beer name off the wall. Then, she starts writing, big, beautiful, loopy calligraphy, touching it up twice until it looks just the way she wants. I'm so fascinated by her, it's ridiculous. I can't look away.

Finished, she glances around, trying to figure out how to drop back down to the floor safely in three-inch heels. Without a thought, I step up behind her, fingers pressing into her waist as I lift her off the counter and set her down on her fancy feet.

"Thanks, Avery." Her eyes crinkle with her smile and she squeezes my hand, a meaningless gesture, but one that makes me want to hold on. She pours everyone a round of beer, not wanting to wait for her own drink. She hands me a Strawberry Grove without asking, knowing it's the one I like. I like it because of her. I think she knows that.

"Two nights out in less than a week?" I ask Casey, trying to tear my gaze off his sister. "Who's got Vivi tonight?"

Casey grins and nods. "I got a taste of what I've been missing." He tilts his head toward Charlee. "Mariana, Charlee's mom, is with Vivi again tonight. Charlee's trying to convince me to let loose once a week." The look he throws Charlee is one of pure longing, and it doesn't go unnoticed by Claire, or Dex. I don't think either of them would be upset to see their siblings get together.

Honestly, good on Dex. If Wyatt tried to get with my little sister, I'd shit a goddamn brick. I trust Wyatt with a lot of things, one of them being accounts worth millions of dollars, but never would I ever trust that man with my sister.

It only takes two beers before Claire lets me pull her out to the makeshift dancefloor. She really doesn't put up much of a fight at all, but then again, alcohol always lowers her inhibitions. I also think she's just learning to let her wall down a bit with me in general.

"Just as I suspected," I murmur as I tug her close, one hand on her lower back, fingers dipping under the ribbon that holds her dress together, while my other hand tangles with hers.

Her nose wrinkles. "What?"

"You're failing, and I'm watching. You're doing a downright *atrocious* job of keeping your distance from me tonight."

She tries so hard to bite back her smile, but those little dimples in her pink cheeks make an appearance. I lean down and kiss one.

"Do you always spend this much time trying to woo a woman into your bed?"

Two weeks? Definitely not. I've never tried harder to nail down a woman in my entire life, and three weeks without sex? It's killing me. "Nah. Usually no more than ten minutes."

She's the one that asked the question, but as soon as the words leave my mouth, I know she didn't really want the answer. It should tell her how different she is to me, but instead it just makes me sound like a self-righteous ass and a manwhore. Which I kinda am, I guess. A manwhore. Or at least was, up until two weeks ago.

So I say, "I'll keep trying and keep waiting, as long as it takes."

I'm not sure that's the right thing to say either, because she won't look at me, and her mouth is set in a pretty damn tight line.

Shit, what's wrong with me tonight? I'm off my game. I need to get her alone.

On a whim, I grab her hand and tug her over to the stairs, towing her along behind me. We pass the second floor, and if possible, it's even rowdier than the first. But the third floor is quiet and dark, almost eerie.

I usher her into her office and close the door behind us. The room is lit from the soft glow of the patio lights outside and the floor lamp in one corner.

"Avery," Claire whispers, hands fumbling in front of her as she takes a step away from me. "I don't...I can't..." Her eyes squeeze shut. She's so nervous, and it tugs at my heartstrings. "I really can't do this. I'm not...I'm not ready."

"I know, Claire." I can see it, her uncertainty, the way she fights with the thoughts in her head. She's not ready to jump back in like that, to take that step and it's okay. "I just wanna kiss you. Can I kiss you?"

I take a step forward and she takes another one back.

"But you want...you want more." Her bright eyes bounce between mine. "I can't give you what you want, not right now. And I don't want to seem..." She drops her gaze to the floor, gripping her arm with her opposite hand. "Selfish."

"If anyone's selfish, it's me. Because I'll take whatever piece of you you're willing to give." I hook my finger at her. "Come here and let me kiss you, Claire. You're exquisite and I can't go a minute longer without tasting you."

She swallows. "Just a...just a kiss?"

"More than one, but yes, just kissing."

She sucks her bottom lip into her mouth as she considers me, considers this, and I think tonight is the first time I've really grasped the severity of what her ex has done to her, the way he's made her second-guess herself. I'm actually considering that she might say no, that maybe I should...back off.

But then she steps forward, tentatively, and I meet her in the middle, sweeping her into my arms. I waste no time, because I never know when the next time I'll get to kiss her will be, and I devour her mouth with mine.

Her slender fingers cup the back of my head while mine skim across her jaw and sink into her hair. I don't think I'll every grow tired of kissing her, but this one is different from all the other times, soft and slow, heated and patient as I take my time exploring her. I love the way she feels in my arms, the way she melts and molds against me, the soft sigh she breathes into my mouth as she gives in to whatever the hell is brewing between us.

Pulling away, I rest my forehead against hers. Our heavy breath mingles, brushing over our swollen lips. Her curious gaze searches mine, that little crease wrinkling her forehead. I know her brain is working in overdrive right now, trying to figure out what's going on between us, just like I am.

"You really are the most magnificent woman I've ever laid my eyes on." I brush my lips across hers in a soft kiss. "And I have to tell you, you make me laugh in the most infuriating way, more than any woman ever has."

Her face explodes with that cheek-splitting, dimple-donning beam of hers that I love, the one that makes me want to drop to my knees and worship her. Her lips part but close quickly when the door opens behind us.

"Oh. Sorry guys. I was just making sure you were okay, Claire. Couldn't find ya."

Regardless of the easy smile Casey gives us from where he stands in the doorway, Claire steps away from me, putting distance between us that I don't want.

It takes no time for things to get awkward, Casey swinging his arms out in front of him, fist clapping into his palm, head bobbing. "And you're clearly fine, so, I'm gonna get going." He thumbs toward the door and starts moving, but stops, glancing back at us over his shoulder. "I like you two together. I can tell how much you like each other, which is saying a lot, 'cause you never smiled this much with...well, ya know." He taps on the doorframe and disappears.

I hate the way Claire stares down at her feet, and even more so the way she pushes my hands away when I reach for her. "I have to get back," she says quietly, slipping by me.

"Hey," I urge softly, spinning so my eyes can track her movement. "Is everything okay?"

She stops in the doorway, gripping the frame with her dainty hand. "I just don't like that it looks like...I don't know. I feel like we're leading people on. My brother likes you. My niece likes you. Everyone likes you."

My hand comes up, rubbing at the back of my neck. "Isn't that a good thing?"

"They think there's something going on between us," she says in a tiny voice.

Stepping up to her, I drink in the woman before me, so lost that she can't recognize how amazing she is. "Isn't there?"

"I'm not sure what's happening, Avery. But I have to go. Okay?"

She doesn't give me a chance to respond, simply turns and heads down the hallway, her heels clicking on the stairs as she makes her way down to the party. I follow a minute later, feeling more confused than ever.

My eyes land on Andre the second I step back downstairs. He moves fluidly across the floor, eyes set on something, grin wide. I follow his gaze and wish I hadn't.

The second he taps Claire on the shoulder, she wraps him in a hug, one he all too happily returns. My chest stretches, stomach clenching, and I hate this jealousy that's only started to rear it's ugly head when I'm nearly thirty.

Why? Why Claire? What is it about her that has me feeling this way?

Wyatt appears at my side, looking a little frazzled. His previously neatly combed hair is a wild mess; I realize why the second he starts tugging on it. "Beck, I'm sorry. I think I fucked up."

"What? Fucked up in what way?"

He runs an anxious hand across his mouth, eyes shifting over my shoulder. I follow his gaze until it lands on a blond bombshell. Her face explodes when she sees me, and she starts slipping through the crowd.

"What the hell is she doing here?" I seethe, my eyes darting back to Claire. Thankfully, but also maddeningly, she's still wrapped up in a conversation with Andre.

"I'm so sorry. She came by the office this afternoon looking for you. Said she was leaving town tomorrow and wanted to see you before she left. I told her you were gone for the day and she asked if I knew where she could find you. I didn't think…I mean, I never thought she'd show up."

A set of arms wrap around my waist, slender, golden fingers gripping me, long-tipped red nails pressing into my torso, and I resign myself to my fate. If Claire was hesitant about me before, this right here just signed the death sentence.

"You're a tough man to track down, Mr. Beck," an alluring voice purrs in my ear.

"Hey Sam," I say softly, noting the way my voice cracks.

Samantha, my casual hook up that I turned down via text on Sunday and every other day this week, spins around my front and throws her arms around me, clinging to my chest.

Naturally, Claire chooses this moment to look up. Why wouldn't she?

Her face breaks right in front of me. It's impossible to miss. Those stunning green eyes flicker, her bright expression and brilliant smile slipping right off her beautiful face. Even from here, I see the heave of her chest, the quiver in her bottom lip.

This is the last thing I ever wanted.

Sam is the last thing I want.

What I want, *who* I want, is the stunning little redhead trying to keep it together twenty feet away from me.

CHAPTER NINETEEN

Claire

And that right there is the reason why I need to stop this, this thing, whatever it is, with Avery.

That's the reason, that gorgeous woman hanging off Avery's arm, running her perfectly manicured fingers over his chest, playing with his collar. She stares up at him with those big baby blues and bats her long lashes, tossing her silky, golden mane over her shoulder.

Her dress dips low down her chest, revealing—you guessed it—a perfect set of boobs, all round and perky. Her skin, just as golden as her hair, ripples over the toned muscles in her arms, in those legs of hers that seem to go on for miles. She's got the most brilliant smile, all red lips and perfect white teeth.

I look down at myself, at my beyond average body, my fair skin, the auburn waves tickling down my arms, the fingernails I painted myself. I'm anything but tall and golden. My curves are too soft. My skin is too flawed with specks of brown freckles.

She's perfect, flawless, everything.

And I'm nothing.

Just another reason for a man to want more, more than me, more than what I have to offer.

My heart tweaks with jealousy as I watch them. Their familiar touches tell me she knows Avery's body in ways I don't. They look perfect together. The golden couple. A god and his goddess.

She molds into him and my stomach knots painfully. I watch him take a step back, and his dark chocolate eyes flick up to me again, like they've done several times over the last few minutes. My cheeks heat at being caught staring, interrupting whatever moment it is they're sharing, and I drop my gaze.

"Dance with me?" Andre reminds me that I'm not alone, that I've been ignoring him for the last couple of minutes while my heart has been trying to crawl out of my chest and wave a white flag. *I surrender.*

"Dance?" I ask.

His brown eyes twinkle with mirth. "Yeah, you know that thing where two people hold each other close and spin around the floor. Dance with me, Claire."

I don't really want to. I danced with Avery already, and he's who I want to be close to, even though he's with someone else, and even though I walked away from him only ten minutes ago.

But Andre holds his hand out to me and I slip mine in, letting him guide me to the floor. It's warm and nice, but I don't feel the same zing that I do when Avery touches me. Speaking of Avery, his eyes follow us across the floor.

"Thanks for inviting me tonight. It's a great party. This place is gonna take off like crazy when you add the restaurant." Andre pulls me close, one hand on my lower back, fingertips ghosting over my skin.

I manage a small smile. "I think so too. Everyone I've talked to tonight is really excited to come check it out when it's done."

"You still feeling good about my proposal?"

I nod with as much enthusiasm I can muster. The proposal is fantastic. Andre's saving us a ton of money, and his ideas are better than what we originally dreamed up. "The proposal is amazing. You've definitely painted a pretty picture for us. We're really excited to work with you."

"I'm glad you approve. I'm really excited to work with you too, Claire."

I don't miss that he singles me out rather than the entire company. He wants to work with *me*.

"Are you still unavailable?" Andre asks boldly, his thumb sweeping absently over my back.

177

I wince, not really wanting to have this conversation. "Yes. I'm sorry. Will that…will that affect this?"

He pulls back and shakes his head. "Nah. I know how to keep it professional, though a girl like you might make it a little bit harder on me. But I can respect your decision. Can I ask why though? Not interested, not even a little?" He flashes me a handsome smile. He's got full lips and straight, white teeth. His warm eyes sparkle down at me.

I could be. Honestly, I probably would be if it weren't for two things: if I were emotionally ready for a relationship, and if I didn't know Avery. That last one is crucial, because I'm *not* emotionally ready, yet I can't stop that thing my heart does whenever I look at Avery, whenever he touches me, whenever his name lights up my phone screen.

"I just got out of a long-term relationship," I tell Andre honestly. "And it didn't end well."

He considers me carefully, studying my face. "Did he hurt you?"

Just fucked with my brain and drove my self-worth headfirst into the dirt. "Yes."

Andre grunts and tightens his hold on me. "Well, tough shit for him, eh? You deserve much better."

My smile feels real, if a little sad. "Thank you for saying that."

"Any other reasons you'd turn me down, say, if that jackass of an ex didn't exist or you were over him?"

My eyes land on Avery. He's full-on ignoring the blonde who does not look happy about it in the slightest. His gaze is glued to me and Andre, confusing me further. Why does he care who I'm dancing with when he's got *that* hanging off his side?

Andre follows my gaze. "Ah. I see."

My eyes shift back to him. "Hmm?"

"You like someone else."

Heat floods my cheeks, urging me to keep my mouth shut. Am I that obvious?

"If it's any consolation," Andre whispers, dipping his mouth to my ear, "I've known Avery a long time, and I've never seen him quite so enthralled by a woman before."

I snort. "Yeah, she's beautiful, isn't she?" *Thanks for rubbing it in, dude.*

His head shakes, eyes alight with amusement. "I'm not talking about the blonde, who he's been actively trying to pay no attention to this entire time, by the way."

When the song comes to an end, Andre and I drift back over to the bar. I slide behind it and pour us each a beer because I need it in me now, not in fifteen minutes when one of the bartenders will be able to get to us.

Our group grows quickly, our corner loud and rowdy, the perfect opportunity for me to sneak a peek at Avery and his friend. I don't want to, and when I do, I really regret it.

I watch as her long fingers slide across his jaw, her red-tipped nails sinking into my favorite mop of dark brown waves. She pulls his face down to hers, their lips mashing together, and something inside of me stops working. It hurts. Tears sting the back of my eyes and I hate myself because I did this. I put myself in this position. I let myself feel things for someone I had no right feeling anything for.

"Excuse me," I whisper to nobody in particular, since most of our group is chatting and laughing animatedly, like my heart hasn't just been stomped on for the second time in a matter of weeks. I drop my beer on a table and turn to leave but a hand wraps around my wrist. I look up at Wyatt's pained, guilty expression.

"Claire…"

I don't need his pity, and I certainly don't want it. I pull my arm from his grasp and slip up the staircase, hopefully unnoticed by everyone but Wyatt, whose gaze I can still feel on me.

I can deny my feelings for Avery all I want, but right now, they're slapping me right in the face.

I slip into my office and pick my bag up off the end of my couch.

I know the exact moment he appears behind me in my doorway. I can feel it, feel him. His presence is overwhelming, just like it always is. The skin on the back of my neck pebbles and I try not to let the shiver that races down my spine shake me.

"Hey."

"Hey," I reply quietly, not bothering to look over my shoulder.

I want this dress off. I want these heels gone. I yank them off my feet and sink three inches to the ground. I slip my old pair of Chuck's on my feet, not caring that I look ridiculous in a glamorous dress and a pair of dirty sneakers. A dress I spent too much money on because I thought about Avery's reaction to it when I tried it on.

The air around me turns heavy with tension as I feel him approach me from behind. With a long, low exhale, I send up a silent prayer. I'm tired of letting men break me, and the last thing I want to do is let him those broken pieces that only become more jagged with time.

"Look, Avery, I didn't come up here for another make out session."

"I know," he says softly. "Neither did I."

I can't formulate a response, and the last thing I really want to do is engage in a serious conversation right now, so I just pack my things up. My sunglasses, my keys, my clothes from earlier today, my heels—I shove them all in, maybe with a little more vigor than necessary.

"What are you doing?" Avery asks.

I flip the top over my leather messenger bag and sling it over my shoulder. "Leaving," I tell him, turning and brushing by him, managing to avoid his gaze.

His fingers circle my elbow, stopping me. "Why are you leaving? This is your party. You worked your ass off to plan it with Charlee." His suit jacket is gone, drawing my attention to the red lipstick stain on his shoulder, the other one on his collar. "You can't leave yet, Claire."

I can't? Orders aren't going to work for me, not tonight, not right now. My eyes flick up to his, anger making my jaw clench. The problem is, as soon as I catch sight of his soft mocha eyes, my anger mixes with heartache, and I hate it. It makes me weak. Being weak is what got me into this mess in the first place.

"Just stay, Claire," he pleads quietly. His hands smooth up my arms, squeezing my shoulders. "Come on. We can grab a drink, talk."

I take a step back, holding my hands out in front of me to keep distance between us that I'm in desperate need of. I can't touch him. He can't touch me. I can't *think* when he's touching me. My heart tells my brain what to do and my brain listens, and I just can't have that anymore. I'm losing brain cells, connections are severing.

"Avery, stop. I'm done, okay? I'm exhausted and I need to go home."

"I'll come with you," he says, pulling his phone from his back pocket. "I can have the car here in a few minutes."

I shake my head and wave my hands. "I can take an Uber."

His brows dip with confusion. "But we're going to the same place. My driver—"

"*No*, Avery. I can get home perfectly fine on my own. I don't need your driver, and I don't need you!" Ouch. Even as I say it, I know I've packed a little too much punch.

A pinch of hurt shades his handsome features. He reaches for my hands. "Claire…"

"Look," I sigh, gently removing my hands from his. I smooth the wisps of hair away from my face and take a deep breath. "I don't know what's going on here. There's obviously…something. Chemistry, maybe, but nothing more. Because just like you said earlier, all you wanna do is fuck. I've already told you that's not me. I'm sorry I've been giving you mixed signals, because I admit my body seems to keep getting a little carried away with you. I don't do casual, Avery, and I don't really wanna go falling in love with someone who just wants to screw until he finds someone better, and it looks like you have plenty of options." I hate that I even mentioned the *l*-word, but at the very least, it should scare him off. Avery doesn't fall in love; that's not what he's looking for.

My gaze floats down to my shoes, because the hurt that dances across his features makes all the thoughts in my head swirl. What right does he have to be hurt? It's stupid to even think that question, because honestly, what right do *I* have to be hurt? We aren't anything, right? That's what I just said. That's what I keep saying.

"Enjoy the rest of your evening, Avery. Please close my door when you leave."

Eyes cast downwards, I head down the hallway, trying not to fall apart. My sneakers padding on the hardwood is the only thing I can hear up here, even with the party raging on the floors below. When I reach the top of the stairs, I hear the quiet click of my office door.

I also hear the quiet crack of a tiny piece of my heart. At least I think I do. If I don't hear it, I definitely feel it. It hurts more than I care to admit.

Two weeks. I've known this man for two weeks and he's thrown my entire world off its axis.

I jog down both flights of stairs and take a sharp turn around the bottom of the staircase on the main floor, slipping unnoticed out the back door. Part of me wants to walk. The night air is fresh and just the right amount of cool, and I need it. I gulp it in, trying desperately to shake away the tears that want to crawl out of my eye sockets.

But it's Toronto, and it's late. It'll take ten minutes of walking to hit downtown, where the foot traffic is alive and well and I'd feel safe enough. I'm not stupid enough to walk through these streets alone in the dark, so I dig my phone out of my bag and order an Uber.

It pulls up two minutes later in record time, and I ignore his eager attempt at small talk the entire ride home. He probably thinks I'm a bitch. I don't care. I just want to cry like the foolish, weak girl I am, preferably into a tub of Ben & Jerry's while soaking in bubbles up to my neck, bottle of wine at my side. No glass needed.

At home, I strip off my dress and throw it in a corner, completely missing my laundry basket. I wash my face and brush my teeth, pulling on a comfy sweater and flannel pants. I want to be warm and cozy tonight in bed. I don't want to feel cold and lonely.

Deciding against the wine, I walk to the kitchen and pour myself a glass of water, swallowing down some ibuprofen, because my head is pounding and all I want to do is climb into bed and drown myself in sleep.

A soft knock on the door has my head jerking up.

I creep quietly across the room and press up on my tiptoes, peeking through the spy hole.

Avery's standing there in a faded blue t-shirt that ripples across his broad chest, and a pair of gray track pants. He's already been up to his condo. I've been home less than ten minutes. That means he followed me out, left right after I did. He didn't stay to play with that girl.

He knocks again and I cover my mouth when a surprised gasp tears through my lips. His eyes flick up to the door and I wonder if he heard me. He looks exhausted, about as exhausted as I feel. He's not smiling, and I have to say, he doesn't really look like his usual self.

He gnaws on the inside of his cheek and tugs at the dark waves on top of his head, messing them up. I love those waves, love running my fingers through them.

His shoulders sag with a low sigh. "Alright buddy," he whispers, looking down. "She doesn't wanna see us. Let's go for a quick walk."

My brows furrow. Us? A walk? It's midnight.

Avery turns and walks away, towing a large black dog with a white and brown nose and matching paws down the hallway and toward the elevator.

He has a dog? Somehow that makes Avery Beck so much more human.

I briefly consider throwing open the door and calling him back, but I know I need to let this go. I need to go to bed and try to do better tomorrow.

I'm just not really sure what my version of *better* looks like.

CHAPTER TWENTY

Claire

I'm seriously contemplating calling in sick this morning, and the reason is my sometimes-terrifying best friend.

Scrubbing my sore, tired eyes, I pull my phone off the nightstand and reread her messages from last night.

Charlee: *Where are you???*

Charlee: *Avery took off, looking pissed. Or sad. Not sure. Barely said bye.*

Charlee: *Are you okay?*

Charlee: *Talked to Wyatt. Got the low down on the blonde bimbo.*

Charlee: *Would absolutely love it if you could respond to my texts.*

My mouth twitches. Blonde bimbo. She was beautiful, but Charlee would say that just to try to make me feel better. But her last message has me chewing my thumbnail. She's not happy.

Thunder rumbles, growling in the sky outside. I let my head flop to the right, staring out the window with no feeling. It shouldn't be, but it's dark out. Lightning flashes, the sky glowing for a split second, and the heavy pattering of raindrops starts slapping against the glass. Fitting weather for how I'm feeling this morning.

Yes, I'm still stuck in pity-party mode. Is it ironic that I'm more torn up about Avery than I was about Aaron, the guy I gave three years of my life to? Ironic or pathetic; one of the two.

Deciding against calling in sick, I begrudgingly roll out of bed and stalk off to the bathroom, stepping into a warm shower. Part of me thinks it would be more fitting to just go stand on my balcony and let the rain do the job.

While I'm toweling off, my phone vibrates on the bathroom counter.

Avery: *Morning. Can I give you a ride to work? It's raining pretty hard out there and I know you normally walk.*

I honestly don't think he's ever sent me a normal text message without some sort of hidden—or in plain sight—innuendo. This is a first. It's a sweet gesture, but I can't. I should also get rid of those stupid emojis from his name, but I can't bring myself to do that, either. I click my screen off and get ready for work.

Forty minutes later, I'm sliding into an Uber out front after successfully avoiding any happenstance run-ins with a certain someone, like a stealthy little ninja. I close my umbrella and say good morning to my driver, looking up just in time to catch Avery watching me from under the condo awning after he steps outside. There isn't a single trace of a smile on his face. He knows I'm ignoring him. Avery climbs into the back of his car after one last glance at my fading ride.

I'm a little bit late today and am relieved to see that Charlee's already gone off to visit some vendors this morning, so I'm safe from questions for the next few hours. That means I have the morning to work uninterrupted on Andre's contract, so I do, and an hour-and-a-half later, I take it to Dex.

He looks up from his desk when I knock on his door, his bright smile lighting up his face. "Wasn't sure you'd be in today. How you feeling?"

I lift a shoulder. "A little tired and a lot hungover." It's the opposite, actually, because I didn't drink that much, and I had a terribly unrewarding sleep. I'd prefer not to disclose that I flopped around restlessly thinking about a certain man and his dog. "It was a great party, Dex. You must be thrilled with the turnout."

The publicity the brewery received last night was incredible, and we've been tagged in over five hundred pictures on social

186

media so far. People are excited about our new ventures, and that's always promising.

"You and Charlee know how to plan a great party," Dex says.

I grin, lifting one brow. "You know as well as I do that it was all Charlee. I'm just here to reel her in when she gets out of control."

"Which she always does, so you have your work cut out for you." He winks. "You deserve a raise. Remind me to talk to the owner for you."

Laughing, I take a seat across from him, placing the contract down on his desk. "This is fantastic. I can't believe it."

Dex takes the papers, flipping through them. "Avery always has the best connections. Don't know how he does it."

I clear my throat, crossing one leg over the other. That man can talk himself into and out of anything, so I assume that's where his connections come from, among other things.

Dex's gaze lifts, studying me curiously above the papers. He sighs, setting the contract down. "Look, Claire—"

I hold up a hand, cutting him off. "Let's not go down that road."

The corner of his mouth lifts. "I'm older and bigger than you. If I want to go down that road, we will." He chuckles at the way I huff and roll my eyes toward the ceiling. "Avery didn't mean to hurt you last night."

"He didn't hurt me," I lie.

"Right," he says slowly. "So you saw him kissing another woman and took off five minutes later with him hot on your tail because…?"

"He can kiss whomever he likes. We aren't dating."

"But he makes you happy," he murmurs. "I can tell. And you make him happy, too."

"Yeah, well, once upon a time Aaron and I were happy, too." I don't really mean to say it out loud. I don't want to go here, to have this conversation. Not today, and not with Dex. It's not as if he doesn't know how badly Aaron wrecked me. He was the one that held me when it all went down, after all.

"Avery's not Aaron," Dex replies quietly. "I had my reservations about his interest in you, but I've known him a long time. I can tell it's different with you."

"Did he say that?" I'm being saucy, and the way my leg bounces, slung on top of my other one, my arms pinned over my chest, says as much.

"Well, no, but—"

"Exactly." I stand, straightening my skirt. "Avery's never been about settling down, and I'm not about to believe that I'm the person who has made him want to change that when I couldn't even get my long-term boyfriend to settle down." I catch the flicker of Dex's eyes before I turn toward the door. "I'm gonna get back to work. Just wanted to drop off the contract."

I make it all of five steps before his fingers wrap around my arm, stopping me.

"I didn't mean to make you upset, Claire. I would just hate to see you let Aaron ruin any future relationships."

"It's been two weeks," I murmur weakly. I'm not sure if it's for myself, or for Dex. "I've known Avery for two weeks. And it's been less than three weeks since Aaron...since he..." My face heats with a mixture of anger, betrayal, and grief, and I glue my gaze to the ceiling to force those tears back where they belong.

Dex presses his hand to my lower back, leading me over to his couch. "I'm sorry. I'm not rushing you, not at all. You take your time, however much of it you need." His fingers drum on his knee. "How's your dad doing? He keeps sending me pictures of his cigar collection. I need to get back there for a visit."

"He'd like that, Dex. You know how much he loves his boys' nights."

"And his appointment last week? Casey said he's been fine."

"Casey is exactly like Dad, and you know what Dad's like. He'll lie and say everything is fine because he hates worrying anyone. He was in a good mood but seemed a lot more tired than usual. The doctor thought it was too early to run tests."

I think back on my Dad's appointment with his oncologist last Friday and the same frustration creeps through my bones now as it did a week ago. When is it every too early to run tests when a two-time cancer patient who's in remission starts displaying symptoms again? The grip my dad had on my hand was the only thing that physically kept me in my chair and out of the doctor's face. The doctor promised to run tests in three months if the symptoms persisted, since my dad is an otherwise healthy guy and in good shape, and my dad thought that was reasonable.

Dex picks up my hand, giving it a squeeze. "Your dad is the strongest person I know, Claire. He'll be okay."

Dex is right in that my dad's strength is unmatched. He's been through so much and keeps going with a smile on his face. I wish I had even a quarter of his strength.

"Why don't you take off early today?" Dex tugs on the tip of my ponytail. "You've been working your ass off. Head out at lunch, go home, take a nap, drink a bottle of wine."

My nose scrunches with my giggle. "A bottle?"

He winks. "A bottle."

"I don't know, Dex." I hate feeling like I'm taking advantage of him, the relationship we share.

"C'mon, Claire." He stands, taking both my hands in his, hauling me off the couch and down the hall. In my office, he pulls my chair out and forces me down to it. "One hour. Finish up whatever you need to and then get the hell outta here. I know you've got Vivi tonight. And Charlee," he adds with a look of fear. "You're gonna need your rest."

"Are you sure?"

He nods. "I'm sure." He digs his hand into the bowl of jellybeans on my desk, tossing them into his mouth as he heads toward the door. "Gonna eat these all when you leave."

Laughing, I watch him leave, and a half hour later, his sister strolls in, shutting the door behind her a little harder than necessary. She sinks to the couch under the windowsill without so much as a word or a look in my general direction, instead checking out her nails.

"Morning," I finally try, because the silence is painful.

Charlee glances up at me, two perfectly groomed brows lifting on her forehead. She crosses one leg over the other and sits back, lacing her fingers together on her knee.

Here it comes.

"You don't get to run off without telling any of us where you're going," she says rather simply, but utterly harshly. "That's not cool, and I certainly don't appreciate that you then ignored my messages for the rest of the night. I was worried sick about you, and so was your brother."

I hate disappointing Charlee, which is probably why I cringe. She loves me fiercely, and when she's firm with me, I know I could have made better decisions.

"I'm sorry," I genuinely apologize. "I wasn't thinking. I just wanted to go home."

She nods once, curtly. "I get it, Claire, but use your words." She pats the spot next to her.

I sidle over there pretty damn slowly, like a puppy who knows it's in trouble. When I reach her, she tugs me down to the couch and wraps her arms around me.

"What's going on with you? Why can't you just admit that you like him?" She knows she doesn't need to say his name.

"Because I shouldn't. I barely know him. I'm not supposed to be getting involved in anything right now." A stupid tear rolls down my cheek. I don't know where it came from. I mean, my eye,

190

obviously. "How can I like him so much, so easily? And why do I have to fall for someone like that, someone who bounces from girl to girl, after I just got cheated on?" I shake my head and swipe at my cheeks, unimpressed at the amount of tears falling now. All I'm thinking about is how perfect Avery looked with that blonde, and the lipstick stains on his shirt.

"The world's a wild place, isn't it?" Charlee rests her head against mine, speaking softly. "He came out of nowhere, and he might seem like the wrong fit at the wrong time, but I don't think he is at all. I think you two suit each other really well. Even your brother sees it. Even Dex, though he hates to admit it. You're like magnets."

What she says resonates with me on some level, a deeper one than I'd care to admit. Avery just strolled right into my life and as terrible as the timing feels, he's also brought me a lot of carefree happiness when I've needed it the most. He's pushed every one of my limits, challenged me endlessly, and as much as I've tried, I can't shake him.

"Wyatt felt awful about last night. He told me about that girl. Her name is Sam."

I shake my head, my eyes fluttering closed. "I don't really want to hear about her."

Charlee grips my jaw and lifts my face. "You do, and I'm gonna tell you, and you're gonna listen. Got it?" When I just stare at her with wide eyes—'cause she's kinda scary—she gives me a smile. "She's from out of town. I guess her and Avery have been casually hooking up for the last couple years whenever she's been here for work. Nothing serious, but she texted him Sunday that she was in town for the week. Asked him to meet up. Asked him a couple times, actually. He said no every time. She showed up at his office yesterday afternoon when he wasn't there, looking for him. Wyatt mentioned that she wouldn't be able to see him because he was out at some meetings, and then had the party last night. Well, Wyatt guesses she took that as an invite. I'm not sure how she got through the door without a pass, but she did."

I can guess. She probably batted her pretty blue eyes and long lashes, flashed her pearly white smile, maybe did a little twirl in her stunning, clingy dress.

"Avery had no idea she'd be there and had no intention of seeing her while she was in town this time. Wyatt feels really bad. He thinks he fucked things up."

"It's not his fault," I point out.

"I agree, it's not, but regardless, he knows how much Avery likes you, and he saw how upset both of you were by the situation."

I'm feeling really torn right now. Tension knots in my stomach like a rope. My head hurts. My mouth feels too dry. On one hand, this makes me feel better. Not only did he not invite her and not want her there, but he'd already turned down her propositions.

But the other part of me is gnawing at my insides, wondering how much longer he'll hang on for before he says *fuck it* and sleeps with her or someone else. I'm not ready, and I can't ask him to wait for me to be ready.

I'm not even sure what I mean when I say I'm not ready. Ready for what? A casual fling? Or a new relationship? I don't think Avery Beck is a relationship kinda guy. In fact, I'd be willing to bet money on it.

"Have you talked to him?" Charlee gives my fingers a reassuring squeeze.

I shake my head. "He knocked on my door last night. Did you know he has a dog?"

Charlee's smile is bright. "No, but I can totally see that. I think he's a big teddy bear under all that hard muscle and deep, penetrating gaze. He's kind of a big softie with you. And with Viv."

The more I think about it, the more I think Charlee might be right. Avery's sweet comments, the slow kisses he gave me last

192

night, the hug he wrapped Vivi up in and how he smiled at her, just watching, soaking in her wild.

"You didn't answer the door, did you?"

"No," I admit. "I wasn't ready to talk, to see him." I pull my bottom lip between my thumb and forefinger. "He texted this morning, too. Wanted to know if he could give me a ride in the rain." I glance sideways at her. "I ignored him."

Charlee's eyes dim and I can't tell if she's disappointed or sad. "Oh, Claire. Give him a chance, would you?"

"A chance at what though? I don't even know that he's interested in anything more than sex. For all I know, the only reason he's still hanging around, besides the obvious professional side to our relationship, is because I haven't given myself up to him yet. The moment we have sex, there's a pretty good chance he disappears."

Charlee frowns. "I really don't think that's it, and Wyatt doesn't either. Casey said he saw you guys kissing in here last night. He said it looked intimate."

I roll my eyes and curl my feet up under my butt. "Can you all stop talking about me?"

She snorts out a laugh. "But you're such an interesting topic."

My desk phone beeps and Julie, the secretary, starts talking. "Claire, there's someone here with your lunch order. Can I send him in to drop it off?"

"Lunch order?" I look at Charlee. "I didn't order anything. Did you?" She frowns. "Weird. Yeah, Julie, send him in, please."

A few moments later, a teenager who looks like he hasn't showered in two weeks, judging by the sheer amount of grease in his hair, peeks into my office, wearing his Uber Eats shirt. He holds up a giant bag from Taco Bell and grins sheepishly at Charlee and me.

Scratching his chin, he reads the paper attached to the bag. "Uh, Claire? Here's your order." He meets me halfway across the floor, handing me the greasy bag, and laughs. "You must really like Crunchwraps."

My brows pinch. "Thanks…"

I open the bag and dump the contents onto my desk, Charlee hanging over my shoulder.

"What the hell?" There are six Crunchwrap Supremes, a large order of chili cheese fries, and two orders of cinnamon twists. I look up at Charlee. "Did you do this?"

She shakes her head but starts laughing. "I promise I didn't, but I totally know who did. I told him on Monday that Crunchwraps are your weakness. I can't believe he remembered."

"What? Who?"

Charlee rips off the paper attached to the bag, her lips moving as she reads it to herself. "Yup. I was right. Ugh, adorable." She presses a hand to her heart.

I snatch the paper from her fingers, searching through the receipt for the message typed at the bottom.

Claire,
I hope this brings a little bit of sunshine to your day.
You looked beautiful last night, but you always do.
Happy Friday.
Avery

CHAPTER TWENTY-ONE

Avery

I can't remember the last time I left the office before five. If I'm not in the office in the afternoon, it's because I'm meeting with clients elsewhere. I don't duck out early, and I sure as hell don't take sick days.

But yet, here I am, dragging my tired ass through the front lobby of the condo at 3:13pm on a Friday afternoon, feeling rightfully wrecked.

The nagging feeling in my stomach that told me I'd fucked things with Claire beyond repair, not on my own accord, had been sinking into my bones since she walked out of her own party last night, one I knew she'd spent months planning with Charlee.

The feeling only intensified as today wore on. Her *Thank you for lunch, Avery*, text lacked her normal sass and the emojis she's become so fond of. The last thing I want to do is break her, someone who's already been broken, someone who never should've been broken in the first place.

Fix it, Wyatt had said simply to me this afternoon after calling me a miserable sack of shit.

I want to. How do I? How can I make her listen? I don't even really know what words I'm trying to say to her, and I think that there is my first problem.

Maybe that's why I haul Sully down to the parking garage and load him into my rarely used truck. Maybe that's why I'm currently heading to spend my Friday evening with my parents. Because at heart, I'm a bit of a momma's boy and I always will be, and tonight I need her usually unsolicited advice. It'll be a night she'll never soon let me forget, that much I'm aware of. Desperate times call for desperate measures, or something like that.

And because my mom is my mom and she's overbearing and likes to insert herself into my life, I don't even have to bring it up. In fact, it only takes her seven minutes to approach the subject of my bachelorhood. A new record.

She stirs a pot of pasta sauce on the stove, ushering me to a chair at the kitchen table. She wipes her little hands on her apron before popping her fists on her hips and scrutinizing me carefully, like she's trying to find something. She releases the heaviest of sighs.

I roll my eyes. "*What?*"

"Oh, nothing," she says passively, baiting me the way she always does. She pulls out a chair and sinks to it with another dramatic sigh, shoulders sagging. "It's just, you're so handsome, Avery, and so sweet, and—"

My sister strolls into into the kitchen, snorting as she pulls a water bottle from the fridge. "Sweet? I don't think there's a girl alive who would use that adjective to describe your son, Mom. Nice? Sure, sometimes. Funny? Eh, he's alright. Playboy? Absolutely. Sweet? Hell fucking no." She sticks her tongue out at me, daring me to argue with her.

"Do you still live here, Harper? You're twenty-five. Shouldn't you be moving out?" I flick my brows up at her.

Mom clutches Harper to her chest. "Don't take my baby away from me, Avery."

"She's not a baby anymore, Mom. She's an adult who still freeloads off her parents." I watch my sister as she sinks into the chair beside me. "You know, the offer still stands to come work with me."

She narrows her gaze and scoffs, letting me know exactly where I can shove my offer. "You say work *with* you, but what you mean is *for* you. I don't want you to be my boss."

I shrug. "Wyatt can be your boss."

"Like that's any better. He's just as much a playboy as you are. I don't wanna be subjected to your sordid affairs at work."

"The fact that you think we bring hook-ups to our office only speaks to your level of professionalism, or rather, your lack thereof." Although, Claire and I did make out there a week ago. But that's beside the point. She's not a hook-up. "I'm just saying, if you have any desire to be your own person and be independent of your parents, there's a job waiting for you."

Mom reaches across the table and pinches my forearm, glaring at me the way only moms can. "Don't be mean. Stop trying to take her away from me. I'll lose you both soon enough to marriage."

You've never seen an eyeroll until you've seen my sister eyeroll. Her entire body slumps forward with the motion, a groan building in her toes and rippling through her until it bursts from her lips. The entire performance lasts eight full seconds. I've timed it before.

"Mooom, enough with this! We've discussed this—I have lots of time and Avery's a playboy!"

"I'm not a playboy," I insist quietly, earning a skeptical look from both women. "What? I'm not. So I like women; that's not a crime. I don't play anyone, and I never have."

"Sure, but you've never been monogamous either," my sister points out.

"I can be monogamous if I want to be." And I do want to be. It's terrifying. I try to say the words out loud but they're not coming. My throat feels dry. I reach forward and tear Harper's water out of her hands, draining the rest of it.

"Oh, honey. You've always had such a wild heart, but you have such a sweet soul." My mom pats my hand lovingly. "They're both good things. It means you'll make a passionate lover and devoted husband to your woman one day."

My dad waltzes through the kitchen. "What the shit kind of conversation is this?" His head pinballs between the three of us before he shakes it. "I'll be out back. Avery...I'm sorry, son. I can't help you with this one tonight."

My mom dismisses him with a wave and then flips him the bird when he can't see her. It's everything I can do to keep from laughing.

"I just want you to find yourself a good girl, honey. Someone with a big heart, but someone who challenges you, too. I'm not sure if you know this, but you can be a bit of an arrogant asshole sometimes." She smiles sweetly, as if that'll soften the blow. "You get it from your father, of course."

"*Of course.*" Yet as I consider my mom's words, *someone who challenges you,* I know who that is. I watch my fingers drum at the oak table. "What if I've already found that person?"

"What?" Mom leads forward, eyes huge and round.

Harper's body stills beside me. "Huh?"

I don't know if they're being jerks or if they genuinely didn't hear me; I did kind of whisper it. I clear my throat and repeat myself.

My mom launches to her feet, slamming her palms down on the table. "You have a girlfriend? Oh my God! Oh my *God*!"

Harper sits in stunned silence beside me. When she finally looks up, her expression is pure betrayal. "Traitor," she seethes.

"Claire's not my girlfriend," I insist weakly.

"*Claire*? Oh my God! She has a name! Claire! What does she look like? What does she do? Is she a family girl? How did you meet? Oh my God, I love her already!" Mom paces back and forth in the kitchen, wearing a hole right through the old hardwood, fanning herself with her hand.

Well, this was a huge mistake.

"I said she's *not* my girlfriend."

Mom halts her movements, frowning. "I don't get it. You said you found your person."

"Sure, but that's about it. I don't really know where to go from here," I admit, lifting one shoulder and letting it fall. I'm going for nonchalance. Not sure it works.

Harper snorts a laugh. "What do you mean you don't know where to go from here? You ask her out. Have you seriously been fucking and chucking so long you don't know the basic premise of dating?" Mom swats her with a dishtowel.

"Yes, Harp, I know what dating entails." I place my hand on my knee, trying to still its bounce. "What I mean is, I've asked her out. More than once. She keeps saying no."

Harper keels over the table, slapping it while she laughs a loud, ridiculous, patronizing laugh. I resist the urge to flick her in the face. "Sounds like she doesn't like you. That must be incredibly difficult for you to wrap your thick skull around." She taps a finger to my temple before I can swat her hand away.

"That's not it. She likes me, I know she does. We've…kissed. A few times. She just thinks it's not a good idea."

"I don't understand, honey," Mom says, finally sitting back down. "If you both like each other, why wouldn't it be a good idea?"

"She recently got out of a relationship and her ex…cheated on her."

Realization dawns on my mom's face, and maybe a bit of amusement, too. "Ah. I see. So she doesn't trust you because of her ex, and because you're a playboy."

"You're supposed to be on my side," I remind her.

"I'm always on your side, Avery. You're my son and I love you. But your sister is right—you haven't had a girlfriend since high school, and you do have a bit of a reputation with the ladies. My goodness, you're with a new one every week." I hate that my mom knows this, and I honestly don't know how she does.

"But I haven't been with anyone since I met Claire," I admit sheepishly. My right hand's been cramping up, but I'm not going to share that with my mom and sister.

Mom's face softens, and I think I even see Harper's eyes flicker. That admission right there tells them everything they need to know—that I'm serious about Claire.

"I don't really know where to go from here. I'm not ready to throw in the towel. I've never felt this way before. But I don't know how to make her understand that I'm not here for casual, that I want to…be with her. Only her." I avert my gaze, suddenly interested in the soggy paper label around the water bottle. I start peeling it, shredding it to pieces.

Mom's hand settles on top of mine, her attempt at steeling my nerves. She gives me a gentle squeeze. Her brown eyes are tender and kind, full of love. "You just need to make sure she sees the real you. If that takes a little bit of time, so be it. Is she worth it?"

"Yes," I say without hesitation. Claire is worth every minute, day, week, or month I have to wait.

"Then keep trying. You have to wear your heart on your sleeve, Avery, not hide it in your chest."

And there it is, the simplest, most profound bit of advice I needed, the one only my mom can give. I need to show Claire how I feel, need to make sure she has no doubts about my intentions.

"Not in your pants, either," Harper adds. "Your heart is different from your dick, in case you weren't sure."

So incredibly profound.

CHAPTER TWENTY-TWO

Avery

I'm a determined man on Saturday morning.

More determined than that time I orchestrated an acquisition of one popular toilet paper and paper towel company by another, and then released their shares onto the stock market. Within a day, their stock prices had tripled, and we'd made a cool million by the end of the first week. It didn't stop there.

Yes, today's Avery Beck is even more determined than that man.

To be honest, I was a determined man last night, too. When I got home from my parents, I went straight to Claire's. But just as I raised my fist to knock, I heard shrieks of laughter that could only belong to sweet Vivi, fits of giggles I immediately associated with both Claire and Charlee.

They were having a girl's night. I couldn't interrupt. My determination had to wait.

But this morning? There will be no stopping me this morning, Vivi or no Vivi.

I got up at the crack of dawn to take Sully for a nice, long walk, and once he'd found his way back to his bed—because he's lazy and the walk more than did him in—I headed right back out for a run.

Here I am, finishing up my fifth mile, people starting to pour onto the busy downtown streets to enjoy the warm sunshine, and my only plan is to knock on Claire's door and demand her time, demand that she hear me out about Thursday night, and demand that she admit her feelings for me.

I might not use the word demand.

Okay, I'm absolutely *not* going to use the word demand. My goal is to talk to her, not have her slam the door in my face.

The only decision left for me to make, as I approach the condo and slow to a walk, stretching my arms out over my head, is how long I'll wait before I appear at her door. An hour? Three hours? Ten minutes? Who knows? I'm flying by the seat of my pants today. I'm gonna hop in the shower and let the cool water decide for me.

Except the world is actually in charge, and it's deciding I'm not going to wait at all. The world is telling me it's happening now. Right now. Keep up or get left behind.

Because the front door swings open and two beautiful redheads come tumbling out, one miniature and the other…well, the other also not very tall.

Claire and Vivi are a sight to see. Vivi looks like she could be Claire's daughter, the similarities uncanny: the ginger tresses, wild green eyes, and dimply smile.

Claire looks…adorable. Her beauty is so effortless, so casual. She doesn't need tight dresses and high heels to turn every head. This morning, she's wearing a lilac tank top underneath a pair of overalls, the ripped hems cut into shorts, showing off a gorgeous pair of legs. An outfit that would be impossible for me to get into, and I don't care in the slightest. Her auburn waves are piled on top of her head, along with a pair of oversized sunglasses stuck in there. As always seems to be the case whenever she wears her hair up, several loose curls tumble down around her neck, framing her face and tickling her shoulders.

My grin widens at Vivi's blue princess dress, her pink cape and matching pink gloves that reach her elbows. She's donning two braids and a tiny tiara on top of her head. I want to scoop her up and give her a big kiss on both of her chubby cheeks.

I could watch them like this forever, swinging their twined hands back and forth while the two of them giggle.

202

And yet, as much as I don't want to interrupt, I plant myself in front of them, crossing my arms over my chest as I wait for Claire to look up, or for her to run into me with the stroller she's maneuvering with just one hand while she holds Vivi's in the other.

And when she does, she jerks to a stop. Her smile melts right off her face. It would hurt my feelings if it weren't for the way her eyes dip down my body, the ruby red flush of her cheeks as she meets my gaze and watches my smile grow. And grow it does, because I can't help it. My heart beats a little faster for both of these Thompson girls.

The smirk on my face has Claire rolling her eyes before either of us can open our mouths to speak. She actually has the balls to try and turn and walk the other way, but Vivi's not about to let that happen. Her huge, sparkling greens settle on me and her face splits in two with that grin of hers.

"A'wy!" she shrieks, shoving Claire aside as she comes barreling toward me.

I crouch down and catch her, spinning her in the air before clutching her to my chest in the biggest hug I can muster. "Well, hey there, beautiful little lady!" Vivi giggles, squeezing my cheeks together with her satin-clothed hands. "Are you a princess today, Vivi?"

"I Pwincess Anna," she says matter-of-factly. She shoves a finger toward Claire. "Care Bear Queen Elsa."

Ah, I know these names. What's the movie? Frozen? I give Claire an assessing once-over. "You're the ice queen, huh? Fitting," I add with a wink, because I can throw shade just as well as she can.

Claire's eyes roll, arms folding across her chest, hip jutting out with attitude. But the corner of her mouth twitches, threatening to show me how much she enjoys our banter, and how much she loves seeing me with Vivi.

"What are you two up to today?" I ask.

203

"Nothing," Claire replies much too quickly.

Vivi looks between Claire and me. "A'wy come wif us?"

Claire's expression softens right before my eyes. She can't say no to her niece. She steps up to us, fingering the end of one of Vivi's braids. "Oh, honey, I bet he'd love to but I'm sure he's very busy today." She shoots me a dangerously slanted look, one that tells me to lie if I need to. She's going to try to pass the heartbreaking of that little munchkin off to me.

Unfortunately for Claire, pissing her off is my new favorite past time. She gets all riled up when I crawl my way under her skin. I suspect it's because it's so easy for me to do.

When Vivi pouts up at me, I tap her nose. "As luck would have it, Princess Anna, my schedule is wide open today. Where are we going?"

Claire groans, sagging forward. "Look, Avery," she starts laying it out for me. "We'll be gone pretty much all day. We're going for breakfast, then to the market. We're going to the zoo at High Park, picnic lunch afterwards, that kinda thing. It's going to be a long, busy day."

"Cool. When are we leaving?"

Vivi vibrates with excitement in my arms. "Right now!"

"Well, I'll tell you what. I'm a little sweaty right now. Do you think you could wait for me while I take a quick shower? I wouldn't want to be stinky around such beautiful princesses."

Vivi's head bobs about a hundred times.

Claire reaches for her. "We'll just wait out here for you." Stubborn.

I ignore her by turning away, spying the stuffed dog in the stroller. Claire follows my gaze. Her mouth opens and I know she knows what I'm about to do, because I know she knows, after she spied on me through her peephole on Thursday night, that I have a dog.

"Vivi, do you like doggies?" I ask.

204

Vivi's eyes widen and her jaw drops. She holds her pink hands up as if they were claws and yell-barks, "Woof, woof! Woof, woof!" Then she leans forward and…licks my cheek.

"Oh, God! Vivi! I'm so sorry, Avery." Claire looks downright mortified. She pulls Vivi from my arms and sets her on the ground, crouching down to eye level. "Vivian Thompson, you cannot lick people," she states firmly, shaking a finger at her. Then her voice drops, soft and quiet, and she smooths her hands over Vivi's braids before taking her tiny hands in hers. "Personal bubble, Vivi, remember, sweet pea?"

Claire plants a kiss on Vivi's pout and both eyelids before tears can spill out. She glances up at me and winces. "Sorry. Grandpa has a dog at home and all those two do is lick each other's faces."

The laugh that rumbles in my chest and tumbles from my lips is hearty and genuine. Everything about this is the best. I love how expressive Vivi is about all things, and I love watching Claire parent her, a little bit of chastising followed by utter love and sweetness. It's classic Claire.

I hold my hand out to Vivi. "Come on, Vivi. There's someone I want you to meet."

I'm a little on edge, for more than one reason, when I open the door to my suite. As a Bernese Mountain dog, Sully's a hundred-and-thirty pounds of fluff, love, and slobbery kisses. I'm worried that his size alone will be enough to scare little Vivi. I'm also nervous about Claire seeing where I live for the first time. It feels kinda intimate, and I wonder if she feels it, too.

Sully is waiting at the door like he always is, and Vivi flings her arms around his neck before collapsing to the floor in a fit of wild, shrieking giggles as he assaults her face with his big pink tongue. I should've known Vivi would be fearless.

Claire's face bursts at the seams as she watches them. She sinks to her knees and buries her hands in Sully's thick, black fur when he gives her attention. I watch her lean forward and press a kiss to the tip of his wet nose. "Hey handsome," she murmurs.

My heart kicks it up a notch, and I turn my attention back to Vivi. "What kind of dog does Grandpa have?"

"Gamps has Tookey," she tells me.

Claire giggles and smiles up at me. "My dad has an Australian Shepherd named Turkey." At my quizzical smile, she adds, "He was born on Thanksgiving."

Chuckling, I jerk my head down the hall. "I'm gonna go hop in the shower. I'll be quick. You okay out here with Sully or do you want me to take him with me?"

She shakes her head. "We'll be fine, don't worry." She strokes the spot between his eyes before lifting her gaze back to me. "Sully like Monsters Inc.?"

I smile. "You got it, beautiful Claire."

There's that blush I love. And because I can't resist feeling that heat—or her—I pull Claire to her feet and take her face in my hands. She swallows hard and licks her lips, dazzling eyes staring up at me. She can deny whatever this is all she wants, but this girl wants me to kiss her right now.

"I missed you," I whisper honestly. She looks as surprised as I am by my confession. I guess it goes with the whole *wear your heart on your sleeve* thing.

Claire's tongue swipes across her bottom lip. "I…I've been right here."

"I know, but you were being a brat." Before she can say anything, I kiss her warm cheek and pull her against me for a hug.

And I'm struck by the feeling that right here, right now, with her in my arms, there's nowhere else I'd rather be.

CHAPTER TWENTY-THREE

Claire

There's an exceptionally large part of me that feels like I don't belong here, not in this incredible penthouse, staring out over the Toronto Harbour skyline. Everything about Avery's apartment is breathtaking, and I'm afraid to touch anything.

That doesn't stop me from pressing my hands up against the glass of his floor-to-ceiling windows, though.

"I told you I have an amazing view," Avery murmurs in my ear, making me shriek and jump. His hands, cool and damp from his shower—also unnaturally large and magical—wrap around my waist, steadying me. His touch lingers, as does his gaze, both of them making me quiver the way they always do.

With an amused and arrogant smile—also charming as hell—he steps back, tugging a t-shirt over his head.

But not before I get a good, hard look at his chest, chiseled to an utterly annoying level of perfection, the six-pack that decorate his torso. No, eight-pack. Dear God. My fingers curl at my sides, itching to reach over and *feel him*, run my fingers over every curve of muscle, through the patch of hair that runs from his belly button down to his—*oh God, Claire, don't you fucking look. Abort, abort!*

I hate the way my mouth hangs as I watch a drop of water dip toward that stupid V-muscle that I love/hate. The droplet keeps moving, like a river etching a path through the mountains of his abdomen, until it disappears into the waistband of his underwear, which are just peeking out the top of his shorts. Calvins, obviously.

The spell I'm under should be broken when his shirt settles around his lean waist, effectively covering up that bronzed skin I wanna lick—*oh, gross, Claire, come on*—except then I look up. I'm unimpressed with the tiny whimper that tickles my throat and puffs past my lips when my eyes land on that wet, drippy mop of dark waves on top of his head, and he has the nerve to smirk.

And just like that, the spell is broken. Well, kinda. Not really, but it should be.

I pin my arms to my chest. "You did that on purpose."

"Did what on purpose?" Smug amusement drips from his husky voice like the water dripping from his hair.

"You know what." When his brows inch up, I roll my eyes and drop my arms, poking his chest. It's mostly an excuse to touch him. "You could have put your shirt on in your bedroom."

"Well, excuse me for being comfortable in my own home. I wasn't expecting to come out here and be ogled. Didn't anyone ever tell you it's rude to stare?"

My jaw drops in a fusion of mortified rage. "I'd like to see how well you'd fare if I did the same thing."

His curiosity is piqued. He grabs my shoulders and starts shuffling me down the hallway. "Tell you what, Claire Bear. Let's test your theory. You go hop in the shower and come out here half-naked. We'll see if I stare or not."

"I already *know* you'll stare." I put the brakes on, digging my heels into the gray hardwood planks, slamming my palms into either side of the wall. When he finally stops, his fingers dip below my overalls and settle softly on the tank top covering my ribs.

His chin lands on my shoulder. "You're not ticklish, are you, Claire?"

If I were smart, I'd swallow the involuntary gasp that flies past my lips. But I don't, and that there is a mistake. My hands rocket to his, trying to rip them away. "Don't you *dare*, Avery!"

"I'm not scared of you," he whispers softly against my neck.

I open my mouth to detail all the ways I plan on dismembering him if he even so much as attempts to tickle me, but his fingers start moving. He gives me no lead-up. He doesn't start slow, choosing instead to go right for the kill, his fingers fast and furious as they scour my ribcage. I shriek with laughter, warm tears streaming uncontrollably down my face as I try to claw his hands off me.

"Stop, stop! Please!" I somehow manage between cries.

He hooks one arm around my chest and under both armpits, hoisting me into the air and tickling with his other hand.

"Avery! Please! I'm...dying!" I can't stop. I can't breathe.

My heads falls back onto his shoulder, eyes rolling up to his face. His face may be blurry through all the tears, but the tender expression that lives there while he watches me in his arms and at his mercy is confusing, to say the least. Wearing the softest, sweetest smile on his face, this man right here looks like he wants to kiss me. I wish I could stop laughing/crying/shrieking.

"P-p-please!" I sputter, my hand sliding around the back of his neck.

His smile grows into beaming grin and his fingers slow. He squeezes me to his chest, pecks me on the cheek, and drops me back down to my feet. Wheezing, I keel over, gripping my knees as I gulp down air.

"Auntie Claire like when you ticklin' her, A'wy," Vivi calls from where she's cuddled up with Sully on his dog bed, his tongue lapping at her face. "She laughin'." Climbing to her feet, Vivi thumbs at herself. "But you can't tickle me!"

Avery's eyes glisten as he starts creeping toward her. "Is that right?"

"I too fast for you!"

Avery leaps into action, sprinting across the floor with his long legs while Vivi screams and starts running, giggling. He follows her around the couch and catches her in his arms, lifting her into the air. "Gotcha, little Miss Vivi!"

She rolls in his arms, shrieking with laughter, legs kicking, and my ovaries burst. My heart, too. It's doing this super weird thing. I think it might be growing. At the very least, it's throbbing.

How much longer am I going to deny my feelings for Avery? Pretend it's just physical, that there's nothing more going on?

What I'm most scared of is not being able to tell real from fake. I couldn't see it with Aaron and we were together for three years. What makes me think I know Avery any better, or even remotely close?

If I've learned anything, it's that I can't trust what I can see with my own eyes, because all they've done is deceive me. What if it's all about the chase for Avery? What if I give in and he…disappears? The thought alone creates an ache deep in my chest. I rub it, trying to make it disappear.

I watch Avery help Vivi with her shoes, and when she climbs to her feet, she slips her hand into his, his massive one swallowing her tiny one right up.

She holds her free hand out, beckoning to me. "Come, Care Bear. We hol' hands. It's safety."

Avery's eyes flicker at her words and the corner of his mouth tilts up. He just adores her, and so does anyone who meets her. Nobody is immune to her charm.

Of course, at the diner, Vivi insists on sitting beside Avery. Except she winds up crawling into his lap and I can't force the smile off my face at the way his arms wrap around her body so he can cut up her pancakes. Every single female in the restaurant is giving him what I affectionately call the *fuck me eyes*, including me.

I snap a sneaky picture of Avery and Vivi and send it to Charlee, letting her know I *absolutely* have baby fever.

Avery peeks up at me and smiles. "Did you just take my picture?" He grins at the way I fumble over my lack of response. "Too cute to resist, eh?"

I groan and fold over the table. "You two are adorable." I sweep one arm out, gesturing around the restaurant. "Can't you see what you're doing to all these women?"

My phone vibrates in my hand.

Charlee: *Oh. Em. Gee. Ovaries = bursting.*

I hold my phone up to Avery. "See?" I immediately regret it when his brows quirk while his eyes scan my message. I just told Charlee I had baby fever. It sounds like I want to have Avery Beck's baby. My cheeks flood with heat and I tuck my phone into the chest pocket of my overalls.

"Can you send it to me?" he asks quietly as Vivi's sticky, syrup-covered hand grips his.

I blink twice. "Oh. Sure. Yeah." I send it to him and read Charlee's newest message.

Charlee: *Also...are you guys on a date right now...?*

Ignore.

When the waitress brings our bill—one bill, snatched out of her hand by Avery before I can reach for it—she *ooh*'s and *aah*'s over how sweet Avery looks with a baby and how good of a dad he is. She touches him seven times—but who's counting—as if I'm not sitting right across from him.

"She looks like you," the ebony-haired beauty says, twisting back and forth while she twirls her hair around her finger, smiling at him like a lovesick teen, and I just barely swallow my snort.

"You think so?" Avery asks. I'm about to jam my foot into his shin when his gaze floats to mine and he smiles, smooth chocolate eyes dancing. "I think she looks more like my beautiful wife."

My jaw unhinges. The waitress stops twisting. She glances my way—for the first time *ever* since taking my food order.

Her eyes drift over my face, my hair. "Oh. Right. I guess."

Vivi pipes up, because why wouldn't she? "They like to kiss and tickle."

I choke on the water I'm busy drinking to distract from the fact that Avery just pretended I was his wife. Avery chuckles under his breath. The waitress gives us a smile so tight it looks painful, then turns and stalks off.

"Well, that was fun," Avery says, mouth set in a permanent, crooked grin as we walk toward the market.

I snort. "Does that happen everywhere you go? Women touching you and flirting so blatantly with you, regardless of your company?"

He presses a hand to his chest. "Why, Claire, if I didn't know any better, I'd think you were jealous."

I roll my eyes. I do a lot of that with him. "Not jealous." *Lies.* "Just annoyed." *Not a lie.*

"Mhmm. I don't think I've ever really thought about it, but, yeah, it does happen a lot." He wags his brows. "Guess I'm gonna need to start bringing my wife and daughter with me everywhere I go."

Vivi, who's riding on his shoulders, curls over his head, one thumb in her mouth and her free hand wrapping around his jaw in the weirdest but cutest display of affection. "I luh you, A'wy."

The look he gives her is so sweet and full of wonder. "I love you too, princess," he tells her softly. He tips his head up and she plants a smooch right on his lips. *Fucking ugh.*

I wish I were more coordinated, less easily distracted, but I'm not. That's why my feet somehow tangle together and I stumble forward. Avery's hand wraps around my elbow, steadying me without any effort on his part.

We're only an hour into our day. How am I going to survive this? These two need to tuck their cute away.

At the market, we pick up fresh buns and meat and cheese for sandwiches, fruit, and some drool-worthy, gooey, freshly baked cookies. When we're done, we head back outside to wait for our Uber so we can make our way over to the park.

I spy a dark-haired beauty catch sight of Avery. Her eyes widen and she sizes him up before her face splits in two with her huge, perfect, pearly-white smile, and that green monster inside me rears its ugly head. I hate that I can't tamp it down, make it disappear.

"Avery?" she calls with wonder as she approaches us. She's definitely not deterred by our presence with him, so I don't think his fake family plan is working the way he thought it would.

Avery's eyes flit to me, and I notice the unease he wears on his face, making the knot of tension in my stomach tighten.

"What are you doing here?" She crosses her arms over her chest, smirking at him, one perfect eyebrow arching. "And with a tiny child, no less."

She's beautiful, incredibly so, but she feels familiar, too. I can't quite put my finger on it. Her deep brown eyes drink me in, and I feel suddenly very self-conscious.

She tilts her head to the side, her smirk turning into a curious smile. "Is this Cl—"

Avery cuts her off, wrapping his arm around her neck, his big hand swallowing up half her face while she tries to pry his fingers off her. He lets out a nervous laugh and looks at me. "Claire, this is my sister, Harper. Harper, this is Claire."

Sister? Yeah, there's that big sigh of relief. The fist that was clenching in my stomach unfurls and my shoulders drop.

It's no wonder she seemed familiar. With the same wavy brown locks, the dark chocolate eyes, that teasing smirk, the two of them could pass for twins, though his sister looks to be a few years younger than him.

Harper holds her hand out, grinning. "Hi Claire. I've heard *so much* about you."

"For fuck's sake," Avery buries on a low groan, averting his gaze.

With a sheepish smile, I shake her hand. "It's nice to meet you, Harper."

She crouches down in front of Vivi. "And who might you be, little princess?"

Vivi puffs her chest out. "I Pwincess Anna!"

Harper slaps the heel of her palm to her forehead. "Oh! Of course you are! And where's your prince? Where's Kristoff?" Using her hand as a visor, she pretends to look around.

Vivi wraps her arms around one of Avery's legs. "A'wy my pwince."

Harper presses a hand to her heart, peering up at me. "She's absolutely adorable. Avery didn't mention you had a daughter."

"Oh, no." I shake my head, feeling a little flustered. "Vivi's my niece. I'm watching her for the weekend."

"Well, she looks just like you. You're both beautiful." She straightens and checks out the partway loaded-up stroller. "What are you three up to today?"

"We went for breakfast, just hit up the market, and now we're heading to High Park," Avery tells her.

Harper's dark brows inch up her forehead. "Wow. Look at you guys. You're like a cute little family."

Avery reaches forward and pinches her arm. She slaps his hand away, face twisting in pain. "Ow, you fuck—" Her eyes slide to Vivi. "Oops. You…poop head."

Vivi explodes in a fit of giggles. "Poop head! A'wy, you not a poop head! You a toot head!"

He touches his chest and gasps in mock hurt. "I am not!"

Harper laughs, her head shaking. "I can't even handle this. This is adorable. Avery, who the hell—heck—knew you were so good with kids?"

He shrugs. "Beats me."

"He turned quite a few heads at breakfast," I tell Harper.

She snorts. "Yeah, I'll bet. Trust me, Claire, it's always been like that, our whole lives. Growing up with him as my older brother was hell." She looks at her phone. "Shit—shoot—I gotta go." She kisses Avery on the cheek and squeezes my hand. "It was so nice to meet you, Claire." She crouches down in front of Vivi. "Princess Anna, it's been an honor."

In true Vivi-knows-no-boundaries fashion, she launches herself at Harper, wrapping her arms around her neck. "Buh-bye, Happy!"

"Happy?" Harper meets my eyes. She looks like she's going to die from cuteness overload.

"She misses some letter sounds sometimes. Kinda makes her own words and names up as she goes."

She taps Vivi on the nose. "You just made my day, little princess." With a smile and a wink, she turns and strolls off down the street.

Hesitantly, Avery twists back to me, rubbing at the back of his neck. "Sooo…that was my sister…"

"And you talk about me to your sister?" I tease.

His eyes narrow and he grabs me by the shoulders, turning me toward the car that's just pulled up beside us. "Mind your own business, Claire Bear."

Oh, but I think I *like* this business.

CHAPTER TWENTY-FOUR

Claire

I have a serious love/hate relationship with how easy Avery is to be with. Our morning together passes so quickly that I find myself wishing it would slow down. It's a dangerous train of thought, almost as dangerous as the permanent smile etched on my face.

Even Avery comments on how he's never seen me smile so much and how we must be breaking some sort of record for number of hours passed without me scowling at him. The record is broken when I turn my scowl on him for that comment.

After a couple of hours at the zoo visiting with all the animals and another hour at the playground, we find a shady tree in the park to set up a blanket and have a late picnic lunch.

I post a few pictures from our day to my Instagram, including one of Avery and Vivi, and one of the three of us with an ostrich poking its head over my shoulder. Avery smiles over my shoulder while I post them, and I feel his lips brush against my cheek before he turns back to Vivi and the fake tea party they're currently having. He's such a good sport.

My post earns me three text messages in rapid succession.

Casey: *Is my daughter third wheeling on your date?*

Charlee: *So you ARE on a date.*

Aaron: *Are you kidding me? You're already dating someone? That's the same guy from the bar. I remember him. Fuck you, Claire, you fucking slut.*

I simply can't with Aaron. I can't spend any amount of my downtime with a man while I'm single, yet it's perfectly acceptable for him to sleep with other girls while he's in an actual long-term relationship? How delusional can one man be?

Clenching my teeth, I stuff my phone into Vivi's bag before I give into the desire to chuck it at a tree.

Avery's hand settles on softly on my knee, drawing my gaze to his face. "Everything okay?"

"Oh, yeah. Everything's fine." I'm sure the way my voice crackles and my hands flail around my face let him know that everything is *not* fine, but I'd rather not go down this road with him.

"Claire."

"Avery."

"Come on," he urges, giving my knee a gentle squeeze. "What's up?"

It's real weird to go this long without taunting and teasing each other. He's actually ridiculously nice when he's not being so smug. Maybe that's why I find myself pulling my phone out, navigating to Aaron's message.

He takes it from my hand with a curious look, and I watch as his lips move while reads. His pupils dilate, taking his eyes brown a rich, milk chocolate, to a starless night. His fingers start flying over the screen, typing furiously.

"What are you doing?" I lean over him, but his hand comes out, pushing on my chest to keep me away while he finishes whatever the hell it is he's doing. "Avery, what are you doing?"

Tension creeps up my spine when I hear that familiar chime my phone makes when I've sent a message.

Avery deposits my phone in my palm and goes back to drinking his fake tea, pinky out and everything, just like Vivi taught him.

Bringing my phone to my face, my suspicions are confirmed: Avery responded to Aaron.

Me: *Hey bud. I'm sure you're aware, but you had your chance with Claire and you blew it. You fucked up royally. I suspect, from your message, that you realize that. You don't get to make her feel guilty about her decisions just because you threw away the best thing you've ever had and you're trying to backtrack now. Claire is amazing, sassy, hilarious, kind, and with a huge heart. But you already know that. If I find out you ever speak to her or about her in that manner again, you and I will be having this conversation face-to-face, and I won't be so nice. Sincerely, the guy from the bar.*

Heat floods my face as I reread those words over and over again, my hand settling at the base of my throat. Is it weird that I'm oddly turned on right now? Angry, defensive Avery is…I mean…*wow.*

I watch those three little dots wiggle on my screen, indicating Aaron's typing a response. They stop and start again three times. Then they stop for good. No message comes through.

A drop of water splatters to my phone screen and I reach up to touch my fingertip to the corner of my eye, where that traitor has accidentally leaked from.

"Hey." Avery's patient, tender voice coaxes my gaze to his as he threads his fingers through mine. "I didn't mean to…I…I'm sorry, Claire. I didn't mean to overstep. I just—"

"No." My head wags back and forth. "You didn't. I'm just…surprised. That was really nice of you. No one's ever stuck up for me like that. Thank you, Avery."

"I won't let him talk to you like that."

My swallow is thick and dry as his deep stare holds mine.

Until I can't anymore. I don't know what's happening, why he's looking at me like that, why *I'm* looking at *him* like that. The thoughts in my brain swirl, making it feel like a muddled mess, and I avert my gaze in an attempt to break the connection, whatever connection there is.

I busy myself with my sandwich and my thoughts, and I'm not sure how much time has passed when Avery speaks again, his voice quiet and pensive.

"Do you still have feelings for him?"

My head lifts. Vivi is now curled up between his spread legs, her cheek resting on his strong thigh. Avery's fingers are in her hair, twirling the tip of one of her braids while she sleeps. Aaron was never like this with Vivi. He avoided her, and most family gatherings, at all costs.

So, do I still have feelings for Aaron?

"No." I hug my knees to my chest. "Things weren't right for a while. Looking back, I don't think they were ever really that good. I just got stuck, I think. Stuck in the familiarity of it, the routine I was comfortable with." My shoulders pop up and down. "It was a safety blanket, even if it wasn't healthy, and I didn't leave when I should have." I sigh quietly. "I'm an idiot."

"There's no shame in staying in a relationship longer than you should have when you're just trying to hold on to the good stuff, when you're trying to make it work."

I rest my cheek on my knees so I can look at Avery. He's not at all what or who I thought he'd be. I've been surprised by him nearly every day, but today more than ever.

"I guess so, but I hung on about a year-and-a-half too long. At some point it feels a little less like hope and a lot more like desperation, stupidity." My cheeks blaze with my truth. If Avery wanted me for more than sex before, he won't now. I'm undecided if that's a good thing or a bad thing.

His mouth quirks to the side while he thinks. "I disagree, but I won't argue with you."

My brows lift. "You won't? But arguing's what we do best."

He lets out a soft chuckle. "We do argue well, but I think there's a few other things we do well besides our witty banter."

Like what? Kissing? Touching?

"Like this," he continues, sweeping one arm out. "Right now, talking without chewing each other's head off. This is nice, just being with you. And Princess Anna too, of course," he adds with the tilt of his mouth.

"Of course," I murmur my agreement. I study him carefully, because if this is Avery—this handsome, kind, sweet man beside me who instills just enough petulance in me to evoke raging passion in my bloodstream—how the hell is he single? "What about you?"

"What about me?"

"Any relationships you stayed in longer than you should have?"

He makes a sound, half chuckle, half throat-clearing. "Uh…" He scratches his jaw.

"Don't tell me you've never been in a relationship?" I sit up straight, kicking my legs out in front of me, resting my weight on my palms.

Avery gives me a half smile, like he's not sure whether honesty will be the best policy in this moment. "Not really, to be truthful."

"How come?" Give me all the details, Avery. Tell me how you love women too much to ever commit to just one. Remind my brain why it needs to tell my heart to back the hell off.

His gaze wanders before focusing on Vivi in his lap, the copper braid he's twirling over his fingers. He glances up at me. "Honestly?"

"Of course."

"My parents are and always have been the best example of true love. I've never doubted their commitment to each other. It's always seemed like…more. More than just love and a desire to be together, physically. They're best friends and I've always been able to see that. They bicker like crazy, tell each other off when they need to, and they're always honest. They drive each other insane, but they love each other just as fiercely. There's just always been…passion between them. It's never been difficult to see." He lifts one lazy shoulder, letting it fall. "I guess I just…what's the point if it's anything less than that? I think it needs to be more than just wanting to be with someone. More like…*needing* to be with

220

them. I've never seen the point in wasting my time on anything less."

I'm floored by the sweetness tucked into his truth, his reason why, because it's not at all what I was expecting. A grin explodes across my face and Avery smiles, tapping the corner of my mouth.

"What are you smiling at?"

I shake my head. "Just surprised."

"That I have a heart?" he teases.

I giggle. "I knew you had a heart. I just thought your dick was bigger than your heart."

If he's shocked by my words, his expression does nothing to show it. "Trust me, Claire, my dick is plenty big. I can show you, if you like."

"You've got my two-and-a-half-year-old niece in your lap," I remind him.

He looks down at her with total adoration, stroking her pink cheek. "Where is her mom?"

I don't realize I've sidled my way up to him and leaned into his side until he winds his arm around my waist, holding me close to him. Looking down at the tiniest person to have ever owned my heart, I sigh.

"My brother dated this girl Angela for a short time. It wasn't working out and he was planning on breaking up with her. I think she knew it. She showed up one day and told him she was pregnant. Literally said *now you can't leave me*. It was almost as if she planned it, but we'll never know for sure, of course."

Casey was twenty-six at the time and had just moved to Toronto a few months prior to be on his own. Dex was about the only person he had in the city, aside from Angela.

"The thing is, Angela didn't actually want the baby at all. She just wanted Casey. When it was clear that Casey wanted to be in his baby's life, but not with her, she decided to get rid of it…of Vivi."

A stabbing tightness swells in my chest as I imagine a life where she'd gone through with the abortion, where Casey wasn't able to convince her to keep the baby, a life where Vivi didn't exist and light up my entire world. I don't realize a tear trickles from my eye until Avery's thumb sweeps across my cheek, catching it.

"Casey begged her not to have an abortion. He said he'd keep the baby and raise him or her himself, that she could go on with her life and not be involved in any way. It took him two months of convincing before she finally agreed. She was just awful. He'd catch her talking to her stomach, calling Vivi stupid, saying that she hadn't fixed anything like she was supposed to.

"The week before she went into labor, she decided she wanted to give Vivi up for adoption. She didn't want Casey to have her if she couldn't have him. He was a wreck. She actually lined up a family and everything. He scrambled to get a whole bunch of legal documents together with help from a lawyer, paid out the ass for help, and then she backed out at the last second and gave him the baby anyway. She didn't even want to see Vivi. Didn't look at her once, didn't touch her. She signed over all parental rights to Casey and took off two days after she gave birth."

Avery's quiet for a few minutes, his heavy hand resting on Vivi's back as it rises and falls gently in her slumber. "I can't imagine anyone ever turning their back on her," he finally whispers. "She's perfect in every single way. I can't believe how much she makes me smile."

I beam up at him. "She's the best at making people smile."

The way Avery's mouth turns up in the corners, the way his eyes flicker as he looks down at me, dropping for the briefest of moments to my lips before bouncing back to my eyes, makes my stomach dance, my heart thrum wildly against my chest.

His fingers splay out over my waist, his grip tightening just marginally, enough that I can feel that zing of electricity that passes between us, reminding me of the power he has over me, the control of unwillingly and unknowingly handed over.

"You're pretty good at making me smile, too," he tells me, his voice low, husky.

Oh, crap. My heart. Yep. I like him. Like, a lot. A lot, a lot. It's official. Super official. As if it wasn't before.

"Can I kiss you, Claire?" He's already leaning toward me.

"You never take no for an answer, so why are you asking me now?" My question comes out barely more than a wispy exhale, and I blame it on the fact that this wasn't the direction I imagined my day heading in.

His gentle smile splits into a crooked grin. "You're right. No has never been an option when it comes to you."

The tip of his nose sweeps across mine before he presses a kiss to my lips, delicate, like he's testing the waters, giving me one last chance to change my mind. But I don't think I want to change my mind. I just want to stay like this, wrapped up in him, forever.

His hand leaves Vivi's back and comes up to cup the back of my head, holding me to him while his tongue slides along the seam of my mouth. When my lips part, his tongue sweeps inside, caressing, laving. He tastes sweet like the peach iced tea and white chocolate macadamia nut cookie he had with lunch, and I lean into his touch, his kiss, craving more, wanting it all.

Pressure pushes on my knee before tiny hand grabs at my shoulder.

"You guys kissin'," Vivi's voice mumbles, raspy with sleep. She stretches out like a sleepy kitten. "I wanna kiss."

We break apart, laughing when she crawls into Avery's lap, sticking her face between ours. Avery grabs her cheeks in both his hands and plants loud, sloppy kisses all over her face. She eats that shit up, giggling and kissing him back before throwing her arms around my neck.

"Now you, Care Bear!"

I fall into Avery's lap while Vivi climbs onto my belly and attacks me with kisses. I'm laughing so wildly I almost miss when Avery aims his phone at us.

"My turn to take a picture."

After we pack up our picnic and tuck Vivi into the stroller—she's out again within minutes—we make our way through the park. The afternoon sun is hot and bright with June's arrival, and being the fair-skinned girls we are, a day in the sun always drains Vivi and I.

Pushing the stroller with one hand, Avery slips his free hand into mine, our fingers lacing together. It feels so natural, so right, I don't even question it or the butterflies that slam against the walls of my stomach.

"What are you guys doing for dinner?" he asks.

"Probably just gonna order a pizza." I swipe my fingers across my eyes and stifle my yawn. "I'm too tired to cook."

He chuckles. "Yeah, being a parent for a day is exhausting, isn't it?"

"I always admire Casey so much more after I have Vivi for a day or two. I don't know how he does it."

"He's a good dad."

My head bobs. "He's the best. She's his whole world."

"Well, if you're too tired to cook and you're planning on pizza, you should know I make the very best homemade pizza." He flashes me a cheeky, all-too-enticing grin.

"Is that so?"

"Yup," he replies, chest puffing with pride. "Think I even have all the ingredients at home."

"Is that your way of inviting yourself for dinner?"

He shrugs casually. "If you want the best pizza to have ever ignited the taste buds on your tongue, then you want me there, trust me."

I laugh softly, peeking up at him from below my lashes. "Aren't you sick of us yet?"

The look he gives me has me questioning my own sanity. "Not even remotely, Claire."

I hesitate for a moment, mulling over our day, the night I have planned with Vivi. It includes a one hundredth showing of Frozen, for which I'm sure she'll demand that he stay. His ability to decline her requests were shot to shit the second she hopped across my office floor to him and demanded a hug. That means we'll have spent at least twelve straight hours together by the time this day is over.

"Okay," I finally say. "Vivi would like that. And, um…" I reach up, tucking a loose tress behind my ear and clearing my throat. "So would I."

At the condo, Avery follows me into my apartment, keeping his eye on a still-snoozing Vivi for me while I run her a bath. When I return from the bathroom, he's unloaded all of our leftover picnic supplies into my fridge, even though he paid for them all.

"Please keep them." I start unpacking them, trying to stuff them back into his hand. "You paid."

He bumps me out of the way with his hip, re-loading my fridge. "I don't mind. Besides, my fridge is full." He pats his rock-hard torso. "Need to keep it fully stocked at all times."

I roll my eyes and snort a laugh, poking his belly. "Yeah, sure looks like it there, big boy."

"I'm gonna take Sully for a quick walk since he's been home alone all day."

"Are you going to bring him down with you after?"

He pauses, tapping his fingers on my kitchen island. "Would you be okay with that?"

"Of course. I think Vivi will keep him more than entertained."

He laughs. "He'll sleep all day tomorrow after a few hours with her." He picks his keys up off the counter and turns to the door.

"'Kay, I'll be back in about a half hour and we'll get our pizza on."
He leans forward and sweeps his lips across mine before disappearing into the hallway.

I'm not sure if this day has made things infinitely clearer for me, or a thousand times more confusing. My feelings for Avery are clearer, the knowledge that they're not fleeting, but rather growing deeper every day.

The bigger problem lies in me not trusting my own judgment, not being able to tell what's real from what I simply *want* to be real. If I've learned anything recently, it's that my perception of reality is skewed. I thought I meant something to Aaron, and that couldn't have been further from the truth. How do I know if I mean anything more to Avery than a pleasurable means to an end?

A steady vibration followed by a quiet chime has me reaching for the phone on the counter. Except my hand pauses, hanging in the air when I realize my phone is tucked into the chest pocket of my overalls.

It's Avery's phone. He left it on the counter.

I wish I could keep my gaze from sliding to his lit-up screen, but I can't.

It feels like a mistake. I'm probably not going to like what I see there.

And I'm right, kinda. I don't like it.

I love it.

CHAPTER TWENTY-FIVE

Avery

The door is unlocked for me when Sully and I arrive back at Claire's apartment, armed with all the fixings to make homemade pizza. It's nothing special, but it makes me kinda happy, the thought that she's expecting me to just walk in.

As soon as we're through the door, Sully glues his nose to the floor and takes off, familiarizing himself with the space for the second time in the last week.

I drop the bag of groceries on the counter as my gaze floats around Claire's small apartment, something I haven't really had the chance to do despite having been in here a few times. It's homey and warm, glowing with floor lamps and a set of twinkly lights framing her sliding balcony door. Everything is hues of light blues and creams and there's a large bookcase in one corner, so filled to the brim that books spill over onto her coffee table. The wall behind her couch is covered in dark wooden shelves that look ridiculously similar to the furniture Casey makes, and on each shelf are pictures and little artifacts.

Inspecting each picture carefully, I smile at the way Claire's personality bubbles over into each one. There are pictures of her and Casey when they were little, and her and Charlee all the way from kids to adults, and tons of pictures of Vivi. I chuckle at one picture of Claire locked in a headlock by Casey while Vivi hits him over the head with a shoe.

Then there are the pictures of her parents. Her mom is her twin, just as Vivi is. That long, wavy mess of auburn, those piercing, bright green eyes. She's even got her dimply smile. The shelves overflow with photos of the woman I'll never meet, but the one that makes my heart ache is of her in the hospital, head wrapped in a scarf, eyes sunken in. She looks exhausted but, my God, nothing can wipe the smile off that woman's face when she's got her kids flanking either side of her bed, Casey's lips pressed to her head, Claire's cheek resting on her shoulder.

"Aaahhh!"

I spin at the wild cry, finding Vivi tearing down the hallway, arms in the air, wrapped up in footie pajamas, her damp hair combed back. Bending, I catch her in my arms, hugging her tight as I lift her in the air. She smells so good, so fresh, and I cuddle her harder, burying my face in her hair.

Vivi touches her finger to a photo of Claire's mom. I remember that Claire said she died six years ago, so I know that Vivi's never met her, but she still says, "That's Gamma." She points to the ceiling. "She in heaben and she bootiful like me."

I kiss her nose. "You are so right, darling."

She squeezes my cheeks with her chubby little hands. "We hab pizza?"

I lean my forehead against hers and whisper, "Uh huh. And guess what else?"

"What?" she whispers back, wide eyes darting between mine.

"Ice cream sundaes."

Her sweet face lights up with a gasp. Then she screams in my face. "Auntie Claire! We hab i-cweam!"

Claire walks into the room, laughing. "Ice cream? Oh my goodness, you're being spoiled, you lucky little girl!" She gives Vivi a quick tickle.

"I show A'wy Gamma in heaben," Vivi says, thumbing proudly at her chest.

Claire's eyes flicker, gaze settling on the picture of her mom in the hospital bed. She clears her throat, looking between us. "And did you tell Avery that you're named after Grandma?"

I widen my eyes and gasp theatrically, because kids like that kind of shit. "You are?"

She grins and nods, dimples popping. "Bibian."

Claire giggles and tucks a loose tress behind Vivi's ear before kissing her tenderly on the forehead. Her lips linger there, eyes fluttering closed. "Vivian. Just like Grandma." She turns to me and smiles after a quick pump of her chest. "Thank you for bringing everything. I feel badly."

Vivi slides down my body and runs over to Sully. The two of them drop to the floor and start rolling around. They're adorable together.

"Why do you feel bad?" I ask as Claire follows me around the island, watching me empty the ingredients onto the counter.

"Because." She gives me a sheepish smile, fiddling with the messy bun on top of her head. Pink tints her cheeks. "You paid for everything today, and now you're bringing over your groceries and making us dinner."

"So? I don't mind."

"I know, but…" She doesn't finish her thought. Her palm presses into the counter while she crosses one ankle over the other. She pinches her bottom lip, eyes on nothing in particular.

I pull her hand off her mouth. There's no reason for her to be embarrassed. I don't often throw my money around, but a cheap diner breakfast, food from the market, passes to the zoo, and ingredients to make pizza literally don't make a dent in my wallet, whereas it probably would to her. Though she'd probably never say it or complain, because she likes to have these special days with Vivi, I can tell that much.

"I'm not concerned about the money and I like to do it. Don't worry about it, please."

Her eyes lift to mine. "Okay. Thank you."

I'm actually surprised she can afford this place. It's one of the smaller units, but this city is ridiculously expensive on a normal day. Toss in a newer, high-end condo smack dab in the middle of the action in downtown Toronto, and shit, it's not even close to affordable unless you're making six figures, or damn well close to it. I know Dex pays Claire well, but…not that well.

"Weekends with Vivi take their toll financially," Claire admits quietly. "I know I don't have to do all this stuff, the breakfasts out, the zoo, and Casey always tries to pay me for babysitting, but…" She shrugs. "I like to, and I don't like to ask for help." She peeks up at me, her expression stuck somewhere between timid and grateful. "You helped me out, but that wasn't my plan when I invited you today. I don't want…I don't want you to think I'm using—"

I cut her off before she can even finish that sentence, because that thought has never once crossed my mind. With other girls? Yes. In fact, almost every single girl I meet. But Claire and I had already had many…*physical* encounters before she discovered I was rich. She was quite literally shocked speechless when she found out I lived in one of the penthouses. But even so, I suspect she still doesn't fully understand how financially blessed I actually am.

"I don't think that, Claire, and I never would. First of all, you didn't invite me today—I invited myself. I mean, for fuck's sake, you tried to run in the opposite direction, or have you already forgotten?"

A soft giggle puffs from her mouth as she runs the tip of one fingernail over her plump bottom lip. "I did no such thing."

I arch a brow and grip her elbows, tugging her into me until our noses touch. "You did, actually. It's a good thing I do whatever the fuck I want."

Her breath hitches in her throat. "Yeah. It's irritating."

"You're irritating," I counter.

"Only because you irritate me to the point that I need to become irritating."

"I like to irritate you."

"I know. That's what's so irritating about you."

"How many times are we going to say the word irritating before we kiss?"

Her brow quirks, that coy redhead biting her lip. "Waiting for you. It's *irritating.*"

Cheeky girl. I grip her neck and bring her lips to mine. They're soft and welcoming, like they've been waiting for me all this time. I don't know how to describe it, she just feels so…cozy. Like I'm right where I'm supposed to be every time I'm kissing her. I've honestly lived through my twenties not knowing if I'd ever feel this way about a person, and now here she is, in my arms after appearing out of thin air. The last thing I ever want to do is let her go.

Vivi tugs on my shorts. "You guys kissin' again?" She holds her palms up in a confused, innocent shrug. "I fink we was habin' pizza."

I snort a laugh. She's the cutest kid I've ever met, and her bluntness is oddly endearing. "I'll get right to it, princess."

Claire puts the Frozen soundtrack on the TV, videos included, and Vivi dances around the living room while I make the pizza dough. While it's rising, Claire leans her elbows on the counter, watching me cut up an assortment of different toppings.

"I didn't know you could cook."

"There's a lot you don't know about me." I wink. "Maybe you'll give me the chance to show you."

Her cheeks flush, nose scrunching with her smile. "How can I help?"

"Um…" I purse my lips side-to-side, eying the ball of fresh mozzarella. "Wanna shred the cheese?"

Straightening off the counter, she laces her fingers together, stretching out her hands. "Big job. Think I can handle it?"

"Smartass," I quip with a smile and a peck on her cheek. Both cheeks warm under my lips before her gaze falls to the floor. "Why do you do that?"

"Do what?"

"Blush and look away every time I kiss you when you're not expecting it."

Yup, there she goes. Her cheeks flame red as she trains her gaze on her pretty pink toes. I tip her chin up, forcing her to look at me. I want an answer.

"I don't know. It just...catches me off guard, maybe?" She doesn't even know why.

"Then maybe you should just expect it always from now on, so you're never caught off-guard," I suggest. *Because I want to kiss you always, every time I see you. I want you to be mine, Claire.* I'm so close to saying the words, but I've got to be honest: I'm a little scared. I've never been scared before, not in this respect, and it's not a feeling I'm comfortable with. I'm still trying to navigate through the newness of these feelings, what this could mean for me, for us.

For the first time in a long time, I feel like I have something to lose, and that's simply unthinkable when it comes to Claire. Sure, the speed with which she tore into my life, took over my brain, carved a direct path to my heart is confusing, but now she's there, and the thought of this not working out is just kind of...terrifying. Plain and simple.

While the pizzas are in the oven, I get a front row seat to Vivi's dance recital. It's...interesting. And hilarious. Claire's seen it a thousand times, so her eyes are trained on my face, watching my reaction. I'm smiling so hard my cheeks hurt, and I have to rub at my eyes to keep the tears from leaking. Claire's sitting there grinning like a goofy, beautiful idiot while she watches me watch Vivi.

"Good, isn't it?"

"I'm not sure there's an appropriate word to describe this," I admit. "I need to show your brother." I pat my shorts down, looking for my phone.

"Oh," Claire murmurs, suddenly all bashful, twirling a wave around her finger. "You left it on the counter when you went to get Sully."

I haul my ass off the couch and retrieve my phone all while wondering why talking about my phone has Claire shy right now. And then I see the text message from my mom on my locked screen, sent over an hour ago.

Mom: *Care to tell me why your sister got to meet Claire before your own mother did?!?! What have I ever done to deserve this? I BIRTHED you!*

I glance up at Claire who immediately looks away, twirling a loose wave around her finger, telltale sign that she's seen this message. Oddly enough, I don't give a shit. Harper already ratted me out this morning. Maybe if Claire knows I've talked to my mom and sister about her, she'll finally understand that I want something more with her.

I mean, I haven't given up on fucking her. As soon as she gives me the go-ahead, I'll be inside of her in two seconds flat.

Still, I record Vivi's dance and send it off to Casey, telling him how fantastic his daughter is. He responds almost instantly with a text and a picture of him and his dad, cigars in their mouths and beers in their hands. I'm a little jealous.

Casey: *Shit dude, looks like you got stuck with babysitting duty. Would have been better off with us.*

Me: *Hahaha. Looks fun. Next time.*

Casey: *Definitely. Who's driving you crazier, my sister or my daughter?*

I topple to my side on the couch when Claire practically crawls onto my lap, pushing on my shoulder to read my messages. I hold the phone away from her and cock an amused brow. "Excuse you."

"Stop texting my brother!" She swipes for my phone and I grab her wrist, holding her hand above her head as I fire off another text message, one she can see clear as day.

233

Me: *Your sister. Always your sister.*

"You ass!" She knocks me backwards and climbs on top of me, grabbing at my phone.

Leaning backwards over the couch with my arms above my head so I can keep texting, I enjoy the way Claire squirms all over me. It's doing a lot of things to my body, naughty things that should never happen in the presence of a toddler.

"Don't swear," I mock. "Your niece is right there."

"She can't hear," she seethes. It's true. Vivi's so wrapped up in her dance, screaming her lungs off to the music.

Casey: *My dad says if you can handle Claire, you'd be a worthwhile reason for him to come to Toronto for a visit.*

I flash my screen at Claire. "Your dad wants to meet me."

"Urgh!" She presses her chest to mine, wriggling all over me while she reaches for my phone. My dick jumps in my pants. He wants to play, and I can't say I blame him.

Laughing, I flip her over, pinning her beneath me on the couch. "Gotcha."

Claire's ankles hook behind my knees, her eyes hooding as her tongue peeks out, dragging across her lower lip.

"You want me to kiss you right now," I murmur.

Her eyes move between mine. "Yes."

"Say it," I order softly. "Tell me what you want."

"I want…I want you to kiss me, Avery."

Well, I'm sure as hell not gonna turn down that opportunity. I bend my neck, the tip of my nose grazing against hers, our mouths just barely brushing. Her lips part on a raspy exhale that makes me smile, makes my chest roar with need. I slant my mouth over hers and—

The timer on the oven goes off. Fucking timer. Fucking pizzas.

"*Pizza!*" Vivi shrieks. She runs over to us, grabbing my arm, giving it a violent shake. "Pizza time! Pizza time! I luh pizza time!"

She rubs her belly with her little hands while she sings her pizza song and then pretends to bite at the air, making munching noises.

The spunk that lives in this one has me wanting to be damn daddy one day sooner rather than later, and I realize I'm well on my way to certifiably insane.

Vivi and Claire both hum happily while they eat their pizza, and by the time we're done with ice cream sundaes, Vivi looks like she needs another bath. She's covered in strawberry ice cream and chocolate sauce, a couple rainbow sprinkles glued to her sticky chin. Claire takes her to the bathroom to clean her off and quietly warns me that Vivi will probably ask me to stay and watch Frozen with them. She tells me she's giving me a heads up in case I need some time to think of an excuse to get out of it.

Vivi shuffles down the hallway with her dog stuffie and a blanket tucked under one arm, her thumb in her mouth. "You watch Fwozen wif us, A'wy?"

"I would love to," I tell her honestly, scooping her up in my arms. I don't miss the hint of a smile that plays on Claire's lips when she realizes I'm not leaving. I also sure as shit don't miss that she's changed into pajamas—tiny little shorts and the same baggy concert tee from the spider incident. She looks ridiculously and effortlessly sexy, her face scrubbed fresh, cheeks pink and freckly from our day in the sun.

I settle on one end of the couch with Vivi in my lap, and when Claire curls up on the opposite end, Vivi holds her hand out and gestures to her.

"Over here," she tells Claire. "Sit wif us."

Claire clears her throat and slides slowly across the couch. Too slowly. I wrap one arm around her waist and she lets out a little yelp as I jerk her over to my side. She slides her arms around Vivi's body, holding her close, and then lets me hold the both of them in my arms.

235

I'm struck again with the feeling that this is exactly where I'm supposed to be, right here, right now. Three weeks ago, I would have laughed in someone's face if they told me this is how I'd be spending a Saturday night.

Vivi passes out thirty minutes in, snoring softly against my chest, leaving me free to ignore the movie, although it is surprisingly entertaining. Disney did good.

"How long have you lived here?" I ask Claire, looking around her lived-in apartment.

"Three years," she answers, curling her feet up under her butt.

"Do you like it here?"

"I love it as far as condos in Toronto go, I guess. I mean, I'm more of a country girl, or suburbs at the very least, but it is kinda fun to be in the middle of all the action. It's so busy here. And loud," she adds with an unimpressed face, nose scrunched up.

My hand trails along her shoulder, finding a loose strand that's tumbled down her neck. I twirl it around my finger. "It is loud. I've lived here all my life, but in the suburbs with my family until I moved out for school. You get used to the noise eventually."

"Yeah, I think I kinda already am." She's pensive for a minute. "I'll miss this place though. It's been a good home to me for the last three years."

My fingers halt in her hair. "Miss it? Are you going somewhere?"

"No. Well, yes. Well…I don't know. I think I'll probably…have to. Soon, anyway."

"What do you mean?" I don't want her to leave.

"It's just, I mean…this condo was kind of a gift. An incentive, I guess, from Dex. Part of him coaxing me here was that he paid the first year's rent on this, and the security deposit. After the first year, Aaron moved in. But now…" She shrugs. "I just don't know how much longer I can keep up the rent on my own, that's all."

"Maybe Charlee can move in?" I suggest.

Her brows rise. "Avery, there's only one bedroom."

"Oh. Right." I flash a wicked grin. "Not that close, huh?"

Her eyes narrow and she pinches my shoulder, making me laugh.

"Well, I've got three bedrooms, two of them unused. You can use one of them. Or you can use mine." I wag my brows.

"Very funny," she murmurs, turning back to the TV.

I have to actually shake the idea from my head, because it doesn't sound half bad. We're not even dating. She won't even admit she likes me.

When Vivi stirs a few minutes later, Claire scoops her up to take her to bed. I kiss the bleary-eyed redhead on the forehead and watch as Claire carts her off down the hallway.

She comes back ten minutes later and I'm sitting there awkwardly, wondering if she'll want me to leave now that Vivi's gone to bed. Truthfully, it's the last thing I want to do. The time on my phone tells me we've been together for a little over twelve hours, and I'm not even close to being done with her.

She pauses to pat Sully on the belly and scratch behind his ear. He gives her a long, lazy lick up her arm and then drops his head back to the rug. Poor guy's done in after all the dancing and rolling around with Vivi.

Claire lets out a tiny yawn and shakes her head as if to shake the sleep away as she walks over to the couch.

"Is that my cue to leave?" I ask her, but she sinks down to the cushion beside me.

"Not if you don't want to."

"I don't want to," I whisper.

Pulling her against my chest, I lie down on my side and curl my body around hers. My eyes are on the TV, but I don't have a clue what's happening with the talking snowman and the funny reindeer anymore. All I can concentrate on is the way beautiful woman I'm currently snuggling the shit out of feels in my arms.

"Are you even watching?" Claire asks after a few minutes, her body trembling under my fingers as they run a path up and down the outside of her thigh.

"Not even a bit," I admit.

She giggles, wriggling free of my hold, and reaches for the remote on the coffee table. When she turns the TV off, the room settles into a soft darkness, lit only by the lingering bits of the fading orange sunset, the floor lamp in the corner of the room, and the twinkly lights around the patio door. Her face glows in the dim light and she gives me the shyest little grin, though she's trying so hard to bite it back.

"Setting the mood?" I ask, my lips grazing her ear. "Or going to sleep?"

"Not sure yet," she breathes.

"Can I make the executive decision?"

She shivers in my arms. "Okay."

CHAPTER TWENTY-SIX

Avery

Sweet holy hell, I'm about to have an uninterrupted, sober, take-my-time make-out session on the couch with the girl of my dreams. I'm pretty fucking psyched about it and I think she knows it by the way her breathy giggle washes over my face when I flip her onto her back and settle between her legs.

"No Vivi to interrupt my kisses?"

Claire shakes her head, fingers dancing up my neck, sinking into my hair. "Fast asleep."

"Mmm." Dropping my lips, I kiss along the edge of her jaw. "Nobody trying to bust through the office door?"

"Nuh-uh."

My teeth graze her earlobe. "And you're not gonna push me away and pretend you don't like me?"

"That's always a possibility," she says on a sharp inhale. "I can never be sure."

I chuckle, low and throaty, in her ear. "You always surprise me, that's for sure." I bury one hand in her hair, tugging her elastic loose, and my other hand slides under her shirt, grabbing her waist. "You are truly the most beautiful woman I've ever known, Claire."

Her fingers slip from my hair, falling to grip my biceps as she flusters, the smiling on her face turning into a frown. "I-I...I'm...not," she finally finishes quietly, her voice laced with sadness, heartbreak.

Rocking back on my heels, I pull her onto my lap. "You are, actually. For a thousand reasons, from the freckles on your nose right down to the way you treat Vivi as if she were your own." My nose skims across her cheekbone and I let out a soft exhale. "I'm sorry about Thursday night, Claire."

She turns rigid on top of me. "Oh, no." She dismisses me with the wave of her hand and then tries to scoot off my lap. I grip her hips tight, refusing to let her go anywhere, to lose this moment. "You don't owe me an explanation."

"I do, actually."

"No, it's…I mean…Wyatt talked to Charlee about it, so…it's all good. Plus, it's not my business anyway, even if she was your…date."

"But she wasn't my date and it is your business. I had no idea Sam was going to be there, and I declined her invitation to see her several times prior to that. I spoke to her before I left and told her I wasn't interested."

She's quiet for a moment, her green eyes lifting to mine, studying me with a little crease in her forehead. "You didn't have to do that. We're not…I mean, you know." The word she's looking for is *dating*, and I know that, of course. The thing is, I think that's exactly what I want to be doing with her.

"I wanted to. I only have eyes for you, Claire. You were the only woman I wanted to be with on Thursday night. And last night. And today."

Her mouth pops open, forming a little *o*.

"I didn't like seeing you so upset. Can you forgive me?"

"There's nothing to forgive," she says with the soft shake of her head. When I give her a look, one that tells her that her forgiveness is what I need, she smiles up at me. "I forgive you. Can you forgive me for not answering the door when you came to talk to me after?"

My eyes narrow playfully. "I knew you were hiding behind the door." I sweep a kiss across her lips. "I forgive you. I also forgive you for blatantly ignoring my offer to drive you to work the next morning."

Her eyes roll up, hands plunging into my hair with a gentle tug. "Shut up and kiss me before I kick you out."

"Yes ma'am."

Kissing Claire is like seeing in color for the first time. I've done this countless times with countless women, but it's never been like this. It feels new and exciting, exhilarating, like I'm not sure where each turn is going to take us. Each sweep of my tongue is cautious but purposeful, the dust of my fingers over her side, her silky skin, familiarizing themselves with her body, memorizing it.

My hands slide over her ass as I gently tip her onto her back, laying her down on the couch. Her legs fall open for me, inviting me between them, and the second I settle there, her heels press into my ass, forcing me closer. I close my eyes and pull away at the warmth that spreads from her center to mine, reminding me to take this slow before I accidentally pressure her into taking this somewhere she's not really ready to go.

"What?" she muses, fingers raking through the waves on top of my head.

"I just..." I lick my lips, peering into her gaze as it swims with desire and curiosity, an enticing mixture. "I'm happy to be here with you. That's all."

Her smile lights up her face. "Stop being cute, Mr. Beck. It does things to me."

"What kinda things?" My body quivers under her touch as her hands snake under my t-shirt, fingertips ghosting over the muscles in my abdomen, my back, like she's memorizing me just like I'm memorizing her.

She blushes at my question, and at my unrelenting gaze, turns her head away.

"Don't do that," I whisper. "Don't be embarrassed. Look at me."

She's stubborn though, and I think she always will be, at least in some ways. That's why I have to slide my palm along the edge of her jaw, turn her face back to mine. The questions that dance in the shadows of her face, causing her brows to furrow, the hesitation that brings about the crease in her forehead, has my mind racing.

Is it just physical for her? Or is it more? I need to know.

241

I sweep my lips across hers and then move down her neck, teasing and kissing until I find the pulse point in there. "Does it do things to you here?" I ask, though I already know the answer—I can feel it pulsing wildly against my lips.

"Yes," she says on a wispy sigh.

I make my way down her body, pushing her shirt up her ribcage. My eyes settle on her creamy stomach, the soft curve of her hips, the jewel in her belly button. I kiss a path around her belly, finishing in the center. "What about here?"

"Yes."

Finding her hip bone, I bite down gently before covering it with my tongue, sucking on it. She moans and writhes beneath me. Lifting her leg, my lips trail down the center of her silky thigh, then back up the inside, enjoying her garbled cry when I shift her sorry excuse for pajama shorts and close my mouth over the juncture of her thigh.

"And here?" I press a delicate kiss to the spot between her legs where I know she's positively aching for me right now. The material is warm and damp against my lips and I can smell her arousal. She's wet, and the thought alone makes my cock jump in my shorts.

The muscles in Claire's stomach jump and she whimpers, fingernails biting into my shoulders as she watches me between her legs. "Yes," she squeaks in a tiny voice.

I sit up on my knees and grab hold of her hips, tugging her down the couch to me. Leaning over her, I pull the neck of her oversize tee off her shoulder. Brushing my lips over top of her heart, I swear I can hear it, feel the way it hammers away in there. "What about here, Claire? Does it do things for you here?"

Her mouth opens and closes like she's not sure how to answer, or maybe she's just surprised by the question. Her sage eyes bounce between mine, cheeks rosy as she fumbles for words. "I...I..."

"I need to know, Claire. I need to know if I do the same thing to you that you do to me."

"The…the same thing?"

I nod, placing her palm over my heart. If it's beating as wildly as it feels like it is, throwing itself at my sternum like it's trying to jump right out of my chest, I know Claire's going to feel it.

And the look on her face tells me she does. Her fingers curl over my shoulder and her palm presses flat to my chest. Her lips part with a soft, "Oh," and she sucks in a shuddering breath.

"Yeah," I say on a quiet chuckle. "That's all you, sweet strawberry." I smile down at her while I smooth my hand over her hair, curling the tips around my finger. "Tell me you feel it, too."

"I…I do, Avery."

And that's all I need to know. I haul her up to me with a grunt and our slow, steady make-out session turns wild and frantic, tongues shoving, fighting for power, hands everywhere. Claire grabs the hem of my shirt and rips it over my head, throwing it somewhere behind me. Her fingers run all over my chest, my abdomen, curving and dipping along every ridge, making me crave her touch.

"You're so ridiculously good-looking it's not even funny. I fucking hate how perfect your body is," she growls, shoving me backwards and climbing on top of me.

I laugh, deep in my throat, my hands sliding over her ass, squeezing her to me while she assaults my neck, my chest, licking, nipping. "Really seems like you hate it."

"No. I love it. It's infuriating." Her mouth opens on my shoulder, tongue lashing out, teeth pressing into my skin, causing my fingers to dig into her plump cheeks before I deliver a swift slap to the ass.

"You bite, I bite back," I growl into her neck.

"Counting on it," she taunts.

Flipping Claire onto her back, I crawl over her. "This shirt is coming off." I yank it over her head. "And this bra." It follows the shirt quickly.

I have to sit back and drink her in. I've touched her, sure, but I've never seen her like this, so openly on display. I've never seen the perfect swell of her tits, the little pink rosebuds that decorate them, tightening right before my eyes. She's so perfect staring up at me, her unruly waves fanning out around her, teeth pressing into her bottom lip, those damn dark lashes she's peering up at me from beneath.

"Perfect," I mutter before dipping my head.

The second my mouth closes over her nipple, a moan rips up her throat, tumbling from her lips as she arches up off the couch, pushing further into me. Her fingers plow through my hair, legs wrapping around my back while I take my time teasing each nipple. I pinch, I roll, I tug. I suck, I nip, I lick. Claire goes wild, wild, wild.

She's making so many noises, whimpering above me, whispering my name, and my ego soaks every bit of it up. My mouth moves down her body, tongue swirling, tasting, and her stomach clenches beneath my lips. I pause over her shorts, my fingers curling over the sides of her waistband, and peek up at her.

Her cheeks turn rosy as she bites her lips and nods.

Pulling those sorry excuse for pajamas down her legs, I groan and drop my forehead to her stomach when I find she's not wearing any panties.

"What?" she asks quietly, voice barely a whisper.

"I've been waiting since the moment I laid eyes on you to get you naked. And now here you are."

Her thighs squeeze together, and she shifts backwards, pushing lightly on my shoulders.

"Underwhelming, right?" Claire has the audacity to cough and avert her gaze. Her hands move to cover herself up.

I make a sound in my throat, half growl, half groan, and grab her hands, lacing my fingers through hers. "Nuh uh. Fuck that, Claire. You're a thousand times more perfect than I could have ever imagined. I'm gonna love on every single inch of this body."

Before she can object, I get to work on my promise, two fingers swiping through her wet folds, enjoying the whimper that tumbles from her lips when I spread her arousal over her clit, swollen with need. I watch her face as my thumb circles her tight nub, pink painting her cheeks as she holds my gaze. When I plunge two fingers inside of her, her lips part with a soft cry, her head falling back into the cushions.

Her hips arch up, pushing me deeper into her like she just can't get enough of me. I can't get enough of her either, so it's cool. For the first time since I've known her, I feel like we're on level playing fields.

Her walls start tightening around my fingers, pulling them deeper, her mouth opening as I slap my free palm across it, stifling her cry as my name comes spilling out.

Claire pushes up, her mouth capturing mine in a searing kiss, and the second I remove my hand from between her legs, her fingers start fumbling with the button on my shorts, hands sliding over my ass, pushing them down my hips.

I don't really know what's happening, where this is going. Does she…does she want to have sex? This isn't exactly how I pictured our first time, on her couch while her niece snores forty feet down the hall. But the rest of it is exactly how I pictured it—wild, frenzied, frantic. Two people who need each other more than anything and are finally giving in.

With two hands on my chest, she shoves me backwards and crawls between my legs, licking her swollen lips. Her eyes widen when they settle on my cock, standing tall and proud.

"You're so…you're so…" She lifts her apprehensive gaze to my face.

I smirk. "Stroke my ego, baby," I say with a wink, 'cause I know what she's thinking. I am the opposite of small, just like the rest of my body.

She rolls her eyes. "You are such an egomaniacal ass sometimes," she says, but her teasing tone tells me she doesn't really mind, and when she dips her head, I hold my breath.

Until my morals kick in, reminding me she's still hurting, unsure. I grit my teeth, dropping my head back with an inner groan. My dick wants to punch me in the face for what I'm about to do.

My hands find her hair, lifting her face. "Claire, baby, what are you doing?"

Her brows tweak and she sends a pointed glance at my cock. "Returning the favor?"

"It's not *a favor for a favor* type of deal. It's just about enjoying each other, enjoying this. You don't have to do anything you don't want to."

"Okay," she says slowly as I pull her in, kissing her softly. "But Avery?" She pushes at my shoulders, prying her mouth from mine. The corner of her mouth lifts in a smile that's nothing but cheeky, a wild girl ready to make some naughty decisions. "I want to."

"I—" My sentence dies on the tip of my tongue the second her hand wraps around my shaft, and I'm already ready to blow. This isn't going to be good.

No, that came out wrong. It's going to be fan-fucking-tastic. What's not good is that I'm about to last an embarrassingly short amount of time. I've been dreaming about this fucking hand wrapped around my cock for the last two weeks, and it's finally happening.

Claire's hand moves slowly, up and down, her thumb sweeping over the head of my cock, spreading a drop of liquid over my tip. Her eyes lift to mine, that sparkle that shines there letting me know she's been thinking about this as long as I have.

"Fuck," tumbles aimlessly from my mouth, and I hiss as her tongue darts out, licking up that drop of liquid. Her mouth sinks slowly, taking me in, and I gather her hair up, gripping it in my fist so I can see her.

I swear to fucking God, I've never seen anything more beautiful than Claire. I wish I could take a picture so I could remember this moment, the way she's staring up at me, watching me come undone at the mercy of her perfect lips wrapped around my cock, her tongue swirling over my length.

With my hands tangled in her hair, she lets me guide her up and down, showing her how I like it, though it's really unnecessary— she's doing a bang-up job all on her own. She pauses on the tip, sucking it, rolling her tongue along the slit, and then takes me as deep into her throat as she can handle.

"Okay, okay," I cry, pushing her off me and sitting up. "You're fucking killing me." As much as I'd love to come in her mouth, I'm not ready to wind this up just yet. I'd prefer a little more unrestricted time with her and her magnificent body.

Claire giggles and licks the moisture from her lips, climbing onto my lap. Her arms wind around my neck as she settles on top of me, rocking her hips while we kiss. I grab a handful of her ass, rolling into her, and kiss along the edge of her jaw until I find the spot below her ear I'm looking for. She throws her head back and moans when I suck on it, grinding her center down on mine.

I'm well aware that I don't have a condom on and my dick is rubbing all up over her, slipping through her wet folds, brushing against her clit. Before it slips inside, I need to wrap it up, but I don't have a condom here because, oddly enough, this is not at all how I thought this day was going to end when I went for my run this morning. I'm also not sure this is where we should take this tonight, that this should be anything more than pleasing and teasing, hot and heavy without the fucking.

247

I tip her backwards and open her legs, settling between them. Gripping the base of my cock, I sweep the tip over her drenched pussy, both of us groaning, because I at least need to fucking *feel her*, get this close. And fucking Christ, she feels amazing.

Claire sucks her bottom lip into her mouth, and I see those wheels turning, working, as she mulls over the same unasked question as me: what are we doing here? Where is this going? How far are we willing to take this tonight?

"Avery," she whispers, timid fingers climbing up my chest. "I want you to…will you…fuck me?"

I try not to let my body go rigid with pure shock and wild anticipation. I cup her head and kiss her tenderly. "It's okay if you're not ready, Claire. I can wait. We can wait. I'm fine with waiting." I think the amount of times I just said that word tells her waiting is the very last thing I want to do right now.

Her eyes flicker, and I watch that self-doubt creep in. I know I'm not the one that put it there, but still, I hate that it exists. "Do you want me?"

My fingers wrap around her biceps, keeping her in front of me when she tries to shift backwards. "Do I fucking want you? I've wanted you ever since you walked that ass into that bar two weeks ago. Haven't I made that obvious?"

My mouth dives down, kissing her hard. Breathless, I tell her, "The second I saw you, I wanted you. You strolled in with this shy smile on your face and I swear every fucking head turned to look at you when you threw your head back and giggled. I watched you talk to the bartender and all I wanted to do was throw you over my shoulder and walk out of there with you and you hadn't even looked in my direction yet." I push her hair off her face, gathering it in my fist. "I want you, Claire. I want you so fucking much. All of you."

Her eyes soften and glisten, and my heart feels like it's swelling with…something…inside of my chest. What is that? Why does it feel that way? Instead of sinking inside her, all I want to do suddenly is scoop her up into my arms, kiss her all over, hold her, ask her to be mine.

She strokes the side of my face, her fingers moving over my jaw, brushing across my lips, and something catches in my throat.

"I like you so much," I blurt out. Who the hell am I? God, this is maddening. I don't know how to do this. Am I messing everything up? Are things going too fast? Am I saying too much?

She blinks up at me, heat creeping up her neck. Her mouth opens and—

Vivi's sudden, loud cries pierce the air. "Auntie Claaaire!" she wails. "Claaaire!"

Our eyes lock for a long moment before Claire lets out a soft exhale. "Yes, baby?" she calls back to her niece.

"I…hab…nightmare!" she chokes out between heartbreaking sobs.

Dropping my head, I reach for Claire's shirt on the floor and tug it over her head, shifting it down her stomach, around her hips. Covering her up is the last thing I want to do, but this is important. Vivi's distressed and she needs her auntie.

Claire's gaze swims with guilt, and maybe a bit of disappointment, too. At least I'm not the only disappointed one here. Though I'm sure it would be perfect, this isn't how this should go anyway, so I'm taking this as a sign. I want to have her all to myself, wine and dine her, show her just how much I want her, how much she means to me.

"I'm coming, honey," Claire assures Vivi.

Pulling her up off the couch, I crouch on the floor below her, dragging her shorts back up her legs.

"I'm sorry," she mumbles, one hand raking through my hair.

I cup the back of her neck, pulling her forward for a kiss. "Not a thing to be sorry for."

Once I'm dressed, I join Claire in the bathroom, washing my hands while she frantically brushes her teeth, cringing at the way Vivi sobs, waiting for her.

I place my hand on her back when I'm done washing my hands. "I can get her."

She shakes her head, gathering her hair over her shoulder as she leans over the sink and rinses her mouth out. She washes her hands and pats herself dry on the hand towel sitting on the counter. "Thank you, Avery, but it's okay."

Nodding, I watch her disappear into her bedroom before I head down the hallway, gathering up my things from the kitchen. I look up when Claire walks back in with Vivi on her hip, all red-eyed and sopping cheeks, clutching her stuffie to her chest.

Sully wakes, stretching in his spot on the rug, and ambles over to Vivi, his head tilting to the side like he wants to know why she's crying and how he can make it stop.

She drops her hand, letting him lick her, and lets out a weak giggle. "Silly Sully bear." She sniffles and wraps her arms around Claire's neck, hugging her tight while she looks at me with the most heart-wrenching expression on her beautiful angel face. "I hab nightmare," she whispers.

I step up to her, rubbing my palm over her back. "I'm sorry, baby. It wasn't real. You've got Auntie Claire now. She'll keep you safe, snuggle you right up in bed."

"You too?" she asks, her hopeful voice cracking.

My mouth tugs up in one corner and I pull her from Claire's arms, hugging her against my chest. Claire watches us with an expression I can't quite decipher. "I'd love to, but I've gotta take Sully home to bed."

Vivi peers up at me with the most ginormous eyes, tears still streaming down her pink cheeks. "But what if dere's monsters?"

"Impossible. I just did a quick monster check. But if you need me, you let Auntie Claire know and I'll come right down to save you. Promise."

"Otay," she says quietly. "I luh you, A'wy."

"I love you too, sweet girl." I squeeze her once and kiss her nose before handing her back to Claire, who looks near tears herself. I pull her into me, pressing my lips to her cheek, and then her lips. "Goodnight, beautiful ladies."

"Goodnight Avery," Claire murmurs. "Thank you for spending the day with us."

I pause in the doorway with Sully at my side, smiling back at that breathtaking woman. "Thank you for giving me the best day I've had in a long time."

CHAPTER TWENTY-SEVEN

Claire

"You've reached Gavin. Sorry I can't come to the phone right now. Leave a message and I'll call you back. Unless you're one of my kids, then I'll probably leave you hanging for a while." My dad laughs to himself on his voicemail recording. *"I'm just kidding, Claire. Don't yell at me."*

The recording manages to tip one side of my mouth the way it always does, but it doesn't stop the drum of my fingers on my desk as I end the call. I open my message thread with my dad, gaze falling over all those unanswered text messages. It's not like him to not answer, which is why that pit in my stomach sinks a little deeper with worry.

My dad has always been the kind of parent you dream of having. Devoted, supportive, full of unconditional love and ridiculous Dad-jokes. Leaving my hometown to move to Toronto was one of the hardest things I ever did, but he pushed me the way he knows I need to be pushed sometimes. Still, I hate being away from him, and we talk all the time.

I fire off a text message to my brother, letting him know I still haven't heard back from Dad. He responds nearly right away.

Casey: *I'm sure he's fine, Claire. We had a busy weekend. He was tired when I left yesterday afternoon.*

I know that, of course. Building furniture and staying up too late to smoke cigars and drink beer with your son will do that to you. Still, it isn't like him to not respond for so long.

Casey: *Vivi and I can head down later today if he still hasn't answered.*

I head to the lunchroom to make myself a cup of coffee in an attempt to clear my head and relax. I'm sure it'll have the opposite effect.

I look up when Dex pops his head into the room.

"You okay?" He gestures at the Keurig machine that's currently brewing heaven. "That's, what, your third cup?"

"Guilty," I murmur. I wrap both hands around the warm mug and inhale with a content sigh. "Can't help it today."

"Still haven't heard back from your dad?"

I shake my head and lean against the counter. "How did you know?"

"I was talking to Casey earlier." He grins. "He might've mentioned something about you driving him nuts."

I roll my eyes. "I'm worried; that's all."

Dex nods and glances at his watch. "Hey, why don't you take off? Go home, check on him."

"I can't do that, Dex. It's only two."

He waves me off, striding toward me and prying my mug from my hands. He dumps it into one of the tumblers from the cupboard, screwing the lid on before he shoves it back in my hands. "Take your coffee to go and give Gavin shit. Nobody makes Claire Thompson wait."

Chuckling, I wrap an arm around his middle. "Thanks, Dex."

Jordan Valley is less than an hour away, nestled in the heart of wine country in Niagara. Unfortunately, traffic is an absolute crapshoot out of Toronto on any given afternoon, which means that a commute that takes fifty minutes on a good day takes me over two hours today.

I pull up the long gravel driveway, spotting my dad's truck, and I'm out of my seat and flying up the steps of the porch before I know it.

Turkey, my dad's dog, leaps to his feet the second I fling through the door. Whimpering, he bolts across the old hardwood, leading me into the living room, where my dad is…fast asleep on the couch.

I crouch down in front of him, examining the deep lines on his face, the sun he got this weekend. With my hand on his shoulder, I give him a gentle shake. "Dad."

His eyes flip open and he jolts in place. "Claire." His arms come up, nearly knocking me to my ass as he rubs at his face, then sits up. "Claire, honey, I didn't know you were coming over. What time is it?" He fumbles with the strap on his wrist.

"It's almost five, Dad. On Monday."

He blinks his bleary blue eyes at me. "Ah, shit. Did you call me?"

"Several times," I tell him with the arch of my brow as I take the spot he offers next to him on the couch. "Casey left twenty-four hours ago." I bury my fingers in Turkey's fur. "Please tell me you haven't been sleeping this whole time."

Dad shakes his head and gestures at the dog. "He woke me up for his breakfast and his usual run around the yard, but then I guess I…I was still tired, so I laid down for a little rest…" He climbs to his feet and I shoot up, steadying him as he wobbles. "I'm fine, I'm fine," he insists stubbornly. "Gotta get his dinner ready and let him outside."

I push him back down. "I'll do it, Dad. Just relax." Patting my hip, I call Turkey into the kitchen with me and fill his food and water dish. When he's done devouring his dinner, I let him out into the yard. Checking the fridge, I discover nothing but fruit and veggies, which is great, except that my dad needs to eat something of substance. I run my fingers along the edge of my mom's apron, which still hangs from its spot on the wall all these years later, before I head back into the living room.

"Do you wanna go out for dinner, or stay in and order pizza?"

Dad's face cracks with his wide grin. "You're staying?"

"Of course I'm staying." I wink at him. "Word on the street is you've got a fridge full of cold beer in the garage."

Dad stands, embracing me in a hug I can't help but sink into. He's warm and safe, one of my favorite places to be. "Pizza and beer with my favorite daughter."

"I'm your only daughter," I murmur against his shoulder.

"And that's why you're my favorite."

"How you doing, gorgeous gal?"

With my cheek pressed to the cool walnut desk, my eyes lift toward the voice in the doorway, calling out to me. Charlee takes one look at me and grins, rolling her eyes as she strides toward me, the largest iced coffee I've ever seen in her hands.

"You're being dramatic," she says, slapping the sloshing, enticing liquid down in front of me. "Get up. You'll be fine."

"Fine?" I doubt it.

She plops down in the chair across from me. "Yes, fine. You, Claire Thompson, will be fine." She gestures to the giant coffee that's calling my name. "And now you can't complain that you're too tired to go."

She's got me there.

With my palms flat on my desk and my head tipped down, I slurp greedily at the iced coffee. The sound I make when that delicious vanilla cold brew coats my throat is something akin to the noises that were flying from my mouth on Saturday night when Avery's magical fingers went to town between my legs.

"I just think maybe I should go home. You know, get an early bedtime. I need it." It's not a lie. By the time I made it back to Toronto last night after leaving my dad's, it was nearly midnight. I don't know if you know this about me, but I get myself easily wound up. It was after one in the morning by the time I was finally able to drift to sleep. I normally need a solid eight hours to function properly.

"So why don't you head home now and take a quick nap before you go? Dex won't mind."

I quirk an amused brow. "Oddly enough, I feel responsible for working the hours your brother pays me for."

"Yeah, but this is technically work tonight."

I snort-choke on my iced coffee. "Right. If you believe that, you're just another victim who's fallen into Avery's trap."

Speak of the sexy devil, my phone vibrates next to my elbow, Mr. Beck's name scrolling across my screen. Actually, it's not his name. It's his picture. Specifically, him and Vivi eating pancakes at the diner. I don't know why I did that—take the picture, set it as his contact picture. I've been staring at it for the last three days.

"What?" I grumble in a tone that is not at all conducive to what's going on in my body right now at the thought of talking to him on the phone, or seeing him in a few hours.

"Oh Claaaire, you know what it does to me to hear that sweet, chipper voice of yours," Avery teases.

I bite back my groan and fold over the desk, cheek back on the wood, right where it belongs. "What do you want, Avery?" My eyes flick up to Charlee when she starts snickering.

Avery chuckles. "Just making sure you're not backing out on me."

"And why would I do that? It's just work, right?"

"Yup. Work." I can hear the stretch of truth in his words.

"You know I can see the stupid smirk on your face right now, don't you?

His laughter fills my ear after a short pause. "I just had to actually check that I didn't accidentally have you on FaceTime. It's for work, Claire, I promise. Ask Dex if you don't believe me. He wants to get started on the expansion of the patio right away."

I grumble a bunch of words that aren't words at all. I know he's telling the truth. Dex already has a contractor—once again, courtesy of Avery—who can start next week, but we need to

256

finalize some plans. The contractor said he can have it done in two weeks if he hauls ass, which means it'll be ready before the Canada Day long weekend, giving us time to get all the kinks worked out so we can kick off summer appropriately here at the brewery.

Which is why Avery texted this morning saying he needed me to come by his office this evening to help him out. That's the excuse he's using, at least. It definitely has nothing to do with me turning down his request for a dinner date on Sunday and Monday. Last night, I had a good reason not to, but Sunday? None. No reason other than that I was trying desperately to convince myself that the universe had thrown me a sign on Saturday night when Vivi woke. A sign that I wasn't ready, wasn't prepared to handle whatever bits Avery had to offer.

And I'm *not* ready. Not ready to open myself up to the chance of my heartache, to show him the parts of myself that I'm not sure he'll like. Hell, I'm not even sure *I* like them.

"I'll see you in a bit," I tell him. "And I'm tired so I'm not in the mood for your games tonight," I add with conviction. Loosely translated: *I don't have the strength to ward off your advances today and my heart can't take having your body, so please, for the love of God, keep your hands to your hot-ass self tonight.*

Avery just laughs. It's rumbly and sexy and irritating. "Sure thing, little Miss Strawberry. See you later."

Tossing my phone down, I slink back in my chair with a groan, tipping my head backwards.

"Literally the most dramatic person I've ever met," Charlee murmurs.

"Avery? I know."

"No," she laughs. "*You*. Why are you dreading this so much? You had an amazing day with him Saturday."

"He paid for everything," I say, absentmindedly twirling a lock of hair around my finger while I think back on Saturday. "I feel so

257

guilty. Vivi reels him in with her sweet baby talk and that little pout of hers, and he winds up dishing out all this dough."

"I don't think money's an issue for Avery Beck, Claire."

"I know he makes a lot, but still. He probably spent a couple hundred bucks, if you include the pizza and ice cream sundae stuff he brought over later, too. That's a lot. It makes a dent in anyone's wallet."

Charlee snickers, stretching her arms across my desk. "You know how much money he makes, right?"

"I don't know, a couple million? Maybe five? Five million?" I'm just throwing out numbers here. I have no freaking clue, but he lives in a penthouse and has a car that drives him around at his beck and call. Then again, five million seems like a lot, so I'm probably wrong.

Charlee's snicker turns into a full-blown howl as she drops her face to her hands. When she looks up at me, she wipes actual tears from her eyes. "Claire, Dex told me Avery and Wyatt each took home thirty-two million last year, *after* business expenses."

I don't know how it happens, because I'm sitting down. I'm literally sitting my entire ass in a chair, but somehow, I wind up clutching the edge of the desk, fingernails biting into the wood to keep me from tumbling straight to the floor when the chair flies out from underneath me.

Thirty. Two. Million. In one fucking year?

"I can't believe you didn't know."

"Well, excuse the shit out of me for not going around asking people how much money they make!" I'm shrieking. I can't control my pitch. It just makes Charlee laugh harder, clutching her stomach while I'm over here vibrating with shock. "Stop laughing!"

Her hands come up in surrender. "Sorry, sorry. I can't help it. Well, at least we know you don't like him because of his money." She wipes at the last of her tears. "So, are you gonna sleep with him?"

258

My eyes flip up to hers. I'm still reeling over his salary, and she wants to know if I'm going to take him for a ride? "No, Charlee! That's a thirty-two-million-dollar penis!" Probably worth every damn penny, too.

"Expensive dick aside, for the last three days you've been whining about how much you like him. I'm impressed and quite frankly proud of you for finally admitting how bad you've got it for him. He told you he likes you, which means the feelings are mutual."

Dropping my gaze, I watch the way my fingers drum the desk. "I'm pretty sure that Vivi interrupting us was a sign."

She nods. "I agree. A sign that you shouldn't fuck when your toddler niece is down the hall. That was the sign." She shrugs simply. "Now she won't be down the hall. You can be as loud and as rough as you want."

"He doesn't really like me," I murmur. "He just got caught up in the moment."

Even as I say the words, I'm not sure I believe them. It was in the way he studied me so intently, brows drawn together, like he was trying to figure me out, or maybe his feelings. I can understand that, at least, because I've been trying to figure out my feelings for him since he walked into the brewery that fateful Monday and I realized he wasn't going to be a man that I just kissed and would never see again.

It's not that I don't want him, that there's no part of me that doesn't want to see where this has the potential to go. But I just can't. I'm falling. I know that now, after everything on Saturday. Hard and fast. Avery may think he likes me, but chances are, after he has me, the feeling fades and he realizes I'm just another girl. There's nothing special about me, and I don't really want to be around when he figures that out, just like Aaron did.

I glance up at Charlee when I realize she's been silent for a long time.

"What?" I ask quietly, my cheeks warming as my nerves get the best of me, wondering about the expression she wears, a mixture of disappointment, grief, and exhaustion.

Her mouth twitches with a small frown as she shakes her head. "I just hate what Aaron did to you. And I'm not talking about cheating, though I also hate that. I'm talking about the way he knocked down your self-esteem to the point that you can't fathom that Avery would actually have real feelings for you despite his words, which he's adamantly backing up with his actions. That you're not allowing yourself to give into happiness and the possibility of new love, all because you're afraid it'll be pulled out from underneath you at any moment. You're living your life waiting for your next heartbreak. I hate that Aaron did that to you."

I know she's right; it's not even up for debate. The problem is that I don't know how to change that. I thought it would be easy to get rid of him. And he might be physically gone, but the effects he's left on my brain, my body, my heart are lasting, and maybe permanent.

I don't want to give him that control over me, let him own these parts of me. I need him to take that shame and dread and self-doubt and get the fuck out.

But it's so much easier said than done. The damage is done, etched into me.

Sometimes I'm not sure I'll ever find my way back to myself.

CHAPTER TWENTY-EIGHT

Claire

"Good evening, Miss Thompson." The doorman at the foot of the building sweeps me inside, leading me over to the elevator.

"How do you know I'm Miss Thompson?" I ask while I wait, watching the numbers creep down as the elevator makes its way to me. My fingers are tapping away a random, irritating beat on my messenger bag, because—*surprise, surprise*—the walk over here did absolutely nothing to clear my head or steel my spine. I thought the fresh air would be good for me. Instead, I sucked in every breath the way I did my inhaler after my cross-country meets back in elementary school.

He gives me a sheepish smile. "Mr. Beck, uh…he described you to a T." He gestures to my hair. "Your hair, and your, uh, freckles." His anxious chuckle is oddly endearing. "Plus, I remember you from the first time you were here. Can't forget a smile like yours."

I smile back at him. He's sweet and friendly; his face says it all. "Thank you, Kirk," I murmur, eyeing his name tag as I climb into the elevator.

My heart thuds as the elevator climbs to the forty-first floor. Is everyone this nervous when they're on the way to see their crush, or is it just me? Also, what if I need to get out of here quickly and the elevator's all the way downstairs? What will I have to do—run down forty-one flights? I'm wearing three goddamn inches on my feet. Why is Avery up so high?

The elevator dings, doors sweeping open, and I'm greeted by a ridiculously jovial Wyatt.

"Well, hey there, sweet thing," he says with amusement glittering in his soft eyes, scooping me into his arms for a hug.

"Can't you stay?" I kind of whine.

He chuckles in my ear before he pulls away. "Scared of being alone with him, eh?"

"Psssh." I wave him off. "Of course not." *Terrified.*

"No toddler to chaperone? There's no telling *what* might happen," he says with the flick of his brows over his wide baby blues.

"Oh, shut up." I shove him on the shoulder and strut by him. "I thought I liked you, Wyatt."

His grin is devilish as he disappears behind the elevator doors, his words following me down the hall. "Have fun!"

The glow of the evening sun and the soft light filtering down the hallway from Avery's office are the only thing going on in Jones & Beck tonight. The floor is empty and eerily quiet, so silent I can hear the swift strokes of Avery's fingers on his keyboard.

Part of me considers turning around and making a run for it down those stairs I was just hating on in my head, but if I can hear him working on his keyboard, that means he definitely heard me and Wyatt. He knows I'm here. Running and hiding seems futile at this point, and I'm wondering if that feeling is indicative of more than just this night together.

So I inch my way down the hallway at a ridiculously slow pace. When I reach his door, my fingers curl over the frame and I peep inside.

Ugh. Fucking ugh.

Those glasses. I swear to God, you think the man can't possibly get any more attractive, and then he throws on those dark-framed reading glasses and my heart drops right out of my vagina, slithering its way across the hardwood floors to him. Probably not the best visual, but an accurate picture nonetheless.

Avery's eyes are trained on his computer screen, his fingers— though I can't see them—flying over the keyboard at a wild pace. How does that impress me? I don't know, but it does. Fast typer?

Apparently that makes me wanna drop my panties. It's a new one, even for me.

His suit jacket is nowhere to be seen and his crisp white shirt is unbuttoned at the neck, his light blue tie hanging loosely.

"You gonna come in or watch me from the doorway?" he asks without lifting his gaze.

I falter for a moment before I tell him to shut up and stroll into his office, slinging my bag down and collapsing onto the couch, crossing one leg over the other, as well as my arms. I glance up to find him watching me with his stupidly adorable little side smile. I look away and pretend to be interested in his office décor, as if it's my first time seeing it. It's not.

My hands glide over the cool leather cushions. I've never felt anything so soft in my life. It's like butter. I bet it was more expensive than my rent.

"Is it satisfactory?"

"Huh?" Our eyes meet, and the air is knocked from lungs. He's so handsome, it hurts.

Avery inclines his head toward where I'm sitting, brown eyes shining with mirth. "The couch. Is it to your liking? You're really feeling it up over there."

"Feels like butter," I muse, sweeping my hands over it again. "Speaking of butter." I flop over onto my belly, kicking my heels off and swinging my legs in the air. "Got any popcorn for me?"

His brows rise. "Speaking of butter, got any popcorn?"

"Yeah. Leather, butter, popcorn. You see the connection, don't you?"

He laughs softly and pulls open a drawer. He looks at it, maybe a little too thoughtfully, one finger tapping on the edge of his desk while he chews his bottom lip, and then closes it. "Nope. Sorry. Fresh out of popcorn."

I pout, clutching a fluffy throw pillow to my chest, burying my cheek in it. "Any other snacks?"

"None. Did you not eat?" Could he not look at me like that over the rim of his glasses?

I shake my head. "Just a giant iced coffee." The effects are finally starting to wear off and I'm slowly coming down from my caffeine high. All I can think about is food, which means we need to get this over with so I can go home and devour the Lucky Charms cereal in my pantry. I say it's for Vivi, but…it's for me.

"Well, that's sure to tide your hunger over," he retorts, tone laced with sarcasm.

Sitting up, I pull my bag onto my lap and pull out my trusty binder, organized to a ridiculously obsessive-compulsive level. Projects at work are the only thing I'm this anal about organizing, and I don't know why. Maybe it just brings me a sense of calm to be able to control one area of my life without much push-back.

"'Kay. Let's get to work." I flip open the cover, running my finger down the color-coded tabs until I land on the bright yellow tab. Yellow for sunshine, sunshine for patio. Everything makes sense in my head.

My mouth opens with a sound of revelation as my head slowly rises. "Purple for patio. That woulda made so much more sense."

Avery's quizzical gaze lands on me. "I'm not even gonna ask," he murmurs, before unplugging his MacBook and sinking down beside me. His arm and thigh brush up against mine with annoying zing that makes my skin sizzle. He flashes me a crooked grin. "Hi."

"Must you sit this close?" I'm distracted by that tiny dimple in his chin, right underneath the light dusting of scruff on his jaw. My teeth skim my lower lip without my permission.

"I must."

My brows inch up. "You must?"

He leans forward and brushes his lips against mine. "*Must.*"

Trying so desperately to smother my smile, I dive right into the work before us. We go over Dex's hopes for the space and Avery shows me three different plans from the contractor, with three drastically different price points. He also shows me the email from Dex saying to let me choose.

"How can I choose?" I ask, exasperated, as I look at the options for what feels like the hundredth time. I roll my bottom lip between my thumb and pointer finger. "This is so much money and it's not mine to spend. It's not my brewery."

"No, but Dex trusts you and your opinion."

"Do you have a limit? You know, how much you guys are willing to give him."

He shrugs. "Sky's the limit as long as we think it's worth it."

Leaning over Avery so I can stare at his computer screen, I examine my favorite option all while trying not to get high on the smell of him. Cedarwood, lime, and just…sexy man smell. So delicious and enticing, I could bathe in it.

"That one's your favorite," Avery observes quietly. "You can't stop looking at it."

"It's also the most expensive," I reply with a heavy exhale.

"Sure, but why do you like it?"

My fingers trace the wooden archway that looks toward the harbor, the stone walkway leading to it, the beautiful garden the contractor thought would be a nice addition. Scrolling over, I study the amazing outdoor bar. The space, this way, is massive and incredible.

"I think this one would be perfect for weddings and big events. It's almost two different spaces." Pointing to the walkway, the garden, the wooden arch, I say, "This could be for ceremonies. And this—" I gesture to the big patio, the bar, the addition of the built-in fire pit, "—could be for receptions, parties. If we really want to expand that way, I think this one makes the most sense."

Avery's head bobs. "I agree. I think it would be a mistake not to choose this one. It opens the space up and allows for a higher head count, which means more money in the summer, regardless of whether or not there's a wedding. But I also think it would be a

265

mistake *not* do weddings and big events. It would open up a whole new business for Cherry Lane."

"Yeah," I agree, stifling a yawn. "You're kinda smart. Who knew?" I tap his chin dimple, unable to hide my smile.

"And you're kind of smartass," he says with a chuckle. He moves back to his desk and I watch his forearms flex under his rolled-up sleeves while he types away, barely blinking at the screen. He stops every few minutes to readjust his glasses and glance my way.

I know I should be doing something, but I'm crashing right now. The sun is dipping low and the little sleep I got last night is hitting me hard. I think that coffee might have been a terrible idea. Now I just feel hollow, hungry, and a little braindead.

I rub my eyes and curl up on my side, snuggling into a pillow.

"What's wrong?"

"Hmm?" I murmur sleepily, gaze drifting across the office, catching the way Avery's watching me.

"You're tired and...not snarky."

I sit up slowly and shake the sleep from my head. "Sorry. I had a really long day yesterday."

"Physically long or emotionally long?"

I wonder how he knows to ask that question. More than the day being long and physically taxing, it took an emotional toll on me, which is really what's knocking me out today. I feel mentally fried.

"Both," I admit quietly.

He takes his glasses off and looks at me. I mean, *really* looks at me, gaze drifting up and down my face, my body. Turning back to his laptop, he clicks around on it for a moment before snapping it shut and packing it in his bag. He climbs to his feet and stretches his arms over his head, scrubbing a hand across his torso.

Dear God, he's flawless. Could those pants fit him any more perfectly? I can almost see the outline of his—

Don't go there, Claire. Don't fucking go there.

266

Retrieving his suit jacket from a closet I didn't know existed, he slings it over his arm and strides over to me, holding out his hand. "'Kay. Let's go."

I blink up at him. Three times, in case I'm dreaming. It's fairly likely I've passed out here on his couch. "Go? You're ready to go home?"

"No, I'm ready to take you to dinner."

"D-dinner? What? No." My head wags back and forth. "I can't—"

"You can't or you don't want to?" Taking my binder from my lap, he stuffs it into my messenger bag.

"It's not that I don't want to," I insist meekly. "It's just…we can't." I rub my forehead and avoid his gaze.

"We can, actually, but why don't you tell me why you're so adverse to going on a date with me." He crosses his arms over his chest and stares down his nose at me, mouth set in a firm line. "It's just dinner. I like you. You like me."

He actually seems a little mad, or maybe it's hurt. Maybe both. It's possible I've finally pushed him too far. Maybe he's finally getting fed up with waiting for me.

But I never asked him to wait.

"We just spent thirteen hours together on Saturday and it was great," he continues. "Or is it because we'd be alone?"

"No." The lie tastes bitter. It's definitely because we'd be alone, and in a romantic setting, without work to divide us. I don't know how to be alone with him. Not without falling more in—

No. Nope. Nuh-uh.

Three weeks, Claire. It's been three weeks. Stop yourself right there, little lady.

But his big brown eyes are peering down at me, and the confusion that lingers there makes my knees weak. I hate that he looks hurt right now.

"It's just, I…I…" My brain searches for an excuse, and the one it comes up with is piss-poor at best. "It's just that I'm not hun—" I stop mid-sentence when my incredibly loud, grumbling stomach cuts me off.

Avery cocks one self-satisfied brow, the corners of his mouth lifting. "Hungry?"

Shit.

CHAPTER TWENTY-NINE

Avery

Ladies and gentlemen, I did it. I fucking did it.

Right now, Claire Thompson, my favorite little redhead, is sitting beside me in the back of a car, on our way to a restaurant.

For dinner.

It's fucking happening.

Turns out, all I needed to do was get her incredibly tired and hungry. She gave in pretty easily. Lesson learned. I'm locking that one up top for future reference.

She sits in silence, fingers drumming on her bare knee, emerald eyes suspect as they flit around, but she's here, so that's all that matters. She keeps glancing over at me, opening her mouth like she wants to say something, but then clamps it shut, shaking her head and proceeding to stare out the window. I have to fight the urge to laugh at her several times throughout the fifteen-minute car ride.

Taking her hand, I lead her into the restaurant and request a quiet booth in the back corner, which only serves to spike Claire's anxiety. She can say that it has nothing to do with not wanting to be alone with me, but I wasn't born yesterday. I know she's afraid of admitting her feelings for me. What I don't know is whether she's more afraid of admitting them to me, or to herself.

The waitress brings over a bottle of red wine and I watch Claire shift back and forth in the booth, pinching her bottom lip between her fingers. I can't handle this, the nerves, the uncertainties, so when the waitress leaves, I slide up beside her and watch her eyes widen.

"What are you doing?"

"Sitting beside you."

"I can see that," she says with a hint of snark.

"Then why did you ask?"

"Oh my God." Her jaw snaps shut and she rolls her eyes. Her shoulders sag before she gives me a sweet smile, dimples popping in those freckly cheeks of hers. She's a freaking conundrum. "You drive me crazy."

"Likewise," I murmur, throwing her a wink that only makes her smile broaden.

This is what I need, her giving it up, dropping those walls, being herself, sass and all. She needs to relax, and when she's pulling on her lips and barely speaking, I know she's anything but relaxed.

"Now kiss me."

She blinks those soft, sage eyes up at me, lashes fluttering. "Pardon?"

"You heard me." I take a sip of my wine, waiting. Her face is priceless.

"But I…if…" She flusters, stopping to lift her glass to her lips for a long pull. She drains half the glass. "If you want to kiss me, why don't you just kiss me?"

"Because I want *you* to kiss me."

"We're in public."

I raise my brows, making a show of looking around. "And?"

"Well, I—"

"I don't care where we are or who can see. And by the way, I can be just as bossy as you. So fucking kiss me, Claire, *now*."

Her head goes backwards like I've just slapped her. She blinks a few times, face riddled with shock.

But then she leans forward, one tentative hand sliding over my thigh, the other curving around my neck. Her lips touch mine timidly at first, once, twice, and I think that's all she's going to give me when she pulls back a fraction.

But then she dives in, her tongue sweeping inside my mouth. Frantic hands grip the collar of my shirt and she shifts, turning in the booth until she's practically crawling onto my lap.

Chuckling, I cup her face and push her back just a touch. "Easy. We're in public," I tease, throwing her own words right back at her.

Her cheeks tint with color and she raises a trembling hand to her swollen lips. "I'm sorry."

"It's all good. Just trying to remind you how you feel about me." I flash her a cheeky grin.

She folds her arms over her chest. "In case I've forgotten?"

"Well, yeah. It took me, like, four hours to get that far on Saturday."

Her face breaks and she smiles. It turns into a snicker and her arms fall to the table, fingers wrapping around her wine glass. "You act like I'm so tough to crack."

"You are *incredibly* tough to crack. I've never met a more hard-headed woman in my life. Except maybe my mom, my sister…Yeah, you'd fit right in with them."

"Trying to fill your life up with stubborn, hotheaded women?"

I press a kiss to her lips. "That's exactly what I'm trying to do."

It's interesting to watch Claire open up, to watch her slowly melt into a state of comfort. The more she talks, the more those green eyes of hers light up. She gradually sinks against my side, though I'm not sure she even knows what she's doing. Her hands wave wildly around her face when she talks about growing up with Casey and Charlee and Dex and all the trouble the four of them got into.

"Once we had a huge kegger when my parents were away. It was wild. I mean, with three years between us, something like a hundred people were there."

"You had enough room for that many people?" I ask, swirling some of her sweet potato fries in her chipotle mayo before popping them in my mouth.

She shakes her head, stabbing at my goat cheese stuffed chicken, and I watch her lips close over her fork. She moans, eyes falling closed. "Mmm, so good. No, our house wasn't super big or anything, but we lived on a nice property. An acre and a half and no close neighbors. Our parties were famous at our high school."

She offers me a slice of her pork tenderloin, and I take it off her fork.

"Anyway, the cops showed up. We ran. Me, Casey, Charlee, and Dex, all of us." She lifts one shoulder. "It worked out because they couldn't give us a ticket because there was nobody home at the time that lived there. We sat in a Tim Horton's until almost four in the morning and ate, like, twenty Timbits each. By the time we got home, I'd completely forgotten about a hole in the wall some drunk idiot put there with his elbow. I was freaking out. Casey took a piece of paper, drew a big happy face on it, slapped it over the hole, and told me to chill the fuck out," she says with a laugh, eyes sparkling at the memory.

"You guys have always been close? You and Casey?"

Reaching over my plate, she scoops up some of my loaded baked potato and I watch her push it past her lips.

"Uh-huh," she mumbles. "Always. But even more so when Vivi was born. Dex actually let me reduce my hours for a while so I could help Casey out. Watching my brother learn to be a dad was so much fun. I remember this one time, Vivi was only three days old, and we were arguing over how to put her diaper on best. We were literally screaming at each other, getting right in each other's faces."

"I can't imagine that," I say sarcastically while I let my mind conjure up the scene she's describing. She might be half her brother's size, but she's a sassy ball of fire when she wants to be.

"Shush," she orders after a giggle, nudging my shoulder with hers. "Anyway, Vivi all of a sudden just pooped everywhere. Like, all over the place. It was green and black and all up and down her legs. It smelled so bad that we both started gagging and Vivi just laid there and stared at us with those huge green eyes of hers, spit bubbles pouring out of her mouth. We ended up laughing so hard I couldn't breathe. I was crying hysterically. Once we put her to bed, we drank two bottles of wine and talked about how awful we were but how much we fucking loved her."

"You do love her," I say softly.

She nods, the corner of her mouth curving. "Like she's my own."

"You'll be a good mom one day."

Her nose scrunches. "Is it weird that I worry about having kids one day? I look at Vivi and I honestly can't imagine loving someone more than her. It's kinda scary, loving someone so much."

I can't stop staring at her. She's fucking stunning and every word she says just makes her even more so. A light blush creeps up her cheeks when she catches me.

"Stop looking at me like that," she whispers, spearing my chicken again.

I pop more of her sweet potato fries into my mouth. "Can't help it.

A giggle to our left makes us both look up.

"You guys are super cute," the waitress says. "Do you always share your food?"

I'm never surprised by Claire's ability to take her blush and amp it up a good couple notches. Her eyes shift to mine and she gives me a nervous, wobbly smile. I smile back. This is the second time we've been out at a restaurant together, and the second time we've shared meals.

"Always," I answer the waitress. "She's a food thief."

"Am not!" Claire gives me a swift smack to the chest.

I give the waitress a wide, pleading look. "That's what she does to me when I don't share."

She laughs and continues on her way, leaving Claire glaring at me.

"You're an ass," she says like that's the last thing she actually thinks, trying to smother her laugh. She heaves a sigh and pats her belly before giving me a loopy, carefree grin, her forest eyes twinkling. "I'm so full."

I brush my thumb across her bottom lip. "You look happy."

"I...I am. I wasn't having the greatest day. You turned it around."

"And to think, you tried to say no." Taking her hand in mine, I trace over each slender finger. "What was up today? Why were you so tired? Physically and emotionally," I add, remembering how she'd nearly passed out on the couch in my office. She'd looked dead to the world, like she just couldn't be bothered. Beautiful, always, but worn out.

She studies me, gnawing on the inside of her cheek. "It's my dad," she finally says. "Casey left there Sunday afternoon. I called my dad in the evening but he didn't answer. Tried him a whole bunch yesterday. Nothing. Casey couldn't get a hold of him either. I was losing my mind. I took off from work a couple hours early and drove out through all that traffic. He was fucking sleeping. For almost twenty-four hours, aside from getting up to feed the dog." She shakes her head and sighs, pulling her hand back to scrub both of them down her face.

"Wow. He must've been tired, I guess."

"It's not that. I mean, it is, but...it's more than that." The heavy exhale she releases drains her in a way I don't like, a way that makes me worry about her. "I told you my mom died from cancer."

I nod. "Ovarian. You said it was kinda fast."

"Well, my dad had leukemia. Twice."

Oh, shit.

"Once when I was in high school, and again after my mom died. He's been in remission for a few years, but I've been worried about him lately. Sometimes he's fine for weeks at a time, and sometimes, like Sunday and Monday, he doesn't get out of bed for twenty-four hours. I think…" She sucks in a shuddering breath. "I think the cancer might be back, but I went with him to an appointment the other week and the doctor just kinda waved it off. Said we'd wait and see if anything changed in a couple months." Her brows pull together, creasing her forehead. "How stupid is that? Cancer's not something you wait for, especially with a man who's already battled through it twice. But my dad just keeps dismissing it, saying he's fine, not to worry."

Claire stares down at her hands for a moment before meeting my gaze again. "I'm just a little scared, I guess," she admits in the softest voice. "I don't want to lose him, too." She swipes at her eyes before her tears have the chance to fall. I wonder if it's less about trying to be strong and more about not letting me see the bits of her she tries to hard.

Her pain picks away at my heart, straining against my chest with a tightness I'm not familiar with. I can't imagine the struggles she's faced, the pain that's gripped her so tightly, the worry that seeps into her everyday life. Sometimes I wonder if she knows how strong she truly is.

Slipping my arm around her waist, I pull her into my side and kiss the top of her head. She makes a little noise in the back of her throat and melts into me, resting her head on my shoulder.

"That's really tough, Claire," I whisper into her hair. "He sounds like a fighter. Strong just like you and your brother."

"He is. The cancer doesn't bother him all that much. Losing my mom is what crushed him. But Vivi…she helped. I think she helped us all, really."

"She's one amazing, wild little girl. She can make anyone's day brighter."

"You really like her," Claire observes slowly.

"That's putting it lightly." That tiny spitfire owns a chunk of my heart.

Claire declines dessert, telling me she feels like she's popping out of her dress, and we ride back to the condo together in a comfortable silence, her hand tucked into mine.

In the elevator, my gaze never leaves her reflection. She keeps giving me the eyes, glancing up at me, biting her lip, and then looking away. She tries to say goodbye to me from the elevator, but I drag her down the hallway toward her door, brushing off her weak attempt.

"Whether you agree or not, this was a date, and I'm walking you to your door and kissing you goodnight."

And I do just that, pulling her into me by her hips, brushing my lips softly against hers at first, before I coax her mouth open, slipping my tongue inside. She sighs against me, and when she rakes her fingers through my hair, a shiver rolls down my spine.

I pull back and kiss her once, twice, three times on the lips. "Goodnight Claire."

She opens her door and slips inside, peering up at me from beneath her thick lashes, one dimple popping with her sweet, lopsided smile. "Thank you for dinner. I'm happy you were bossy tonight." Pressing up on her toes, she touches her lips to mine. "Goodnight Avery."

I watch her nose twitch with her bright-as-hell grin as the door closes, slow as fucking molasses, like she doesn't want to say goodnight yet.

And what the fuck am I doing? *I* don't want to say goodnight yet.

She's happy I was bossy tonight? Well, she's about to see a whole new level of bossy.

CHAPTER THIRTY

Claire

He's not asking to stay. He's not asking to come in. He's just…leaving. He's watching me shut the door in his face, and he's doing it with the goofiest grin on his handsome-as-sin face.

But it's the last thing I want to do. I don't want to say goodnight.

With a quiet, barely-there sigh, I push the door the rest of the way closed.

At least I almost do.

Until an arm shoots forward, shoving the door open, and Avery pushes his way inside.

He doesn't just come in. He pulls off his suit jacket and tosses it across the room to my kitchen island. He starts loosening his tie, stalking toward me while I stumble backwards, my anxious hand at my throat, feeling the wild thrum of my pulse. His once goofy grin is now a dangerous mix of dark and devilish, playful and needy, his wicked espresso drowning with desire.

"See, the thing is, Claire, I don't wanna say goodnight right now."

He whips off his tie and drops it to the floor. His fingers start working the buttons on his shirt and I watch, absolutely riveted, as each tug reveals a little more of his golden skin, the light smattering of chest hair, the hard lines of his collarbone, his glorious pecs. He keeps moving toward me, and I keep backing up. His eyes follow my every move, white teeth pressing into his full bottom lip when he flashes that sexy smirk.

"Y-y-you don't?" I sputter.

"No. Not at all."

"What do you wanna do?" It's a stupid question. I know what he wants to do. The same thing I want to do.

His smirk grows more wicked by the second. He clicks his tongue with the tilt of his head. "You know exactly what I wanna do."

"Me?" Feeling bold, even though I stammered the damn two-letter word.

He nods. "You."

Avery reaches for me and I freak out, blurting, "I don't have a condom!"

He growls and grabs my hips roughly, flinging me effortlessly over his shoulder.

"What are you doing?" I gasp, my arms winding around his middle.

He doesn't answer me, just stalks toward the front door, yanking it open and letting it slam behind him. He struts right for the elevator, doors sweeping open and revealing a young couple staring at us with the most stunned expressions I've ever seen.

I can only imagine how this looks. I'm hanging halfway down Avery's back, one of his strong arms wrapped around my knees while his free hand covers my ass—which is in the air—keeping me locked to him. His shirt is unbuttoned halfway down his torso, revealing how hard he works to look the way he does.

Avery gives the couple a nod. "Nice night, isn't it?"

The young man stammers for words, only coming up with sounds, while the girl beside him giggles.

"Not as nice as yours," the boy finally manages, his eyes sparkling with humor.

The girl whacks him hard on the shoulder, and I manage a snicker, even in this ridiculous situation.

They get off a few floors later and we continue up to Avery's suite. Sully barely lifts his head off his bed when Avery plows through the door. Kicking off his shoes, he strides down the long hallway to the last door on the right. He throws me on the bed and I bounce twice with a yelp.

"Take off your dress," he orders, peeling off his shirt.

"Bossy," I murmur, reaching back for my zipper.

His grin grows. "You have no fucking clue, Claire, but you're about to find out."

Apparently, I'm not moving fast enough. Avery grips my hips and flips me over, tugging the zipper down my back and yanking my dress over my head.

"Fuck," he mutters. A glance over my shoulder finds him scrubbing over his mouth with his hand. His eyes flick up. "Do you know how perfect you are? Don't fucking know if I can handle it."

His fingers make quick work of my bra, and suddenly he's curled over my back, tugging me up to all fours, palming my breasts while his lips slide down my spine. He pinches my nipples, rolling them between his fingers while I groan, pushing my ass back into him. I can feel him growing, the weight of him pressing into me.

He pulls my panties down my legs, pressing his lips to my backside, nibbling, kissing. His hand swipes over me from behind and he groans while I let out the world's loudest moan. I'm already ready to beg for more, to plead with him to never, ever stop touching me. Why in the hell have I been denying him this? Denying myself?

"Already. Fucking. Wet." He moves back up my body, his hot breath grazing my ear when he whispers into it. "I'm going to fuck you, Claire. I'm going to fuck you senseless, and you're not going to say no, are you?"

I whimper, because I can't with words right now. My body's going crazy. I feel like a live wire dipped in water.

"Tell me," Avery demands. "Tell me I can fuck you."

"Please, Avery," I cry out, fingers clutching the sheets. "I want you to fuck me."

He lets out a sinister chuckle. "Yes, baby.

I'm well aware that he's only said a few sentences, but nobody's ever talked to me like this during sex. Never. Sex with Aaron was always so...monotone, routine. The same, always, as if there were specific, set instructions that needed to be followed at all times. It was okay for a while, when it was still new, but even then...it wasn't great. I faked more orgasms than should be legal.

"First, I'm gonna fuck your pussy with my tongue," Avery says slowly, licking a path down the center of my spine. He gives me a sharp smack to my ass and dips one finger inside my heat, making me gasp and wiggle.

Fingers digging into my hips, I feel his hot, damp breath on my ass when he settles behind me. His tongue licks a slow, torturous path from my clit through my drenched, aching folds.

And then he feasts. His tongue is everywhere, swirling over my clit, diving inside me. It's too much, all at once, and I can't take it.

With a shove, he pushes me down onto my belly and flips me around.

"Head on the pillows," he directs with the jerk of his head while he drops his pants and boxers to the ground. He grips the base of his long, thick cock as it pulses and grows impossibly bigger before my eyes. Licking his lips, he watches me settle myself on the pillows.

"Open your legs, Claire. Let me see that pretty pussy."

Fuck, fuck, fuck. Is this for real? This is what I've been missing? I can already tell he's going to ruin me for every other man for the rest of eternity.

But I do as he says, spreading my legs wide for him as he crawls toward me. Sliding his arms under me, he loops them over top of my thighs and jerks my hips down. His grin is pure evil as he sinks to the mattress, his face disappearing between my legs.

"Tell me something, beautiful," he murmurs at the apex of my thighs. He lifts his head to peer at me, licking his glistening lips. He spears me with two fingers, and I cry out, clawing at his shoulders. "The first night we met, when I touched you, you were soaking wet. Do you remember that?"

I can't speak, so I just nod my head. Like, seventeen-thousand times. He smiles, because he knows.

"You seemed surprised, shocked even. You looked up at me with the widest eyes." He plunges his fingers deeper, harder, and bends his head to suck my clit into his mouth. "Why?"

I let out a low hiss at the feel of his voice reverberating against me, his hot breath rolling over my wetness with a sting, making my whole body tremble. "I…it's…it's embarrassing."

He thrusts hard, peering up at me with hooded eyes. "Tell me, Claire." The noise I make is stuck somewhere between a moan and a scream when he twists his fingers inside of me, curling just right and hitting that spot that makes my vision blur. "*Claire.*"

"I…he…he couldn't get me wet!"

Avery's eyes flicker but he never stops moving, making me shake, my walls clenching around his fingers, pulling them deeper.

"We had to use lube," I wheeze. "Otherwise, it…it hurt."

With a slight smile touching his lips, he bends and flicks his tongue over my clit. "But you're always wet for me."

"Always." It's a problem. Like a faucet with a drip I can't quite fix.

"Is that just because he wasn't a good lover, or is there something special about me?" His teeth press down on my swollen nub, tugging and pulling.

"Avery," I cry, my fingers pressing his head into my pelvis. "I can't…I'm gonna…"

"Tell me," he growls.

"It's both! Both! Please!"

"You wanna come?"

"Yes, yes! Ohhh, f-f-fuuuck," I stutter. My legs start trembling, sending me well on the way to noodle-leg territory, just like that night in the elevator.

Reading my mind, he pulls his fingers out of me and smooths his hands down my quivering thighs, murmuring, "Noodle legs," before he closes his entire mouth over my entire pussy.

And I'm coming. Jesus Christ, I'm coming.

I bend forward, tugging at his shoulders, trying to tear him up to me. "Please," I beg. "Please, Avery, I need you."

"Need me how?" he asks, wiping his mouth on the inside of my thigh. He climbs to his knees, sliding his hand up and down over his hard length.

Licking my lips, I reach for his hips. I need him closer.

He clicks his tongue and shakes his head once. "Use your words."

With a growl, I push up against him, grabbing his neck and jerking his face down to mine, smashing my lips to his. He grips my chin and rips my face away, holding me tightly.

"*Words*, Claire."

I don't think I've ever glared so hard in my life. I don't want to say the words, because I don't want to need someone the way I need Avery right now. It gives men a certain power of you, parts of your body, your heart, your brain. Parts I'm not ready to give up control of.

And when Avery chuckles at my expression, it just makes me angrier, livelier.

So I tackle him backwards, straddling his hips as I grind all over him.

But Avery's not having that. Quicker than I can say his name, I'm pinned beneath him, one hand wrapping around the base of my throat, his strong thighs squeezing my hips.

"I had a feeling it would be like this," he whispers.

I pant, swiping my tongue across my lips. "Like what?"

His face dips, tongue slipping into my mouth. "Passionate. Frantic. Obsessive. Wild. Because that's you and me, Claire. That's us. It's like we live in our own little wild world."

282

I groan, dragging my nails down his back. It's so true.

With a fistful of my hair, he tugs my face up to his. "Tell me what you want, Claire."

"I want *you*," I snarl, letting the words tumble from my lips. "I want you to show me how badly you want me. I want you to fuck me, and I don't want you to be gentle about it."

"Well, far be it from me to say no to you, my queen." He presses a lingering kiss to my scowling pout and rolls off me.

"Where-where are you going?" Desperate for his touch, his warmth, his body, I reach for him, unable to stop myself. *Fuck, Claire.*

His mouth tilts with a crooked smile, eyes drawing up and down my body. Opening his bedside table, he pulls out a condom, ripping it open and sheathing himself in one swift movement.

On his knees, he makes his way back to me. "I've been dreaming about this since I laid eyes on you. You have no fucking clue how much I want you, Claire."

"Then I guess you better show me."

He crushes me to the mattress under his heavy weight and I run my fingers up his arms, over the curves of his biceps, his muscular shoulders. I didn't know shoulders could be so sexy, but his are, all corded and knotty. I dig my fingers in, pulling my body up, rubbing myself against his cock.

"Are you nervous?" Avery asks, shifting back on his knees, wrapping my legs around his hips. Taking his cock in his hand, he rubs the tip over my clit, pushing through my folds, sitting just outside my entrance.

I should be, because that's all I've been feeling about this every single time I think about it, but... "No. Not anymore."

He smiles down at me. It's different, this one. Genuine, sweet and soft, just like his eyes right now, the crinkles around the edges. He looks...happy.

"Me neither, baby." He sweeps his lips over mine. "I feel like I'm right where I'm supposed to be." He smooths a hand down my hair and skims his fingers over the side of my face. "You sure you're good?"

I have to giggle. Ten minutes ago, this man told me he wasn't going to take no for an answer. Now he's giving me one last chance to change my mind, to back out. But I'm not going to. Not tonight. I'm taking what I want, because, shit, what if the world ends tomorrow and I never have another chance to feel this man moving inside of me?

Pushing up on my elbows, I whisper against his lips, "I've been dreaming about this just as long as you have."

Ah. There's that devilishly smug grin, the one that makes my panties wet. Except I'm not wearing any, and I'm already soaked.

And with one determined thrust, he slams into me, both of us moaning at the sensation of him filling me up, stretching me. I feel complete, fuller than I've ever been. It's like he was made for me, even though I shouldn't be thinking that. I shouldn't be thinking that at all.

But for tonight, I'm going to allow myself to pretend, to pretend that Avery is mine, that I'm his. That we belong to each other.

"Shiiit," he exhales, his lids fluttering closed. "Perfect. Just like I thought, Claire. Fucking perfect."

And when he begins moving inside me, my world starts to come tumbling down, one deep thrust at a time. Gripping my hips so hard I think I might bruise, he drives his cock into me, over and over again, each stroke harder and faster than the last.

Avery grabs one leg and throws it over his shoulder, leaning into me, his pelvis rubbing against my clit with each plunge, every roll of his hips, taking me right to the edge. I teeter, looking down, and then I free fall into oblivion.

His name falls from my lips as I explode around his cock. He swallows my screams with his mouth, and when he breaks away, he pulls out, flipping me over and jerking me to my hands and knees.

He pulls my head taut, his teeth grazing my ear. "Not done. Not fucking done, Claire. You're going to come for me again."

Without warning, he slams into me from behind, and just when I thought I'd felt it all, his body shows me just how much more there is. He hits every spot, making me tingle from the inside out with each powerful thrust. How does he know me so well? How does he know my body, like he designed it himself? He knows exactly how to work it, how to make me moan, shake, scream.

His hand glides around my hip, sliding over my belly, finding my clit. He rubs fast, furious circles while he moves inside me until the sensation is too much. I'm going wild, on the verge of collapsing. I can't support myself anymore. I start sinking down into the mattress and he growls, yanking me right back up.

"Don't you fucking dare." He curls overtop of me, teeth pressing into my back, tongue lashing out, covering the sting.

"Avery," I plead, fingers ripping at the sheets.

"You gonna come again for me, baby?"

"Yes, yes, yes," I chant, slamming my ass back onto his cock. Wrapping my hair around his fist, he keeps my head taut while he works my clit, his pulsing length swelling inside of me.

"Look at me," he demands. "Look at me when you come with me inside you."

As soon as my eyes hit his—like molten lava, so hot I feel them searing into my skin—my entire body shakes like an earthquake. I try to bite back my scream but my lip slips from my teeth on a strangled breath. His mouth closes over mine as I cry out his name and come undone around him.

Avery rips his mouth away with a curse, burying his face in my neck with one, two, three more destructive plows, and then he collapses on top of me, his arms like a vice around my body, his cock still throbbing inside me.

"Christ, Claire," he wheezes between panting breaths.

His lips sweep across my shoulder, up my neck, planting hot, wet kisses all over. I don't think I can move. My whole body is limp. I just breathe heavily, sucking in each breath like it might be my last.

"You okay?"

My grunt should be answer enough. No, I'm not okay. Never have I ever been fucked like that. Every fiber of my being is alive right now, sizzling.

Avery's low chuckle tingles against my neck. Pushing one hand between my belly and the mattress, he presses me to his chest as he turns us onto our sides. He nuzzles my neck, kissing me softly below my ear before tugging my lobe between his teeth.

"I didn't…I didn't know it could be like that," I finally manage.

"Mmm, me neither." I want to call bullshit on that. The man knows how to fuck. He's clearly…experienced. An expert, even. He *knew* it could be exactly like that. But he slips one hand under my cheek, turning my face to his, lips moving on mine. "There's something about you, Claire. I'm not sure there's even an explanation, but…you do something to me. To my body. You fucking wreck me."

You fucking wreck me. It's quite a euphemism. It's also exactly how I feel about him. Wrecked, like I'm not sure I'll ever survive him, but don't think I can survive without him, either.

Turning in his arms, I slide my hand along his jaw until my fingers thread through his messy waves. And I kiss him, slow and purposeful, wanting to feel, taste, every single bit of him. I suck on his bottom lip, nibble it, caress his tongue with mine. The kiss turns hungry quick, and Avery pushes me back down on the pillows, climbing over me as his mouth glides down my throat.

Slipping my hand down the hard lines of his abdomen, my fingers close over his thick cock, feeling it grow and twitch all over

286

again while Avery groans in pleasure, lips vibrating against my collarbone.

Sully trots into the bedroom, whimpering at the foot of the bed. He rests his head on the mattress, looking up at us with enormous dark brown eyes, tail wagging. Avery's gaze slides to mine and I give him a smile.

"I gotta take him out for a pee and get his dinner. But…" He dips his head, sucking one nipple into his mouth. His tongue swirls over my bud before tugging it between his teeth. "I don't wanna go anywhere."

With a giggle, I push him off of me. "Go take care of your dog."

Avery flops onto his back with an exaggerated sigh, one arm over his face. "You won't go anywhere, will you? 'Cause I wanna do that, like, twenty-five more times."

"I won't go anywhere," I promise him. "Except maybe to the kitchen for some water. I feel like I haven't had a drink in days."

He gives me a cheeky grin and rolls back on top of me. "Wore ya out, did I?"

"*I* wore *you* out."

"Yeah." He pecks my lips. "You did." Avery pulls himself from the bed and finds a t-shit and a pair of track pants, letting them hang low on his hips. Fuck, he looks so ridiculously good in sweatpants and an old tee. How is that even possible? He kisses me again. "Help yourself to whatever you want. I'll be back."

Climbing out of the bed when I heard the click of the apartment door, I let myself take in his space. His bedroom is massive, with a glorious en-suite bathroom, a glass shower with marble tiles. Opening up the balcony door in his bedroom, I step into the dark, starry night, letting the warm air wash over my naked body.

Walking down the hallway past the two other bedrooms, I find what I already know from being here on Saturday morning—his open-concept kitchen and living room is just like mine, except four times the size, with a dining area to boot. His space is impeccably decorated, perfect in every way.

I fill and refill a glass of water three times, draining each in a matter of seconds, gasping for air after I polish them off. Then my stomach grumbles. I don't know how I'm hungry; it wasn't that long ago that we ate.

Then again, he just fucked my brains out, so, I guess that earns me the right to a snack.

Pulling open his pantry, I grin when I find a box of popcorn. I shove a bag into his microwave and lean back on the counter, tapping my fingers on the cool marble while I wait, inhaling the buttery, salty smell wafting through the air as if it were a drug.

The second I shove a greedy, hot handful into my mouth, the condo door opens and Sully comes bounding in. Avery pauses in the doorway and takes me in, naked in his kitchen, shoveling popcorn down my throat.

"I'm sorry," I mumble around my mouthful of food. "So hungry."

His grin grows tenfold as he stalks toward me, taking me into his arms. He squeezes my ass and kisses my salty lips. "You can eat my popcorn any day, Claire."

Moving to the fridge, he pulls out some sort of raw meat and starts preparing Sully's dinner. "You better be finished that popcorn and back in my bed by the time I'm done feeding Sully," he throws over his shoulder.

"Is that an order?" I tease, throwing another handful into my mouth.

The only thing that moves is his head, twisting to look at me, all devil, no angel. "Yes, Claire, it is." Turning back to the bowl in front of him, he adds quietly, "You have approximately thirty seconds to get there."

"Thirty seconds? I can't possibly finish and get there in thirty seconds. You're setting me up for failure."

"You're wasting time, lovely Claire," he murmurs. I watch him bend, setting the bowl in front of Sully. He washes his hands before turning slowly to me, pulling his shirt over his head. He cocks one brow, looking a lot like he's about to devour me as he licks his lips. "You still standing there?"

The hand that's full of popcorn stops midway to my gaping mouth. As if I can move when he's standing in front of me, shirtless. I'm pretty sure I'm gawking, gaze falling to that V that's like a landing strip, leading right to the wildest ride of my life.

"Where should you be right now?" Avery stalks toward me and my breathing falters.

"Well, you…you…" I honestly don't have a single clue what my mouth is trying to say. I don't think my brain is even working.

"Where," he repeats slowly, "should you be…right now?"

I blink up at him when he stops in front of me. God, has he always been this tall? I'm craning my goddamn neck to meet his gaze, which is entirely intimidating, maybe even a little terrifying. "In the bedroom?"

He nods. "That's right. In the bedroom. Now go."

I keep staring, my jaw still hanging.

"*Go*, Claire, *now!*"

With a squeak and a jump, I throw my handful of popcorn in the air and take off at a run down the hallway, Avery hot on my heels. He catches me in all of three steps, throwing me over his shoulder. He tosses me down to the mattress and rips his pants off before pinning me to the bed with his muscular thighs, holding my wrists above my head.

With a smirk, he dips his head, running the tip of his nose across my cheek, down the line of my jaw. He pauses at my ear, his breath making me quiver with fear and lust. "I'm gonna fuck you so hard, all night long, tomorrow you'll need to sit your pretty, round, peach of an ass at your desk all damn day long because your legs will shake when you try to stand. How's that sound?"

"Don't make promises you can't keep," I whisper, trying my luck as I push his thick waves off his forehead.

His lips curl. "Baby, I've never wanted to keep a promise more in my life. Trust me."

And I do, because he does. Dear Lord, does he ever make good on his promise.

It's nearly three in the morning when I'm finally certain he's fallen asleep, one arm draped over my slick, sweaty body, his slow, steady breath coating my neck.

And that's when I start coming down from my high.

Avery's like my own personal drug, pumped up in my veins, coursing through my blood. But I'm already going through withdrawal, just thinking about tomorrow, or the next day, the next week, when he's had his fix and starts his detox, pulling away. The thought makes my stomach turn and my chest tighten.

So, very carefully, I peel my body from his, slipping out of his bed. Sully looks up at me, cocking his head to the side. He opens his mouth and lets out a long, squeaking yawn, shaking his big, burly head with a slow blink.

Finding my clothes on the floor, I dress silently, give Sully a kiss on his head, and disappear down the hallway and out Avery's door.

It's better for both of us this way; I'm sure of it.

CHAPTER THIRTY-ONE

Claire

Is this what people mean when they say they're walking on cloud nine? Are they secretly talking about that post-coital, *I just got fucked straight into next week* feeling? That high you never wanna come down from? 'Cause that's kinda exactly how I'm feeling this morning.

Despite the fact that I know my time with Avery just got an expiration date and I'm going to watch it tick down like a time bomb, I'm feeling pretty out of this world.

My mind drifts to that dark spot in my brain, that nagging piece of me that's wondering how long it'll take for Avery to start pulling away. How long until he's bored, ready for his next adventure? I'm not entirely sure if my reason for leaving last night was to guard myself, or to leave him wanting more, hanging on just a while longer. The latter would be stupid of me. In the end, I'll only wind up digging myself a deeper hole, one I'm eventually unable to pull myself out of.

And that can't happen.

In truth, Avery's been nothing but kind to me, with a side of sass, as is the relationship we share. But I know what kind of lover he is. And while he's a fantastic lover, what he really is, is a lover of women, a lover of variety, no strings attached, no commitments. He's a lover of freedom, making his own rules. I've reminded myself of this six times already in the hour that I've been awake this morning, convincing myself that if I keep that knowledge at the forefront of my mind, then maybe I won't be so crushed when all he is to me is an acquaintance I have to deal with at work occasionally.

My phone buzzes on the counter, making me smile. I know exactly who it is.

Charlee: *K. Wtf Claire? I call you three times last night to find out how it went with Avery at his office. No answer. Then you text me back at 3am saying "good"???? Get your sweet, perky ass to CLB. You have some 'splaining to do.*

Charlee: *PS. I'm gonna wear my sexy librarian glasses today because I feel like I'm going to want to give you a stern look overtop of them. Is that right? Should I wear them?*

Me: *Wear them.*

Charlee: *Best. Hump Day. EVER.*

Laughing, I tuck my phone into the back pocket of my jean skirt and pack an entire box of Lucky Charms into my messenger bag. Yeah, that's happening today. No qualms.

Slinging my bag over my shoulder and slipping a pair of sandals on my feet, I tug the door open.

I jump backwards with a shriek that echoes down the hallway, all while clawing at my throat.

Avery leans in my doorway, arms crossed over his chest, one sexy eyebrow arched high on his forehead, and a delectable, jerky smirk painted on his ruggedly handsome face.

"Fuck, Avery, you scared the shit out of me." I press a palm to my chest, feeling the way it heaves, before I reach forward and swat his shoulder.

My gaze trails a burning path down his body, looking sexier than ever in his perfectly tailored wine-colored suit. It's a bold choice, and naturally, he makes it work. Flawlessly. His hair is disheveled in a way that makes it look like he had sex exactly seven times last night, and he's got a delicious five o'clock shadow lining his jaw that I want to scrub my fingers along.

"Did you sneak out on me last night?" Avery asks, voice gravelly and thick with sleep, like he was up all night. Fucking.

"Nooo?" I flash him a teeth-gritting grin and lock my door, strolling past him instead of jumping him, wrapping my limbs around his body and begging him to screw my brains out in the elevator, which he conveniently follows me to.

"Hmm." He stuffs his hands in his pockets, looking ridiculously relaxed and unfazed as we wait for the elevator doors to open. When they do and we step inside, he asks, "Did you leave in the middle of the night?"

I clear my throat. "Yes."

"Was I sleeping?"

I pretend to think, squinting and tapping my jaw with one finger. "Think so."

"Were you being careful not to wake me?"

Busted. "Maybe."

When he turns to me, his grin is all devil. "So you snuck out."

The elevator dings and opens, and I dash away from him, which is stupid, because: A) we're going in the same direction, out the same damn door; and B) his legs are twice as long as mine.

He follows me onto the sidewalk, matching my pace. I'm glad I wore my sandals today—high heels would not fare me well in this situation, because I'm fumbling around like a mad woman. Also, because I got fucked straight into heaven last night, and my legs are all limp noodles.

"You're going to miss your ride," I tell him, pulling my phone and earbuds out.

"Nah, Jacob's picking me up at the brewery."

I swat Avery's hand away when he reaches forward, touching two fingers to my jaw and tapping it shut. "Why? We don't have a meeting today."

"Nope. Just walking to work with you."

"What? No. Why? What are you doing?" I'm confused.

He simply loops his arm through mine, tugging me down the sidewalk. "So we can talk about why you snuck out on me in the middle of the night."

"I didn't sneak out on you," I argue.

"We've already deduced that's *exactly* what you did, Claire. No point in arguing about it."

"Well," I start, holding up a finger. "I wouldn't call it sneaking out. Just, you know…" Where am I going with this?

"Sneaking out?"

My nose scrunches with my glare, and I catch sight of Avery's handsome smile before he presses his lips to mine. It's fleeting, because we're mid-stride, and I probably shouldn't let him do that because kissing me in public on a Wednesday morning…that's the type of thing that feels all relationship-y and screws with my head. But I take it, simply because I want it.

"Why'd you leave? Am I not a good snuggler?"

I giggle quietly. "You're an excellent snuggler, Avery. But isn't this…wasn't that, you know, for the best? We didn't have to do the awkward morning-after-the-one-night-stand stuff."

His forehead creases, and I swear I see the beginning of a frown tugging at the corners of his mouth. "One-night stand?" He recovers quickly, slapping a smile on his face. "That wasn't a one-night stand, Claire. I plan on having you for many, many more nights."

"Bet you say that to all the girls," I murmur, half teasing, half actually wondering.

"Literally none of them. Just you."

Peering at him out of the corner of my eye, I examine this man. I want to say he smirks, flashes me a coy grin, looks anything but genuine, but he doesn't. He's quiet, pensive, teeth working that bottom lip. He looks anxious, unsure. My stomach flip-flops when he looks like that.

I don't want him to get tired of me. What I was is him. I want him so much it actually hurts thinking that I can't have him, not permanently, at least. It hurts thinking that one day soon he'll be inside of another girl, whispering the same words in her ear, making her feel like the most beautiful woman in the world.

I squeeze my eyes shut and turn away, willing this feeling in my stomach, in my heart, to just go away. Why did this have to happen to me? Why did I have to fall for someone right after being cheated on, when I can't possibly trust anyone, let alone someone who doesn't do commitment, who's successful at picking up girls at the bar and taking them back to his place?

"You're doing that thing where you think too much," Avery says quietly. "Just relax and enjoy what is. You had fun last night, didn't you?"

I nod because I did. Of course I did. It was what I needed, I think, and I can't remember another night where I felt more free, free to go after what I want, to embrace my needs.

"Then what more is there to worry about? We had fun together. Just relax."

There it is, the reminder about what exactly this is between us: fun. Nothing more than a couple of exciting nights together. I should take his advice and just relax, stop overthinking. But I can't, not really. Because it's too late for that. My heart's already involved.

And that's the problem. And I knew that would be the problem right from the beginning.

You know what the scariest part is? I can't remember ever feeling like this about Aaron, ever being so goddamn wrapped up in him, even in the beginning when everything was new and exciting. Even the first time we told each other *I love you*. So what does that mean for me? For us, me and Avery?

It means I'm fucking terrified of my heart and the way I feel like a loose cannon because of this man beside me, currently holding my hand, being incredibly patient with me right now.

"What do you normally listen to on your way to work?"

I look up at the sound of Avery's soft voice. He motions to the earbuds I've been clutching in my fist since I opened my door. When my fingers unravel, he takes one bud and pops it in his ear. A smile tugs up the side of my face as I put the other one in my ear and fish my phone out.

My walking to and from work playlist is actually, I'm sure, the weirdest, most makes-no-sense playlist in the world. It's only four bands, and while my love for music is wide and extensive, these are the only bands I like to listen to while I'm pounding the pavement. The Tragically Hip, Pearl Jam, Red Hot Chili Peppers, and Blue Rodeo fills the list. I press shuffle and the familiar opening chords from Better Man fill my ear.

Avery listens for a moment and then gives me a quizzical smile, gaze drifting over my face. "Pearl Jam?" He lifts the hand he's holding to his mouth, brushing a kiss across my knuckles, and I feel it right between my legs. "I love everything I learn about you."

We walk in silence, weaving in and out of traffic, Avery humming along to every single song. When we stop in front of the brewery, his driver, Jacob, pulls up at the same time, almost as if he was hiding in the shadows, just waiting for us to show up.

Avery gives me back my earbud and takes both my hands in his. With a smile that looks nothing short of tender, he asks, "Do you regret it?"

Do I regret it? It's an interesting question. I regret walking into this whole thing with my heart left wide open when I knew better. I regret staying in an unhappy, unhealthy relationship with Aaron for far too long. I regret not knowing my self-worth. But do I regret last night?

"No, Avery. I could never regret that." Pushing up on my toes, I press a kiss to his lips, my palm curving over the back of his neck. "Have a good day at work. Thanks for walking with me."

I climb the stairs to my office, and those butterflies in my stomach turn to rocks, dragging me down, making my feel heavy and unsure. It matches perfectly with the ache in my chest.

I stop short when I open the door to my office to find Charlee sitting on my couch, hands folded on top of her crossed legs, her thick frames bordering those huge brown eyes of hers. She shifts them down her nose and raises her brows at me, a tiny little smirk playing on her ruby red lips.

"Well, Miss Thompson? Were you a bad girl or a good girl last night?"

CHAPTER THIRTY-TWO

Avery

"Happy fucking hump day, buddy. Did you see how much money we already made this week?"

Wyatt slaps down his laptop, showing me the stocks, his cursor circling over Galvin Pharmaceuticals. I smile at the little arrow that's pointing up toward the sky beside all those points. Company shares went public on Monday morning, and fifty hours later, Jones & Beck Investments has already raked in three-point-seven million dollars. This is, by far, going to prove to be one of our biggest deals ever.

I already had an ecstatic Troy Galvin on the phone twice this week, offering me the use of his private villa in France and the beachfront one in Hawaii.

"It's looking prettier and prettier by the hour," I observe.

Wyatt slumps down in the chair across from me. "When we started this company, did you ever think we'd be here? I mean, I knew we'd make money. I figured we'd make enough to live comfortably here in Toronto, buy a nice house, not really worry about anything. But I never imagined we'd be *here*. And in a matter of years. Shit, we aren't even thirty yet." He runs his fingers through the blond mess on top of his head. "I honestly don't even know what to do with all the money I make."

"You sound like a rich snob. No wonder you have so much trouble nailing down a girl."

"I have no trouble nailing down a girl. I just don't *want* to nail down a girl. All they want is my money. Rather keep doing what I'm doing."

"Sticking your dick in anything warm and wet and with a nice set of tits and then never seeing them again?"

"Don't forget a nice, juicy ass." He leans forward, swiping my phone off my desk. "And you're one to talk. Up until a month ago you were doing the same fucking thing. Now…" He unlocks my phone. I change my password every week and the fucker guesses it every time within the first three tries. He flashes me the screen, showing me the picture I'd been staring at the last time it was opened, as if he knew. "Now you just sit here and stare at *this* like a fucking pussy."

I pluck my phone out of his hand, taking one last look at the picture of Claire on my lap, her head thrown back while she laughs wildly, Vivi showering her in kisses at the park. I clear my throat when I catch myself smiling and shove my phone in my desk drawer.

Wyatt's brows rise slowly as he looks me over. His elbows hit the desk as he leans toward me. "Unless you're still sticking your dick in something warm and wet, with a nice set of tits and a juicy ass?"

"A gentleman doesn't tell." I lean back in my chair, lacing my fingers behind my head.

"Good thing you're not a gentleman." He shakes his head. "You fucked Claire. I can't believe it. Spill. How was she? As feisty in bed as she is all day long?"

I'm not sure feisty covers it, and I think the expression I'm wearing says as much.

A sly, crooked grin slips up Wyatt's face. "Knew she'd be wild." He plucks my apple off the desk and takes a big, juicy bite, not looking the least bit apologetic.

I hesitate, mulling over my next words. They slip from my mouth before I have the chance to decide whether or not I even want to say them.

"She snuck out in the middle of the night."

He slaps a hand over his mouth, covering his choking cough. "She snuck out?"

299

"She sure as shit did."

I'd rather not get into detail about the momentary rage that rolled through me when I woke up in the middle of the night to an empty bed. I had half a mind to go down to her apartment, guns blazing, demanding to know what the hell was up before dragging her back to bed with me.

Luckily, I rarely ever act on impulse, and the five minutes I took to cool my jets reminded me that this was all new to her, sleeping with someone without any type of relationship status, and that she was probably freaking out a bit.

I gave her the space she clearly needed, but I've only got the one free pass up my sleeve.

"You pissed about that?" Wyatt asks, tossing the apple core in the trash. "Her sneaking out?"

I shrug noncommittally. "I know what she's like. She's freaked out and afraid of commitment right now. Can't really hold it against her, I guess, but we talked this morning, so I doubt she'll do it again. I think she thought it was what I wanted, too."

"Normally it would be what you wanted," he points out, relaxing back in his chair. He kicks his feet up on my desk, because he's way too comfortable here.

"Normally."

"But not with Claire."

"Not with Claire," I agree.

Wyatt considers me carefully, lacing his fingers together behind his head. "You really like her, eh?"

"You could say that." Whatever it is I'm feeling for Claire is so totally different from anything I've ever felt that I don't really know the words to describe it.

He stands, rapping his knuckles against my desk. "Well then. Guess you better nail her down, eh? Just don't expect me to follow suit anytime soon, 'kay?" He runs a palm down his chest and strolls toward the door. "This man can't be tamed."

Nail her down is exactly what I need to do, which is why I shoot her a text later while I'm cooking dinner over my stove.

Me: *Can you come up for a min? Need your signature on a doc for the patio.*

Claire Bear: *Seriously??*

Me: *Seriously. Don't have time to stop by the brewery tomorrow. Please. It'll be quick.*

Claire Bear: *How do I get up there? You can't possibly expect me to walk up 21 flights of stairs. I'm supposed to be relaxing in a chair all day, or did you forget that you fucked me until you were satisfied that I wouldn't be able to move properly for days?*

As if I could ever forget that.

Me: *I didn't forget, noodle legs. Elevator code is 212871. Door's open.*

Me: *Hurry up.*

Claire Bear: *Don't tell me what to do.*

Little does she know I'm going to spend all night telling her what to do, something along the lines of *get on your knees, sit on my cock,* and *come for me, baby.*

Five minutes later, I glance up from the stove when I hear the soft click of my door opening and closing. Sully springs to his feet and trots over to Claire as she drops to her knees for kisses and pets. When she stands up, I get a look at her outfit.

"Ready for bed?" I tease.

She looks up at me through slanted eyes, fists planted on her curvy hips. "I like to get comfy when I get home from work, and I wasn't changing just for you, and certainly not for something that's going to take me two minutes to do."

"You don't have to change for me. I love your outfit." Love those skimpy excuse for pajama shorts, the oversize concert T-shirt hanging off her shoulder, giving me a glimpse of those golden freckles that dot her skin there.

301

She pads over to me in her bare feet, sticking her head around my arm. "Whatcha makin'?"

"Chicken cacciatore," I tell her, pressing my lips to her silky hair.

She inhales deeply. "Smells delish." She claps her hands. "Where are the papers?"

"Huh?"

"The document you needed me to sign right this minute," she says impatiently. I can practically hear the word she wants to add to the end of that sentence: *duh.*

"Oh. Right." *That blatant lie.* "I'll get it later."

"Later? But you said it would be qu—" She stops mid-sentence, gaze settling on my dining table, where two places have already been set, with a bottle of wine and a couple of candles. She shoves a finger into my chest. "This is an ambush!"

My eyes fall closed with a rumbling laugh. "You act like you've just been surrounded at gunpoint instead of surprised with a romantic, candlelit dinner."

"What if I already ate dinner?"

I give her a look that says I call bullshit. "Judging by the entire box of Lucky Charms that was poking out of your bag today? I'm gonna go out on a limb and say that's a lie."

A smile tugs at the corner of her mouth. She crosses her arms over her chest, nose pointing toward the ceiling. "I happen to like Lucky Charms."

I snort. "Clearly. Marshmallows for breakfast. Breakfast of champions, is it?"

She narrows her eyes then pouts, tugging at her top. "I'm not dressed for a candlelit dinner."

I shrug. "Doesn't matter. You're not going to be dressed for all that long anyway. In fact, if you're more comfortable, you can go ahead and strip down now."

Her jaw drops. Then she reaches out and smacks my shoulder.

"*Ow*! Hey! No hitting!"

I drop the wooden spoon I'm pushing the chicken around with and grab for her waist. She ducks away just in time, but her legs aren't long enough to let her take more than two steps before I wind an arm around her middle and drag her back to me.

Trapping her against my chest, I drop my lips to her ear. "I know you like it rough, Claire," I murmur against her skin, "but I had planned on getting through dinner before I threw you around. Your choice, though."

She shivers and wiggles against me, puffing out a breath. "You're such an arrogant ass."

"You love it."

"Cocky."

"You mean confident."

"Self-righteous."

"Know what I'm good at."

Claire makes a sound that can only be described as inhuman before she growls out, "I hate that I don't hate you," flipping around in my arms. She shoves me back against the counter and pulls my face down to hers, devouring my mouth.

"You're so pushy," I say against her lips, grinding her hips into mine.

"*I'm* pushy?" She climbs up my body like she's climbing a damn tree, pushing down on my shoulders. I lift her ass, letting her wrap her legs around me. "You're a bossy, domineering egomaniac who expects everybody to do what you say, when you say it, without questioning it."

"You're damn right, Claire." I nip her bottom lip and drop her to her feet. "Now take off your clothes and bend over the couch."

I watch with a wicked grin as she immediately drops her shorts—not wearing any panties, how lovely—and reaches for the hem of her top, too. She catches the expression on my face, realizes what she's doing, and stops.

303

"Oh, you ass." She backs away from me, shaking her finger. "Oh, no. Nuh-uh. I'm not doing anything you say."

"You can and you will." I flip the stove top off and shift the pans off the heating element before stalking toward her, because, safety first. "You know you want to, or else you wouldn't already be half-naked. I bet you're already soaked and ready for me."

"N-no." The way she stutters tells me I'm right.

Her calves hit the couch and she topples backwards, legs in the air. I follow, sinking to my knees on the leather, crawling toward her while she does the crab walk toward the other end of the couch. I grab her ankles and drag her to me.

"Open," I order. She does, knees falling to the sides. I smirk up at her.

She gasps and clamps her legs shut. "Stop it! You're getting in my head and you're not allowed to be there!"

Prying her legs open all too easily, I tell her, "I think you would allow me *anywhere.*"

A shudder shakes her entire body and a tiny moan pushes past her full lips.

"Are you wet for me, Claire? From our little make-out session just now? From us arguing? From me telling you what to do?"

Her chest rises and falls too quickly. "No."

"No? Really? You wouldn't lie to me, would you?"

She pins her arms to her chest, that stubborn chin pointing to the ceiling. "I'm not lying."

"So then you wouldn't mind if I check?" I don't need to check; I can smell her arousal from here. But she wants to play this game. She *likes* to play this game. She knows she's wet, and she knows I'm going to find out.

She opens her legs nice and wide, letting me run my hands up and down the inside of her thighs, getting closer and closer with each pass.

"If you're lying and you're wet…I'm going to tease you all night long and never let you come."

Her eyes widen, dancing with fear and a whole lot of lust. "*What*? No! No, I don't agree to that!"

"Well, it shouldn't be a problem. You said you weren't lying, right?"

She snaps her legs shut and scurries backwards. Turning over, she tries to pull herself over the edge of the armrest, but I wrap one arm around her, pinning her to my chest, burrowing my face in her neck.

"I'll give you one last chance to tell the truth," I whisper. "If you do, I'll be kind and let you come. If you don't…well, it'll be a long, grueling night for you. It's up to you, Claire. You choose how this goes."

I slip my hand up her shirt to find she's not wearing a bra, which I already suspected when she climbed me in the kitchen, and pinch one nipple. She gasps, arching into my palm. I love how responsive her body is to my touch. I make her just as wild as she makes me.

Dragging my hands over her curves, I pull her shirt up and over her head. With her back pressed to my chest, I let my fingers explore her sizzling skin, ghosting over her nipples, her quaking belly. I'm dying to sink my fingers inside her, but I need to hear her words first, so I let the tip of one broad finger circle gently around the edges of her pussy.

"Do you want me to touch you?"

She makes a garbled sound and squirms under my hands.

"It's just a yes or no, Claire."

She groans deeply, her fingers wrapping around my forearms as my hands scour her. Her forehead dips in defeat. "Yes."

"Are you wet?"

She flips me a threatening glare and growls, "Why don't you just check for yourself?"

Chuckling, I kiss the scowl right off her face and release her from my arms, climbing to my feet. Pulling my shirt over my head, I shove my hand down my boxers and gesture to the end of the couch. "Stand up and bend over."

She scrambles to her feet but doesn't bend. Part of me thinks it's on purpose. She likes me bossing her around, taking control, a stark contrast from our day-to-day.

"Bend over," I repeat, moving toward her.

She meets my gaze, dropping her hands to the armrest, *barely* bending, testing. "Make me," she whispers like the wicked little devil she is.

It takes everything in me to hold back that grin that wants so desperately to shine. Moving behind her, I grip one hip and a fistful of her hair, pulling her against me. She teeters on her toes, hands reaching out for something to grab onto.

"What did you say?" I ground out in her ear. "*Make* you?" My tongue presses against her neck and licks up. A burst of air shakes past her parted lips.

I shove her straight down to the couch, ass in the air over the armrest, and let my hand come down hard on her perfect, heart-shaped ass. She gasp-moans while I admire my red handprint, one fingertip tracing the lines. Then I jerk my pants down my thighs, grasp my cock, and slam into her from behind with no warning.

Claire cries out, her fingers clawing at the leather, gouging it. I don't give a shit. Something to remember, and hopefully, there will be a thousand more nights like this, opportunities to tear my leather couch apart.

Honestly, I was planning on gentle tonight, but now…now I pound into her with reckless abandon, my eyes darting back and forth between my hand in her hair, pushing her into the couch, and the spot where my dick fills her, moving in and out of her. With each thrust, Claire's pleas get louder, each wheezing breath more strangled than the last.

My eyes roll up. She feels fucking amazing, so tight and warm, hugging me perfectly. I could keep my cock buried inside of her forever. Her ass is perfect, all full and plump, like a juicy peach I wanna sink my teeth into. My hand slides around her hip, curving over her ass until my thumb finds that tiny pink rosebud that's peeking up at me. I press against it.

Claire tries to shoot up off the couch with a cry of pleasure, but I push her back down. Her ass wiggles against the pressure of my thumb and she stares up at me from where I'm pressing her cheek into the couch. She's flushed a delicious shade of crimson while she pants, her tongue sweeping across her lips.

"Do you like when I touch you there, Claire?"

Sucking her bottom lip between her teeth, I loosen my hold on her hair just enough for her to nod.

"Has anybody else touched you there?"

With a whimper, she shakes her head. "Only you."

The thought of having a piece of her that no other man has had ignites a fiery part of me. It's fucked up, I realize, because I've had more than my fair share of women, but the thought of another man being inside of Claire, touching her, kissing her…it nearly sends me off a cliff. There's no part of me that wants to share any bit of her.

Reaching around, I grip her neck and bring her up to me, kissing her fiercely, claiming her mouth. I've claimed every part of her body; there's only one more piece of her I want to make mine. The only problem is I can't just reach out and take it, and if there's one thing I know, it's that she has a fuckload of walls surrounding it that I've been working on tearing down since we met. Watching her give into our chemistry one moment and then work so hard to fight it the next hasn't exactly been easy.

On the contrary, it's been exhausting, leaving my head spinning most of the time. Sure, I have her in my hands right now, naked, filled with me, but I'm not naive enough to think that means I *have her.* She still needs convincing that I want her, not just her body, that I'm not gonna do the same thing her ex did.

My hand dips between her legs, rubbing circles around her clit while I pump into her with everything I have. The sound of our skin slapping together, my heavy breathing, Claire's begging whimpers fill my ears like the best song I've ever heard.

Claire winds one arm backwards around my neck, burying her fingers in my hair, her free hand clutching at mine on her, trying to rip my fingers off her pussy. "Please, Avery. I'm gonna come. I…I can't…"

I push her forward, grab her hips, and drive my cock into her. It starts twitching, kicking when she starts clenching around me, and a ball of fire roars to life at the base of my spine as my orgasm starts to barrel through me. Bowing over her, my teeth latch onto her neck, sucking her skin to keep me from screaming as we come together, filling her with my…

Filling her…

Filling…

Shit.

Slowly, I pull out, my grip on Claire—and maybe sanity—suddenly feather-light. I scrub my palm over my mouth when I watch my glistening cock slide out of her.

Fucking shit.

I bend and press a light kiss to her heaving shoulders. "Claire," I whisper carefully. "Are you on the pill, sweetheart?"

"Yeah," she wheezes. "Why?"

My sigh of relief deflates my whole body.

She looks at me over her shoulder. "Why?" she asks again.

"I'm so sorry, Claire. I got a little carried away. I forgot…I forgot to put on a condom."

Thankfully, she doesn't look too concerned about any oopsie-babies. But then her brows pinch and something indecipherable crosses her features. Shame, maybe.

"I got tested after…after…" After her boyfriend cheated on her? "I'm clean." She glances away, but not before red heat climbs like a vine up her neck and into her face.

Capturing her jaw, I pull her face back to mine and kiss her. She has no reason to be ashamed. If anyone should be, it's me. She got tested because she got screwed over by someone she trusted. I get tested because I've spent too many years fucking around.

"Me too," I tell her. "I promise. But I'm still sorry. I lost my head there for a while." She has that effect on me, I'm aware, but never have I ever been so wrapped up in somebody that I've *forgotten* to put on a damn condom. I'm more careful than that.

She looks up at me, her expression soft and understanding. "It's okay." She cups my cheek. "You know, you go from drill sergeant to sweet with the snap of your fingers."

"Drill sergeant?" I grind my half-hard erection against her ass.

"Oh my God." Her eyes roll, just the way I like. "I meant bossy! Not *drill* sergeant."

"I think both meanings work." I lick the spot on her neck where my teeth were when I came inside her. It's quickly turning purple. *Mine.*

"Come on, gorgeous. Let's eat."

CHAPTER THIRTY-THREE

Avery

I can't keep my eyes off Claire while we eat. She's lounging on one of my dining chairs wearing nothing but my T-shirt, one knee pulled up to her chest while her other leg swings down below. I'm not sure I've ever seen her so loose and carefree, humming happily around each bite.

"This is so good," Claire tells me for the third time. She toes the fur on Sully's belly where he's waiting patiently by her side, hoping for some scraps. "How old is Sully?"

I lift a shoulder. "Not sure, but the vet thinks around four or five."

She washes down her bite with a gulp of wine, dragging her tongue over her bottom lip to catch that drop of red that clings there. "You didn't get him when he was a puppy?"

I shake my head. "My sister showed up at my doorstep one day begging me to take him."

"He was Harper's dog?" Claire asks, surprising me by remembering my sister's name.

"Nope." Chuckling, I think about how Sully and I came to be. I have my crazy sister to thank for my burly, lazy, best bud.

"When Harper was eight, she came home with four kittens, two tucked under each armpit. She walked right by my parents in the kitchen, singing a song, and took them straight to her bedroom as if she didn't have four animals in her arms that didn't belong to us. She found them in a box by a dumpster in an alleyway. What an eight-year-old girl was doing in an alleyway by herself is beyond me, but she heard the cats crying and refused to leave them. My dad was allergic and told her they had to go. She cried for hours until he gave in, saying we could keep them only until we found them homes. We found homes for three, but she refused to let the last one go." I smile to myself, thinking about the fluffy black-and-white cat with piercing green eyes. "We had Clyde for thirteen years."

"I thought your dad was allergic?"

"He was, but the rest of the family ganged up on him."

Claire bounces in her spot with an airy giggle. "So how did Sully come to be?"

"Well, that started Harper on a whole new path. We always joked that she was like a Disney princess. She's just always had a way with animals. They flock to her. Everywhere she went, she had her eyes peeled for animals in need, and our home became a sort of sanctuary until my parents could get them vetted and into new homes. Of course, like Clyde, a few of them wound up finding their home with us.

"Two years ago, right after I moved in, Harp showed up at my door, soaked to the bone, with the shaggiest looking dog at her side. Between the two of them, you'd never seen such sad, huge brown eyes. My parents had two dogs and a cat that they hadn't been able to get rid of, as well as an entire litter of kittens Harper was caring for. There was no room for Sully. She'd seen his picture on Facebook at a high-kill shelter. They'd given him a week to find a new home. She drove seven hours to get him."

Claire's eyes widen. "She went to get him without asking first if you'd even take him? What if you said no?"

I roll my eyes. "Harper knew I'd never say no to her, especially with him at my door." To say that my sister hasn't taken advantage of my love for her, and animals, a few times in my life would be a blatant lie. I've housed my fair share of stray kittens for her over the years when my parents' place has been jammed. "I took one look at those big brown eyes and sank to my knees. The rest is history."

311

I glance up to find Claire resting her chin in her palm, her green eyes smiling across the table at me. "You're a big softie, aren't you?"

I throw her a wink. "Don't tell anyone." Stretching back in my chair, I lace my fingers behind my head, watching as her eyes drift over my bare abdomen. "What about you? Any pets growing up? I know your dad has his dog Turkey now."

She flashes me that toothy, dimple-popping grin, head bobbing happily. "Cats and dogs. I love them both. I always wanted a bunny, too." Her nose scrunches with the memory she replays to me. "My dad said if I could catch one of the ones that were always running through our backyard, I could keep it. I once spent an entire summer trying to catch one, getting up at the crack of dawn, setting booby traps."

I cough a laugh into my fist. "Booby traps?"

Her smile splits her face in two. "Yeah, those wild bunnies are fast as hell. Chasing them around was exhausting."

Dipping my head, I let out a long, hearty laugh, imagining a young Claire running in circles, screaming after a tiny, scared animal. I also know what she means about the chase being exhausting; I've been trying to catch her for nearly three weeks now.

She reaches across the table and swats at me. "Don't laugh at me."

"I'm just picturing it, that's all. You and your potty mouth, yelling at the bunny."

"My dad has a video. Maybe I'll show it to you one day." She makes a face, seeming to rethink that last statement. "Or maybe I won't. It'll just fuel your fire. The camera is shaking so badly because my dad is howling with laughter. You can hear my mom slapping him over and over again, telling him to stop, but she's laughing, too." She gets this faraway look in her eyes, like she's reliving the moment. "And then Casey sprays me with the hose."

"Alright, I *need* to see this video."

"Nope. Not gonna happen. Changed my mind." She taps my nose—I find it oddly endearing for some reason—and stands, grabbing our plates.

I follow her to the kitchen, trying to tug the dishes from her grasp. She throws her elbow up, nearly hammering me in the throat.

"You don't need to do that, Claire. I can clean up."

"You cooked; I'll clean." She bumps my hip with hers and shoves her way in front of the sink. "It's called compromise."

"Compromise? You? Claire Thompson?" I wrap my hand around her forehead. "Are you feeling okay?"

"Oh, shut up." She slams her ass backwards and jams an elbow into my ribs.

"Did I fuck the fight right out of you?"

"Keep talking. See where that gets you." She flicks her brows up at me in a way that says *fucking try me.*

Laughing, I wrap my arms around her and nuzzle into her neck. "I didn't invite you over here to clean up my mess."

"No, you invited me over here to sign a document that I'm beginning to think doesn't even exist."

"Bingo," I whisper. "Just wanted you all to myself."

Claire doesn't say anything, but I feel the heat on her cheek when I press my lips there.

"And while I'm admitting things, I might as well tell you the drawer in my desk at work is *full* of popcorn. I saw your hunger as an opportunity last night, and I took it."

She turns toward me, cheeky grin exploding off her face. "You sneaky little…" The threat dies behind the hungry mouth that devours mine, her fingers plowing through my hair, my hands on her ass.

With the kitchen cleaned, we move to the balcony to have a drink and watch the sun set over the harbor. Claire lets me pull her

313

down between my legs, resting her back against my chest. With a happy sigh, her head flops into the crook of my arm.

"Your view is way better than mine," she murmurs, the tips of her fingers tracing the length of each of mine. "It's amazing. And your balcony. I don't have words for your balcony."

I love my balcony. It spans the entire length of my condo and winds around both corners, which means not only do I get this amazing Toronto Harbour view, but I also get a glimpse of the city lights and the CN Tower, depending on where I choose to sit. For the most part, I sit right here, staring out at the quiet water, forgetting for a moment that I live smack-dab in the middle of Canada's busiest city.

I focus on Claire's quiet breathing, the way her body lifts and falls in my arms. She lets out a little yawn and snuggles deeper into me, making me smile. She's tired, as am I, because we fucked for, like, five hours straight last night, with no more than twenty-minute breaks in between each round. Somehow, this is better than that.

"I've never done this before," I confess, tightening my hold on her.

"Mmm, done what?"

"This. Just sitting. Talking. Fuck, making dinner for someone. It's…nice."

A soft laugh washes over the inside of my bicep. "You mean you've never dated? Because that kinda stuff is kind of a requirement."

"Not really," I admit. "Never had an urge to do any of it with anyone."

Her hands slide along my forearms where they hold her around her chest, the tips of her fingers tickling my skin with the warm breeze. "Why are you doing those things now?" I almost don't hear her, her voice is so low, so timid, like she doesn't want to hold out hope for a certain answer.

"Because you're not just anyone. You're you, and I like spending time with you." The words come out easily, but my stomach tenses and knots, wondering how she'll respond.

"Even though we push each other's buttons?"

With a quiet chuckle, I tell her, "It's called chemistry, Claire. We have it. A lot of it. You push my buttons; I push right back."

"And then we make out?"

"And it's fantastic."

She quiet for a moment, those wheels turning. "So, we have good chemistry...and that's it?"

I tip her chin up until our gazes lock. "No, Claire, that's not it."

I gaze down at her, her wide, uncertain eyes, her flushed, freckled cheeks, and my heart swells in my chest. Tracing the shape of her lips with the pad of my thumb, I wonder just how to tell her how I feel. I've always been able to talk my way into anything. One of the perks of the job, I guess. But this...this feels different. This is unchartered territory for me. One wrong word, one step out of line, and this whole thing can detonate, blow up in my face.

Before I can find the words I'm looking for, Claire turns in my arms and crawls onto my lap, sliding her fingers along my jaw before she claims my mouth. It's not frantic or wild, but it's perfect. Without words, she's found the meaning I've been looking for.

Warm hands sweep along my collarbone, over the plains of my chest, and she dips her mouth to kiss me there with small brushes of her soft lips. Pushing herself against me, I feel wet heat press against my lower abdomen.

Cupping her bare ass under my shirt she's still wearing, I pick her up and walk toward the far end of the balcony, heading straight into my bedroom.

Gently setting her on the bed, I watch as she pulls the shirt over her head while I drop my sweats and boxers to the ground, stepping out of them. I climb on top of her, pushing my fingers through her tresses, my tongue plunging into her mouth.

But I need something. I need something to assure me that this can be more, that she's willing to take this to the next level with me.

"Claire…" I brush a soft, closed-mouth kiss to her plump, wet pout. "You're going Friday night, right?"

Her brows pinch together and then relax. "To the Sick Kids fundraiser?"

I nod. There's a huge fundraiser for the children's hospital in two nights that Wyatt and I always attend. We donate a percentage of our earnings from the year before. This year, we're collectively donating three-point-two million.

"I'm going," she confirms, pushing my waves off my forehead. "Charlee and Dex and I, and a few other people from the brewery."

"Would you go with me?" I force the words out of my mouth before I can overthink them.

"With you?"

"With me," I nod. "As my date."

Her jaw hangs. "You…you want me to be your date?"

"Yeah." I pull my bottom lip into my mouth but resist the urge to chew on it. "I do."

"Like…"

"Like I pick you up at your door, we ride there together, dance together, spend the night together in public. I get to show you off on my arm. Like a date," I add with an amused arch of one brow, and maybe the hint of a smirk. I'm the one that's new at dating, yet she's the one who seems totally lost right now. I kiss the lines off her confused forehead and finish with the sweep of my lips across hers. "Say yes."

Her fingers find her lower lip, rolling and pinching. I pull her hand away.

"Okay," she whispers, finally meeting my gaze.

My grin is so big it's actually painful. "Okay?"

She nods, the corner of her mouth lifting. "Yeah, okay."

I drop my smile to hers. "Thought I was gonna have to beg on my knees all night."

"You can spend the rest of the night doing so if you'd like." Her teeth press into her lower lip with her mischievous grin. "You know, for good measure."

My chest vibrates with a low purr. I trail my nose down the length of hers, my hand covering her hip. "For good measure? In case you change your mind?"

She lifts a lazy shoulder. "Eh, you never know. You really grind my gears."

"Oh, I'll fucking grind your gears."

"As long as you're on your knees when you do it."

With a snarl, I devour her hot, filthy mouth, and then spend the rest of the night doing as asked: begging for her, on my knees. Well, the next hour-and-a-half, because we're both pooched from last night still, and after four orgasms, Claire can barely keep her eyes open.

It's just after eleven when I get back from taking Sully out for one last bathroom break and climb back into bed.

"Can you plug my phone in over there?" I hand it to Claire and watch her plug it in on the bedside table.

"Am I on your side?" she asks, fingers gripping the sheets. "Do you want me to move?"

"Nah, it's cool. I want you to stay right there." I scoop her up in my arms and curl my body around hers, hoping to God she doesn't try to make out like a bandit in the middle of the night again.

Reading my mind, she whispers, "Maybe I should go home."

I snuggle her harder. "Nope."

But my grip loosens as I start to fall, unconsciousness claiming me. I don't know how long it's been or what time it is when I feel Claire shift, the mattress dipping, and I realize my arms are empty.

317

I fling an arm across the bed, catching her around the waist and yanking her back down to her side. I crush her back to my chest and nip at her ear. "Nice try."

She makes a tiny sound and I wrap my hand around the base of her throat. I can feel her pulse beating wildly in there. Her fingers won't stop moving, her legs shifting.

"Would you just fucking relax and go to sleep? I'm not going to hurt you. I just wanna hold you."

Leaning over her, I kiss her, pushing my tongue past her lips. With one final sigh, her body lets go of that tension, sinking into my hold.

"Go to sleep," I say against her lips.

"Avery?" she whispers, right when I think she's asleep.

"Yeah, baby?"

A sigh. "Thank you for dinner."

"Yeah, baby." I kiss her shoulder. "Thank you for staying."

With Claire warm and snug in my arms, sleep envelops me in minutes, my body overcome with a quiet calmness I'm not sure I've ever felt before. My heart rate slows to a soft kick, like it's finally found its place in this wild world.

But it feels like no time at all has passed when a blaring ring fills my ears, telling me it's time to wake the hell up, signaling the end of my newfound peace.

With a groan, I roll over, slapping around for my phone to silence my alarm. And when I find it, when I blink through the glaring morning sun filtering through the wall of windows, that's when I see the two missed FaceTime calls and the text message I received at 12:37am.

Samantha: *Been thinking about you, handsome. Miss you & that divine mouth of yours. Thought we could video chat ;)*

That's also when I realize that the other half of the bed is empty.

Claire's gone. Again.

318

CHAPTER THIRTY-FOUR

Avery

"Morning Mr. Beck."

I grunt at Jacob as he opens the door to the Bentley for me. It's not my typical greeting, nor is it my finest hour.

Sliding into the backseat, I bury my face in my hands. What a fucking clusterfuck this has turned into. How the hell did I wind up here after the last five days? All the progress I thought I'd made with Claire is gone just like that.

"Jacob, take me to Cherry Lane, please."

"You got it, sir."

I'm not in the mood for this today. I try my best to suppress a groan and an eyeroll, because none of this is his fault. He's not the person I'm upset with. "Jake, man, it's Avery. Please."

"Right. Sorry, Avery." He clears his throat and looks twice before pulling into traffic.

My thumb hovers over Samantha's contact on my phone. I shouldn't have to do this. It's ridiculous. She always knew this was casual. We only saw each other a couple times a year. I thought it was pretty clear that I wasn't interested when I left the party at the brewery after literally telling her I wasn't interested.

I click the call button and hold the phone up to my ear while it rings.

"Well, hello there, Mr. Beck," Sam purrs. "You're a hard man to get a hold of. I have to leave for work in fifteen, but if we're quick—"

"Sam," I sigh. "You've gotta stop this."

"Stop what?" I can practically see her fluttering her long lashes at me in mock confusion.

"This." I circle my hand in front of me, which is stupid, 'cause she can't see me. "Whatever this is you're doing. Showing up at events I'm at when I tell you I can't see you, calling me in the middle of the night."

"But I thought that—"

I clear my throat and pinch my nose. "I thought you understood that what we had in the past was casual. You've always been okay with that."

"Well, yeah, but I thought…Wait, what do you mean *in the past*? Are we…do you not want to…" She trails off, her voice cracking.

"No, Sam, I don't want to. Not anymore." I watch Jacob's eye flicker to mine in the mirror. He knows Sam. He knows Claire. He's also been privy to many conversations about Claire between Wyatt and I in this backseat. He knows how I feel about Claire, and he knows how I don't feel about Sam.

Silence. For a long moment. And then, "Is it something I did? Is it because I showed up at that party? I just wanted to see you before I left town."

"No, Sam." I press the heel of my palm to my forehead. This is painful. "Actually, you know what, while we're on it, yeah, it wasn't cool of you to show up like that. And it really wasn't fucking cool of you to kiss me." I should have had this conversation with her then, but when I saw Claire take off up the stairs to her office, all I could think about was following her up there. And then when she left and went home, I'd followed right behind her, with nothing more than a quick *I'm not interested* for Sam. "I was there with somebody."

"You were there with somebody? Like…"

"I'm seeing someone," I finally blurt out. I'm not sure that Claire would agree with that statement, especially given the circumstances, but I don't give a shit. I'm spending time with her and her alone. She's the only one I'm kissing, holding, sleeping with. Except we aren't doing much sleeping. "She was there that night and saw you kiss me. And she saw your text message last night, too."

That last one is unconfirmed so far, but I'm willing to bet that's the reason Claire disappeared in the middle of the night again after finally falling asleep in my arms. My phone was on the table right by her head, and a text like that would be more than enough to send her running for the hills.

"Wow," Sam muses quietly. "I…I'm sorry, Avery. I didn't…shit. I didn't think…well, to be honest, I didn't think it was possible."

"Yeah. You and me both."

There's a little puff of air and then a small giggle. "She must be something special to nail Avery Beck down."

I snort. "Yeah, she's special alright. Just gotta try and salvage this now."

"Oh, Avery. I'm sorry. I really didn't mean to mess anything up for you. Can I help in any way? Do you want me to reach out to her and—"

"No, absolutely not. It's more than you, Sam. There's more than that going on." I scrub my jaw. There's *so* much more than that going on. Claire's insecure, and I get that. But her constant flip-flopping between returning my feelings and running away from me like I'm chasing after her wielding a weapon has my head spinning.

"Don't give up without a fight, Avery. I've never known you to turn down sex with a beautiful woman before, so…I guess that's saying something."

I laugh at that. Sam's confidence is one of the things that drew me to her. She's a bombshell and she knows it. She's also fairly easy to talk to, which is why we'd been mutually interested in repeated hook-ups whenever she was in the city. I would clear my schedule and blow off semi-important things to accommodate her, the sex was that good.

But it was nothing like what I have now with Claire. Not just the sex, but the chemistry, the connection, the draw to her that I can't explain. I can't put into words how I feel about Claire, or why I feel this way. It isn't one specific thing, because wouldn't that imply that without that thing, the feelings would vanish? I'm sure that isn't the case, not with Claire.

It's...everything. Everything about her, rolled into one phenomenal woman who makes me laugh, shake my head, grit my teeth, and smile all in the same day, over and over again. Everything about Claire draws me to her like a magnet.

The car rolls to a stop and I glance out the window to see the old-time charm of Cherry Lane staring down at me. "I've gotta go, Sam. Are we good?"

"Yeah, yeah. We're good. I guess I won't be seeing you anymore. But, you know, if things don't work out..."

I know she means well, but I'm not in the mood. I'm not in the mood to even consider that this might not work out. This *has* to work out. Claire and I *have* to work out. There's no other way; I'm sure of it.

"Have a good one, Sam."

Her small sigh tells me she knows it's final. "Goodbye Avery."

I tuck my phone in my pocket and lean forward between the front seats. "Can you stick around? Might be a while."

"Of course. I'll go grab a coffee. You want anything?"

I pull out a bill and pass it to him. "You know what I like."

Walking rapidly across the first floor, my pounding footsteps echo off the empty brick, matching the trotting that's currently going on in my chest. I take the stairs two at a time, sprinting up them, and nod at the secretary as I move past her.

"Good morning, Mr. Beck," she says, standing and raising a finger as if trying to stop me.

"Morning, Julie," I toss over my shoulder. "Just going to see Claire."

"Um, right, but she's not feeling well today, so, she asked for privacy. I can tell her you're here and see if she—"

I slice my hand through the air. "No thanks. She's expecting me." I fucking know she is.

I burst through her office door without knocking and Charlee's head shoots up from her spot on the couch. Her jaw drops, eyes darting to Claire, who's much slower to move. Her elbows are up on the desk, face buried in her hands. She looks about as wrecked as I feel.

"Morning, Charlee." I nod in her direction. That gets Claire moving. Her head snaps up in my direction and she quickly swipes at her eyes before pasting on an impenetrable mask. "Mind if I have a few minutes alone with Claire?" Holding the door open, I sweep my arm out in front of me.

Charlee scrambles to her feet, meeting me at the door. She opens her mouth as if to say something but then shuts it and frowns. She glances back at Claire, who's shaking her head, her green eyes huge, scared, begging.

"Charlee, no. You don't have to—"

"Charlee, I need a few minutes, please."

Her eyes bounce between us. "Uh…I'll just be outside, Claire, okay? Just right outside the door." The look she gives me lets me know that she'll be listening and that she won't hesitate to jump in if she thinks she needs to.

"Charlee, *no*." Claire stands and takes a step toward us but then seems to reconsider. She doesn't want to come near me. "You-you should go, Avery. I'm busy. I can't talk right now."

"You can and you will." I look at Charlee and shift my gaze to the door. "Charlee, please."

She chews the inside of her cheek like she's really not sure what to do, who to give in to. Then she nods. "Right outside," she reminds us both, pointing to the door. She gives me one last assessing survey, and her eyes flicker, softening.

I'm sure there's nobody who knows Claire better than Charlee does, which is probably the only reason she's agreeing to leave right now. Because as much as she loves her, Charlee knows that Claire isn't always right.

I shut the door behind her, flipping the lock. Claire immediately cowers into the corner.

"Why did you lock it? You don't need to lock it. Why are you here? You shouldn't be here." Her hands fumble at her stomach, the one I spent hours kissing on last night, and her gaze moves around the room, landing anywhere but on me.

I'm so torn right now. Looking at Claire in this moment, how obviously scared she is, it fucks with my head. I don't want to hurt her, and I sure as hell don't want her to be frightened of me. But this shit can't go on anymore. It needs to end, and the only way that's going to happen is with a real conversation. My jaw ticks with anger on its own accord, probably because Claire intends on ending this *without* a real conversation.

Hands in my pockets, I take a few calculated steps toward her. "Did you seriously leave me in the middle of the night again?"

"I-I…" She takes a deep, steadying breath and points that stubborn nose at the ceiling. "You got what you wanted. It was time for me to leave."

"Got what I wanted? What the fuck are you talking about? I didn't get what I wanted at all, or I would have woken up with you still in my arms this morning."

Her eyes land on me, flashing with rage, nostrils flaring. "So you could have me again? The last two nights weren't enough for you? Didn't have your fill of me yet?" Her shoulders tense and she takes a step toward me. "Because it's you who gets to decide when you're sick of me, right? Wanted to use me a few more times before you tossed me out?"

"You can't be serious, Claire. What are you saying right now?"

I cross the room to her in three strides, expecting her to back off, but she just puffs her chest out, determined to stand her ground, even if it shakes. It's one of the things I love about her—her ferocity, feistiness, tenacity. But right now, I hate it, because it's exactly what's keeping us apart.

"You heard me. You got what you wanted, what I've been denying you all this time. You finally fucked me. Now the chase is over." She waves one loopy hand through the air. "You can go have video sex with your fuck buddy, or better yet, bring her to your next event, sneak off somewhere private, and remind her how *divine* that mouth of yours is. Shit, maybe she's available tomorrow night." She pins her arms across her chest, huffing every breath as if she's just run a five-minute mile.

"Great, so you saw the message. Did you open it up and see the five times I turned her down before that? Or would you like to text her now and ask her about the ten-minute phone call we just had where I politely told her to fuck off because I was seeing someone?"

Her eyes widen in surprise, arms falling to her sides. She blinks rapidly, looking a little lost for words. Finally, she stutters out, "We're not…we're not together."

My brows jump. "We're not?"

"N-no." She looks like even she doesn't know what the hell is going on.

"Like fucking hell, Claire. What was that on Saturday, you, me and Vivi? What were the last two nights?" I refuse to believe that time together meant nothing to her, and she's ridiculous if she's trying to convince herself of that. Truly, if it meant nothing to her, she wouldn't give two shits about Sam.

"What was it? It was a mistake, that's what it was. It was you pushing your way into my life where you don't belong, all in the name of fucking me." She shoves an angry finger into my chest.

With a growl, I grab her by the shoulders and back her up against the wall. "It has *never* been just about fucking you since the night I put you in that cab and sent you home."

"Bullshit," she spits, shoving back against me. "You saw a challenge and made me your mission. That's all I was to you. I'm not stupid! I know you must think I am after I let someone cheat on me for so long, but I'm not, and I refuse to let it happen again!" Pain slashes her features, but she shakes her head furiously, trying to clear it before I can see it.

It's too late; I've already seen it.

"Claire," I plead, trying to control the way my voice shakes and breaks, all of the anger I was feeling a mere moment ago dissipating. I'm desperate, and I hate to see her hurting. "I would never—"

"Save it, Avery." Her voice is soft now, tiny. She drops her gaze.

I clasp at her hands, bringing them between us, shaking my head. "No. You have to listen to me."

"I don't have to do anything!" She wrenches her hands free and pushes away from me. "This—" she circles her hand around the air between us, "—this whole thing is meaningless. You can be with whoever you want. You can have phone sex with whoever you want, screw whoever you want, date whoever the hell you want."

"I want to date *you*."

She barks out a laugh. "No. You don't. You wanted to fuck me, and you did. It's over now."

"It's not anywhere *close* to over." Closing the space between us, I grab her face in my hands. Her eyes flicker, her forehead creasing. "We have something. I don't want anybody else. I want you. Please, tell me you want that too. Tell me what you want, Claire."

I search her expression, watching her eyes bounce between both of mine, her bottom lip clamped between her teeth. She's right there, right on the edge of giving in.

326

Her hand comes up to rest on mine and I feel the warmth that spreads from her fingertips into my hand, up my arm. She leans her cheek into my touch and for a second, I think I've got her.

But then she takes my hand off her face.

"I want you to see other people."

CHAPTER THIRTY-FIVE

Claire

I'm not inside my apartment for a minute before I'm stripping off my clothes and running a bath.

Naked, I pull down a bowl from my kitchen cupboard, dump a whole bag of chips in it, top it off with two handfuls of mini rainbow chip cookies, crack open my favorite Strawberry Grove beer, and plant myself in the tub even though there's only three inches of water in it so far.

"Claire Thompson, pity party for one," I murmur, tossing a mixed handful of cookies and chips into my mouth. A mini cookie falls into the water. I pluck it out and toss the soggy treat in my mouth. Yep, I fucking do that.

With my toes, I somehow manage to squeeze out a generous helping of bubbles into the running water and sigh as they start to foam up around me.

"Hey Google!" I yell unnecessarily loudly. It's only on the counter, not five feet away. "Play my walking playlist!"

"Okay, here's a shuffle of your playlist called walking."

"Thanks, Googs." In goes another handful of junk, followed by a long pull on my ice-cold beer as I sink deeper into the too-hot bubbles.

My phone starts vibrating on the toilet lid, rumbling toward the edge. I scramble for it, throwing my bucket of snacks across the floor, not because I don't want the phone to fall, but because I think/hope it might be Avery. Fucked up, right? Yeah, I'm a hot mess.

But it's not Avery, of course. It's Charlee.

"What are you doing?" she asks as soon as the call connects. I hate how uppity she sounds right now, but it beats the harsh tongue-lashing I got when she stumbled back into my office after Avery whipped the door open and stormed out.

"Drowning my sorrows."

"With?"

"Beer, chips, cookies, and bubbly water up to my belly button because I couldn't wait for the bath to fill before I got in."

She chuckles. "Well, get out and dry off, babe. You're coming over."

"Charlee." I huff a loud, drawn-out sigh, patting at the fluffy bubbles. Like the schoolgirl I am, I start etching Avery's name into the thick softness. "I'm really not up for it."

"I don't give a shit, Claire. You fucked up royally this morning and then moped around the rest of the day with your head up your own ass. So now you're gonna come over and I'm gonna tell you how the hell you can make it right."

"That sounds like a lovely night but—"

"We're having a girl's night. It's mandatory." She pauses, then laughs at something, probably herself. "And when I say girl's night, I mean wine blackouts in my living room with nineties hits blasting. Bitch, get your sweet ass over here."

Well, when you put it like that...

Tugging on a Cherry Lane tank and a flimsy pair of running shorts, I fill my backpack with snacks and alcohol, in case Charlee's not prepared, though she always is. I make the fifteen-minute trek to her place, squinting through the bright sun. It's not fair. I mean, it feels like it should be rainy and gray, not all blue skies and sunshine. Nature should always match my feelings, then I could walk through the rain and pretend like I'm in an emotional music video, singing about all the mistakes I've made and how my heart will never be whole again.

But Charlee doesn't let me wallow. She yanks me through her door, tunes blasting from her TV, a giant, steaming pan of nachos waiting for me on her kitchen island.

"Yesss," I groan, dropping my head backwards and grabbing a greedy, cheesy handful.

She hands me a tall drink. It's an alarming shade of mud brown, with a hint of rust.

I make a face. "I'm not drinking that."

"You are." She dips a crazy straw into it. I watch her slurp her drink, the liquid moving through the loops of her straw. Squeezing her eyes shut, she shudders. "So good," she chokes out.

"Yeah, no. Not happening. When Charlee Williams gags at a drink, it's *definitely* not happening for Claire Thompson."

"Don't be such a pussy." She clamps a hand over her mouth. "Oh, I said the p-word. Even *I* don't normally say that word." She giggles at herself. "But you are being a little pussy. Not just about this, but this drink is the easiest thing to fix right now. So drink up, Claire Bear, or I'll hold you down and pour it down your throat. I'm not above doing that and you know it."

I do know it. Otherwise I would've never wound up stripping down to my bra and undies and running through my high school parking lot on a dare one night in eleventh grade with about fifty juniors and seniors cheering me on. So maybe that's why I close my lips around the straw and suck it back.

It's truly disgusting. I gag. I cough. I die a little inside.

And then I finish it. And then I drink three more. And each one tastes better than the last, until they taste like I'm simply drinking root beer. Not good. Not good at all.

"You love him," Charlee slurs, nuzzling her face into my shoulder after a good hour of shaking our asses. We're both sticky with sweat and breathless like we just had the best sex of our lives, which we did not. And also, we're super drunk.

I start to wag my head back and forth. It's all slow and lazy. "Nnnn-yes." I do. Fuck me.

She sits up and grips my shoulders, giving me a fierce shake. "I just don't understand you. Why are you running from the very thing that makes your heart beat faster?"

It's a good question, and a deep one, one I can't really comprehend right now. Why am I running away from the person who makes me undeniably happy when we're together? Why has it taken me so long to even *admit* that he makes me so happy?

"Because he can't love me back," are the words that tumble from my lips. "And even if he thought he could, he'd realize it soon enough, and then he'd leave."

You know, I haven't always been such a cynic with love. I believed in it wholeheartedly, believed in all of it. Love at first sight, jumping right in, happily ever afters, monogamy.

Now I'm just not sure.

Charlee's entire body rolls with her theatric sigh, starting with her shoulders. "Maybe it would be easier if you put it down."

My face scrunches with confusion. "Put what down?"

She boops my nose. "All your self-doubt."

Ha. I wish. Easier said than done, I suppose.

"Do you think I like feeling this way? This has been the longest month ever since Aaron. And not because I miss him, but because…because…" My bottom lip does that quiver I hate, and I feel that familiar sting in my eyes and nose. I try to hold it in; I swear, I do.

But comes rushing forward in a barking sob, and Charlee flings her arms around me.

"I feel so worthless," I cry, swiping furiously at the tears that stream down my cheeks. "I don't care that he's gone, Charlee, I really don't. I care that he made me feel like gum on the bottom of his shoe. That he made me question everything about myself, including the things I used to love."

How can I even begin to attempt to let someone else love me when I'm not even sure I love myself?

331

"Claire, fuck that guy! It has nothing to do with you and everything to do with him. And all the things that Aaron was too busy missing out on, other people were busy loving. Me, Casey, Dex, Vivi…Avery. We love you for you and we always have, always will." She squeezes my cheeks between her palms, her boozy, hot breath coating my lips, infiltrating my sense of smell. It makes me woozy. "Let Avery show you that those things you used to love about yourself are still perfect and worthy of so, so much love. Not just his, or another guy's, but your own."

She pats my head affectionately and gives me a sad smile. "You don't actually want him to see other people."

"No," I choke, head wagging back and forth wildly. "It would kill me."

"Then why? Why did you say that?"

I hold my palms up. "I have no fucking clue. It just seemed…it just seemed easier. Like, if I was the one to push him away before he could get too close."

"If you could leave him before he leaves you? That maybe it wouldn't hurt so much?"

Wiping the heel of my palm up my snotty, sniffling nose, I nod.

"*Claire.*" She smooths my hair back from my sopping cheeks. "Honestly, how do you sleep at night?"

Oh, that's an easy one. "I sleep at night knowing I'm irreparably damaged and will most likely die surrounded by twenty-five cats due to my inability to communicate, accept love, or behave in a socially acceptable manner."

Charlee laughs, her forehead hitting my chest. When she straightens, her expression is both soft and firm, full of love but unwilling to let me go on like this. "I see your pain, Claire, and I know it's big, just like your fears. But I also see your love, your heart, and that's so much bigger. Sometimes I worry that you don't see that, that you don't see your strength, your ability to keep pushing forward. Have the courage to try this, to open yourself up.

Don't let somebody tear you down. I know this is hard, but sometimes the hard things wind up being the best things."

"But…it's too soon, isn't it?"

"Too soon for what?"

"I don't know…everything?" I scratch my head and then gnaw on a Twizzler while I think. "Too soon for me to be in a new relationship. Too soon for me to trust again. Too soon for me to…fall in love? I mean, I've only known Avery a few weeks and we spend half our time fighting with each other."

Charlee snickers. "You don't fight; you bicker like an old married couple. You tease each other. It's different. I mean, that thing this morning was a fight, but everything else…that's just chemistry. Two people wild for each other." She grabs her own Twizzler and takes a bite before pointing it at me, right along with her brows. "You have to learn to loosen your grip a little bit and let go, let things happen the way they're supposed to."

"Lets the chips fall where they may?"

Her licorice turns into a happy little whip when she smacks me in the shoulder. "Exactly. Sure, the timing isn't right, or at least that's what you think. It's too soon, you just had your heart broken, you're not ready, blah blah blah…You could come up with a million excuses, and I know you have. But what if the timing is exactly right? What if Avery came into your life at the moment you needed him most? To remind you what it feels like to be alive, to show you what love and real passion looks like?"

In all her highly intoxicated state and mine, Charlee's making a load of sense. A boatload. Like, toss me overboard because I just truly realized how hugely I fucked up and it's about the size of the ocean.

"He asked me to be his date to the fundraiser tomorrow," I murmur, pulling my lip between my fingers.

333

"Do you want to be with him, Claire? Like, really be with him? All the way? Because after today, you can't just stick your toe in the water. You have to dive right in."

"How do you manage to give such good advice after an unprecedented amount of shady brown liquor that tastes like a mixture of death, gasoline, and fire?"

Her shoulders pop up and down. "It's a talent of mine."

I bite my lip. I chew on it. I gnaw on that thing until I taste blood. "Yes," I finally say. "I want to get on the diving board."

Her brows pinch together. "You lost me."

"Well, you said that thing about diving…" I slice my hand through the air. "Ah, forget it. I want to be with Avery." I swear there's a whooshing feeling coming from my chest. I clutch it and let out a nervous giggle. I shake out my arms, my shoulders. "Holy shit. That feels so good to say."

Charlee bounds forward, tackling me to the floor. "See how good it feels when you're true to yourself? Look at you, my little Claire Bear!" She gets all up in my face, trying to pinch my cheeks. "I'm so proud of you!" Rolling off me, she shoves my phone into my chest. "Now call him."

Giggling, I press one hand to my hot cheeks while my thumb hovers over his contact, the picture of him and Vivi I took last weekend. I pause. "Shouldn't I talk to him in person? And preferably when I'm sober?" Something tells me he'd appreciate that more than a drunk phone call.

The dip of Charlee's brows tells me that she's disappointed she won't get to sit in on the phone call. She sighs, shoulders sagging. "Yeah, you're right. Being sober definitely seems important. Bet he'd appreciate a grand gesture at the fundraiser."

I'm not big into grand gestures, but I'm sure it'll be the perfect time to talk to him, to make this right, so long as he's willing to hear me out after a day to cool off.

"Yeah, I love this plan," Charlee says, head bopping, even though she's the one that came up with it. She shoves a handful of popcorn into her mouth before grabbing her phone. "I'm gonna text my brother to let him know that you and I will be needing lots of extra breaks tomorrow and a greasy breakfast spread." She points her phone at me. "Pose with your drink so he knows I'm serious."

Grinning at the camera through my still-watery, swollen eyes, I hold up a handful of licorice in one hand and my drink in the other.

"Oh, this is fantastic. You look like a hot mess. Dex'll never deny us now. He'll probably buy us lunch, too."

It's after eleven when I'm stumbling down the street toward my building, which is way too late for me on a work night, especially with the little sleep I've gotten this week. But Dex, ever the gentleman, assured us a free pass tomorrow, promising greasy food, iced coffees, and a quiet day locked in our offices. So we accidentally opened a bottle of wine.

I've drunk an unholy amount of alcohol tonight, and my bones are telling me I may never be the same again. It's not great, but the heaviness in my heart has lifted tenfold, and that right there does wonders for a woman.

I'm humming along to my music and doing this little hip sway thing that I'm sure looks less like dancing and a lot more like I'm having some sort of medical attack while walking, but I don't care. I'm happy. It's entirely too freeing of a feeling to admit what's going on in my heart and to finally agree to act on in it in a way that makes sense. All I know is I can't wait to see Avery tomorrow and tell him how I feel.

I grin like the happy I drunk I am—quite the contrast from the sad, pitiful drunk I'd planned to be alone in my bathtub tonight— at a man leaning against the brick of a building two down from mine. He's puffing on a cigarette, his eyes smiling at me while they drift down my body.

When I move past him, he reaches forward and tugs one of my earplugs out, making me gasp with surprise.

"Hey gorgeous," he purrs.

He's not so bad looking himself, tall, but not as tall as Avery, cute smirk, but not as irritating as Avery's. I'm also not a fan of smoking, which I've just made obvious by choking on the thick air and waving my hand around to try and clear it. He chuckles and throws his cigarette to the ground, stomping on it with his shoe.

"Whatcha listenin' to?" He pops my earbud in.

Ew, gross. Those are definitely going in the garbage.

His lips curve up. "Tragically Hip, huh? Good taste."

He hands my bud back and I curl my fingers around it because, like I said, there's no way I'm putting that thing back in my ear.

"Where you off to? It's kinda late to be walking around by yourself. Need me to escort you?"

I point to my building. It's, like, a hundred steps away, but it suddenly feels like a hundred blocks. "No thanks. Pretty much home already." Crap, I'm still slurring my words. They're slow and lazy as I sway a bit in my spot. He reaches out and wraps his fingers around my elbow, steadying me. I don't know if I appreciate it or not.

"You look a little drunk. How 'bout I help you get upstairs?" His eyes scroll up and down my body, lingering on my legs, or my ass, I'm not sure. "Those are the tiniest shorts I've ever seen."

"Oh, uh…thanks?" I tug on my jogging shorts, suddenly feeling incredibly uneasy and a little too exposed. I may be drunk, but I'm with it enough to realize this situation is quickly becoming uncomfortable.

"You've got nice legs." He moves behind me and whistles. "And that ass. Shit."

When he comes back around and stops in front of me, he's biting his knuckles. A tremble shakes my spine and goosebumps dot my flesh.

"Right. Well, thanks." I thumb toward the condo. "I gotta work in the morning, so…" I teeter back on my heels before taking a step forward. I wobble just a bit and his hand catches mine.

"Let me walk you upstairs," he suggests again.

"Oh, no, it's okay. I got…I mean…my…I told my boyfriend I'd text him and he'd meet me downstairs to let me in." I fumble for my phone in my back pocket.

Except I don't have back pockets in these shorts. My phone is in my backpack.

Panic sets in when the man's lips curl into a menacing smile and his grip on my hand tightens. He takes a step forward and I mirror his movements, backing up. I try to tug my hand free.

"Please," I say. I hate how weak it comes out. I hate that I drank like I was in high school tonight. I hate that I've made mistake after mistake lately. "You're hurting me."

"Well, I wouldn't want that. I just wanna make you feel good, beautiful. Unless you like it to hurt a little bit. I can handle that." His eyes darken, tongue swiping across his lips.

My chest tightens past the point of painful.

The man jerks his head toward my building. "Come on, gorgeous. Show me your apartment."

"I don't fucking think so," a dark, husky voice spits out from behind me.

A warm hand slips under my backpack and lands on my lower back, sweeping me forward while my hand gets ripped out of the other man's tight grasp. Something fluffy rubs against my leg. I look down at Sully, his chest puffed out while he stands on guard, growling at the man I'm desperate to get away from.

"Keep your fucking hands off her," Avery snarls. "Claire, let's go." He pulls me tight into his side and stalks off toward the building, my feet barely touching the ground as he drags me along with him.

Avery pushes me through the front doors and jams his finger into the elevator button about twenty-five thousand times. "What the fuck were you thinking?" He glares down at me, lips curled back over his teeth. His chest lifts and falls rapidly with each heavy breath.

I'm feeling a little bit intimidated by him right now, mildly shocked by what just happened outside, and a lot drunk, so I sway backwards on my feet.

Avery catches me, his grip tight on my arm, midnight eyes flicking over me. He leans closer. "Are you drunk right now?"

My eyes widen and I open my mouth to speak but no words come out. The elevator opens and he scoffs, forcing me through the doors. He steps in after me and mutters something under his breath.

"What?"

He turns on me, looking downright livid. "I said un-fucking-believable, Claire. You walked home by yourself in the middle of the night in downtown Toronto." He waves his hand over my body. "You're fucking trashed."

"I am...not." I lean back on the wall, because I have to, and he twists away, shaking his head. Our eyes stay locked on each other in the mirrored walls. The elevator feels like it's moving faster than normal.

My face lights up when I realize Sully's staring at me, panting happily with his tongue flopping out the side of his mouth. I crouch down and reach for his face while he trots over to me.

"Sully, *leave it*." Avery tightens his hold on the leash, stopping Sully. He whimpers and my face falls. I'm an *it* and Avery doesn't want me near his dog. Avery sighs and grumbles something I can't hear before giving the leash some slack. Sully comes bounding into my arms while I sink to the floor, burying my face in his fur.

"You didn't have to ride with me. You could have...took...your fancy elevator."

338

He snorts. "Little late for that, isn't it?" I lift my eyes to find that we're only five floors away from mine. "And clearly you need someone to make sure you get home safely."

Okay, now maybe I'm not entirely in my right mind right now, but the words I want to say to him are right on the tip of my tongue. He looks pretty freaking angry with me and if telling him now instead of waiting 'til tomorrow ends this madness, I'm game for it.

Except that I'm *not* in my right mind so I'm not sure how much he'd appreciate the sentiment right now. So I zip my lip and lock it, throwing away the fake key. Avery's eyebrows skyrocket while he watches my reflection. I think I even see the corner of his mouth twitch while he tries to fight a smile.

The doors ding and before I can even attempt to pick myself up off the floor, Avery's fingers curl around mine, hauling me to my feet. He ushers me out into the hallway without another word.

Feeling a little dejected—although rightfully so after my performance this morning—I mosey on down to my door, putting a little extra saunter in my step.

It's actually not a saunter at all. I'm pretty sure it looks more like a cop pulled me over and asked me to walk in a straight line while touching my nose with alternating hands. I'm failing miserably.

I shove my key in the lock and glance over my shoulder to find Avery's head peeking out the elevator, one big, strong, masculine, magical hand holding it open. When I disappear—backwards so I can still watch him—into my apartment, his shoulders sag, he breathes a sigh, and the doors slide closed in front of him, but not before I hear him murmur, "Goodnight Claire."

Aw, crap. I think I love him a lot.

CHAPTER THIRTY-SIX

Avery

It's a beautiful day, which is absolute shit for my mood, because I feel like a bag of hot garbage, and it would be fantastic if the weather could more accurately match that feeling. Instead, I'm sitting on the patio in the sunshine, soaking it all up, wishing I was at home doing a whole shitload of nothing.

It's not like me. I'm not lazy. I don't like to sit around with nothing to do, that's why I rarely do it. I like to be busy. I like to work my ass off. I like sitting here every Friday with Wyatt while we drink good alcohol and eat good food before heading back to the office for the last few hours before the weekend hits.

Today, though? Today I don't wanna do anything. I sure as shit don't wanna go to this fundraiser tonight where I'm somehow supposed to act like I don't see Claire, like I don't want to be the one spinning her around the dancefloor, pulling her in for a kiss. Thirty-six hours ago, she was supposed to be my date tonight. We were moving forward, or so I thought. Instead, we took, like, ten giant leaps backwards.

The waitress sets my scotch down in front of me with a wink. "Back to scotch, huh? Off that beer kick?" Her face screws up with distaste. "That Strawberry Grove is so disgusting and sour, I don't know how you drink it." She juts her hip out and tosses her straight, golden locks over her shoulder.

"I like the sour," I mutter, taking a sip of my scotch. But the thought of drinking that beer today makes my throat feel itchy and I need something stronger right now.

"Mhmm, whatever you say. I like you better as a scotch drinker."

Great, I don't give a fuck. That's what I almost say, and Wyatt knows it's on the tip of my tongue, because he's smirking at me over the edge of his glass, one brow creeping toward his hairline.

Instead, I give the waitress a tight-lipped smile and raise my glass. "Thanks for the drink."

Her lashes flutter as she pats my shoulder. It's not so much a pat as it is a slow slide from the back of my shoulder, over my chest, giving my pec a rub for good measure. I drop my gaze so she can't see the look on my face right now which is stuck somewhere between *what the fuck* and *please don't touch me.*

When she walks away, I squint up at the sun, licking a bead of sweat off my top lip. It's fucking sweltering out, but why wouldn't it be? Noon in June. Shit, that rhymes.

"Why the fuck did we sit outside for lunch?" I complain.

Wyatt gives me a short, quiet chuckle, glancing down at his drink before back up at me. "Shit, you're pretty wrecked, aren't you?"

"What?"

"Pretty torn up over this Claire shit." He waves his hand through the air, gesturing at me. "Never seen you so fucking grumpy. You're like a teenage girl on her period."

"I'm fine, and I don't wanna talk about it." I swirl my drink around, watching the ball of ice smack off the round glass. I put it down with a sigh. "It's just that I don't understand why this is so difficult for her, why she won't admit how deep her feelings run, why she's playing this off as if it's nothing."

I'd like to wipe Wyatt's shit-eating grin right off his face. "Thought you didn't wanna talk about it?" He blows out a breath. "And just how deep do *your* feelings run, Beck? Seems to me you might wanna be sure of that before you lure her into this, whatever this is with you."

341

I sink back in my chair, staring him down. "Trust me, I'm sure of my feelings. Otherwise I would have given up on this chase a long time ago."

Wyatt gives me an assessing once-over. "Ah. You're in love with Claire."

My eyes flip up to his, then drop back down to my drink. I don't answer him, but I guess that alone is answer enough.

He taps a finger on the table, eyes never leaving mine. "Gotta say, I saw this coming from a mile away when you took off the first night to help Charlee find Claire when she fucked off with her ex."

"No you didn't," I scoff.

His head bobs with a nod. "Did too. Normal-you would have said it wasn't your problem. Instead, you jumped into action." He sips at his drink. "So…I think you knew even then that this was gonna be something more with Claire."

Did I? I mean, I knew Claire was different from the moment my gaze fell on her when she strolled into that bar, those green eyes floating around like she didn't have a clue how to act in here. She turned nearly every damn head in the place without even trying, and truthfully, the attention made her a little bit uneasy, like she was confused why anybody would be interested in her.

I thought about Claire on and off all weekend after that. I wondered if she made it home okay, if she cried when she got into bed, if she gave that asshole another chance the next day. I wondered if she thought about me. And I wondered how the fuck I was going to find her again in a city with over six million people when all I knew was her first name.

And then fate had dropped me on her doorstep on the Monday morning. Or, rather, the doorstep of a brewery.

So yeah, maybe Wyatt is right. Maybe I knew right from the beginning that there was going to be more to Claire, more to us than sex, more than a one-night stand.

"I'm not ready to give up." The words fall off my tongue at the same time the thought flits across my brain.

Wyatt simply lifts his shoulder. "Then don't. Have you done everything you can?"

"I guess not, but…what more do I do? She told me to see other people."

"You don't believe she actually wants that, do you? Shit, look how she reacted when Sam kissed you at the birthday bash."

"No, I don't believe her at all. I don't know why she would even suggest it." But it hurts all the same. She won't put a single bit of trust in me, in whatever this has the potential to be.

His brow quirks with amusement. "Really? You don't know why?"

When I don't answer, he groans, stretching his arms out over the table, head dipping like he can't believe he needs to spell this out for me. "She just got out of a long-term relationship with someone she trusted after she found him balls-deep in someone else. You're not exactly a saint and she knows that. Christ, you asked her to go back to your place and fuck when you'd known her for all of five minutes. She doesn't want to get hurt again, Avery. She's pushing you away before you can."

"But I won't—"

Wyatt holds up a hand. "I know that's not your intention, and I bet deep down she knows that, too. But that doesn't change the fact that it's on her mind. It happened once; it can happen again. I'm sure she's just as upset about your fight as you are."

Scrubbing my hands over my face, I laugh. It's not a *haha* laugh, but more of a *I can't believe this is fucking happening* laugh. "She fucking infuriates me, you know that? I took Sully for a walk late last night and found her getting man-handled on the street by a guy she didn't know. She was trying to get away from him but he wasn't giving up and she was drunk. She was fucking trashed, walking home alone in the middle of the night. How could she be so stupid? And what would have happened if I hadn't been there and stepped in?"

Wyatt takes a drink with an audible, smacking sigh when he puts his glass down. "So, let me get this straight. You two had your big blowout, then she went out, probably with Charlee, and got absolutely wasted?"

"Right."

"Well, there ya go. That just shows you she was upset. Needed her best friend and a shitload of booze to get her through the night. Was she upset to see you? Annoyed?"

"She seemed relieved. Maybe a little scared, because I was pretty angry. She actually looked like she wanted to say something to me." I smile a bit, remembering how she'd zipped her mouth, locked it, and then threw away the metaphorical key. Then she'd walked backward into her apartment just so she could stare at me with that goofy, doe-eyed expression on her face. I wanted to be so mad at her in that moment, but she was so fucking cute that I'd nearly chased after her and kissed her, begged her to give me a chance.

"Sounds like she just needs a push in the right direction."

"What do you mean? A push how?"

"Well, you know she likes you. I mean, we all fucking know. We have these things called eyes on our face, which makes it incredibly helpful for seeing this shit." Wyatt's eyes twinkle with sarcasm as he lifts a lazy shoulder and lets it fall. "She thinks she can handle seeing you with other people? Test that theory."

Blinking at him, I let his words sink in. "Are you telling me to make her jealous so she realizes she wants to be with me?"

"Yup. That's what I'm saying."

"I honestly don't know if that's brilliant or the stupidest, shit advice I've ever received."

His grin is a challenge as clinks his glass off mine. "Only one way to find out."

The waitress, Gwen, appears at our table, a platter on each hand. "Hey there, handsome men. Food's here." She flashes me a pearly smile, pouty lips painted red, and slides our lunch onto the table.

Gwen's been mad at me for the last few weeks, ever since I ignored her advances and she caught me kinda dirty texting with Claire. Not that I've cared in the slightest. But today she seems to have decided to put that all behind her.

My eyes flick up and down her body. She's always been good-looking, which was why we had flirted every Friday, pre-Claire, when Wyatt and I came here for lunch.

But now I feel nothing when I look at her.

Her cheeks turn pink from my gaze. "Like what you see?" She bites her red lip and twists in her spot.

I meet Wyatt's eyes and his brows quirk in a way that says *here's your chance.*

My head already hurts from what I'm about to do.

But I open my mouth and do it anyway.

"Are you free tonight?"

CHAPTER THIRTY-SEVEN

Avery

I already know I've made a huge mistake based on how anxious I am right now, my eyes darting around the ballroom as I adjust the button on my suit jacket for the third time, hoping like hell Claire's still hungover from whatever the hell happened yesterday evening and has decided to skip tonight's fundraiser.

"I'm a fucking asshole," I mutter, feeling a lot like I just swallowed my heart after I spot a redhead who thankfully happens to *not* be the girl I desperately want to/do not want to see tonight.

Wyatt glances my way. "Already? She's not even here yet."

"I know, and that's a problem. She's not here yet and I feel like a fucking dick." I push out a heavy exhale and my fingers plow through my hair, one hand scrubbing at my jaw. I'm beyond agitated right now. "I'm not sure this is the right way to go about this."

"Just go with it, Beck. It'll be fine. She'll see you, get jealous, and that'll be it. She'll tell you how she feels and the whole thing will be over in two minutes."

Sophie, Wyatt's date, snorts. "For the record, Avery, I'm not on board with this. Yeah, it'll probably make her realize how strongly she feels for you, but she's also probably gonna want to punch you in the baby-maker. So…" She lifts her wine glass to her lips and tilts her head at me with the arch of one perfect brow. "Be prepared for that."

I groan and rub the back of my neck. Fuck me. I also feel shitty for leading Gwen on. She's been bouncing on her heels all night, bubbling with excitement. Normally, a girl knows exactly what I'm after—one night, no strings. Gwen and I didn't have that discussion, and it's not like I'm even after the sex tonight. She keeps pouting up at me, trying to wrap her arms around my neck. Keeping her at arm's length is exhausting as hell.

Gwen catches my eye as she makes her way back from the bar, a glass of wine in each hand, which she waves wildly over her head, grinning. "Did you miss me?" she asks, sidling up next to me. She rubs her chest on mine and goes in for a kiss. I turn my head and she gets my cheek.

Wyatt nearly spits his drinks out and Sophie hides her snicker with an exaggerated cough.

"Uh, yeah. Missed you tons." The lie curdles in my stomach like sour milk.

"Hey, can you hold these for me? I'm gonna go to the bathroom." Gwen shoves her two stems into my hands and I immediately set them down on the cocktail table we're standing around. I don't know why she couldn't do that herself.

"Again?" I ask. We've been here for all of forty-five minutes and she's already gone to the bathroom three times. Each time she returns, her lips are painted a different shade of pink as if that's the one that'll get me to kiss her.

"Gotta stay pretty." She taps my nose and runs off.

"Dear fucking God, I could not have picked a worse date," I breathe out, dropping my head back, mortified.

Sophie laughs and licks her thumb, wiping my cheek. "Can't have lipstick on you when your girl comes in. That's one step too far."

"Thanks, Soph."

I like Sophie. Her and Wyatt have some sort of agreement where she comes to events as his date and they fuck like rabbits after, but both of them are good with not dating. They say they're just really good friends. I can see it. I mean, Sophie is fun and easy to talk to, and she couldn't give two shits about how much money Wyatt makes, which is always a bonus. She gets a fun night out of it, and that's more than enough for her. I think they're probably the only two people in the world who make friends-with-benefits work.

Wyatt lets out a low whistle. "There she is, Beck. Shit, she's dressed to kill tonight."

"That's Claire?" Sophie's hand lands on my forearm, gripping it. "Holy hell, Avery. She's stunning."

"What? Where?" I crane my head around the crowd, trying to get a look at my girl.

And when I do…Christ, somebody help me.

Claire looks…dazzling. She's a tall glass of champagne, and all I want to do is toss her back and get drunk on her. The shimmering material draped over her milky skin dips low down the center of her chest and clings to the curve of her hips, thin straps showing off her delicate, freckled shoulders. With every step she takes into the room, her smooth legs peek through the high slit running up the front of her dress, showing off the matching, strappy golden heels on her feet.

I can't help it. When Dex wraps his arm around her waist and pulls her into him, bending to whisper something in her ear and making her laugh, jealousy flares in my chest, making my fists clench.

Claire steps away from Dex, surveying the room, looking for…me? Yes, me. Her lush forest eyes light up when our gazes lock from across the room and a brilliant smile spreads across her face. I'm real fucking confused right now, and especially when she starts making her way over to me, peeking up at me every few steps from beneath her thick, fluttery lashes, a coy smile curving the corner of her mouth while she tries so hard to stop those teeth from gnawing on her crimson lips.

"Uh, that doesn't look like a woman who doesn't know whether or not she wants to be with you, Avery," Sophie mumbles beside me. "She looks pretty sure of herself about who her man is. You might wanna reconsider your plan."

"Don't reconsider," Wyatt insists with a pointed eyeroll directed at his date.

I'm fucking considering reconsidering. I *am* reconsidering. I don't want to do this. This feels wrong. Fuck. Shit.

"I'm telling you to fucking *abort*, Beck," Sophie grinds out, gripping my arm, long nails gouging through my suit jacket. "Abort this mission," she hisses. "Ditch your date! Fast!"

Shit, shit, shit.

I don't have time to make a decision.

Claire stops in front of me, Charlee and Dex flanking her sides. She opens her mouth to say something, but Wyatt wraps her up in his arms.

"Claire, you are absolutely stunning, as always." He kisses her cheek.

"Nobody compliments me as much as you do," she says with a giggle. Her gaze bounces between me and Sophie, a silent question.

Wyatt puts his hand on Sophie's back. "This is my date and good friend, Sophie. Sophie, this is Claire."

I absolutely don't miss the look of pure relief that paints Claire's features when she realizes Sophie is with Wyatt and not me, her eyes brightening, lips parting in a grin.

Yeah, I don't want to do this. Is there a way I can sneak out of here with Claire before Gwen gets back? I start looking around the ballroom, planning my exit strategy while Claire and Sophie embrace, and Wyatt continues with introductions.

Claire steps in front of me, cheeks flushing when she tips her head backwards to smile up at me. Fuck. She's perfect. Her smile, her pink, freckly cheeks, her ruby red lips. She fiddles with a loose tendril of hair that's spilling down the side of her face. Most of it is twisted away from her face in some sort of wavy ponytail, sweeping down her back and over her shoulder. I want to yank the pins free and bury my hands in it.

"Hi Avery," she says quietly. "You look very handsome."

"Thanks," I croak. I'm a goner. "You look…um…" I scratch my head, totally lost for words as my brain shuts down on me. "I mean, wow."

Her giggle is low and anxious. "Thanks, I think." She reaches for me but pauses, looking unsure. Her fingers curl back into little fists, and I notice her perfectly shaped fingernails match her toes and her eyes—hunter green. "Um, do you think we could—"

"Thanks for waiting for me, babe." A pair of lips land on my cheek, an overpowering floral scent invading my nostrils, overwhelming my senses to the point that I feel woozy.

Claire's eyes widen as Gwen wraps her hands around my elbow. I watch those emeralds move rapidly between us. Those teeth Claire was trying to keep from her lower lip descend, trying to still that slight tremor.

I know this was the exact reaction I wanted, but this feels nothing like how I thought it would. I try to shake Gwen off me, but her talons just dig in, holding on for dear life.

"You…um…is this…" Color paints Claire's face as she trips over her words. Her throat works with her thick swallow. She can't finish her question.

Gwen sticks her hand out to Claire. "I'm Gwen. Avery's date."

"Your…date."

I can't take my eyes off those glistening orbs. Claire looks…utterly devastated. Those gorgeous eyes that I love redden right in front of me. I open my mouth to say something, anything, but nothing comes out. See: brain walking out on me two minutes ago.

Gwen snickers. "Yeah, he's been flirting with me for ages. Finally got the courage to ask me out today, didn't you?" She rubs my chest and grabs my face, kissing my cheek again.

Claire's gaze flips up to mine, and there it is. Betrayal. Hurt. But worst of all…defeat. She's done.

"Claire, I—"

She plasters on a fake smile and blinks back her tears while everyone else looks like they'd rather be anywhere but here, except Charlee, who seems to be running through a thousand different scenarios in her head on how best to cut off my dick and feed it to me.

"I hope you two have fun tonight. Excuse me." Claire turns on her heel and quickly disappears into the crowd.

"Huh, that was weird." Gwen drags a fingertip along my jaw, making me shiver with displeasure. "I think somebody has a crush on you. Too bad you're here with me, eh, handsome?"

I shrug out of Gwen's death grip and sidestep away. Dex looks like he's about to ask Charlee what plan of attack she's decided on and how he can help. I need to get the hell out of here, preferably with Claire by my side, even if I have get down on my knees and beg.

"Charlee, can you—"

"See if she's okay?" she spits out. "Sure. Wouldn't want you to have to leave your *date*." She storms off after Claire, the crowd parting around her as she goes.

What. The. Fuuuck.

I'm so confused. I mean, I know why I feel like an asshole. I don't know why the hell I did this, why I ever thought hurting her as a means to getting her was a good idea. But this is exactly what Claire said she wanted, isn't it? She's the one who told me to see other people. I wasn't expecting her to come here looking all happy to see me, wanting to...what did she want to do, anyway? *Um, do you think we could*...Gwen had cut her off before she could finish. Did she want to talk? Dance? What?

I need to find Claire.

I take one step and Gwen slips her hand into mine. "Let's go dance, Avery."

I look down at our joined hands. "Uh, I don't think—"

351

"Come on," she pouts. "You brought me here and you don't want to dance with me? I got all dressed up for you. Don't you think I look nice?" She smooths her hands down her torso and takes the long red skirt between her fingers, fluffing it out.

I've never been a bigger asshole.

With a sigh, I tell her, "You look very beautiful. But Gwen, I'm—"

She grins, clasping her hands under her chin. "Thank you! Let's dance!" She yanks me out to the floor, wrapping her arms around my neck.

Very carefully, I put my hands on her waist, touching her with only the tips of my fingers as we start to sway back and forth to the music. Well, she sways; I just kind of shift on my feet, just like my eyes are shifting around the room, on the lookout for Claire.

As if thinking about her is enough to conjure her up, she sneaks out of the bathroom with her head down, Charlee at her side, holding her hand and clutching her elbow. I watch them find our small group, and that's the only place I want to be, too. Wherever she is.

I can't tear my eyes off Claire, but I should, because the second she looks up and sees this, me and Gwen, the last thing I want to see is the hurt that's bound to slash her face. I'm a fucking coward. I chose to do this; I should be able to take it, own up to it.

But I can't. I can't stomach hurting her. I'm just like Aaron right now, and that's the last person I ever wanted to be to her. I've spent these last weeks trying to convince her that I'm different, that I won't hurt her the way he did, but this right here is the exact opposite.

I try to focus my attention on Gwen as she chatters away, but I can't. She doesn't feel right in my arms at all. She feels foreign and unnatural. My body aches to get away from her, to wrap myself up in Claire.

"You know, you can shift your hands a little lower," Gwen purrs in my ear. "I don't mind."

I'm about to tell her I'm good here and that maybe we should take a break, when her hands drop to mine, pressing them flat on her waist, dragging them over her hips, settling them on her ass. Naturally—because I really fucked myself here—this is the exact moment Claire's roaming gaze lands on us.

I rip my hands off Gwen. She grabs my face and pulls down, smashing her lips against mine.

I bounce backwards, hands in the air.

"Claire! Claire, come back!"

"I'm leaving," a broken voice chokes out.

I spin frantically, watching Claire hurry past us.

Charlee halts in front of me, jabbing a hard finger into my chest. Charlee's usually so happy and friendly. Right now, she's anything but, probably because, above all, she's fiercely protective of the people she loves. "You're acting like a jerk! What the hell are you doing, Avery? Do you get pleasure in making her cry?"

"Cry?" I turn, searching desperately for Claire. I can't find her. "I didn't mean…I mean…" I tug at my hair. "Fuck, I was just trying to get her to realize that she has feelings for me." I gesture at Gwen haphazardly. "I was just trying to make her jealous."

"*What*?" Gwen fumes.

"I'm sorry," I apologize sincerely. "I'm so sorry. It was a mistake. I shouldn't have ever asked you to come here tonight."

Charlee shoves my chest with both hands. "She doesn't need you to do *this* to make her realize it! She already knows exactly how she feels about you! Newsflash: she feels pretty fucking seriously about you."

I blink. Once. Twice. "What?"

Charlee throws her arms up in the air and makes an irritated, furious noise. "Are you kidding me? First of all, it's plain as day how she feels about you. Second of all, she talks about you all the time. All. The. Fucking. Time." She punctuates each word with the sharp jab of her finger. "She's just been terrified that you're going to hurt her!" Charlee gives her head a soft shake, her voice dropping to a heartbreaking volume. "And it looks like she was right all along. Congratulations, Avery. You hurt someone whose heart was already broken."

"No, Charlee, I didn't mean to." I shake my head rapidly. "Please, I—"

"You didn't mean to?" One hand on her hip, the other rubs at her temple. "How did you think this was going to play out, Avery? I mean, really." Her unrelenting disappointment in me right now has me more ashamed than I've ever been. I deserve it all.

"She told me...I mean, you heard her. She told me she didn't want me. She told me to see other people. I don't want anyone but her." If I sound destroyed right now, it's because I am.

"For the record, Avery, she came here tonight to tell you how she feels and that she wants to be with you. She was so excited. She was going to tell you last night, but she had—" she coughs, looking slightly guilty, "—a little too much to drink. It might've taken her a while to get here, but all things considered, I think she did pretty well. She knew she made a mistake, and she wanted to make it right, own up to her feelings."

"She really wants to be with me?" I grab Charlee's hands, feeling hopeful for the first time since Claire walked in here. I pull her in, her gaze drifting over my expression, assessing me.

"Is this really happening right now?" It's Gwen. She's still standing here, listening to everything. "Avery's with *me*, not her!"

Charlee rolls her eyes at her. "Oh, fuck off, Gwen. Haven't you heard a single word of this conversation? He's taken." She yanks her hands free from my grasp and pops two fists on her hips. "You want her, Avery, you better fix this. Fix it *now*."

"Yes. Okay." I nod about a hundred times. "I will. I'll fix it."

I spin, looking for the exit. We've got a bit of a crowd gathered around us now, most of them looking anxious. Wyatt's jaw ticks while he scrubs the back of his neck. I point at him. "Worst advice you've ever given me. I don't know why I listened to you."

He throws up his hands, managing to look both guilty and innocent all at once. "Man, I don't fucking know! I don't have a girlfriend! I don't know how this shit works."

Sophie chuckles and pats his arm affectionately. "It's true. He doesn't have a romantic bone in his body. Avery, go get your girl."

Dex wraps his hand around my arm, his expression and tone laced with warning. "You better fix this, Beck. I warned you."

"I will." A promise I have every single intention of keeping. I look to my date. "I'm truly sorry, Gwen. What I did was wrong. Wyatt, can you make sure she gets home tonight?"

I catch Wyatt's curt nod while Gwen seethes, "Don't you *dare* think about coming back to the restaurant unless you're ready to grovel at my feet."

Yeah, that's not gonna happen, but I'm not about to keep this conversation going and longer than necessary. "Understood," I throw over my shoulder, heading for the door.

It's still early, which means the sun hasn't fully set yet. The sky is red and orange with wisps of lavender clouds, and the air is hot and sticky, making me feel constricted in my suit. I tug at my tie, desperate for some air.

It takes me all of three seconds to spot Claire down the street, head buried in her hands. Her body is shaking, quiet, heart wrenching sobs echoing along the quiet sidewalk.

Everything hurts. I never meant for this to happen.

I go to her, and fuck, I don't think I've ever moved so fast.

A cab stops in front of her and she lifts her head just enough to grab for the back door.

"Claire," I plead, reaching out for her.

She pauses halfway into the car, head down.

"Claire," I repeat softly. "I'm so sorry. I'm sorry, Claire. Please, talk to me. Let me explain." She jerks her hand away the second I reach for it, her silky skin slipping through mine.

She inhales deeply, the sharp breath crackling, and climbs into the car. When she reaches for the door to tug it closed, she looks up at me.

The pain that swims in those massive green eyes, red-rimmed and bloodshot, kills me. Crimson lips swollen, beautiful face soaked to the bone with tears, Claire is an utterly beautiful and heartbreaking mess.

"*Claire*," I choke out. "Please don't go, baby, please." I'm about ready to drop to my knees and beg her to stay here with me, to just be with me. If that's what it takes, I'll do it. I'll do anything for this woman.

But Claire raises one small hand, swiping her fingers across her wet eyes, spreading black mascara around. She sniffles, breathes out a husky *goodbye Avery*, and shuts the door.

The cab drives away, with Claire and my heart in it.

CHAPTER THIRTY-EIGHT

Claire

I thought I knew heartbreak when I found out Aaron had been cheating on me, deceiving me, using me, lying to me. I thought I knew. I was so sure it couldn't get any worse.

But I was wrong. This is worse. This is so much worse.

This hurt I'm feeling right now from seeing Avery and that girl together, dancing, kissing, is so physically painful I actually consider that I might be having a heart attack. Everything hurts. My chest is tight. My back aches. I can't stand up straight. It feels like my heart is being pulled from every angle, seeing how far it can be stretched. My stomach is all knotty and tumbling to the point that I'm clutching it with one hand while I run toward the front doors of the condo building, waiting for my body to decide that it can't take it anymore before I finally either vomit or my legs give out.

The door opens and the concierge ushers me in. "Are you okay, Miss Thompson?"

"Just fine," I manage without looking at him as I tear across the front foyer, slamming the elevator button a thousand times in three seconds. One set of doors opens right away. At least something is working in my favor tonight.

"Claire!"

My head whips up without my permission to find Avery running toward me, looking wild and distraught. I start hammering on the *close doors* button over and over again. I can't do this right now. I can't see him. I can't let him see what a mess I am over him.

"Claire, wait!"

The doors slide closed right before he reaches the elevator and I jump back when I hear a pounding thud on the other side and a loud *fuck!*

Sinking back in the corner, the tears keep flowing, louder now, wracking my body, and I just pray nobody else gets in this elevator before the twenty-sixth floor. In this elevator. *This* elevator. The very one where Avery gave me a mind-numbing orgasm down on his knees. The very one where, last night, I just about blurted out that I love him.

Love. *Fucking love.* Is this some kind of a cruel joke? That I would fall in love with someone like Aaron who would hurt me, destroy me so permanently, make me vow to never want to fall in love again, only to do it right away and with the worst person imaginable for me, for my stupid, fragile heart?

When the elevator stops on my floor, it takes me a few moments to get enough of a hold of myself to drag my feet out and down the hallway, still barely seeing through the pools in my eyes. I'm sure I look like a vision right now, snot dripping from my nose, face blotchy, raccoon eyes. I rub at my face and—sure enough—my fingers come away black.

Resting my forehead on my door, I take three deep breaths, hiccuping between each one.

And then another set of elevator doors spring open.

Avery steps out.

No, he doesn't step out. He dashes out, making a beeline for me.

Shit, shit, shit. I fish my keys out of my purse and try to shove them in the lock, but my hands are shaking so violently that I drop them to the ground. I bury my face in my hands, crying harder, because I'm just falling apart at this point.

I bend, reaching blindly for my keys, but Avery swoops in, scooping them up in his big hand.

"Give them back," I plead, reaching for them. He holds them away, his free hand wrapping around my wrist.

"Can I come in?" His smooth chocolate eyes beg me, more distressed than I've ever seen them.

He cannot be serious, and the look on my face must be answer enough.

"I'm not giving them back. Not until you talk to me, Claire. I'm not letting you walk through that door and watching you slam it in my face."

With two hands on his chest, I shove him as hard as I can. He doesn't even budge. "Fuck you! You can't do this! Give them back," I sob. "Please, Avery."

"We need to talk about this, Claire. We need to talk about us." His throat bobs with a swallow, chest heaving. He catches me around the shoulders, squeezing tightly. "Please, Claire."

"No," I croak out, long and slow. "You're just going to lie to me."

He grabs my chin, forcing me to look at him, his eyes no longer soft, but hard, impossibly dark, a raging storm, like whatever the hell is going on in my stomach right now. "I would never lie to you, Claire, and I never, ever have. I promise you that."

His lips are on mine suddenly, hungry, demanding, possessive, and I hate myself for melting into him, moaning into his mouth. Why does this man have such a carnal effect on me even after seeing him with another woman?

Our tongues duel viciously, fighting for control while I try to fight the desire to crawl up his body and latch onto him. My hands are buried in his hair, just like the words I want to say to him are buried in my throat, begging to be released.

I love you.

When he pulls back, both of us breathless, our chests lifting and falling erratically, I swipe at my wet lips and watch him walk away from me.

"I'm going upstairs." He presses the call button for the elevator and covers my keys in his fist. "When you're ready to talk, you can come up. I'll leave the door unlocked for you." He glances at me before he steps inside. "The quicker you throw out your stubborn attitude and come up, the quicker we can both put ourselves out of this misery."

Oh my God. He did not just—

"Avery!" I run toward him as the doors start sliding shut. "No! You can't! *Ugh!*" I bang my head off the closed stainless-steel doors and immediately regret it—because, fucking *ouch*.

I become a caged animal, pacing up and down the hallway, growling, snarling, crying.

Why? Why does it have to be Avery? Why is he the person I fall in love with at the worst possible time?

I slink against the wall, sliding down to my butt, face in my trembling hands. Everything Charlee said last night about Avery rang true. Every single thing. I've been stupid to try to stay away from him, to deny my feelings for someone who made me feel so genuinely happy.

But now? Now what? Was it all a lie? Everything he said to me? I've never been more confused in my life. On the one hand, he looks destroyed. The pain that flashed across his face when his date stepped up to his side, kissed his cheek, introduced herself to me…he looked like I felt on the inside—crushed.

Charlee told me I still needed to tell him how I feel, regardless of this mess. That I need to get it off my chest, be honest, even if only for myself, to know that I've done everything I should.

I don't know if I can bring myself to do it, not now. All I'd needed to do was admit to him that I cared for him, that I liked him. That was all he'd asked for in my office yesterday morning.

But that's not accurate. Those words aren't strong enough for what I'm feeling. Even if I didn't already think that it was love, the pain pulsating through my body would be enough for me to realize it now.

No, I can't do this right now.

Climbing to my feet, I tug a pin from my hair, bending one end backwards. Planting my palms flat on my door, I stare at the lock, tipping my head side-to-side, the tension in my neck cracking. I have no idea how to do this, but they do it in the movies, so...I shove the tip of my pin in the lock, twisting it desperately.

Nothing happens. And then it snaps in half.

Growling, I try again. The second pin joins the first on the floor.

Pulling my phone from my purse, I do a quick YouTube search for *how to pick a lock with a bobby pin.* Yeah, I really do that.

But even the video with sixteen million views and a handful of comments like *I can't believe this actually worked!* and *Got it on my first try!* is absolutely useless to me. Or maybe it's just me that's absolutely useless. All I know is fifteen minutes later I'm out of pins and my hair is an unruly mess down my back and around my shoulders, really adding to the whole wrecked hooker vibe I've got going on right now.

With a deep belly groan and the realization that I'm out of options if I want to sleep/collapse in an actual bed tonight, I drag myself into the elevator, smashing in every number in Avery's penthouse code.

Upstairs, I cross the hall to Avery's door, bracing myself against the frame. I have two options here: I can knock quietly, let him speak, and then politely excuse myself with my keys, or I can bust through there, guns blazing, and demand my keys back.

I go with option three, which I just made up now.

I try the handle. It's unlocked, just like he said it would be. With a tiny push, the door creaks open. My eyeball peeks around, but I can't see much from my spot. The sound of the shower running softly in the distance gives me enough courage to open the door just wide enough for me to slip in.

I don't see Avery. It's quiet, save for the pitter patter of running water coming from down the hall. The gentle throb between my legs tries to coax me to the bathroom to sneak a peek.

Not now, vagina. Didn't you get the memo? We're done with him.

Done. Done with Avery. There's not a single part of me that likes the way that sounds. A deep frown tips my mouth and my heart pulses erratically.

Tiptoeing into his space, my head swivels around, looking for my keys. I spy them on the island and start creeping over. Sully comes bounding over, big pink tongue lolling out the side of his mouth, and I can't help it—I drop to my knees and bury my fingers in his soft, fluffy fur.

"Hey Sul," I whisper, kissing the tip of his nose. I smooth my hand over his floppy ears and rub the white stripe that runs between his eyebrows and over his snout with my thumb. "You're such a handsome boy. I'm sorry, but I can't stay."

I press my lips to his wet nose again and straighten, snagging my key ring with my pinky. Like the stealthy ninja I think I am, I turn on my toes and creep with my head down back toward the door, mentally high-fiving myself for getting out of here unscathed, Avery's plan foiled.

Until I bounce off something hard, rigid, and scrumptious smelling.

I see the bare toes. I see the long, lean legs, the muscular thighs. I see the navy-blue boxer briefs and the impressive package inside. I see that fucking V, see those chiseled abs and all their ridges, the dark patch of hair circling the world's sexiest belly button—I know, who knew belly buttons could be sexy? I accidentally groan when my eyes find those pulsing, corded forearms, crossed over a rock-hard chest. And when I see the that stupid, sexy smirk, that cocked eyebrow, set over impossibly dark chocolate eyes, I lose it.

"Going somewhere?" Avery asks, tone laced with ice and a touch of mirth.

My heel catches on my dress when I step backwards, and I fall straight to my ass. Could this night literally get any worse?

No, I take back that question. I don't need to tempt fate.

I just stare up at Avery, not blinking, and he stares right back. Then he crouches to the floor and I think he's going to help me up, but instead, he takes my ankle and starts pulling my heels off. I try to jerk my foot away, but his fingers curl tighter.

"What are you doing? Let go of me!"

"I'm taking off your shoes, because you're not going anywhere, Claire."

"Like hell I'm not!" I try to scoot backwards on the hardwood, but he drags me right back.

Avery leans over me and my heartbeat kicks straight into high gear, as if it wasn't already there. Looking me dead in the eyes, he rips my shoes off and throws them over his shoulder.

"You're here, and you're staying. You're not going anywhere until we fix this."

His tone leaves no room for argument, but like the stubborn bitch I can be, I cross my arms over my chest and jut my chin out. "You can keep me here, but you can't make me talk."

Avery laughs, low, throaty, and a little bit scary, warm hands sliding up my legs, squeezing my thighs as my dress falls away. "I have never, *ever*, met a more stubborn, hard-headed woman in my life," he breathes. "You annoy the shit out of me sometimes."

"Well then, I wouldn't want to stay any longer and *annoy you* more than I need to. I'll just be on my way."

I twist onto my hands and knees, trying to crawl away from him. It's a stupid move. He grabs me around the waist and pulls me to his bare chest, curling over me until I can feel his hot breath tickle my neck. His lips graze the shell of my ear and I tremble in his arms. I think he's just going to try to fuck this problem away until he whispers against my skin.

"I'm sorry I hurt you tonight, Claire. I'm so sorry." Voice cracking, he buries his face in the crook of my neck, his arms winding so tightly around my body, holding me to him. "Please forgive me."

And that about does it. I'm a blubbering mess all over again, breaking down right here in his arms, on his floor. His own body starts shaking, or at least I think it does. It feels like he's vibrating, but it could just be because I'm a quivering blob in his arms.

But then I feel something wet where my shoulder meets my neck, and I know there's no way my tears got there. My resolve starts crumbling like a sandcastle.

"I was trying to make you jealous, and it was the stupidest thing I've ever done."

I pause. My heart stops. My anger flares. I turn around and shove him off me, baring my teeth as I climb to my feet. "You were trying to make me jealous? You did this on purpose to hurt me? How dare you," I growl, shoving my finger in his chest when he stands. "You bring a date to rub it in my face, to make me upset." Another jab. "You put your hands on her." I jab him again. "You *kiss* her." One more for good measure.

"Stop it!" Grabbing my hand, Avery tugs me into him. "I didn't kiss her; she kissed me. And for the record, I pushed her off."

I scoff and roll my eyes. "She can hardly be blamed for kissing you, since you, you know, *asked her out*! She obviously thought you liked her or wanted to get in her panties."

"I already told you it was fucking stupid. I was angry with you and hurting because of what you said to me in your office yesterday. You told me there was nothing going on between us. You told me you wanted to see other people."

And I regretted it the second the words were out of my mouth, but he doesn't know that. "And you said you didn't want to, and yet, there you were, thirty-six hours later, with your hand on some girl's ass."

"I fucked up, Claire. I did. I'm admitting it. It was so incredibly stupid of me, but I was at a loss. I didn't know how to get you to come back to me. I didn't know how to get you to admit you have feelings for me." He grabs my face in his hands, his eyes scouring mine. "But I've never lied to you. Never. Honestly…you're the one not being truthful. Not with me and not with yourself. I know there's something between us, Claire. It's…it's…" He trails off, his head just barely shaking while his eyes move between mine, desperate. "It's more than *something*, Claire. There's magic between you and me. You can't keep denying it." He takes my hand and holds it to his heart. "Please, tell me you feel it."

I feel the warmth of his skin against my palm and I press harder, my fingers curling over his collarbone on their own accord, feeling that steady thump beneath my touch. My heart stutters at the sensation, at the feel of his heartbeat, the vulnerability in his words.

"I…I…" I swallow thickly. Why can't I just say the words? Why can't I tell him how I feel? Why can't I just admit that I was wrong, that there's something here, that I want him? I squeeze my eyes shut when the tears start threatening again. His warm, smooth hands cup my face, thumbs sweeping underneath my eyes, catching my tears.

"Why is it so hard for you to admit?" His quiet question is a sincere plea.

"Because…because you might break my heart," I blurt, choking on my words, gripping his biceps when I fold forward.

"No I'm not. I promise. I'm not him, Claire," he insists, his tender voice as soothing as the palm he smooths over hair. "I'm not going to hurt you. I'm not going to leave you. If anybody, it's going to be *you* who breaks *my* heart." My eyes open to find Avery staring down at me, his brows knit together, face sheathed in pain as he brushes my hair off my face. "You kinda already have, several times over."

I open my mouth to deny it. I would never hurt Avery…

Except the agony behind that deep gaze tells me he's not lying.

"I know why you did it, Claire. I know you were just trying to protect yourself. You were already hurting, and you didn't want to trust anyone. You tried to push me away. But you hurt me, and I think you hurt you, too. Am I right?"

I bring a trembling hand to my lips. I nod. It's so minuscule, so tiny, but he sees it. His forehead relaxes just a touch at my admission, and I realize what a small amount of my truth means to him.

"I don't need a rebound," I manage between hiccups, melting into his feather-light strokes down the side of my face.

"That's fantastic," Avery starts softly, "because I don't want to be your rebound. I want to be your partner."

"I'm scared," I admit quietly.

"I'm fucking terrified."

A tiny laugh bursts past my lips and the corner of his mouth curves up.

"Tell me what you're feeling," Avery whispers, pressing his lips to my temple, hugging me. "Please, just tell me everything. Help me understand, Claire."

My stomach starts tumbling, cartwheeling, free-falling. I take a step back and start pacing, thinking, my mind racing. "It's just that…it's so soon, you know. I got out of this awful relationship. He cheated on me. I don't…" I stop, shaking my head, swatting at new tears. Fuck, why won't they stop? I drank a ton of alcohol last night; I should be way too dehydrated to cry today.

"I don't feel good about myself. I don't know what's wrong with me and I'm worried if we…if me and you…I'm worried you'll realize whatever he did." I close my eyes to the brutal truth of my confession. "You'll realize I'm not worth it. You'll leave, and I'll be broken all over again."

"*I won't.*" Avery steps toward me as I step away. "Claire, that guy's an absolute idiot if he didn't realize what he had when he had you."

"Is he? Or did he realize *exactly* what he had and got the fuck out of Dodge in the most cowardly way?"

366

He makes a deep, rough sound as his eyes fall shut, like he needs to compose himself before he responds. "Don't you dare talk about yourself like that. You're everything, Claire. *Everything.*"

"You barely know me," I argue weakly.

He chuckles softly. "On the contrary, Claire, I feel like I know you very well. I know that your family—Charlee and Dex included—is the most important thing in your life. I know you'd do anything for them. I know you're competitive and sassy and sarcastic and you swear like a trucker. I don't think you do it on purpose; I think the words just fly out of your mouth, and I think it's because you get so caught up in the passion of each moment. I know you're afraid to open your heart because you're scared of getting hurt, but I also know that your heart is huge. I know that you're strong as hell because you've survived a lot of shit over the years. You're strong because even though you're terrified that being cheated on is going to break you, you're not going to let it happen. You're not, Claire, do you hear me?"

Avery closes the distance between us, taking my hands in his. "I know that underneath your attitude, you're a big softie. You love physical connection, even if you sometimes pretend you don't." His gaze falls to our hands, thumbs sweeping across my knuckles before he brushes a kiss across them. My lashes flutter as I savor the feel of his lips igniting my skin.

"I know you've spent a lot of time being tough, but you crave someone to take care of you some of the time, because you can only be so strong on your own for so long. I know you need someone who's your equal, who's not going to give in to your every whim, someone who's prepared to fight back and occasionally tell you you're fucking wrong." A smile tugs at his face, his eyes crinkling. "Sometimes you're wrong, Claire, you know that? Like yesterday. You were wrong."

"I know. I know I was wrong." I drop my gaze. "I knew as soon as I said it." The word vomit comes when I start pacing again, throwing my hands up, gesturing around like a madman. "I just freaked out, okay? I freaked the fuck out. It all happened so fast. You came out of nowhere at the worst time and in a matter of, what, like, twenty-one days, I'm already falling in lov—"

I stop on a gasp. Both hands fly to my mouth, clasping it tightly before anything else can pour out of it.

Oh, no. No, no, no.

Avery's face tells me he doesn't need me to finish my sentence—he knows exactly what I was about to say. His brown eyes are wide, lips parted.

I can't look at him. This is absolutely mortifying.

"I'm so sorry," I mumble from behind my hand, knees wobbling. "I'm so, so sorry." I stifle a sob. "I told you I don't do casual well." I grab my keys off the floor and push past him, heading for the door. "I'll go."

I just get the door tugged open, defeat making my whole body slump, when his big hand comes down hard and fast, slamming it shut.

Avery spins me around, his wild eyes drinking me in. "Why would you leave now?"

Humiliation has me leaning backwards, away from him. "Because I just—"

"I know what you said. So why the hell would you leave if that's how you feel?"

Because you don't feel the same.

"Do you wanna do this thing with me, Claire? You wanna be with me? You and me, nobody else. Just the two of us."

I nod meekly, my fingers curling and fumbling under my chin. That's as brave as I can be right now.

"Then get your ass over here and be with me."

CHAPTER THIRTY-NINE

Claire

Avery's eyes drag over me, blazing with zeal and ferocity as he steps into me, pinning me to the door with his hips. He rakes his fingers through my messy locks before dragging his hands over my shoulders, down my arms, leaving the skin beneath my dress tingling when he grabs my waist.

"No more of this bullshit. Do you understand me? No fucking more. You want me, you have me. There's nobody for me but you. I'm sure of it."

My eyes bounce between his, looking for any sign that this might not be what he really wants, that maybe he hasn't thought this all the way through. I find nothing. "Avery…"

"*Claire.*" His hands slide up my arms, gripping my jaw as he tips his face down to mine. "I'm going to kiss you now and then we're going to be done with this. We're going to move forward, together. Is that what you want?"

I make a noise, something like a whimper-moan. His lips are an inch away. If I just press up on my tiptoes, tilt my head up—

"Use your words, Claire. Tell me."

"I-I do. I want that. I want…you. I want you, Avery. I want us."

He wastes no time, his mouth crashing down on mine. His tongue pushes past my lips, diving in, his fingers tugging at my hair, just like mine are his. This kiss is wild, teeth clashing, all of that pent-up anger, the passion. His hungry mouth slides down my neck, nipping, sucking at the base of my throat.

He flips me over, pressing me against the door, and yanks my zipper down. His hands sweep across my shoulders, pushing the straps of my dress down my arms until the shimmering material

369

slips over my hips and pools at my feet. He trails a fingertip down my spine, his lips following its fiery path.

"Fucking beautiful," Avery murmurs against the dip of my lower back before hooking his thumbs in my panties, dragging them down my legs.

He turns me back around and sweeps me into his arms, my legs wrapping around his waist. His eyes never leave mine as he walks us down the hallway.

"You've been running my water bill up this whole time," he teases at the exact moment I realize his shower is still running, the steady sound of rain beating against glass gently thrumming in my ears.

Avery walks us into the steamy bathroom and shifts me so that he's supporting me with only one hand, his other pushing his underwear to the ground, and then steps into the gigantic shower. He drops me to my feet and I look up at the rain shower overhead. It pelts my face in the softest, gentlest way and I open my mouth, welcoming every bit of euphoria that washes over my skin.

Avery's thumbs move over my cheeks, under my eyes, and come away smeared with black. I watch the gray water swirl on the white tiles until the drain slurps it down.

"I promise I'll never hurt you again," he whispers, winding an arm around my waist. "I'll never be the reason you cry again. I'm so sorry I hurt you tonight, Claire."

'I hurt me,' I admit. "And I hurt you along the way. I'm sorry, Avery." I take his face in my hands, unsure if I'm blinking through the falling rain or a fresh set of tears. He's so incredibly handsome, his dark waves wet and plastered to his forehead. I push them back, sliding my hand down the side of his face, gripping his jaw. My thumb swipes over his full lips, catching the water droplets that bead off them. "Can I kiss you?"

His smile splits his cheeks. "You never have to ask, especially when you're naked and in my shower."

Before I have a chance to respond, he pulls me into his chest, claiming my mouth, my tongue, my taste. Our tongues swirl together until we're one—one mouth, one kiss, just...one. Me and him, together.

Avery backs me against the shower wall and drops to his knees, his hands running up and down my sides, over my hips, my torso. He sucks on my hipbone, peering up at me. "I was so mad at you last night, Claire. When I found you on the street with that guy. So fucking mad that you'd put yourself in that position. I saw red. I wanted to hurt him." He lifts one leg and rests it on his shoulder, kissing and nipping a path up the inside of my thigh. "What if I wasn't there, Claire? Something might have happened to you."

He presses his tongue to my center and licks, one long, slow stroke from the bottom to the top. I groan and sink lower down the slippery wall, clutching at his wet locks.

"But you were there," I pant.

"You're never doing that again. You're out late at night and you call me. You were drunk, Claire. You scared the shit out of me when I saw him grabbing you, saw you swaying back and forth." He buries his face between my legs, his tongue darting in as he clamps down around me and sucks. "I wanted to throw you over my shoulder, bring you up here and spank you."

I can barely think straight when he talks like that, let alone when his tongue is inside of me, lapping. I love him angry, possessive, passionate. "You can still...you can still do that."

"I will. Tomorrow, maybe, but not tonight." He looks up at me from beneath his dark, thick lashes, water droplets clinging to the tips as he pushes two fingers inside of me. "Tonight...tonight, Claire, I just wanna take my time, love on your beautiful body, every inch of your creamy skin. I wanna find every freckle and kiss each one. You're perfect to me and I don't want there to be a shred of doubt about that by the time I'm done with you. Do you understand?"

"Yes." I already feel perfect when I'm with him. I don't know why or how, insecurities considered, but when I'm with him, I always feel it. The way he appreciates my body, the way he wants me, the way his eyes scour every inch of me, the way he touches me, sometimes as if I'm as delicate as crystal, and other times as though he needs me right that second, like nothing will ever be enough. That's how I feel about him—like it'll never be enough. I'll always want more, crave it. I'll never get enough of Avery Beck.

His lips close over my clit, sucking it between his teeth while his fingers pump faster, pushing deeper, and I can't stay upright anymore. I fold forward, grasping his shoulders as I start shaking from within.

"Avery...p-please. Ohhh."

My eyes roll up when his fingers curl. He pulls out and sucks my entire pussy into his mouth and I come all over his tongue. I'm a writhing, whimpering mess of limp limbs when he picks me up in his arms, flipping off the water and carrying me to his bed, not bothering with a towel.

"I hope you know we're not leaving this bed for the rest of the night." He crawls over me, flicking his tongue over my nipple before kissing his way up my throat, across my jaw.

"What if I get hungry?" It's meant to be cheeky, but it's likely to happen if I'm being honest. I'm pretty sure I burn a thousand calories on any given night when Avery's inside of me. With him, I'm always ravenous.

"Then I'll feed you my cock." He rolls his hips against mine, letting me feel the full weight of his arousal for me as he laughs against my lips. "I'll order pizza and we can eat in bed."

Avery makes good on his promise to find every single freckle. His fingers dance over every inch of my body, pressing on each little star before he covers it with his lips. He takes his time, his mouth washing me, exploring, claiming every inch as his.

"Just seeing if you taste different here," he says each time he sucks at a new spot. By the time he's done, my body is covered in the tiniest purple hickeys. I touch each one when he goes down on me again, and come when his hands close over my breasts, rolling my nipples between his fingers.

Positioning himself between my legs, he sweeps the tip of his swelling cock through my dripping folds, rubbing himself against my sensitive clit.

His eyes flick up to mine. "I know we didn't use a condom on Wednesday, but what do you want to do?"

"I'm on the pill," I remind him, panting and squirming as he teases my nub. "And we're both clean."

He nods and licks his lips but doesn't do anything. He doesn't want any misunderstandings.

"No condom." I pull his face down to mine, kissing him deeply. "I want to feel you, all of you, inside of me."

He groans in my mouth, tongue vibrating against mine, and swallows my gasp as the tip of his cock starts pushing through my entrance. His hands slide along my back, dragging me up to his chest as he fills me with a moan, biting into my collarbone.

"You feel so good. So fucking good, Claire, like heaven. I'm throwing out every single one of my condoms. No more. Never again. Can't go back."

Giggling, I arch my chest into his mouth as he fucks me. It's torturous, each thrust slow and deep, leaving me quivering in his arms, bucking my hips into his. I'm dying, going crazy. I can't take this. I need to come and he's doing his damn best to draw this orgasm out as long as he can.

"More, Avery, please."

He rolls his hips, rubbing against my clit, and I cry out, throwing my head backwards. "You want more? Faster? Harder?"

"God, *yes*." All of it, right now.

373

I feel his smile against my neck. He pulls out, gripping my hips, presses his lips to mine, flashes me an entirely too-wicked grin, and then slams into me, impaling me with his cock, pounding me over and over again without reservation. He bends my knees and shoves them up my sides and I scream at the new depth, the feel of him hitting me so hard. There's nowhere else for him to go, I'm sure of it. He's taking up every single space I have to offer inside of me, stretching me beyond my limits, and it's heavenly.

He presses on my clit—once, just one fucking time—and it sends me into a frenzy, screaming his name and clawing at his back as I soak his cock during orgasm number three.

Avery's thrusts slow, letting me catch my breath, but he never stops moving, sliding in and out of me. "You're gonna come again, baby. You're gonna come with me this time."

I push him backwards until his back hits the mattress. Lifting myself off him and leaning forward, I grip a fistful of his hair and tug his face up to mine. I nibble on his lip then gasp when his palm comes down hard on my ass.

He grins and winks. "Couldn't resist just one."

I bite back my ginormous smile. "You're the devil." And then I sink down his length, throwing my head back with a hiss and a deep belly groan.

"*I'm* the devil?" Avery growls, grabbing my hips roughly and lifting me. "*You're* the fucking devil, complete with fiery red hair and all."

He slams me back down on his cock and I ride him into oblivion. I can't stop the sounds flying my mouth and he can't stop the curses soaring from his. He yanks me off him and flips me around onto my hands and knees, sinking into me without warning, fucking me so hard from behind while he grips my throat, his lips pressing soft, sloppy kisses all over my back.

"Avery," I cry. "I'm gonna come. Please!"

"Yes baby," he hisses, hand dipping between my legs, rubbing furiously at my clit. "Come, baby. Come with me."

He plunges into me again and again, my walls shaking, clenching. My arms give out and I fall flat on my face into the pillow, burying my scream as I come around him. Avery groans, sinking his teeth into my shoulder as he pulses inside me, filling me to the brim.

He slaps my ass once more and rolls onto his back, bringing me with him, clutching me to his chest. He peppers my sweaty face with kisses, smoothing my wet hair back. "Break time," he wheezes.

"Pizza time?" I try with an angelic smile and the flutter of my lashes.

He chuckles and touches his lips to my nose. "Anything for you." Pushing me to my back, he kisses my stomach. "Need to fill you up. You'll need all the energy you can get."

Avery takes Sully out for a bathroom break while we wait for dinner, and then we eat the biggest, greasiest, most delicious pizza in bed. Pizza is followed by an unholy amount of rounds—the man is absolutely insatiable—of whatever wild thing he can think of in bed, until I'm a panting mess, wheezing for air and begging him to stop.

"I think you broke me," I gasp, smoothing his hair down while he rests his head on my chest.

His chuckle tickles at my nipple, making it tighten all over again. "I'm sorry. I could go all night with you. Never stop. But I'm toast, too." He props himself up on his elbows. "Bedtime?"

"For the love of God, Avery, *bedtime.*"

He grins and rubs the tip of his nose against mine. I love it when he does that. It's so sweet and intimate. But I love it even more when he tilts my chin up, touches his lips to mine.

Avery wraps me up in him, so tight. "So glad you're here with me in my arms," his throaty voice murmurs.

375

I skim his cheek with my fingers and kiss him once more. "Me too."

Avery's out in five minutes, and I lie there staring up at the ceiling for the next half hour. As happy as I am, I feel powerless against the tiny ball of unease that creeps into my belly and stretches across my chest.

There's this voice in my head that whispers lies, taunts me that this won't last, that I won't be enough for long, reminding me that he didn't say those three words back.

Squeezing my eyes shut, I shake the ridiculous notion from my head. He wants this. That's what he said, isn't it?

Aaron can't control my thoughts any longer; I won't let him. That self-sabotaging voice that sounds a whole lot like him needs to, quite frankly, hit the damn road.

I'm making the conscious decision to put one foot in front of the other, to put my trust in Avery's words, his intentions, to take this leap with him.

Regardless, when I'm this mentally and emotionally drained, sleep never comes easy. So I slip out of Avery's hold and steal away down the hallway, pouring myself a glass of water.

When I spot my mess on the floor, I tuck my shoes next to the front door and sink to the couch with my dress in my hands, the cool leather a shock to my bare legs, still blazing with heat from Avery's touch. The material shimmers, catching the light of the moon streaming through the wall of windows.

With a soft sigh, I stand. My brain is tired, my body exhausted, and all I want to do is curl back up against Avery, let him hold me until my mind gives in to the need for sleep.

Ready to head back to bed, I turn, only to come face-to-face with a very naked Avery, corded arms folded over his broad chest. The moonlight illuminates his impressive package and the fact that, despite the fact that he looks slightly annoyed, he's ready for another round.

"What are you doing?" His eyes float to the dress in my hands.

"I was just—"

"Get your ass back in the bed."

Oh, shit. "Avery, I wasn't—"

"*Now*, Claire."

Shoving my dress and my glass into Avery's chest, I hurry my ass as fast as it'll go back down the hallway, diving at the bed, Avery's chuckle following behind me.

He slips beneath the covers and pulls me into his arms. "You think you can try to sneak out of here after you tell me you're in love with me?"

"I wasn't leaving, Avery. I promise. And I didn't say…I mean, I said I was…Well, I didn't…" I have no idea where I'm going with this.

"I love you too, Claire." His tender admission melts my heart, the same way his lips melt against my jaw.

My heart jumps to my throat, my hands clammy as they grip Avery's forearms where they wrap around me. "You do?"

"I do."

"Even though it's only been a few weeks? Even though I've been pushing you away? Even though I'm stubborn and argumentative?" If my goal is to give him a reason to rethink this, mission accomplished. I'd stop talking if I could, but I often like to ramble when I'm in over my head.

"Even though," Avery replies with a soft sigh. "No more though. No more pushing me away. I'm in this thing with you, Claire, and I need you to be in it, too. Okay?"

I think of Charlee's words last night. "You can't just dip your toes in; you have to dive right in?"

His quiet chuckle makes my heart glow. "Exactly. I need you to dive in with me."

"Okay."

"Promise me, Claire. It hurts too much every time you run away. I know you're scared, and I am, too. We won't get through this if we don't communicate, if we aren't honest with each other. There's nothing I want more than to be with you, to try this with you. So promise me. Please."

I turn in his arms, taking his face in my hands. "I promise, Avery."

His mouth covers mine, coaxing it open for a slow, lazy kiss. Warm, tender lips slide down my neck before he flips me back over, burying his face in my hair, one hand on the base of my throat, holding me to him.

"I love you, Claire," Avery whispers. "So much I think it might split me right open."

The sleep that follows is magical.

CHAPTER FORTY

Avery

One moment.

One moment is all it takes. One moment to define a distinct ending, a new beginning. One moment to give everything in your world new meaning, to change your entire life for the better.

When she walked into my life just a mere few weeks ago, something shifted inside me, even if I didn't know it at the time. My path started to change, like a river slowly carving a new trail through the ridges of a mountain. It's been a struggle, an uphill battle, but nothing's ever felt more natural than having Claire in my life.

For the first time in my life, I feel like I'm exactly where I'm supposed to be.

I'm still not sure what exactly it is about her, or what it was that night. Was it the way she rolled her eyes at me, shoved away my advances, challenged everything I said? Was it the raw honesty she gave me right from the beginning when she admitted how she'd been broken? Was it her strength, how much she fought like hell with herself against something she wanted, something that would make her feel good, just because she thought it was the right thing for her to do?

I'm not sure, but I'm done looking for answers. The only thing I know, and the only thing I need to know, is that my life-changing moment is sleeping in my arms, cheek pressed to my chest, her small hand covering my heart.

My chest stretches as I stare down at the beautiful woman in my bed, the morning sun casting a warm glow over her face, illuminating the tiny freckles dusting down her nose and across her cheekbones like stars. Her full, pink lips are still slightly swollen from hours upon hours of kissing, and her copper waves are a wild, intoxicating mess strewn across my pillows.

Christ, she's magnificent.

Sully's face, his head resting on the edge of the bed while he stares at her, tail wagging, tells me he's just as happy as I am. He leans forward and licks at her fingers.

Hands curling into her chest, Claire stirs softly with a moan that reminds me via jumping cock that I'm a man, a man who's ready to take his woman for a wild ride should she only ask.

Those mossy eyes flutter open and land on me, that rosy blush creeping into her cheeks.

"What?" she whispers sheepishly, tugging the white sheet up to her chin.

I smile down at her, skimming my fingers along her cheek. "You're still here."

She grins up at me. "You think I'd try to leave after you yelled at me? Plus, I couldn't have gone anywhere even if I wanted to. Your arms were a force field last night."

Laughing, I sink back down beside her, my arms snaking around her waist under the sheet as I kiss her neck. "Didn't wanna let you go."

"Well, you're gonna regret it. Your bed is a fluffy cloud and I'm never leaving."

"Fine by me." I flip her over, wrapping her leg around my hip, and try not to hiss when my cock slips against her center, illuminating the fact that, as always, she's hot, wet, and ready for me. "How are you feeling this morning?"

"A little sore, but I'm fine. You can be as feral as you always are."

I chuckle and kiss her eyelids—they're a little swollen and red from all the tears she cried last night. "I meant emotionally, but good to know, because there's nothing tame about the way I love you."

Third time I've said those words and they taste just as good as they did the first time.

Claire's hands land on my shoulders, pushing me down to the mattress as she throws her leg over me and climbs aboard.

"I really like hearing those words," she murmurs, sweeping a kiss across my collarbone as she slides herself over the length of my cock.

"That's good," I manage, all gravel, fingertips biting into her hips as I watch her sink down, swallowing every inch of me, her head thrown back with her moan. "'Cause I sure as fuck like saying them."

We play for the next forty-five minutes and follow it up with breakfast made entirely of leftover pizza, much to Claire's enjoyment. I can't take my eyes off her while she sits on the edge of my kitchen counter in nothing but my T-shirt, swinging her legs and humming happily around each bite.

After a quick shower, I find Claire on my balcony, knees pulled into her chest as she stares out at the water, one arm hanging lazily as she buries her fingers in Sully's fur.

My teeth graze her earlobe when I wrap her in my hug from behind, and her fingers curl around my forearms as she tilts her head to the side, giving me full access to her neck.

"Feeling like going for a walk with me and Sully before we head to lunch?"

Claire peeks up at me over her shoulder. "Lunch?"

"Uh huh. Lunch. You and me."

Her nose twitches with that bright beam of hers. "I'd love to walk with you two."

She climbs to her feet, stretching her arms over her head with a sleepy yawn. My shirt on her lifts, slipping over her creamy curves, and I'm about five seconds away from scrapping our plans and fucking her in my T-shirt while she hangs onto the edge of my balcony.

381

She rubs her eyes and smiles up at me, lopsided and breathtaking. "I just need to go home and get changed."

"Don't wanna wear your gown?"

"I donno." She crouches in front of Sully, ruffling his floppy ears before smooching the spot between his eyes. "What's the dress code for this walk of yours, handsome? Gown or no gown?" He licks her ear and she glances up at me. "He says it's casual."

My grin is explosive; I can't help it.

While Claire fumbles with her key in the lock at her door, I look down at the mess of broken hairpins on the floor. I quirk a brow in question.

She glances down and then back at me. "Oh, uh…" With an anxious laugh, she sticks her hand in her hair, scratching at her scalp. "I kinda…tried to pick my lock last night."

"You did not."

Claire's answering grin, entirely goofy and way too guilty, tells me she absolutely did. "Watched a YouTube video and everything. Sixteen million views and I still failed."

Chuckling, I push her through her door.

From the edge of Claire's bed, I watch as she brushes her teeth, washes her face, and combs her long waves down her back. She threads her fingers through her hair, looping strand over strand, gathering more pieces along the way until a thick braid hangs over her shoulder, and all I want to do is tug it free and love on her all over again.

Standing naked in front of me, she starts rooting through her dresser, humming to herself. For someone who's been so oddly shy at times, she sure is suddenly incredibly comfortable around me. It's a nice feeling, and I can't fight the pride that inflates my chest, happy that she's chosen me to open up to. I wonder if she just needed to feel loved again to feel a little bit more like herself.

"Grab whatever you need to spend the night again," I tell her, watching her tug on a soft-yellow sundress, lean legs on display.

She twists in my direction wearing an expression I can't quite decipher. "You want me to stay over again?"

I want her to never leave my sight because I think I have a mild obsession, but I can't really say that, can I? "I don't plan on letting you go until you leave for work Monday morning."

"You're going to get sick of me," she murmurs, fingering the scalloped hem of her dress.

Walking over to her, I wrap my arms around her and rest my chin on her shoulder. "Not possible." I kiss her neck and clap a hand to her ass before walking out of her bedroom. "Pack your shit, Claire."

I don't know who spots her first, me or the damn dog. He leaps to his feet, whimpering as he sets his sights on her the second she pushes through the door of the coffee shop.

"She's mine," I remind him as Claire struts toward us with a drink in each hand and a little brown bag tucked under her arm. She brushes a kiss across my lips and hands me my coffee.

I love how much she loves to kiss, the way she craves touch, physical intimacy. It makes me wonder what her relationship with Aaron was like, before everything. Was it anything like this? Did he deny her what she needed, what she deserved?

Breaking off a chunk of muffin, she pushes it past my lips before shoving something into my pocket. I fish it out and glare at the twenty-dollar bill I gave her before she went into the café.

"Claire," I start, swallowing down the delicious decoy. Her hand covers mine the second I reach for her, and she gently shoves the money and my hand back into my abdomen.

"I know you want to pay for this, but please just let me do something here."

"I—"

"Please," she repeats, and the quiet plea, the sincere look in her eyes, has my mouth closing, my hand dropping.

It seems pretty ass-backwards that my money makes her uncomfortable, considering it could make her *very* comfortable, but I don't want to push her. I'll ease her into being spoiled.

So I stuff the twenty in my pocket, then pull her into my side and kiss her temple. "Thank you, baby."

"Well, if this isn't the cutest display of public affection I ever did see!"

When my eyes land on my sister, stopped not five feet in front of us, hands clasped under her chin, my entire body vibrates with a groan.

Sully rips the leash free from my hand when he spies Harper, nearly tackling her to the ground. That big boy will never forget what she did for him.

"Hey Sul!" Harper drops to her knees, scratching his ears while he cleans her face with his tongue. "How's my handsome man? Oh, so handsome! I woof you, Mr. Sully-Wully, yes I do!" She beams up at Claire and jerks her head toward me. "What are you doing still hanging out with this loser?"

"I tried to run." Claire lifts both shoulders. "Didn't get far."

"Mmm, I believe that. Likes you too much. Isn't that right, brother bear?" Harper's scrutinizing assessment of my face and pointed look at Claire's hand in mine, in public, tells me she wants details.

With a heavy sigh and a hand dragging over my face, I say, "Harper, you remember Claire. My girlfriend."

Harper's hands do a slow roll, dropping from Sully, her jaw unhinging. "No. *Way*." She looks at Claire. She looks at me. Back to Claire. Back to me. "You seriously did it? Oh my God. Does Mom know? Oh my God, she's gonna lose her shit. Can I be the one to tell her? Oh my God. *Smile*!"

"What?"

Click.

"*Harper!*" I lunge for the phone she's hiding behind. She spins out of reach, fingers flying over the screen while Claire snickers beside me.

Harper clicks off her phone and tucks it in the back pocket of her shorts. "Sorry, what were you saying?"

"You're kidding me right now. Did you seriously just text Mom?"

She has the audacity to look shocked, one hand pressed to her chest. "Avery, I'm insulted. I would *never*."

My phone starts ringing in my pocket. I pull it out, rolling my eyes at the three-letter word that scrolls across my screen. My sister's toothy grin tells me she's anything but sorry.

"Hi Mom," I sigh into the phone, watching as my sister and my girlfriend stroll down the street without me, their hands tangled together like they're already best friends, my dog trotting along beside them.

"*Girlfriend!*" Mom shrieks in my ear, drawing the attention of at least three innocent passersby. "You have a girlfriend! Claire is your girlfriend! I'm gonna be a grandma one day after all!"

Aw, for fuck's sake.

CHAPTER FORTY-ONE

Claire

"She's *not* volunteering with you at the shelter, Harps." Avery tears the cereal box out of his sister's hands, shoving it back in his pantry.

"Why not? What if she wants to?" Harper opens the fridge, searching through it.

"She doesn't have time."

"But you haven't even asked her," Harper points out, to which I nod, because even though this conversation is about me, I haven't contributed to it at all.

"No, and I'm not going to—" he flashes me an apologetic look, "—because if she starts spending all her free time at the animal shelter with you, I'm gonna be right back to fucking my hand alone in my bedroom."

"Avery," I say on a gasp. "That's your sister!"

"Sorry," he says in a way that tells me he's not at all. He waves his hand down my body. "And the last thing I need is her coming home with an armful of puppies and kittens because they gave her the sad eyes and she couldn't say no."

Ah, he's got me pinned.

Harper plants her fists on her hips. "Well, they need homes, Avery."

His head bobs. "They sure do, but not with us. Not twenty of them."

Harper rolls her eyes and slams the fridge. "Ugh, you're the worst." She opens the pantry, pulling out the box of cereal Avery tucked away only a minute ago.

"Harps, you're driving me fucking nuts." Avery's eyes widen and he wraps both hands around her neck from behind, pretending to strangle her. "We're going for lunch in ten minutes. Stop eating." His dark coffee gaze lands on me. "Why did you invite her?"

I lift a shoulder and let it fall. "I like her."

She irritates Avery, and that makes me laugh. She's also been crawling on the floor, rolling around with Sully, taking pictures of him with an expensive-looking camera while talking to him like he's a baby. She's highly entertaining. Despite Avery's attitude toward her right now, I know he agrees. He watches her and his dog with a smile.

Avery's eyes roll with amusement at my response, and he pulls me into him by my hips. "Fine, she can come." He tilts his face, forehead resting against mine, and gives me a tender smile. "The things I'll do for you."

Click.

"Ugh, adorable. Avery, who knew you had a sweet bone in your body?"

Glancing up at Harper's voice, I find her staring into the screen of her camera, clicking around.

"I'm loving this whole candid thing you've got going on. You guys are naturals behind the camera."

Avery slaps her camera away. "That's because we didn't *know* you were taking our picture." But he slips his chin over her shoulder, peering down at the picture, and one side of his mouth curves before his gaze floats over to me. Then he claps a hand to my ass. "'Kay. Let's get this show on the road."

Harper's eyes roll before she flicks Avery's ear. He puts her in a headlock while she flails around. "Would it kill you to be romantic for more than sixty seconds?"

"I'm very romantic."

"Name one romantic thing you've done for Claire."

"I fucked her brains out last night and then ordered her pizza and let her eat it in bed." Avery looks my way, amusement dancing

387

on his face at the way I'm gaping at him while his sister gags. "You good?"

"I...you...that's..." I shove a finger in Harper's general direction. "*Your sister!*"

"Sure is." He takes my hand before opening the door. "Let's go, baby."

I suppose I should get used to the shock factor that's part of Avery's whole package. I don't really mind the honesty. That part is refreshing. It's the bluntness in front of his sister that's hard to wrap my head around. Casey and I have always been close, but I'll be damned if either of us is going to discuss our sex lives in front of the other.

Twenty minutes later, Avery's sweeping Harper and I into the foyer of the Drake Hotel. The hostess leads us up to the rooftop patio, and the way I'm gripping Avery's elbow, nearly vibrating, tells him how excited I am.

"I've never been here before," I tell him when his quizzical smile swings my way.

"I think you'll like it." He punctuates his sentence with a kiss. The man loves to kiss, and I love to be on the receiving end of his kisses. It makes me realize how deprived I was with Aaron.

"Right this way, Mr. Beck," the hostess says, motioning toward the back corner, where my gaze lands on—

"Ehhh! There they are!"

"Woohoo!"

"Hell yeah! *Finally!*"

"Auntie Claire! A'wy! Dey kissin' again!"

Our friends sit around the large patio table, grinning up at us. I don't know if I'm more embarrassed that our working things out required a coming out party, or if I'm just insanely happy to be surrounded by the people I love. It's definitely both.

Charlee embraces me in one of my favorite hugs, warm and squeezing. "I'm so happy for you, Claire, and so incredibly proud of you for taking control of your happiness."

"Daddy! Daddy, down! Me want down!" Vivi looks to be struggling for dear life in her highchair, chubby cheeks flaming red while she kicks her legs and tries to lift herself out of her seat. Her wild eyes land on me and she gestures a hundred times over with the curl of her fingers. "Me want hug!"

Harper hums appreciatively beside me, shifting her sunglasses down her nose as she gives Casey a once-over. Her elbow nudges my waist. "Your brother?"

"Don't even think about it," Avery grinds out, whether it's because it's my brother, or because he knows as well as I do that Charlee crushing on him in a major way. It's also clearly not one-sided. I mean, for God's sake, Casey can barely take his eyes off Charlee long enough to get his daughter out of her highchair.

With a squeal, Vivi tears across the patio and crashes into my legs. I waste no time scooping her up, holding her tight against me. I rarely go more than a couple days without seeing my niece, but I haven't seen her since last Sunday.

"I missed you, Little Miss Piggy," I murmur against her hair.

She squeezes my cheeks together and oinks twice. "I luh you, Care Bear." Her green gaze lands on Avery and she giggles, batting her long, curly lashes, hands clasped under her chin. Girl's two-and-a-half years old and already knows how to flirt. "I go see A'wy now."

And just like that, I've been replaced. Avery's all too happy to take her, showering her with kisses while she squeals.

Wyatt wraps one arm around my shoulders, free hand running down his chest. "Glad to see the advice I gave Avery worked," he says, voice dripping with arrogance.

"It did *not* work," Avery argues with an outraged snort beside me. "Right, Vivi? Say, bad advice, Wyatt!"

Vivi shakes a finger at Wyatt, face scrunching. "Bad, Wyatt! You a *bad* boy!"

Adopting the cutest mask of shocked hurt, Wyatt slaps a hand over his heart. "I'm so sorry, Miss Vivi. Please forgive me." His face dips to my ear. "Seriously, I'm an idiot. I don't know a thing about women. I can barely handle my own mother."

He might've been the one to give the crap-tastic advice, but Avery's a big boy who makes his own decisions. I also recognize that my actions and words drove Avery to that cliff, to a spot where he felt helpless and didn't know what to do. We both made mistakes, but I think what matters most is how we move past them from here, try to be better together.

I gesture at Sophie, Wyatt's date from last night. She's sitting at the table, chatting away and enjoying a beer. "You must know a little bit to land a girl like that. I had no idea you were dating someone."

"Oh." His light eyes grow, throat bobbing with his swallow. His gaze shifts over my shoulder as he shakes his head. "No, she's not, uh…no. She's not my girlfriend."

I don't have time to ask for clarification. His smile is brilliant as he moves by me.

"Harps!" Wyatt exclaims excitedly, grabbing Harper around the waist. He smashes her against his chest while she groans, moans, and tries her damn best to fight him off, grumbling something about dirty hands and STDs.

"You know you love me," he teases affectionately, nuzzling her neck.

"I know I *hate* you," she mumbles, shoving him off her, although her cheeks are the most interesting shade of pink.

My attention is drawn away when my brother tugs me into him.

He presses a chaste kiss to the top of my head. "Good things happen when you let go of what was never meant to be and embrace what life throws at you." His patient eyes meet mine. "You're the

390

only person that can control your happiness, Claire, but I'm glad you're giving Avery a chance to be a part of the equation."

By the time Sunday night rolls around, my body has been well used in the most wonderful way. Loved on by Avery in every way imaginable, ways I had never been loved before. His searing touch, lingering stares, whispered words have all left their mark on me this weekend.

The tips of his fingers brush down the edge of my face where it's nuzzled into his bare chest, the two of us snuggled up in bed while we watch a movie. He's watching; I'm not. I'm too tired to move, to keep my eyes open any longer. All I can focus on is the way his chest rises and falls beneath the heat of my palm, the warmth of the dog curled up behind my knees.

Soft lips touch the crown of my head. "Bedtime?" Avery prompts gently.

I nod against him. "I'm so sleepy."

He shifts me onto the pillows and turns away, the muscles in his back rippling as he reaches for the lamp, encasing the room in black. His thick arms pull me back into him as his body curls around mine, his lips pressing against my neck.

"Can I tell you something?" he whispers.

"Of course."

A beat of silence stretches between us, and I swear I can hear his heart beating. Sweeping my hands over his forearms where they wrap around me, I lace my fingers with his and kiss his palm, silent encouragement for him to continue.

"I'm still scared I'll wake up one morning and you'll be gone."

My heart stretches in my chest, a reminder that I've been unfair to him, that I've hurt him in ways I never wanted to hurt anyone. Turning in his hold, I lay my palm over his cheek. "I'm sorry I hurt you, Avery. That I gave you a reason to be wary of trusting me."

His eyes shine in the dim glow of the moon that bathes the room. "I know that you were just trying to protect yourself."

I wish I had never hurt him, but I can't say that I regret trying to keep my distance. It's confusing, to be honest, and maybe that's why I don't say it out loud. There's no part of me that wants him to take it the wrong way, but I know how it'll sound. I shouldn't have gone to the bar the night we met, and I certainly shouldn't have gone outside with him, kissed him.

Because what I should've been doing is giving myself time to heal, learning to love myself again, trust not only somebody else, but my own judgment. Because that's part of the battle, isn't it? Maybe the hardest part. How do I let someone else love me when I'm not even sure how to do it? How do I trust my judgment when it's been so horribly wrong in the past?

But it feels right now. Everything feels right with Avery. Not perfect, not by a longshot. I don't think that's how relationships work, and I know we'll have some work to do based on the way ours started, the damage somebody else did that I'm still trying to undo, that Avery wants to help me undo.

But I haven't always been the best at letting people in, and I guess that's where I need to start.

Cupping my face, Avery's thumbs sweep across my cheekbones. "Are you still scared of all this?"

"Terrified," I admit.

"What are you scared of?" His lips dot across every inch of my face before he sits up against the pillows, pulling me into his lap.

His fingers dance up and down my spine as I try to put my thoughts into words. But his touch is magic, lulling me into that safety blanket of comfort that he drapes me in whenever we're together, the one that pushes me to be open and honest instead of retreating back into my shell.

"I'm scared that you're caught up in the novelty, the excitement of a new relationship. I'm scared that you'll miss the freedom that came with bachelorhood. I'm scared that when you find out everything there is to know about me, you won't love it all."

My throat tightens. I try to swallow it down, but it doesn't go anywhere. I don't think it will until I spit the words out. "I'm scared that you won't love all of me, that I'm not…enough. I don't know if I'm enough, Avery." My nose tingles and when I blink, a lone tear rolls down each cheek. I try to look away, but his large hands hold my face, keeping our gazes locked.

"I hate that he hurt you like that. That he took everything that makes you who you are and convinced you it was anything other than beautiful." He brushes the hair off my forehead, nothing but complete adoration and sincerity swimming in his deep brown gaze. "You can't live your life being terrified that somebody won't see you for just as beautiful as you are because one person made you feel anything less than. You are enough. So fucking enough, Claire."

Avery's mouth covers mine, tongue slipping in as our lips move together.

"All I want is to help you rediscover all the things you used to love about yourself, and to remind you just how lovable you are. Because you are, Claire. You're mine, and I love you."

CHAPTER FORTY-TWO

Claire

I'm having the very best dream. You know the kind, where you don't want to wake up because there's no way real life can be better than this.

In this dream, I wake up with Avery's face between my thighs, his tongue lapping at my folds, teasing the tight bud of nerves at the top. His magical fingers, the ones I love more than life itself, trail up my belly, circling my taut nipples, making me arch and moan.

His wet lips press against the juncture of my thigh before vibrating against my center when he murmurs, "Morning, baby. It's Friday."

It sure as hell is. Even dream-Avery is current on the times.

We've spent every night together in our short week, as hard as I've tried not to. I mean, if I'm being honest, I haven't put much effort into it at all. I'm not so secretly terrified that he's going to get sick of me, but he sure does everything in his power to convince me he won't.

I almost won once. Wednesday night. Charlee came over for dinner and drinks. Avery popped down with Sully on their way out to a walk and asked me to reconsider staying over. I stood my ground, which is pretty impressive when you have a six-foot-three wall of muscle ready to get on his knees and beg. Charlee snickered from the couch, throwing handfuls of popcorn into the air and catching, like, two out of twenty kernels, making a mess of my floor. Sully darted in and hoovered it up.

When I curled up under my blankets two hours later, half-drunk and frustrated with myself for making such a big deal about spending the night together, I shot him a bitter goodnight text. I'm proud to say I lasted all of five minutes before dragging my ass out of bed, stuffing my feet in my slippers, and wrapping myself in my blanket. I threw open the door, ready to trudge up to Avery's with my tail between my legs, only to find him on the other side of my door, poised and ready to knock, Sully by his side. Avery grinned, I launched myself into his arms, and he carried me back to bed, whispering against my neck about how he couldn't stay away.

A sharp gasp pierces the air as two fingers spear me. My body shoots up from my spot in bed, fully awake and fully aware that it's not dream-Avery between my legs, but a very real Avery, in the flesh. Literally, in the flesh. He's naked. Just the way I like him.

The grin he flashes me from his spot between my thighs is purely wolfish, brown eyes twinkling, lips glistening while he pumps his fingers in and out.

"There you are," he murmurs, that sexy, husky morning voice thick with sleep, making my insides molten. His tongue flicks out over my tender clit, sucking it between his teeth, and I die on the inside.

"It's Friday," he repeats. "And you're going to your dad's for the weekend."

I flash him a cheeky grin, extra toothy. How I manage it while he's busy setting off fireworks between my legs is beyond me. "Gonna miss me?"

"Nah. I have no intention of missing you."

Excuse me? Well, that's that. I shove his head away and clamp my legs shut. His throaty chuckle tells me he's amused. I'm not.

Fingertips digging into my hips, Avery crawls overtop of me. My eyelids hood with desire as his tongue drags slowly across his lips, tasting my arousal.

"I have no intention of missing you because I'm coming with you. I've been waiting all week for you to invite me, but you're being stubborn, as per usual, and now it's too late to wait any longer, so I'm inviting myself."

My fingers sink into the hair at the nape of his neck. "And you think calling me stubborn is the way to get what you want?"

"Well, I've tried brain-melting orgasms all week long and that hasn't worked, so..." His hips circle, rubbing against me, spreading my wetness.

"Oh, it's worked exceptionally well for me." I swallow a moan, back arching off the bed as he pushes inside me, inch by aching inch.

Looking down at me with that goofy, half-smile of his, Avery sets the pace, painfully slow, torturing me in a way that brings him too much pleasure. My hips lift to meet his thrusts, begging for more, for deeper, for faster.

"Avery, *please*. Fuck me."

"I am fucking you, baby."

The sound I make is stuck somewhere between the deepest groan and a ferocious snarl. "Harder!"

"Harder..." Leaning down, he takes one nipple into his mouth, rolling his glorious tongue around the taut bud. His teeth press down, biting, tugging, all of it hard, making heat lick at the base of my spine. "You like it rough, Miss Thompson, don't you?"

I like it all, anything he gives me, and he gives me everything. But goddammit, right now I just wanna be fucked into this mattress to start my Friday off right. "I like *you*."

"No. You *love* me."

"I do."

"And I love you. That's why I want to meet your dad."

My hips stop grinding. Avery's movements halt, too. His eyes move around my face, trying to gauge my reaction.

"You're serious."

He nods.

"But I..." Aaron never wanted to come home with me. The only time he ever spent with my dad was when Dad came out to take us for dinner, and the time I dragged him to the hospital with me when Vivi was born.

I lift my gaze to meet Avery's, warm and patient. My God, he's always patient with me. "You really want to meet my dad?"

"I do, Claire." He shifts back, rocking on his knees as he pulls me up with him, still inside me. I hiss at the sensation, the depth. "Maybe we could make this a family weekend."

He lifts me and drops me, gently, and I rock on top of him. This is kind of a weird conversation to have while we're doing this, but I'll be damned if I'm going to stop. He feels too good.

"A family weekend?"

"Mhmm." He drags his nose across my cheek before his lips meet mine, tongue delving in. "Will you come to my parents' on Sunday for a barbecue?"

"On Sunday?"

"Sunday."

"For a barbecue?"

He chuckles. "That's what I said." His fingers creep up my back, sliding into my hair. He tugs my head backwards, his hot mouth descending on my neck. "Please put me out of my misery. My mom's called me every day this week."

My laugh shakes me and Avery's answering grin makes my stomach weak. I know his mom's been on his back. I know because I've been sitting beside him during half of those calls. I know because he's forwarded her texts to me. My personal favorite was: *Your clock is ticking. You have seven days to introduce me to Claire or I'll pick back up on the grandbaby conversation. And I'll also slap you upside the head. Love you so much xoxoxo.*

The woman clearly thought her son would never, ever settle down.

But I frown, remembering what's happening this Sunday. And when I frown, Avery frowns. But he doesn't just frown. His whole face drops, those big brown eyes…sad? His hands on me still their caress, and he starts leaning backwards, away from me.

"I have Vivi Sunday," I clarify quickly, not wanting to give him the wrong idea. "I'm supposed to bring her back with me in the morning. Casey's staying with my dad 'til Tuesday. They're working on a project for a winery."

Avery's face lights up. "You have her 'til Tuesday?"

I nod.

"She can come. To my parents' place, she can come. My mom will lose her mind, she'll love her so much. They have a pool, so Vivi can swim. And dogs. Vivi loves dogs. And—"

I cut him off with my lips on his. I can't help it. How much he loves Vivi is one of the things that makes me so crazy for him. "Okay, Avery."

"Okay?"

"Okay. Of course okay. We'll have a family weekend. But make sure your parents are okay with Vivi coming."

He literally shoves me off him, pinning me to the mattress with his body as he climbs over me, pulling his phone from the charger on the table beside me. Five seconds later, he's on the phone with his mom.

"We can come Sunday," he tells her.

"*You can?*" she screams, followed by a bunch of words I can't understand.

"Is it okay if Vivi comes? Claire's niece…Yes…Yes, she calls Harper Happy; she doesn't have all her sounds yet." Avery gives me a wide-eyed look and laces his fingers through my hair, playing with the tips. "Yes, super cute…Uh huh…Two-and-a-half…Mom, if this is going to turn into a baby thing, we won't come."

My cheeks flush with heat. This woman wants a grandbaby. I love her son, but I'm not even going to allow myself to start thinking about that right now. I'm just going to try to enjoy this for what it is, right now, because if I can't live in the past, then I can't live in the future either.

He clicks his phone off after ending the call and tosses it across the bed. Shifting overtop of me, he spreads my legs wide and settles between them. His hips start moving, rolling in that way that makes me throw my head backwards, my eyes unable to go anywhere but heavenward.

"Now where were we…" His hands push between me and the mattress, squeezing, fingers pressing into my ass. "Oh, right. I was about to fuck you. *Hard*."

"I can't stand this giddiness. It's too adorable. You're adorable."

With a sigh, I close my laptop, shoving it into my messenger bag. "You know what I can't stand, Charlee?" I watch the smile slide right off my best friend's face. She's nervous about whatever I'm about to say. She should be. "I can't stand this game you and Casey are playing."

Her face pales. I see her thick swallow from here. "Wha…what are you talking about?" Her hand slides into the messy bun donning her head. "What game? There's no game. What do you mean? Like…hockey?" The face she makes tells me she hears how ridiculous she sounds; she doesn't need me to point it out.

I sweep a hand out in her direction, leaning back in my chair as I watch her flounder. "What's going on with you two? I'm not blind. I saw him holding your hand under the table at lunch on Saturday." It was actually Avery who jammed an elbow into my ribs and pointed it out to me. It was super cute, but the two of them definitely thought no one noticed. "I've been waiting all week for you to tell me what's going on, but you haven't said a word."

"I-I-I, he wasn't holding my hand!" She looks down at both of them, then promptly shoves them behind her back in a move that's entirely too guilty.

At the amused brow I arch, the tension in her face eases. She smiles. She also sinks to my couch with the loudest sigh. "Well, he wasn't *holding* it, he was just…resting his…on top of mine." She fiddles with her dirty-blond locks. "I don't know, Claire. I really don't. Nothing's happened. Nothing like what I…" Her eyes meet mine. She pulls her bottom lip into her mouth, pensive and confused. "Nothing like what I want to happen."

"You like him." I already know she does, of course, but I'd like for her to finally admit it.

A furious shade of red creeps up her neck, staining her cheeks. "I'm sorry, Claire," Charlee whispers. "Are you mad at me? I can't help it. God, it's been years. It's just getting worse."

I cross the room to her, taking her hands in mine. "Mad at you? Are you crazy? Charlee, I would have a fit of epic proportions if you became my sister-in-law. You'd be the best ever mummy to Vivi."

She snorts and starts picking at some nonexistent fluff on her dress. "You're getting way ahead of yourself. I don't think Casey thinks of me that way. I'm just me, his best friend's little sister, his little sister's best friend."

I chuckle, though I know what it's like to be on the other side of this, to not see what everyone else sees. "Charlee, he can't take his eyes off you, ever. He was holding your hand at lunch, for fuck's sake. I'm not the only one who notices. Avery's seen it since day one."

She blushes harder, scratching at her cheek. "It's just, what if…what if…"

"What if what? What if he feels the exact same way and you two start dating?"

Charlee's shoulders sag as she peers down at her lap. "What if things don't work out? He's your brother. He's one of my best friends. He's Vivi's dad. There's so much to lose, Claire, and that's terrifying."

I know she's right to think about it, to consider all the ways it could end. Casey and Vivi are her family as much as they are mine. Though I doubt it would, if it were to go down the wrong way, there's a lot on the line for both of them.

My phone chimes on my desk, letting me know Avery's downstairs.

"That's your ride," Charlee says with a reserved smile.

"It is. I'm sorry. Can we talk about this again though?"

She nods. "I'm just happy you're not mad at me for secretly being in love with your brother."

I snort a laugh. "Hate to tell you this, but it's not much of a secret." I wrap my arms around her and we rock back and forth. She gives the best hugs, all warm and snuggly. "Are you sure you don't wanna come home with us for the weekend? We can stop off at your place and grab your stuff."

"Nah." She waves me off. "I'm not really in the mood to see my own dad."

"You can stay with us," I offer, though she knows she's always welcome. "You know my dad loves you."

She wags her brows in a way that tells me I'm not about to enjoy her next sentence. "And I love Gavin. He's a DILF."

"Aaand I'm done." I push off her and strut to my desk, scooping up my weekender bag that I stowed back there this morning.

Charlee's laughter bounces off the walls as she follows me into the hallway and down the stairs. "Are you nervous for Avery to meet your dad?"

"He already likes him," I tell her, filling a box with my dad's favorite beers from behind the bar. "That's way more than I can say for Aaron."

"Yeah, well, that's not exactly hard, babe. Aaron fucking sucked." Leaning over the bar, she cranes her head, trying to sneak a peek out the windows. "What kinda car does Avery have?"

401

"I actually have no idea." When he insisted on driving, I thought he meant he'd have his driver pick us up in the Bentley. The way he laughed in my face told me how wrong I was.

"Well, knowing Avery, it'll have all the bells and whistles."

I'm sure she's right, but so long as it's safe for Vivi, I really don't care.

I pop the front door to the brewery open, stepping into the hot sunshine, and pause at the sight before me.

"Interesting," Charlee hums approvingly, pushing past me. "Well, well, well, Mr. Beck. Once again, you surprise me. Look at this baby." She pets the hood of his glossy, candy apple red truck. "This thing is huge!" She turns back to me, brows pumping. "Hey, you should take him to the drive-in and let him screw your brains out in the back."

"I like the sounds of that," Avery purrs as he pops a kiss on my cheek. He takes my bag off my shoulder, box of beer from my arms. "What were you expecting, Charlee?"

"I donno, like, an Aston Martin or something. Lamborghini?" She lifts both shoulders. "Those are about the only fancy car names I know."

He chuckles, closing the latch on the truck bed once all of my things are tucked safely away. "I'm rich, not ostentatious."

I try to fight my snort. I swear, I do. But the pointed glare Avery flashes my way lets me know I'm doing a piss-poor job.

Charlee leans through my window. "Have a good weekend, lovers. Say hi to Gavin for me," she adds with the flirty flick of her brows.

"Your dad?" Avery clarifies as Charlee bounces away.

"Uh huh."

"So which Thompson is she after, your dad or your brother?"

I sigh. "Both, apparently."

Avery chuckles, sliding his sunglasses on. God, they really kick that fuck-me status into high gear. He flashes me a ten-out-of-ten grin, the kind that makes me slam my thighs together. "You ready to go home, baby?"

Oh, that sounds good.

"Ready."

CHAPTER FORTY-THREE

Avery

Claire's right leg starts bouncing a mile a minute as soon as we pull onto her dad's street. It's one of those long and winding ones, all tree-lined and quiet. The houses are few and far between. We pass farm fields and a cherry orchard, and Claire points out Charlee and Dex's childhood home, where their own dad still lives.

"We're just up there, on the right." She points to rows on rows of perfectly pruned grapevines and the people in wide-brimmed hats who are tending to them. "Just past the winery."

Looking around, I get it. I understand why Claire told me she was a country girl at heart, why, even after a few years in the city, Toronto is still too loud and busy for her. Even though it's only just over an hour away—if you manage to miss the shitstorm that is Toronto traffic—it's an entirely different world out here. Everyone moves at their own pace, like they're content to just soak up every bit of nature, enjoy the peace and quiet.

We pass the driveway to the winery and an older man looks up from where he's talking with a small group of people, inspecting some grapes. His eyes take in Claire, hanging halfway out the window, and his whole face lights up.

"Hi John!" Claire yells out the window as we drive by.

"You better come see me, Miss Claire Bear!" he shouts back.

My giddy girl twists my way. "That's John. He owns the winery and also a few vineyards in France. I've known him my whole life. He gave me my first taste of wine when I was twelve." Her face screws up with disgust. "I hated it."

Anything I don't already know about Claire, I'm sure I'm going to learn this weekend. I love watching her like this, so relaxed and at home, like she's able to be herself without any reservations.

We turn down a long gravel driveway and approach an old ranch house on a huge slab of land, surrounded by tall pines and oaks, a few perfectly placed weeping willows. The two men waiting on the wraparound porch start making their way down the steps.

Claire's out of the truck before I put it in park, flinging herself from the front seat and making a mad dash the rest of the way up the driveway. She throws herself into her dad's arms and he catches her around the waist, laughing and giving her a spin while she burrows into his neck. She's a daddy's girl.

And suddenly I'm a little bit nervous. I'd like to think I can talk myself into and out of just about anything, but meeting her father? I've never done families before. Aren't dads protective of their daughters? Was this a terrible idea? What am I doing? Fuck, someone help me.

I step down from the truck and watch her dad's eyes peel to me. Before I can say anything or make a move in his direction, a tiny body hurls itself at my legs.

"*A'wy!*" Vivi shrieks.

"Hey there, sweet cheeks!" Scooping her up, I shower her chubby cheeks in kisses.

Her tiny fingers press against my face. I'm afraid to ask why they're so sticky. "You come see Gamps and Tooky?"

"I sure did." A fluffy white dog with black and brown spots prances over to us, sniffing my legs. I drop one hand down to Turkey, letting him lick me before I bury my fingers in his soft fur.

Vivi gives me a toothy grin, jade eyes dancing. "You bwing Sully?"

I shake my head. "No, baby. Sully's having a sleepover with Harper."

Vivi's face falls and she pushes that wet, swollen pout out. "Oh."

405

I kiss her nose. It's so cute and tiny I can't resist. This girl has me eating out of the palm of her hand. "You'll see him on Sunday though, okay? We're going swimming at my mom and dad's."

She squeals with delight, hands on either side of my face as she leans in. "Gamps gimme a pop-icle," she whispers against my lips, sticky fingers explained.

"He did? What a special Gramps you got there, little lady."

"I'm about as special as they come, that's what they say." I look up at the gruff voice, finding Claire's dad stopped in front of me, grinning at me. Or rather, his granddaughter. I'm sure I'm not the one he's grinning at. "Mr. Beck, I presume?"

With a nod, I shift Vivi to my hip, holding out my hand. "Avery, sir. I'm happy to meet you."

His smile widens as he takes my hand, his grip firm. "Gavin, please."

Instead of Casey's copper hair, Gavin's is light brown, peppered with gray around the temples and in the scruff lining his jaw. Rather than green eyes, his are a striking shade of sapphire blue. Other than that, he's all Casey. Tall and broad with the same squared jawline and high cheekbones. He's strong and lean from years of woodworking and doesn't look the least bit tired, despite Claire's worries about his health. He's also got that signature Thompson smile, all goofy and crooked.

"I hear you've been taking good care of my two girls," Gavin says, his lingering gaze both amused and curious. "How the hell you got yourself roped into that is beyond me. Nice man like you? Figured you could find yourself someone a little less stubborn than my daughter."

"*Hey!*" Claire steps up beside us. The indignant fists planted on her hips match perfectly with her displeased scowl and furrowed brows. "I am *not* stubborn."

"Only someone as stubborn as you would say that, my darling." Gavin tickles her chin and throws me a wink.

"So damn stubborn," Casey agrees, clapping me on the back. "Hey Avery."

Claire huffs and throws her arms in the air, stalking off toward the truck bed. "I wish Charlee was here."

"You and me both." I'm not sure who murmurs it, Gavin or Casey, but one quick glance at the two of them tells me it could be either or. They're both donning shit-eating grins.

"It's not too late to run," Casey mutters.

Chuckling, I blow out a breath, the tension in my shoulders easing. "Nah, I like her too much. I'm trapped now."

"Auntie Claire and A'wy like to do lotsa kissin'," Vivi pipes up, nuzzling into my neck. For God's sake, how many times is this little nugget going to say that at the most inopportune moments?

"Uh…" My eyes shift back and forth between Gavin and Casey. They're still smiling, so I guess that's a good thing. Still, my answering laugh is entirely too anxious, and maybe a little shrill.

"Come on!" Claire calls out from the porch. She's got her bag and mine over her shoulder, struggling to hold up the box of beer. She keeps readjusting her hands, knees lifting to help her hold it up. "Or I'll drink all this beer myself and won't share a single sip with any of you!"

Gavin runs a hand through his hair and sighs. "Yup, that's my daughter."

I'm re-evaluating my life choices here. I want a house, a yard. I want to see the stars when I look up at the sky at nighttime. I want to hear crickets and watch Claire read a book on the back deck while I barbecue dinner and the dog runs free.

I don't want the city lights, the never-ending noise, the smog. Don't get me wrong—I love the Toronto skyline. I love the hustle and bustle.

But this? Shit, this is living.

407

My gaze sweeps the yard, the twinkle lights in the distance, wrapped around the back porch, the seas of trees in the black night, the stars, and I feel good. Happy. At ease. And now I know why Claire was so anxious to get back here.

Here, Claire is in her element.

Smiling, I watch her pull her stick back from the fire, tapping on her marshmallow.

"*Ouch!*" she hisses, jerking her hand back. She meets my gaze, grinning like a goofy fool. "Hot."

Laughing, I twist her birthday cake Oreo apart for her, getting it ready for her marshmallow, because regular s'mores are entry level according to Claire. "You don't say. I can't imagine something that comes off the fire being hot…"

"Quiet before I jab you with my stick." She jerks it in my direction for good measure.

Gavin chuckles, watching me smoosh Claire's sticky mess together before handing it over to her. "You two are quite the pair. Nothing like sarcasm and death threats to get the love flowing." He threads his fingers through Vivi's hair while she snoozes in his lap and throws a glance in Casey's direction. "Speaking of love, when are you gonna get your shit together and nail down that Charlee Williams? She's not gonna wait around forever on a chump like you."

It's hard to tell through the glare of the fire, but I'm pretty sure Casey's cheeks tint with color, his eyes shifting to Claire.

Claire licks her sticky, goopy fingers. "Don't look at me, Case. I'd love to officially make Charlee my sister." She looks at her dad and rolls her eyes. "He was holding her hand at lunch under the table last Saturday and thinks nobody noticed."

Casey nudges Claire's knee with his foot. "Shut up, Care Bear. I wasn't holding it, I was just…resting my hand there."

"Uh huh. That's what Charlee said too."

Casey perks up. "She did? What else did she say?"

Gavin barks out a low laugh. "Christ, are you twenty-nine or twelve? Stop making secret passes at your sister's best friend and just go after the girl already." Climbing to his feet, he scoops Vivi into his arms. "I'm taking this munchkin to bed. Don't kill the fire."

When he returns nearly a half hour later, he's shaking his head, wearing a huge smile. "That girl is a con artist." He hands Casey and I a cigar each before sinking into his chair. "Talked me into another popsicle and two more stories after I told her it was the last one."

"You gave her a popsicle?" Casey checks his phone. "It's 9:45! There's no way she's sleeping."

Gavin shrugs. "She's my only grandbaby. I'll spoil the ever-loving shit outta her if I want." He takes a long drag on his cigar, tipping his head back as he puffs the smoke out. "What are you planning for my daughter for her birthday, Avery?"

"*Dad.*" Claire tosses her head back, the sound she makes stuck somewhere between a hiss and a groan.

"Birthday?" I repeat, studying her closely. She sure is doing her damn best to act like she doesn't notice, eyes trained ahead of her as she pokes at the fire with her stick.

Claire tugs her sweater up to her nose, sinking lower into her chair, grumbling something I can't hear.

"Canada Day," Casey clarifies, handing me another beer from the cooler. "You're not trying to hide your birthday from your boyfriend, Claire, are you?" he teases, flicking the ash from the end of his cigar.

Canada Day. That's in...shit, just a few weeks.

"Twenty-six?"

My question is directed toward Claire, but it's Gavin who answers since Claire seems intent not to. "Yup. Twenty-six years of my wild, stubborn, fiery little girl." His eyes linger on her face, the corner of his mouth tipping up. "She looks more and more like her mom every day. And every bit as beautiful."

"Daddy," Claire whispers. They lock eyes, the two of them smiling softly at each other.

Gavin gives her a wink and shifts his gaze back to me. "So, Mr. Moneybags."

"*Dad*! Oh my God." Claire covers her face and nearly disappears into her sweater.

"What?" He sweeps one hand out in my direction. "Big investment banker with his own firm in Toronto? I think that's a fair name."

"I'm not offended," I assure him.

"How'd you get into that, anyway?"

I lean back in my chair and Claire picks herself up, climbing onto my lap and snuggling up. I'm a little surprised she's so affectionate with me in front of her dad and brother, considering she fought like hell against all of this affection in the first place, but if this is her unguarded, I'll take every bit of it. My free arm winds around her as I run my fingers up and down her back. I touch my lips to the crown of her head and she lets out a sleepy, quiet sigh.

"My dad had his own firm for years. Just retired two years ago, actually."

"Ah. So did you take over his firm?"

I shake my head. "No. I own it with my best friend Wyatt. We met in college, which is actually where we met Dex, too. I used to love going to my dad's work with him when I was a kid. I was just enthralled by it all, and it just felt natural to follow in his footsteps. He taught me everything I know. I can't imagine doing anything else."

"Well, I should think so," Gavin says. "Checked out your website. You've landed a ton of huge deals, so that must mean something."

I don't have a clue what's on our website, but I'm sure it looks impressive enough. My mom designs and runs it for us, just like she used to with my dad's. It's how they met, actually. She started as his secretary straight out of school when his company was nothing more than a twenty-by-twenty office space, two desks and a phone. She stuck by him through all those start-up struggles, including missed pay checks. She says it's because she loved him, but my dad says she fought off his advances for an entire year, and she had another boyfriend.

So fucking glad Claire didn't make me wait a year. Three weeks was hell enough.

"What about you guys?" With my cigar, I gesture to Gavin and Casey. "I love those tables and desks you made for Cherry Lane. Been meaning to ask how to get my hands on a few of those."

"Same way you did," Gavin says, kicking his feet out. "Followed in my dad's footsteps and so did Casey. Although he took it a step further than his old man."

"I teach woodworking at the college," Casey clarifies. "That's why I'm in Toronto."

"No shit. I didn't know that. So you're off in the summer?"

Casey's head bobs. "I can teach a summer course, but I pull Viv outta daycare instead and we get up to all kinds of fun shit. More so now that she's a bit older. Get to come down here a lot more too, and we get a ton of work done in the summer." He claps his hands together. "But if you're serious about wanting a couple pieces—"

"Trust me, he's serious," Claire mumbles. "He's constantly petting my desk. It's weird."

"Hey," I whisper, tipping her chin up. "You be quiet there, little lady." I kiss the sleepy, cheeky smile right off her sweet lips. She tastes delicious, like a sugar coma I could get high from.

It doesn't take long for Claire to fall asleep in my lap while I shoot the shit with her dad and brother. I suspect the aforementioned sugar coma. The fact that we've been screwing like wild animals every night this week probably also plays into it.

411

"She seems happy," Gavin observes pensively, eyes locked on his daughter curled into my chest.

Casey's head bobs as he murmurs his agreement. "She was never like this with Aaron. And he sure as hell didn't treat Vivi the way you do." He's pensive as he studies his sleeping sister. "She smiles way more since you came along."

"It's soon," Gavin says quietly.

My gaze snaps to him, nervous he's going to tell me to slow this shit down, which I'm pretty sure is not possible. I'm already well in over my head with feelings I've never felt before, plans for a future I wasn't sure I'd ever want.

But he just chuckles, holding up his hand, putting an end to my worries. "It's soon, but I can see that it's real. And that's all that matters to me. You treat her right, you love her the way she deserves to be loved, and that's it. That's all I need to see."

I peer down at the beauty in my lap, her delicate fingers curled tightly around the collar of my hoodie. Her lips part with a soft sigh when I run my fingers through her soft waves. "I do love her." A small laugh puffs past my lips. "It's kinda scary. Never been in love before, to be honest. But it's not hard to love Claire. I want to give her everything she deserves."

And she deserves the whole world.

When I wake up in the morning, the sheets are cold and I'm alone.

How the hell this girl repeatedly successfully sneaks out of bed is beyond me, considering I have a death grip on her all night long. Also, this bed is tiny and she was practically sprawled on top of me all night.

Making my way to the kitchen, I find the house empty and quiet. There's a fresh pot of coffee on the counter, the robust scent wafting through the air, and a note next to a bowl of fresh berries that says there's breakfast keeping warm in the oven.

Shrieks and giggles filter through the open screen door on the warm breeze. As I step out onto the covered back porch, I'm not sure whether to laugh or sink to my knees at the sight before me. I decide to lean up against the house and fold my arms over my chest while I watch whatever the hell this is unfold.

Claire and Vivi are creeping across the expansive lawn, Claire on her hands and knees, Vivi on her tiptoes and wielding what looks to be a butterfly net.

Vivi turns to Claire, placing one finger on her little pout, and whisper-yells, "Shhh! You gots to be quiet, Auntie Claire. Or else we never catch 'em. Gamps says I keep it if I catch it."

"I know, baby, I know," Claire whispers back much more successfully, just loud enough for me to catch.

Vivi plants one fist on her hip, net flailing through the air, nearly decapitating my girlfriend. "Well, Daddy says you isn't bery good at catchin' wabbits."

I smother my laugh while Claire grumbles something I can't hear, and then Vivi gasps. "You not allowed to say that word!" She taps Claire on the head. "You bad girl!"

I can't fight back that laugh any longer. It leaks out of me with a deep belly rumble and Claire's head swivels around, icy glare landing on me.

Gavin and Casey slink out the patio door, both of them chowing down on bacon while they chuckle and sidle up next to me to watch the show.

"*There*!" Vivi shrieks suddenly, whipping her net around as a bunny goes dashing across the yard. She takes after it like a rocket, screaming, "Get back here, you wascle-y wabbit!"

"My girls," Gavin murmurs with a happy sigh, lifting his steaming mug of coffee to his lips, blue eyes twinkling while he watches those two crazy redheads tear across the yard.

413

My heart stretches as I follow the sound of Claire's laughter, smiling as her and Vivi go tumbling to their knees, rolling around on the grass when the bunny escapes.

I want to give Claire the kind of birthday she deserves, filled with reminders of how special and loved she is, and what I know more than anything is that, to her, there's nothing more important than family.

I turn to her dad and brother. "Can I convince you to take off up to Muskoka for a couple nights at the cottage for Claire's birthday?

Gavin smiles. "I don't need convincing to spend a weekend on a lake in the middle of nowhere, and for my daughter of all people." He claps a hand to my shoulder. "What in the hell she was ever doing with a guy like Adam when you were out there is beyond me."

"Aaron," I correct.

Gavin lifts a shoulder and lets it fall, eyes shining with mirth as he sips his coffee. "I figure *Adam* is better than *cheating piece of shit*, which is what I really want to call him."

CHAPTER FORTY-FOUR

Claire

"Nervous?" Avery reaches over, giving my knee a gentle squeeze as he puts the truck in park in the driveway of a ginormous house tucked back into a cute, quiet neighborhood.

I had no idea neighborhoods like this even existed in Toronto. I thought it was all skyscrapers, concrete, bright lights, and noise. This is anything but. The street is quiet and wide, lined with trees and a big park up ahead. The house is all wooden pillars and big stone, blue-gray siding. It's so…residential.

Anyway. Nervous? Absolutely. Avery killed it this weekend with my Dad. I'm not sure I'll be so lucky. I can be awkward and shy, and I certainly don't command a room the way Avery does. People don't hang on my every word.

"No," Vivi answers for me, bouncing in her car seat while she cranes her head around. "I not ner-bus."

My eyes roll as I bite back my laugh. Of course she's not nervous. Girl's a social butterfly.

Avery swivels around, shaking Vivi's tiny foot in her sparkly purple sandals. "Well, I'm so glad you're not scared, princess. But what about Auntie Claire? Do you think she's scared?"

"Oh. Auntie Claire big scaredy cat." The claws go up before Vivi snarls and meows at us.

"Just the teensiest bit," I admit, resting my head on the seat while my lids flutter closed, taking a moment to steel my nerves.

Avery's hand closes over mine before he lifts it to his mouth, pressing a kiss to my knuckles. "They're going to love you, Claire."

My lids flip open. "You don't know that. What if they hate me? What if they think—"

He cuts me off with the sweep of his lips. "My mom's already planning our wedding, so nix those thoughts right now." He levels me with a serious look, brows dipping as he repeats, "They're going to love you, Claire."

Avery's out of the truck, pulling Vivi into his arms before I can get my stupid seat belt off. I jab at the latch a thousand times. Why the hell isn't this thing—

"Oh," I murmur, peeking up at Avery after he opens my door, reaches across my lap, and unbuckles me with one swift click, all while holding Vivi on his hip, and her bag on his shoulder.

He smiles at me and kisses my cheek. "Stop freaking out and relax, you weirdo."

"Welax, you wea-doh," Vivi repeats.

Avery snickers while I bite my tongue. He leads us down the side of the house and through a wooden gate, and Harper's exasperated voice drifting across the yard.

"Mom, *stop*. You're whacked, lady. Claire's easy to please. She's with your son, after all."

"*Happy!*" Vivi shrieks when we round the corner and spot Harper. She wiggles in Avery's arms until he lets her slide down his body and then takes off across the perfectly manicured lawn on her chubby little legs to accost Harper.

Oh, sweet, holy heavens. I mean, this house, this yard…it's immaculate. The sprawling, two-tiered deck, the gazebo off in one corner of the lawn, the sea of towering old trees that make the yard secluded and quiet, a beautiful, bright garden, and is that a…

"It's a stone pizza oven," Avery whispers, lips touching my ear.

"Jesus," I mutter on an exhale, fingers fluttering to my throat as I take it all in.

And I mean, the pool. There's a freaking waterfall flowing into it on one side.

"*Oh!*" I squeal and jump when something licks my hand. There are two dogs sitting at my feet, neither of them Sully, both wagging their tails.

There's Sully, rolling around on the grass with Vivi.

And there's Avery's mom, looking at Vivi like she's never seen anything more precious in all her life. Is she—

"Aw, Christ, Mom," Avery wails, stalking over to the petite woman as he tows me along behind him. "Are you crying?"

"She cries all the time," a husky voice drawls. "Goin' through the change, I think."

"Oh, you shut up!" Avery's mom twists, and I can only imagine the scowl she hits him with as he steps through the patio door. Turning back to me, she smiles sweetly, clasping her hands under her chin while she moves toward me like I'm some sort of foreign object she's never seen before. "I'm so sorry about my husband."

The man in question steps down the stairs and hits me with a grin that's, quite frankly, just as panty-melting as his son's. They're twins. Big and broad, muscly, that dark, wavy hair. This…this is not fair.

"And *I'm* sorry about my wife's tears."

Avery's eyes shine with amusement at the way I'm standing here, gaping, before he sweeps me forward. "Mom, Dad, this is Claire."

His mom doesn't hesitate to yank me into a crushing hug. She's small but aggressive. I think that's where Avery got his tenacity from. "Hi honey. I'm Jess. We're so happy to meet you. Avery's been talking about you for weeks."

I peek over Jess' shoulder. Avery stuffs his hands in his pockets, dropping his gaze to his feet. "Weeks?"

Jess waves a hand through the air when she finally releases me. "Oh, yeah. Came over here a couple weeks ago looking for advice. Said he found his person."

I've never seen Avery look more uncomfortable than he does right now. His mocha eyes lift to mine before quickly flitting away, focusing on Vivi as she chases all three dogs through the yard.

Me? I'm focusing on the fact that Avery told his mom he found his person. *I'm* his person. Me. His person. My heart stutters and tumbles.

And then I'm swept into another hug. And good God, this one smells so good. Feels so good. So hard. Oh, crap. Does he work out still, at his age? I resist the urge to squeeze a bicep. Charlee would die right now.

"Hi sweetheart. I'm Austin." He's got the best laugh lines in his cheeks, crinkles around his eyes. Different than Avery's, his eyes are a soft, weathered blue, just slightly less. They land on Vivi when she stops at his feet, gazing up at him with wonder. "Would you look at that head of hair! Holy cow!" Crouching, he fingers one braid. "Did Avery do your hair for you?"

Vivi's nose scrunches before she bursts into a fit of giggles. "A'wy? No way! A'wy don't know how to do pwincess hair! Auntie Claire do my pwincess hair for me."

Vivi cocks her head, examining Austin. "You old like my Gamps."

Austin presses a hand to his chest. "*Old?*"

"Uh huh, but you cute like A'wy. Gamps cute, too. I call you Gamps?" Her brows furrow with her question, her entire expression perplexed, one palm turned up.

He wraps her in a hug, and I can't tell who's enjoying it more. "Darling, you can call me whatever you like."

Harper's chin lands on my shoulder. "You fucked up," she whispers.

"I did?" Oh, no. What did I do? I tug on my sundress, cheeks blazing as I drop my gaze.

Harper's laugh is light and soft. "I mean, bringing that little cutie here was a terrible idea. Mom's been on our asses to give her grandbabies for a year now. We thought this might cool her jets. I think it's going to be the opposite." She angles me toward her mom. "That woman wants to keep her forever."

I sputter out a nervous laugh. *Babies*. We've been dating for all of ten days.

Vivi turns her dimply beam on Jess as she attaches herself to her legs. She really knows no boundaries. Stranger danger? Not a real thing. "You a Gamma? My Gamma in heaben." She points one little finger to the sky.

Jess' gaze lifts to mine as tears pool in her eyes. Avery groans beside me. Harper cackles. Austin runs an exhausted palm down his face, breathing out the quietest, *Oh, for fuck's sake.*

"I'm not a Grandma," Jess tells her, sinking to her knees. Her fingers flutter over Vivi's braids.

Vivi looks to me with the most ginormous eyes, expression slightly terrified. "She cwyin'!" She spins back to Jess and throws her arms around her neck. "No cwy. It's otay." She takes Jess' face in her little hands. I hope they're not sticky. Avery gave her a freezie earlier. "You be my Gamma. I hab two. One here and one dere." She points to the sky again. "Otay? No cwy."

The sage wisdom of my toddler niece. She's so far beyond her age sometimes, likely because she spends all her time with adults who have a hard time controlling the words that fly out of their mouths. Vivi has a huge heart and so much love to give. She hands it out freely if she thinks you're deserving.

Jess makes a noise I've never heard before, stuck somewhere between a gasp and a choking sob. This woman is an emotional mess, and Vivi's making it a hundred times worse.

The hold she embraces Vivi in looks crushing, but Vivi's all about suffocating hugs. "Well, aren't you just the sweetest thing."

After an afternoon in the sunshine, in and out of the pool, Vivi eventually falls asleep in Avery's arms under the shade of the deck. When she wakes, she follows Austin into the kitchen and helps him make the pizzas he's going to be throwing in the fancy stone oven. They're quite a pair, those two, just as she and Avery are. There's something about those Beck men; the both of us know it.

"Everyone's coming for the weekend," Avery says as Vivi covers her face in ice cream and chocolate sauce after dinner. "Charlee, Dex, and Wyatt, too."

Harper rolls her eyes, tossing her hair over her shoulder. "Will Wyatt be bringing his plaything?"

Avery ignores her, which is probably for the best. "Me and Claire are staying the rest of the week."

My brows jump. "Oh, we are?"

"Uh huh. Already texted Dex. He said you have tons of vacation days you never use."

What can I say? When you love your job, taking a break feels unnecessary. I'm lucky to spend most of my days with two of my best friends, and at one of my favorite places.

"We're definitely in," Jess says, clapping a hand to Austin's knee, his head bobbing away in agreement. "We don't get up there nearly enough and we have no excuse for that."

"Should we rent another cottage?" I ask quietly, hand on Avery's thigh as I gaze up at him. "So everyone fits?"

"We aren't renting anything," Avery tells me on a laugh that feels entirely too humoring. "Dad and I bought it a couple years back."

And I'm surprised, why? I don't even know why I have expectations anymore. All Avery does is consistently blow them out of the water.

"The cottage sleeps sixteen," Avery continues simply, cleaning Vivi's massacred ice cream sundae off her face. "Tons of room for everyone and every pup."

"Speaking of pups," Harper chimes in, clearing her throat. She drums her fingers on the table, dragging her tongue across her lower lip like she's gearing up for something big. "Are you *only* a dog person, or are you also into other animals, like, oh, I donno…cats?"

"Cats?"

She nods. "Specifically, kittens. Really, really *cute* kittens."

"I luh kitties! Meow!" Out comes Vivi's cat claws for the second time today. She gives the back of her hand a lick for good measure.

Avery shakes his head back and forth. "No. No way, Harps."

"Aw, come on, Ave." She slinks back in her chair with a huff, pinning her arms over her chest.

"Absolutely not. End of discussion."

"End of what discussion?" I'm confused. "I do like cats. I had cats and dogs growing up. What are we talking about?"

I tried to convince Aaron to get a cat, because he said my apartment was too small for a dog. Honestly, it is. It works for Avery and Sully because Avery's penthouse is massive and Sully's also extremely lazy. But the cat? No, Aaron wouldn't even go for that. He told me he was allergic, but several old photos of him with his childhood pet subsequently determined that that was a lie.

"Claire." Avery touches my hand. "Quit while you're ahead, trust me."

Harper shoots up from her seat and dances through the patio door, singing, "I'll be right baaack, with a special surpriiise."

With a deep sigh, Avery flashes me a look that tells me that whatever is about to happen is my own fault. "You walked yourself right into this one. I can't help you now."

Harper returns two minutes later cradling a tiny ball of fluff in her arms. Vivi goes wild, clawing at Avery for help getting down, and nearly takes Harper out by the legs.

"This is Chester," Harper tells us, setting the orange and white fluffball down on the table. He stands on four wobbly legs, bright blue eyes moving around the table.

Vivi climbs onto Harper's lap and reaches her hand out. "Here, kitty, kitty." She looks to Avery. "Maybe Chessy like i-cweam."

Avery dips the tip of his finger in the melted vanilla remnants of Vivi's bowl and holds his finger up. The kitten comes lolloping over, tiny tongue covering his finger. And then Chester saunters right on over to me, climbing up my chest and settling onto my shoulder.

"Oh." I pout at Avery. "Oh my God." I meet Harper's gaze. She's practically bouncing in her seat. "Does he have a home?"

Harper smirks. "I don't know, Claire. Does he?"

"You mean…you want me to take him?"

"I'm bottle-feeding him for a couple more days. You could take him home next weekend if you're up for it. No pressure, though."

I take Chester off my shoulder and check him out, kissing the stripes on his forehead. He looks like a tiny lion with his thick mane.

"Don't look at me," Avery says on a chuckle the second my eyes land on him. "I told you, you walked yourself right into this one."

"I'm at your place every night," I try to bury on a whisper, unsure of how that might sound to his family. "I don't want to leave him home alone all the time."

But then there's Sully. Besides the obvious—Avery's condo being significantly more spacious and gorgeous than mine—the reason we're there so often is because of Sully.

I'm also not fond of the idea of giving up sleepovers with Avery. I've had a taste of drifting to sleep and waking up with his warm body tucked around mine, and there's no part of me that wants to give that up.

"And we wouldn't," Avery insists gently. "If you want him, that's not something you need to worry about. You know I like cats, too." He tucks my hair behind my ear and scratches Chester's chin. "He can hang out at my place."

"What about Sully?"

Avery peels Chester from my grasp and plops him down on the ground where Sully's sleeping. Sully cracks a sleepy lid, lifts his head, and covers Chester's entire face with his tongue. Chester stretches and curls into the tiniest ball, right there in the crook of Sully's neck.

"You want the damn cat?" The curl of his lips tells me he's amused.

I'm sure my grin detonates my entire face. "Yup. I think I want the damn cat."

CHAPTER FORTY-FIVE

Claire

Stifling a sleepy yawn, I slide into the cool sheets. Avery and I just had quiet sex on the couch like a couple of horny teenagers trying not to get caught. I accidentally gouged the leather, which earned me a swift slap to my ass, so I'll probably do it again.

I watch Avery stroll out of the bathroom in only his boxers and my loins start gearing up for round two, except there won't be a round two. They're going to be sorely disappointed when they get the memo, because, hot damn, that man's torso is a chiseled slab of tanned marble.

And he's smiling.

"What are you smiling at?" Besides the obvious, which is my sleeping niece cuddled in the middle of the bed, where Avery's deep brown eyes are glued.

Vivi was supposed to sleep in one of the spare bedrooms. I set it up for her and everything. But she got that wide-eyed look, all wobbly bottom lip, and said that she wanted to sleep with us. As soon as the words left her mouth, Avery scooped her up in his arms and deposited her right here.

It's new for her, he justified.

What he really meant is that he's a giant pushover. I mean, the girl's got far better adaptability skills than anyone I know, including me. For example, the time I moved an hour away from home and my first bright idea was to get drunk and sleep with my best friend's brother.

Me? Not adaptable in any way. Vivi? Made two total strangers her new grandparents in a matter of minutes. Avery's just got a soft spot for her. It's sweet, and I can't blame him.

"Just trying to wrap my head around how much my life has changed so quickly," he whispers, climbing under the covers. He tucks them carefully around Vivi and strokes her pink cheek with his knuckle.

At the apprehension that tenses my body and creeps into my face, tipping my mouth, he reaches across Vivi and cups my cheek. "Hey. It's not a bad thing. Not at all. I love my life right now. Wouldn't trade it for a damn thing."

"Even the cat?"

He chuckles, tugging me up so I can meet him in the middle for a kiss. "Even the damn cat."

We settle into the darkness together, the sliver of moonlight that slips through the shades casting a soft glow over Avery and Vivi. Happiness radiates through every fiber of my being. I know it hasn't been long, and I know it wasn't long ago that I was swearing off men altogether, re-evaluating my life after what felt like the biggest betrayal. And so I'm kinda not sure how I got here but— okay, wait. That's a lie. I know how I got here. I got here because of a very persistent, pushy, arrogant man who refused to take no for an answer.

"What are you thinking about over there?" Avery's quiet voice carries over the mattress, his fingers finding mine on Vivi's back. "I can hear the wheels turning."

"Aaron never did this." The admission slips past my lips before I can stop it. I don't mean to talk about him in front of Avery, but I can't help comparing the two. They're so drastically different, and since Avery walked into my life, I've realized how much I was missing all those years, how our relationship had emptied me of everything I had left.

Avery, though. Avery breathes the life back into me, making it better than it was before. Everything is new and fresh, and I finally feel like I can bloom into the person I was always meant to be.

"Every time Vivi slept over, he disappeared for the weekend. Stayed over with his friends." Or his other girlfriends, for all I know. "He barely spoke to her, hated that he couldn't understand what she was saying. He made her cry once." I'd never thought he was mean until then. I'd just thought he was uncomfortable around babies. I even convinced myself things would be different when it was our own baby. Thank God I never had to find out. But when he made Vivi cry because he couldn't understand her words, that was the last straw. It was only a couple months ago, and I never brought her around him again. I refused to put her through that.

"You love her so much," I whisper as a single tear tracks a path down the side of my face, rolling into my pillow.

Avery's fingers squeeze mine. "I do. And I love you so much, too. I'd do anything for you two." He brings my hand to his mouth, soft lips dusting across my knuckles. "My strawberry girls."

A laugh mixes with a cry and I sniffle, trying to get a hold of myself. I'm so lucky to be where I am now, surrounded only by people who love and support me.

"Can I ask you something, Claire? You don't have to tell me if you don't want to, if you're not ready."

I know where this is going without him saying the words. Quite frankly, I'm surprised we haven't had this talk already. That Aaron cheated on me was one of the first things Avery learned about me.

"You want to know how I found out?"

His answer is a heavy sigh as his fingers trace up and down the length of mine.

I think back to that weekend, the one that would ultimately change my life for the better, even if I didn't know it at the time. I was emotionally devastated for all of two hours, before my sadness flipped to rage. That rage emerged the second Aaron strolled through my door, whistling like he didn't have a care in the world. Until he saw Dex sitting with me on my couch, holding me.

"He said he was spending the weekend at his friend's cottage, helping him get it set up for the season. He didn't even leave the city. How careless is that? I didn't have Vivi that weekend. I could have gone out with Charlee, might have run into him anywhere. But I guess he decided it was worth the risk. Or maybe he just didn't give a damn anymore."

Avery shifts closer, wrapping one long arm around me and Vivi, holding us tight, like he's trying to protect us. He's quiet, just listening patiently while I find my words, tell my story.

Just another thing Avery gives me that Aaron didn't. Listening, patience.

Why do we choose to ignore these things for so long? If I could go back in time and smack myself upside the head, I would.

"Dex went out to a club with some friends. Um, Rebel, I think?" I choke out a bitter chuckle, the irony of the name not lost on me. "Dex spotted him at dinner with a blonde who was obviously not me. Couple hours later, found them on the dancefloor, making out. And then again out back with his, um…hand…inside her—"

"It's okay, sweetheart." Another kiss to my knuckles. "You don't have to say."

I swallow down the lump in my throat. I'm glad it's over, but it still hurts to think about it, how intimate they were in public, for anybody to see. And in the city where we lived together.

"He didn't notice Dex, I guess. Dex came by first thing in the morning. He didn't want Aaron to come home and…he didn't want me and Aaron to have…sex…before I knew." God, what if we had? He always came home extra ravenous after a night or two away. Thinking about that now makes me my stomach roil. How many times did Aaron come home and fuck me after being inside somebody else all weekend long?

A tiny sob squeaks past my lips as I remember how worthless I felt, how embarrassed I was that Dex had witnessed it all, that he had to come over and be the one to break my heart.

The bed shifts and I watch Avery's shadow slink across the room. He rounds the bed and slips in behind me, his body curling around mine. His lips touch my neck as he burrows in, fingers splayed over my hip, my belly.

"I need to hold you," he whispers. Somehow everything is always better when he does.

With Avery's hands on me, reminding me that I'm safe and so very loved, I remember the way Dex held me, let me snot and sob all over him while he promised me everything would be okay. I didn't believe him. I didn't think it would ever be okay. But now I know how right he was. Now it's better than I ever could have imagined.

"When Aaron walked through the door, Dex was holding me. Aaron—" another bitter chuckle, "—accused *me* of cheating on *him* with Dex. He lost his mind, called me a slut, a whore, every name under the sun. Dex had him pinned against the wall in two seconds flat. He told Aaron he'd been at Rebel the night before, to be a man and come clean. He didn't; not really. He tried every excuse in the book. *It wasn't me. I wasn't there. I was drunk. I don't remember anything.*

"I kicked him out for the night. Later, I got a text from a number I didn't recognize. It was another girl. He'd gone there for the night, but turns out her friends had seen him at the club the night before with that other girl, too. She went through his phone when he fell asleep and found out about me." I snicker. I'm glad I can laugh about this now. "She threw a bucket of ice water on him and told him to get the fuck out. And it just kinda went from there. By the morning, I'd found out about four girls in total." I snuggle a little deeper into the mattress, and into Avery's hard, warm chest. "I didn't go to work Monday. I went to get tested for STDs and packed his things. When he came home from work, I told him it was over."

"I'm so sorry, Claire." Avery's lips touch my neck, my shoulder, my cheek, over and over again, his arms squeezing me tight, like he wants me to know he's never, ever letting me go. At least, that's what I hope.

"You know what?" I twist in his iron hold, taking his face between my hands. "I'm not sorry. Not at all. The opposite, really. I'm so, so grateful." I trace the shape of his lips, his jaw, running the tip of my finger over his sharp cheekbones. "I never would have met you."

He breathes out a tiny chuckle. "That's not entirely true. I still would have walked into your conference room on Monday morning. The difference is I would have had to convince you to break up with your douchebag of a boyfriend before I got into your pants. Which I would have, by the way." His mouth covers mine, the tip of his tongue sweeping across my top lip.

"Convinced me to break up with my boyfriend, or gotten into my pants?"

"Both," he says so confidently.

"Arrogant," I murmur against the velvet sweep of his tongue.

"Nah. Just persistent enough to not give up on the things I want."

"I'm glad you didn't give up on me."

"The thought never crossed my mind, regardless of how stubborn you were."

"So stubborn," I agree with a quiet sigh, trailing my lips down his neck.

"It's one of the things I love about you." He hooks my leg over his hip and rolls us both off the bed. Pressing me against the wall in the hallway outside the bedroom, his hips grind into mine. "You're stubborn, I'm arrogant, we fight. It's what makes the sex so damn explosive."

His fingers slip beneath the hem of my top, dancing up my torso until they find one pert nipple, pinching gently. My fingers sink into his hair, nearly ripping it right out of his scalp when he pushes

429

my shirt up, tongue lashing at the taut bud. His teeth pierce my sensitive skin and a puff of air escapes my lips.

A moment later, I'm over his shoulders, and my pajama shorts are on the ground.

"Where are we going?" I ask as innocently as I can manage as he stalks down the hall. Circling my arms around his middle, I sneak one hand into the elastic of his boxer briefs, my fingers wrapping around his thick cock, smiling when it jerks in my palm.

"Somewhere I can fuck your brains out without waking up your niece."

He opens one of the spare bedroom doors, tosses me down on the bed, and licks his lips as he prowls toward me, the glint in his eye all devil, along with the delicious smirk that tips one side of his mouth.

"Now spread those legs and let me see that pretty pink pussy I love so much. I'm gonna show you all the reasons why you'll never need another man but me for the rest of your life."

CHAPTER FORTY-SIX

Avery

I'm distracted this afternoon. That's probably why I'm staring out the window instead of at my computer. It's not the first time I've caught myself doing it today.

I love my job. Really, I couldn't love what I do more. Before Claire, work was my life, the only thing I was so certain of. I was here 'til dark most nights, and often brought projects home with me on the weekends. I didn't mind.

Now I can't wait to get out of here. I never stay past five. I never bring work home with me, unless I have a deadline to meet, and even then, I do it with Claire's head on my shoulder, her body pressed next to mine on the couch.

For the first time in my life, I feel like I'm truly living it, rather than just moving through the days. I never felt like anything was missing, but now I know. Claire was missing. Intimacy. Love. Partnership. The things I never want to go without again.

This last month together has been nothing short of perfect and I can't wait to take off to the cottage this weekend with the people I consider family, real or made.

Begrudgingly, I return my attention to my computer, shifting my reading glasses back up my nose. This acquisition contract I'm typing up is long, tedious, and boring as fuck. But it's going to bring in about five-mill for us, so I gotta get my shit together and get it done.

I'm twenty minutes back into it when the elevator out in the lobby dings and I hear our receptionist dish out a warm welcome before she gasps.

"Oh no, sweetie, you don't look too hot. You're not sick before your big trip, are you?"

I don't need to hear the response to know it's Claire. I wait patiently for her to drag herself into my office, knowing she's moving a bit slow today.

And when she does, it's quite possibly the most dramatic thing you've ever seen. I'd make fun of her if I didn't know how sick she actually is. She's in awful condition. Awful enough to warrant an actual sick day, which Claire never takes. I almost took one too, simply because I didn't want to leave her this morning. She kicked me out. Literally, she kicked me in the ass, chucked a pillow at my head, and screamed, *Out! Get out!*

Claire glides across the room with her head down, shoulders sagging, oversize sunglasses on her face and a bag tucked under her arm.

"Hi sweetheart," I greet her, opening my arms as she drops the bag on my desk and plops down in my lap, nuzzling that gorgeous face of hers into my neck. I pull her legs up and cup the back of her head, kissing her forehead. It's still warm. Hot, actually. She was one-oh-two this morning when I checked her. "What'd the doctor say?"

"Strep throat," she murmurs, nuzzling harder, deeper. My baby's a baby when she's sick. I don't mind. I want to take care of her.

Rubbing my hand down her back, I rest my cheek on her head, holding her close. "Do you wanna postpone? We can go in a couple days when you're feeling better."

She sits up, shaking her head. I pull the sunglasses off her face, finding her eyes all sleepy and bleary. I kiss each one when her lids flutter closed.

"I want to go, Avery. I got a prescription. I've already taken my first dose, and the doctor gave me a shot of vitamin C. She said I should feel like myself by the morning." She grins, dragging the tip of her nose across mine. "She said I won't be contagious by then, either."

432

"Mmm. So I can look forward to sticking my tongue down your throat then?" I haven't gotten more than a closed mouth peck on the lips since yesterday morning, considering she could barely cart herself through the door when she came home from work yesterday afternoon. She didn't eat dinner, passed out on the couch in her work clothes, and I towed her off to a cool bath before I dropped her in bed before seven.

"Uh huh." She drags her closed lips across mine, swallowing back a moan. I'm not sure if it's because she's desperate for more or because her throat hurts. Sighing, she rests her cheek against my shirt. "I'm so tired."

"You should be home in bed, cuddling with the zoo." Chester's awoken a wild streak in lazy, old Sully. Those two are insane together, and when Vivi comes over, all hell breaks loose.

"I wanted to see you." She swings an arm out toward the bag she dropped on my desk, flicking her hand around. "And I brought you and Wyatt lunch."

I ruffle the messy bun on top of her head. "You're a princess."

"I'm a queen," she mumbles sleepily. "Just gonna rest here for a bit, 'kay?"

"Mhmm. You do you, baby. You know I work better with you around." Untrue. She's highly distracting. Still, I'd rather have her in my arms.

She's out cold in two minutes, breathing deeply against my neck, small fist clutching my shirt while I work around her, thinking about how I could do this every day. If she took up every inch of my personal space for the rest of my life, that'd be just fine with me.

Wyatt strolls in with his hands in his pockets, whistling a tune. He halts just inside the door when he sees Claire sleeping in my lap, a smile tugging up his face. "I came to see if you wanted to grab lunch. Looks like you've got your hands full."

433

I tip my chin toward the bag on my desk. "Claire brought us lunch."

"Mmm." Wyatt rubs his hands together and drags a chair up to the desk. Unraveling the paper bag, he inhales deeply. "Fuuuck, Thai food. She's the best." His blue eyes flicker to Claire as he pulls out the boxes. "What'd the doc say?"

"Strep throat," I tell him, saving the document I've been working on before swiveling toward the food. My stomach starts growling as the spices invade my nostrils and I inhale that scent like my life depends on it.

"She gonna be okay for this weekend?"

"Doc loaded her up on meds and said she should be feeling better by the morning, so, I hope so. I know how much she's looking forward to this." I stab at some chicken and shrimp pad Thai. "Sophie coming?"

Wyatt shakes his head, eyes downcast as he shovels food into his mouth.

"She busy this weekend?"

He lifts a shoulder. "Donno. Didn't ask her."

My brow lifts. "You didn't ask her? Why not?"

He shrugs again. "Didn't feel like it. There's lots of us going. It's not like I need the distraction."

I study him carefully, looking for the real meaning behind his words. It's a little odd, at the very least. He brings her to nearly every event, even if their label is purely casual.

"Look at you," he mumbles around a mouthful of noodles, a clear sign the topic is done with. "You're a pussy. How did that even happen? Next time this year, bet you're a married man, maybe even a dad."

"Shut up," I murmur, gently squeezes the back of Claire's clammy neck.

"I'll be walking down the aisle, holding your wedding rings. I have to start prepping my best man speech. What embarrassing stories—"

"Who says you'll be my best man?"

Jaw hanging, the look he wears is pure outrage. "If I'm not your best man, I'll stand up when the minister asks if there's anybody who objects." He pounds a fist down on the desk. "I'll object that shit so fucking fast you won't know what hit you. Claire'll punch you in the dick for ruining her wedding day."

My chest vibrates with a low chuckle. There's nobody else I'd choose to stand up beside me and he knows it. Wyatt's so much more than just my best friend, my partner. He's a brother to me.

Claire stirs with a soft sigh, hand sliding up my chest, over my collarbone. "Wyatt," she grumbles, eyes still closed. Her tongue flicks out, coating her lips. "Shut the hell up, please, or I'll punch *you* in the dick."

I swallow my laugh. Wyatt doesn't even attempt to suppress his. It comes barking out.

"Christ. Haven't even put a ring on her finger yet and she's already a bridezilla. Not too late to get out of this whole relationship shit, Ave."

Claire cracks one lid, just enough to locate my pen, which she promptly flings through the air at my best bud's forehead. Her aim is spot on.

"It's my birthday weekend," she says sadly. "You can't talk to me like that."

"I'm sorry." Wyatt stands and rounds the desk. He takes Claire's face between his hands and pecks both cheeks. "Jesus, your face is on fire," he remarks, eyes widening before he tweaks her nose. "You're right. You're the birthday princess. No teasing. Until tomorrow, at least. All bets are off when we're at the cottage. Also, you're getting birthday bumps. Twenty-six, and four more for good luck." He kisses her forehead. "Thanks for lunch, Claire Bear."

After lunch, I send Claire home in my car with Jacob, and then I rush home to her before five even rolls around. I check her apartment first, though I'm ninety-nine percent sure she won't be there. Sometimes she doesn't even enter her apartment for an entire week.

I want to keep her forever.

And sure enough, she's not there. Instead, I find her passed out, naked, in my bed, Sully at her feet. The cat is nowhere to be found, which is never a good sign.

I find him in the bathroom, sleeping on a pile of shredded toilet paper. Fucking cat. I snap a picture and send it to my sister with nothing but the word *thanks*.

Taking a seat on the edge of the bed, I push Claire's damp hair off her forehead. She's not so warm this time. I lean over, pressing a kiss to her lips, and they part on a sharp inhale.

"Oh," she mumbles, stretching her arms overhead the way Chester does. When they come down, she brings me with them. "You're home."

"Mhmm. How you feeling, beautiful?"

She touches her throat, blinking up at me. "Better, I think. It doesn't hurt as much."

"I'm glad to hear that." The tip of my finger dances over the dainty freckles decorating her nose. "Our cat's an asshole, by the way."

"Did he rip up the toilet paper again?"

"Uh huh."

"I like that you call him *our* cat." She threads her fingers through my hair. Her green eyes are bright and clear, a stark contrast from the hazy, red-rimmed mess earlier today. She's definitely feeling better.

"I want to share everything with you," I tell her honestly, not caring one bit how vulnerable that makes me sound.

"Mmm, so Sully's half mine?"

I roll my eyes, glancing at the obsessed, fluffy black blob guarding her feet while she sleeps. "I think Sully's all yours. He'd choose you over me any day of the week."

"But you're his daddy."

"And you're his mommy."

Her cheeks flush, and she feels like she's a hundred-and-two degrees again. "Stop it. I can't handle your level of cuteness."

I roll on top of her, pinning her wrists above her head. "And I can't handle you being sick, 'cause I just wanna fucking devour you."

Her hips lift, pressing into mine. "You can still devour me, just not my mouth."

"Hmm." My finger trails down her stomach, enjoying the way the muscles there clench and jump. "So I can have *you* for dessert tonight?"

She tosses her head back into the pillows with her throaty laugh. "Will we ever get sick of this?"

"Nah." I suck on her collarbone, marking her as mine, the way I like to in a new spot every day. "I wanna love on you forever."

Her emerald eyes peer up at me. "Forever?"

"Forever."

CHAPTER FORTY-SEVEN

Avery

"Hot. Damn."

I glance at Charlee, sunglasses tipped down her nose while she fans herself with one hand, propping herself up on the dock with one elbow while her legs kick out behind her in the lake.

"There are way too many sexy men in bathing suits," Charlee murmurs, biting on her lower lip. She eyes me up, then Casey, then Wyatt, then Casey's dad, then my dad. It's too much, and I can't help the laugh that bursts pasts my lips. Her eyes glaze over her own brother with a gag. "I mean, don't get me wrong, Dex, you're cute and all, but…"

"Yeah, you really don't need to explain." Dex clears his throat and tugs on his hair. "In fact, I'd prefer if you didn't."

Hanging off the pier, Charlee peeks up at Casey, eyes raking over him on repeat. She opens her mouth to say something while she starts pulling herself up on the dock, but before she can, Claire collides with her back, wrapping her arms around her and propelling them both back into the water. My wild, fiery girl.

"Ew. Stop. That's my brother. Don't you dare call him sexy."

"I only speak the truth, Claire Bear. You know that."

Charlee grips Claire's foot as Claire climbs up on the wood, trying to jerk her back in. Claire scuttles away, cackling, and Charlee's gaze settles back on Casey with a wink.

"You look beautiful too, Charlee, but you always do." Crouching down in front of her, Casey takes her hands and starts pulling her up, but hesitates, his lips to her ear. "You'd look even better without the bathing suit." With a wink as devilish as his sister's, he drops Charlee back into the water.

438

Charlee's curses are drowned out by a gaggle of shrieks. Every heard turns, finding Vivi being chased, hands in the air, by four dogs and one cat who thinks he's a dog. I catch her around the middle and scoop her up when she races by in her teeny tiny frilly bikini.

"A'wy," she wheezes, thumbing over her shoulder. "Dey chasin' me! Dey twyin' to get me!"

"You're too fast for them, munchkin."

She deflates in my arms with a heavy sigh. "I twyin'!" She points to the water, sage eyes sparkling wildly. "We jump?"

"You wanna jump in?"

Vivi's head bobbles up and down. She crooks a finger at me and cups her hands around my ear. "I tell you secwet. I bwave."

God, I love this little girl.

A clicking sound has me looking up, my eyes landing on my sister, her camera pointed at us. We've been here for six hours and she's been snapping pictures nonstop.

"I'm sorry. I can't not. You two are fuck—*freaking*—adorable. God, I gotta get used to the no swearing around kids thing."

Casey waves her off as he takes Vivi from me, strapping her into her Frozen life jacket. It's Frozen everything with this little chick. "Between Claire and I, she's pretty much heard it all by now. I think we've just given up on it at this point. If the worst thing she does is know how to spell fuck by the time she goes to Kindergarten, I'll count my single parenting a success."

"You're a great dad, Case," Charlee says, dripping with water as she kneels beside Vivi. She takes her braids in her hands and tickles Vivi's pink cheeks with the tips. "Right, Viv?"

"Wight! And you a gweat mama, Auntie Cha-Cha!" Vivi throws her arms around Charlee's neck as best as she can in her bulky jacket. "You be my mama. You can kiss Daddy and we can snuggle in bed, like Auntie Claire and A'wy!"

I'm not sure who's cheeks burn brighter—Charlee's or Casey's. Gavin sucks his lips into his mouth, fighting a laugh that shakes his body. Dex claps a hand to his face. Claire snickers and jabs an elbow into his side.

Deciding to put them out of their misery, I toss Vivi over my shoulder while she squeals with laughter. I try to hide my smile at the awkward way Casey helps Charlee to her feet, like they're both suddenly terrified that lightning is going to strike the second they touch.

"Come on, pipsqueak. Into the water with you!"

"I count dem," Vivi murmurs with wonder, tipping her head backwards over the crook of my arm. Her face screws up when she squeezes one eye shut and points her finger up to the black sky, the millions of tiny stars that paint it, making this beautiful summer night glow.

"One...two...free!" She grins up at me. "Dere's free stars, A'wy!"

Chuckling, I hug her against my chest. I'll never get tired of the way she speaks. "Three times a million, baby."

"What's dat mean?"

I shake my head softly, kissing her nose. "Nothing. Good counting. You're such a smarty."

"I like Smarties. Sometimes Daddy lets me hab 'em for bweakfast."

Wyatt snorts beside me and Casey's eyes widen.

"You're not supposed to tell anyone, kiddo," Casey reminds her. "That's our little secret, remember?"

My dad pats his shoulder. "Don't worry. All the best fathers feed their kids chocolate for breakfast. Have you gotten to ice cream yet?"

Casey groans, looking down at his lap while he stretches his legs out in front of him. "She had a strawberry sundae for breakfast on Wednesday. Why the hell is it so hard to say no to her?"

"Uh, I donno, 'cause I cute?" Vivi frowns and holds both palms up in a purely innocent shrug while she guesses at her dad's rhetorical question. "Dat what A'wy says when he gimme i-cweam." Which is often, because, like everyone else, I can't say no to her.

I meet Casey's gaze and shrug. "Sorry, dude."

He only chuckles, pulling himself out of his seat. "Alright, Miss Munchkin. Off to bed with you. Say goodnight to Uncle Avery."

His body tenses at the same time mine does. Maybe he didn't mean to say it, or he's worried I'm not going to be into it.

Claire, who's been relatively quiet beside me, sucks in a breath that catches in her throat, her swinging leg hanging in midair. My mom quite literally whimpers.

Vivi's fingers dig into my shoulders as she stands on my thighs with her little bare feet. She wraps her arms around my entire head, pulling me in for a suffocating hug. "G'night, Uncle A'wy."

"Sleep tight, little princess," I say quietly, touching a kiss on her soft pout.

"Don't let da bed bugs bite!" she squeals, going in for a tickle on my ribs, because that's our thing now.

When Casey returns twenty minutes later, I'm sitting alone on the dock, watching all my favorite people talk and laugh around the fire. It's almost overwhelming sometimes, seeing the family we've made together in such a short time, the way we all fit together perfectly, like missing pieces of a puzzle. Sometimes I just need to step back and soak it all in, appreciate it from afar, my new life.

Casey sinks down to the chair beside me, handing me a cigar. "Sorry about the uncle thing. Just kinda slipped out. I hope I didn't make you uncomfortable."

441

"Not at all," I assure him. "I love your daughter. I'd be honored if you two thought of me that way."

"We do," he says after a moment. "You're family to us. Vivi loves you. She's lucky to add another person to her life that loves her so much." His pensive gaze drifts over the stars above. "Claire, too. They're both lucky to have you."

"I'm the lucky one."

"No, really." His head flops over his shoulder and he smiles. "Thank you for loving them. You'll be a great dad one day."

My eyes travel over the yard, landing on Claire. She catches my eye, I think, because the fire illuminates her grin as she waves at us.

I always figured I'd be a dad one day, but never had any real pull toward fatherhood. Just kinda assumed it was one of those natural steps. You know, meet someone, settle down, get married, have kids. Two months ago, I wasn't ready for any of that, not even step number one.

"I never really thought I wanted kids until I met Vivi."

Casey laughs softly beside me. "She's her own breed, that one. I might be biased, but I think she's the fucking greatest."

I couldn't agree more wholeheartedly. "If my own kids are anything like her, I'll be one lucky man."

"They'll be half Thompson, so, you're bound to get a little wild in there." He clears his throat, like his own words just sank in. "I didn't mean to assume, uh…" He takes a long drag on his cigar, choosing not to finish his sentence.

Grinning at him, I say, "It's all good, man. Nobody else I'd rather do that shit with than your sister."

"Your desk is done, and conference table will be ready next weekend." Casey chuckles, changing the subject. "Wyatt wants a desk now too."

I laugh, puffing out a ring of smoke. "Yeah, he wants to outfit the whole office now. You're gonna need another workshop."

"No kidding." He scrubs a hand over his jaw. "Going back and forth to my dad's is a pain in the ass. When I'm teaching, I can use the woodworking space at the college for smaller projects, but then I'm at work a helluva lot more, and don't see as much of Vivi."

"You in a condo?"

He nods. "Like to get a house with a yard and a decent workspace, but it's so damn expensive in Toronto. Still saving."

"You wanna teach the rest of your life?" I can imagine he makes a decent living as a college professor, but I'm trying to feel out what his long-term plan is.

Casey's quite for a minute while he thinks. "Nah. I just wanna build, create. I only went into teaching because the income was good and steady, which is what I needed with Vivi. I've always wanted to open up my own shop, but Dad says he's too old for it now."

"What kinda shop? A space to build and sell your creations?"

"Yeah, but more than that. I'd wanna sell specialty wood so people could DIY their own projects. Hold workshops and shit. It's fun to see people learn to love it the way I do. The DIY trend is so popular right now."

"Sounds like you got a pretty solid business plan right there," I observe. "Sure you even need your dad?"

He laughs, scratching his fingers through the stubble lining his jaw. "Well, I sure as hell can't pull it off on my own. I've got the ideas, I guess, but I don't really know the first thing about running a business. I also don't have the kind of money needed to start one."

I lick my lips, savoring the robust flavor of the full-bodied Nicaraguan I'm inhaling. It's lush and creamy, with just a hint of sweetness. "So you need a partner?"

"What? No. I mean." He twists, staring at the side of my face. "What?"

"You wanna go into business together, Casey?" My gaze shifts sideways to watch his reaction. I'm not disappointed.

His jaw drops, cigar tumbling from between his fingers, rolling across the dock as he scrambles to pick it up. "Avery, that's not what I meant. Shit, I don't want you to think I was asking you for money. Fuck." He runs an anxious hand through his messy hair.

"Relax," I chuckle. Those Thompson siblings are two peas in a pod with their nerves and money guilt. "I'm the one that brought it up. I'd never think that. I've seen the stuff you build, Casey. It's incredible. An art, and you've mastered it. You already have a huge customer base. I think you've got something here, and it'd be a shame to let it go to waste simply because you can't afford to start up a business on your own." After all if my dad hadn't helped me and Wyatt get started, where would we be right now?

When he doesn't say anything for a long moment, I add, "I think it'd be a big success, Casey."

"You really think so?" he asks quietly.

"I really do."

"So, what? You wanna give me a loan?"

I consider this for a long minute. What do I want? I could give him a loan. Wyatt and I could invest. I know Wyatt would in a heartbeat. He loves Casey's stuff just as much as I do. Or…

"I wanna be your partner."

He straightens, spinning to look at me. "What exactly does that mean?"

"We do it all, together. Except the carpentry shit. Unless you wanna teach me. We look for a place together, open the business together. I can help get everything set up and running, and you can run the day-to-day. You'd be in charge of staff, workshops, all that stuff, and I'd handle the money side of it."

"Do you have time to do all that?"

I shrug. "I manage my time well." I also know how to prioritize and get shit done.

"What about Claire? I mean, do you think…what if you two break up?"

444

I throw a sidelong glance at him. "Do you think we're going to?"

His grin grows. "No, but I think you might consider it a few times when she's driving you up the fucking wall."

I smirk. "When she drives me nuts, I'll come take my frustrations out on some wood."

Casey chuckles. "There's no better stress release than hammering your anger out on a slab of timber."

"We're friends, Casey. I'd like to think we could maintain our friendship even if Claire and I were to break up. But to be clear, in case that's your biggest worry here…I mean, I know it's soon, but I don't plan on letting your sister go." She'd have to change her name and leave the country to get away from me. And even then, I'd find a way.

Casey smiles down at his lap.

"Give it some thought. Quitting your job and opening a business is a life-changing decision, especially when you've got a daughter to think about." I turn toward him, putting the butt of my cigar out. "But let me draw up a proposal, show you what it would look like. You can come down to the office one day in the next couple weeks and we'll go over it."

Casey groans, dropping his face to his palm. "Only if you promise me Claire won't be there that day. I'm never going to either of your offices again if there's a chance you're both there."

I bark out a loud laugh as I stand and stretch my arms overhead, rubbing a hand across my stomach. "Man, it was one time," I argue weakly.

Casey might've walked into Claire's office two weeks ago to find her sitting on top of me with her dress bunched up around her hips and my hands on her ass. I forgot to lock her door that day. She pinched me so hard I bruised, and then put me on timeout that night.

"One time too many," he grumbles, stalking past me as we make our way up the hill toward the others. "I like you, but she's still my little sister. I'd prefer to let myself believe she's waiting for marriage."

"How long's it been since you got laid?"

"Too long," he says on a heavy exhale, his eyes finding Charlee as she throws her head back with laughter. "Way too fucking long."

I pull a sweaty Claire into my chest, molding my body around hers as I kiss a sloppy path across her bare shoulder. "I can't wait for everyone to leave on Monday so I can give you a proper fucking."

"A proper fucking? What do you call what we just did?"

"Quiet and restrained," I murmur, nipping her neck. "And that's just not you. I need you screaming my name while you come all over my cock."

Her lips part on a shudder and she grips my hand, dragging it down her belly, pressing my fingers into her sopping warmth. "God, how do a few simple words from you get me ready to go all over again?"

"You're always ready to go for me." I hitch her leg over my arm and drag my fingers through her slick folds, gathering her wetness and coating the tiny hole between her plump cheeks. She moans and pushes back against my hand as I massage her there. "When you gonna let me in here?"

"You're gonna hurt me," she garbles out.

"I'll be gentle. I promise."

She chokes out a laugh. "You and gentle do not belong together in a conversation about sex."

I laugh against her neck, licking a slow trail up to her ear. "I can love you gentle. I *do* love you gentle."

"No." She shakes her head, fingers sinking into my hair. "You love me wild."

446

"Yeah," I breathe out, rocking my hips against her ass as I lift her thigh. She's not wrong. I'm fucking wild for her. My cock pushes through her slippery entrance. "You're right. I do love you wild."

"Can I ask you something?" I grunt out as I begin an achingly slow plunge into her velvety walls, my fingers rubbing a languid circle around her wet, swollen clit, enjoying every whimper I draw past her lips. "Did Vivi call Aaron Uncle?"

"Nuh-uh," she stutters out as I roll us, propping her up on her hands and knees. "Never."

My fingers grip her hips as I pull out and thrust back in, slow, slow, slow, in and out, in and out while she whimpers for *more, please, Avery, more.*

Leaning down, I flick my tongue over her ear. "Just me?"

"Just you."

"Hmm."

"Is that okay?"

"Uh huh. I'm gonna be the best uncle."

"You already are."

My chest swells with pride as my hand wraps around Claire's face, covering her mouth. I smile against her cheek as her teeth press down on the flesh of my palm. "I'm about to fuck you wild, little strawberry, so be good and stay quiet."

Releasing her, I turn her face to mine, my tongue sweeping into her mouth.

"I love you," she murmurs against my lips.

My hand claps back over her mouth, swallowing up her scream when I pull out and slam into her as hard as I can.

"I love you wild."

CHAPTER FORTY-EIGHT

Claire

Truthfully, I haven't enjoyed a birthday so much as this one since my nineteenth. It was the year I was finally legal drinking age, and my parents and brother took me out and pretended like I hadn't been drinking illegally for the last three years. We spent the day visiting wineries and breweries and went to a fancy dinner overlooking the lake.

I was drunk by the time dessert came around.

After dinner, Casey and Dex took me out. Oh, we also snuck Charlee into the bar. It wasn't hard. The bouncer played hockey with our brothers for years. He winked at Charlee and let her in the back door. Totally illegal.

But every birthday since then has been difficult. My nineteenth was also the last one I celebrated with my mom by my side.

Actually, that's not entirely true. She was there for my twentieth birthday, but she was sick as hell in the hospital, and I didn't feel like celebrating. I snuck off for the day and spent it by myself on the edge of the escarpment, overlooking the town below, the Toronto skyline on the other side of the lake. Casey and Charlee found me just before sunset, towing along a bag of Crunchwrap Supremes.

Now, every year on my birthday, I regret my selfish behavior. I regret letting my emotions get the better of me, because I lost out on one last birthday with my mom. And as much love as I've always been surrounded with on this day, I've always felt incomplete. Something's always been missing.

Charlee's arm wraps around my waist as she tugs me into her side, my head tipping onto her shoulder. I gaze out at the lake, at all the men I love splashing around down there, acting like a bunch of…well, men. I hear a shriek and look over my shoulder.

"Don't you *dare*, Wyatt!" Harper screams, arms braced between them while Wyatt ignores her demand, barreling down the hill toward her. He grabs her around the knees and throws her over his shoulder while she shrieks—whether it's with laughter or anger, I'm not sure. Probably a bit of both. "*Wyatt!*" I swear, her scream echoes across the lake.

He just keeps on ignoring her, flashing us a grin and a wink as he runs past us and launches himself—and Harper—off the dock and into the lake. When they emerge, Harper jumps on top of him, attacking him while he laughs in her face and easily fends her off.

Vivi walks down the hill with Avery's mom's hand in hers, waddling in her life jacket, two buns on top of her head, the sun catching those red strands and making them shine. "Uncle A'wy!" She waves her hands high in the air like she doesn't already have all of his attention. "Uncle A'wy, you catch me? I jump!"

Avery's smile lights up his face as he wades closer to the dock. He opens his arms. "Jump, baby! I'll catch you!"

Charlee moans beside me. "Like, stop it. So freaking adorable. She's so in love with him."

She is. She spends most of her time attached to his hip. Or his knee, because that's about as high as Vivi can reach. She's been glued to him all weekend, and if he minds, he certainly doesn't let it show.

And so, as I take it all in, glued to my best friend's side, looking over the gorgeous lake, I realize how full I am. Utterly happy. Complete.

Beyond that, though, I feel my mom, here with me, with us.

"Look, Claire," Charlee whispers in my ear, nudging me with her shoulder. She points to the sky and I blink through the glare of the bright sun, spotting one small white cloud, and the tiny patch of rainbow that colors it.

449

The day my mom died was a beautiful, sunny day in early February. A balmy fifty-three degrees smack dab in the middle of winter. I remember sitting on my front porch just staring up at the sky, splashing through the puddles from all the snow that had melted from the unseasonable warmth, and laughing. Because the whole thing just felt so surreal, like the worst joke I'd ever heard.

I woke up with the sunrise the next morning and sat on the back porch in my mom's sweater with a cup of tea, and when the sun came up, a rainbow painted the sky, right there in the middle of winter, while tears slid down my cheeks.

"Do you think my mom is with us?"

"Oh, Claire." Charlee squeezes me tight, her temple pressing against mine. "I know she's with us. All the time, guiding you and Casey toward the very best things in your life. How do you think he got so lucky with Vivi? How we *all* got so lucky with Vivi? How you found Avery?"

I'd like to think she's right, that my mom has played a part in all of the very best things. Vivi came at a time when we needed her more than anything. She mended old wounds and brought us all closer together. She reminded us that life was meant for living and loving. And Avery came along and ground that into me when I needed that reminder more than anything, when I'd forgotten the value of a life worth living.

"Hey," murmurs a soft, husky voice, drawing my gaze like a magnet. Avery plows a hand through his soaking ebony waves. My eyes follow the path of a hundred different droplets as they carve a path through the ridges of his chest, his hard abdomen, disappearing into his bathing suit where it hangs low on his hips. It should be illegal for him to be standing here in front of us right now, looking like a snack I wanna eat.

"Damn." Charlee tips her sunglasses down her nose and speaks my thoughts. "You look good enough to eat."

Avery chuckles and pretends to cover himself up with a hand over his chest and one squeezing the bulge in his slick, wet shorts. "I'm not a piece of meat, Charlee." He moves next to me, sweeping my hair off my shoulder before touching his lips to my neck. "Why is the birthday girl crying?"

"I'm okay." I grip the back of his neck, holding him close while his lips move over me. He makes a noise like he doesn't buy it, so I add, "I'm just happy, Avery. Really happy."

His hand slides along my jaw, turning my face toward his. Dark chocolate eyes drift over my face, studying me. The droplets clinging to the tips of his long lashes are distracting. "Promise?"

"Promise."

A small smile tips the side of his mouth before he plants a kiss on my lips. "Okay. I'm happy you're happy."

Charlee leans over with a gag. "Somebody get up here and save me before I have to watch these two give each other a happy ending!"

Avery laughs and flicks Charlee's ear. "You remind me too much of my sister. You're just as annoying."

"But you love me just as much?" She grins up at him, batting her lashes.

"Yeah, something like that." He straightens, running a hand down his torso. "I'm gonna get started on dinner," he calls out, loud enough that everyone can hear. Avery points at Charlee's leg before he turns and walks up toward the cottage. "You've got a bee on your leg, Char. Careful."

"What?" She freezes, hands in the air. "A bee?" Her eyes drop down to her lap in slow motion. And then she shrieks, her arms flailing around before she smacks her leg. "*Ow*! Fuck me! Oh! Claire!" She keels over, clutching her leg. "I've been hit!"

I smother my laugh, because laughing right now wouldn't be nice. "Stung. You've been stung."

She looks up at me with tears in her eyes.

"Oh." I pout at her, reaching for her head, cuddling her close. "I'm sorry."

"Help me," she cries. "It feels like I've been shot." It doesn't look all that great either, but I won't say that. Painting the inside of her thigh and swelling fast, the sting is nearly the size of a golf ball already. An angry, red golf ball.

"Cha-Cha!" Vivi tears a path up to us as she rips her life jacket off and ditches it somewhere behind her. "You otay?" She jerks to a halt in front of Charlee, dropping to her knees. She inspects the bump as if she really knows what she's doing. "Oh, no! You need kiss!" She plants a loud smooch to the inside of Charlee's thigh before she can protest.

Charlee manages a tiny laugh through her tears, smoothing her hand over Vivi's hair. "Thank you, baby."

"You still cwyin'." Vivi gazes up at her, looking a lot like she might cry herself. With the biggest heart there is, this girl feels every emotion. "You need Daddy's magic kiss. Daddy?" Her head spins wildly. "*Daddy!*"

"Christ," Casey mutters under his breath as he climbs up the hill. "I'm right here, Vivi. You don't have to yell."

Vivi's bottom lip quivers, big green eyes welling with tears as she takes her dad's hand and leads him over to Charlee. She pats Charlee's knee. "Cha-Cha hurt. You needa kiss her boo-boo."

When Vivi points out the bee sting on the inside of Charlee's thigh, Casey's eyes nearly roll out of his head. Charlee groans and looks to the sky. Casey kneels at her feet, parting her thighs gently while he examines the red bump.

His cautious gaze flicks up to hers when he speaks so quietly that I feel like I should silently back away and give them some privacy. "You get stung?"

Charlee just stares at him. I watch her throat work with a hard swallow. Oh, this is fantastic.

Casey's thumb sweeps around the bump. He glances up at me. "Can you grab me some tweezers and an ice pack?"

"Uh huh. Sure can." I point at them with both index fingers. "I'll just...yup. I got you." I dart up to the cottage, grab a pair of tweezers, load up a sandwich bag with ice, all while screaming at Avery that my brother's between my best friend's legs. He doesn't understand what I mean, but his laughter floats behind me when I fly back down to them, stopping to suck in air when I spot Casey wiping at Charlee's tears.

It takes Casey all of two seconds to pull the stinger from Charlee's thigh before he covers her red skin with the bag of ice, looking up at her with a smile while she cracks one lid and releases a shuddering breath.

"There. All fixed up," Casey murmurs softly.

"Daddy," Vivi whispers, hugging his middle. She can't get her little arms all the way around his broad body. "You needa kiss her. Don't worry, Cha-Cha. They magic, like Queen Elsa." She pats Charlee's knee. "You be all better. I pwomise."

"Oh, that's, uh..." Charlee's brown eyes dart to mine, pink heat creeping up her chest and into her cheeks. "It's o—"

Vivi cuts her off with a finger to her lips. "Shh. Magic kisses," she insists in a stage-whisper. "Daddy..." Her little brows climb her forehead as her gaze moves between her dad's face and Charlee's bee sting.

I watch my brother's lips press softly to Charlee's thigh, which should be entirely too intimate for a sister to watch, but instead I'm thinking about Charlee's words, that my mom is always with us, guiding us to the best things, the lives we're meant to live. I hope my mom is guiding those three together, because they deserve each other.

Charlee jumps up to her feet. "Uh, well, thanks. I should go—" she jerks her thumbs toward the cottage, "—get dressed, uh, for dinner..." She takes a step and cries out, clutching at her leg.

Casey just chuckles, shaking his head before he bends and scoops her up behind her knees, carrying her bridal style toward the cottage.

"God, they might actually be cuter than you and Ave," Harper breathes in my ear.

Before I can respond, Wyatt winds an arm around Harper's head, towing her away in a headlock while she rips at his hands.

"Wyatt! You stupid asshole! Get your grubby hands off me!"

An arm slings around my shoulders, pulling me close. I inhale the familiar scent I love so much, snuggling into my dad's side.

"You've got quite the bunch here, don't you? Surrounded by lots of love."

My body relaxes with a happy sigh that feels like it melts away every worry in my head. "I was just thinking the same thing."

"Happy birthday, princess." His lips touch my temple. "I love you so much."

"I love you, too, Dad."

CHAPTER FORTY-NINE

Claire

Watching as the last car pulls down the drive Monday afternoon, disappearing through the thick brush of trees, I sink back against Avery's chest, my hands over his on my stomach.

"That was the best birthday ever." I turn in his arms and snuggle into him, enjoying the way his broad body swallows mine up. I never want to let him go, because I never want to lose this insane happiness that I just happened to stumble upon. "Thank you so much, Avery."

Lacing his fingers through mine, we stroll through the cottage. I don't think cottage is even the right word. It's a mansion. In the woods. On a pristine lake. Which, by the way, set off one hell of a firework show last night. Vivi just sat there in utter silence, staring up at the sky with wonder while it exploded with color. When it was over, I couldn't tear my gaze off the stars that dusted across the black, the Milky Way shining right there above me.

"I never want to leave here. I could stay forever."

Avery's eyes crinkle with his smile. "You wanna take an early retirement? We can move out here. I'll work from home and travel into Toronto a couple times a month."

Giggling, I shove his hip with mine. He pins me against the kitchen counter, caging me in with his arms. "Sounds like you've given it some thought."

He lifts a shoulder, looking all too casual. "Little bit. Hard not to think about it when you're out here."

"Hmm. But that would never work."

"Oh? Why not?"

"'Cause I'd never let you leave me," I say simply, not even caring how needy that sounds, because it's true. My need for this man makes me feel insane.

Avery's brows jump, his thumb skimming his jaw. "Leave you? Did you miss the part where I said *we* move here?"

"You don't mean that." I lift up on my toes and kiss his ridiculously full lips before I sneak under his arm and move to the fridge, pulling out a tray of fruit. "You'd get sick of me in a week if we lived together."

"Would I? We already pretty much live together." He watches my face, which I'm trying my damn best to school into a mask of indifference. "Don't we? You're at my place every night. We have a devil cat together." His eyes drift to Sully who's lounging in the sun on the back deck, paws in the air, while Chester jumps at his wagging tail. "And a Sully," he adds with a laugh.

He stalks over to me, gripping my hips. "Are you telling me you don't wanna live with me?"

I grin up at his face, the pout he's got on that could rival Vivi's. I tap it with my finger. "I'm telling you it's a moot point because I can't retire at twenty-six."

"Well, you could," he says slowly, thinking.

"No."

"I'm just—"

"I'm not living off your money for the rest of my life. I love you for you, not your money. In fact, your money is very intimidating. Could you make less, please?" I tease.

"No can do, sugar," he says with a broad grin. "I'll tell you what I can do though."

"Mmm." Licking my lips, I grab a fistful of his shirt and tug him down to me, the fingertips of my freehand dancing across the waistband of his shorts. "What's that?"

"I can fuck you properly now that we're alone."

456

"Properly?" I pop the button on his shorts, fingers creeping down as I palm his cock. It twitches and kicks, growing fast.

"Properly. Sideways. Six ways to Sunday. Into next week. Senseless." His hand slides up the nape of my neck, gripping my hair as he tips me backward, soft lips ghosting over my throat, settling a breath away from my mouth. "Get the picture?"

"Not sure. Can you show me?"

I'm upstairs, naked, and flat on my back before I can count to ten, watching as Avery rips off his clothes and retrieves a black box from the dresser.

"I have one more present for you."

I groan, dragging a palm down my face. "Another? You've spoiled me."

His grin is so wide and calculating that I find myself sitting up, backing into the pillows as he slinks across the room to me. "I think I like spoiling you, so you'll have to get used to it." He climbs onto the bed, crawling toward me on his knees. "But this is a different kind of gift."

Hitting him with a look of pure skepticism, I take the box from his hand, lifting the lid. Inside is a small pink...*something*...half the size of my palm. I hold it up, examining it carefully. It has a small hole with a raised lip running around it, and a button on the opposite side.

"What is—*oh*!" I squeal and throw the toy when I hit the button and it starts vibrating in my hand. "What the hell is *that*?"

I mean, it's a sex toy, obviously. A vibrating sex toy. I have a vibrator at home. One I haven't touched since the first night Avery and I slept together. But...the hole? What the hell is the hole about?

Avery chuckles, picking up the toy as he moves toward me. I crawl further backwards until my back hits the headboard.

"Don't be scared," he murmurs, amused. "It'll feel good. I promise."

"You don't..." I don't know why, but I find a pit of insecurity growing in my stomach, one that reminds me that at one point, not long ago, I wasn't enough for someone. I pin one arm across my chest and pull my knees up to my stomach, trying to quell the ridiculous thoughts in my head that tell me this man feels anything but love for me. "Do you not want to touch me anymore?"

Avery's deep brown eyes flicker and he clicks the toy off before hauling me into his arms. "That's not what this is about at all, Claire. Please don't ever think that. It's physically painful to keep my hands off you. Sometimes I worry how much I love you is downright suffocating."

Oh, he's cute. He's a very hands-on partner, that's for sure. His hands are on me the second he walks through the door when he gets home from work. But suffocating? No. I can't get enough of him either.

"Then what's it for? Why do we need it?" I pry the toy from his fingers, tracing around the lipped hole with the tip of my finger.

Avery's nose drifts along the edge of my jaw. "Can I show you? Or do you want me to tell you first?"

"Tell me first," I breathe out, meeting his gaze. "Please."

I need to envision it before I jump into something like this. I've never used a toy with a boyfriend before. The question—asking Avery if he's used toys with women before—is right on the tip of my tongue before I swallow it down. I don't really want to know, and the man is incredibly experienced, so I likely already know the answer.

He plucks it from my hand and guides me gently down to the pillows. One finger traces the seam of my legs and they fall open for him. His thumb touches the hole in the toy. "This...is all for your pleasure. You're going to hold it right here—" he fixes the hole overtop of my clit, "—while I fuck you right..." Avery's finger slide through my folds—already wet, big surprise—and

458

halts at my tight hole, pushing gently. "Here. With my fingers." His smile is wicked. "You good with that?"

There? Oh. Oh no. I gulp. I scratch my throat. It feels itchy from the inside out. The desire to scream the word *never!* tingles on the tip of my tongue, but the logical—or highly illogical—part of my brain knows that I'd do anything this man asks of me.

But still, trying new things terrifies me. "I...I'm nervous, Avery. I don't want it to hurt."

"It'll be fine, Claire."

I fight the urge to roll my eyes. Actually, I don't. The urge wins. "Oh, right. *Fine.* Because *it'll be fine* is exactly what you wanna hear right before trying some kinky, new sex stuff with your boyfriend."

Avery's head lolls forward with a laugh. "It'll be better than fine. Have I ever let you down?"

Hell no. I'm actually fairly certain my bones have partially dissolved over the last month. Every muscle feels weak after sex with Avery. Sometimes it takes me a day or two to walk properly again. So that's why I grumble out a particularly growly *no.*

"We'll take it nice and slow," he promises, dropping to his elbows between my spread legs where he's still holding the toy. "Easy."

"What if it hurts?"

"It won't hurt. You're going to be overwhelmed by how good it feels."

"How can you say that?"

He bites back his smile. "Trust me."

"Avery, I—"

He turns on the toy.

"*Oh, sweet holy hell!*" I shriek, shooting forward. "Hoooly fuuuck." I smack the toy out of his hand, clutching it tight to my chest before he can send me into overdrive. "What in the fuck is that?" And why does it feel like heaven? It feels like Avery's

459

sucking my clit and rubbing it all at once. "What is this sorcery?" Meant to say that one in my head.

Avery collapses onto his back, body shaking. I'm glad he finds this so humorous. "I told you. You're going to be going wild over that while my fingers are stretching you out. It'll help you take your mind off it."

"What if I'm bad at it?"

"Bad at laying there while I finger-fuck you?" he questions with the quirk of one amused brow. God, he's got such a deliciously filthy mouth.

"I don't know!" I throw my hands in the air and, consequently, the tiny, magical, sucking machine. It goes flying across the room, dropping to the floor. I shift my eyes back to Avery and choke out an anxious giggle. "Oops."

Avery retrieves the toy and takes a seat beside me. Taking my face in his hands, he kisses me deeply. "I would never push you to do something you're not comfortable with Claire. If you don't want to do it, we won't. It's that simple. Okay, baby?"

Swallowing the nerves that make my throat tight, I nod.

The thing is, everything he does feels good. Avery lives to please me. He might take until I have nothing left to give, but goddammit, this man of mine is a giver too. He loves every inch of my body, and every inch of my body loves the sweep of his hands, the push of his hard fingers, the soft brush of his lips, the slow, wet trail of his tongue. He pushes me to my limits, yes, but he's never given me more than I can handle.

"Avery?" My voice is quiet, hesitant. My fingers curl and fumble at my stomach. "Could we...could we try it?"

"Claire, we don't have to—"

"No." I cut him off with my hand on his, my head swinging back and forth. "I want to. It's just...if I ask you to stop—"

"I'll stop. No questions asked." His eyes bounce back and forth between mine as he pulls his lower lip into his mouth, brow furrowed as if he's searching for a hint of duplicity, something that tells him I'm not ready for this.

Nails biting into his shoulders, I push him down my body. "Just do it before I change my mind."

He laughs against the inside of my thigh, sloppy, wet kisses painting my delicate skin, slowly driving me wild. His mouth covers my center, sucking me gently, before he sits up on his knees and turns on the toy. That little thing packs a vicious punch, judging by the sound it's making and the two whole seconds it spent on my clit.

"It has seven settings," he tells me. "Each one more powerful than the last."

Stars burst in my vision the second he fixes it over me, and I shoot up, trying to clamp my legs together and rip him off me. "Is that the seventh setting?" I gasp out as Avery holds me back with his hand on my chest, not letting me get anywhere near that tiny, deceiving toy.

His chuckle is dark and devious as he kisses the inside of my knee. "Oh, baby…no."

I slap a palm across my mouth to stifle the scream the rips its way up my throat as the pulsing, the sucking, gets more intense. "Avery!" I reach for his hand but he captures mine, holding it tight as he presses on the toy a third time. And then a fourth. And a fifth. And a sixth. And holy fucking hell, I'm coming.

I'm coming, I'm coming, I'm coming.

My head tips backwards and my mouth opens. I'm not sure what comes out of it. It sure as hell isn't words, just a bunch of garbled sounds and pleas. Pleas for what, I'm not sure. To stop? To never stop? I have no idea what I'm asking for, but I don't think I've ever come so soon or so violently in my life. And Avery hasn't even put his hands on me yet.

"Shit, Claire. That took you all of fifteen seconds." He pulls the toy off me, giving me a much-needed break. "I'm not stopping 'til you hit five."

"Five what?"

"Five orgasms."

"*Five?*" Five like that? No. I'll die. I. will. *die.* "Avery, no. That's…that's too much. Like that. I can't." My head shakes furiously. "No."

"You can and you will."

"Avery, I—*oh fuuuck.*" The words come out a strangled, choking mess when Avery fixes the toy back on my cramping clit. "Down, down, down," I cry. "Please, turn it down."

I suck in a breath like it's my first one in minutes, or maybe my last, and release it with a sigh when the vibration goes from absolutely detonating to just mildly eruptive.

My eyes snap open with a gasp when Avery's fingers dive inside—three of them—pumping slowly.

"Fuck me, Claire," he groans, nipping at the juncture of my thigh. "You're fucking drenched. So hot. So wet. You like this."

Yes, I like it. I think the river of lava flowing from my vagina is proof enough. But in case it's not, my walls start clenching around him within seconds, hips thrusting, my entire body writhing while I choke out his name on my second release.

"Two," he murmurs, tongue flicking out to lick me up. He pulls away with glistening lips, his tongue dragging across them, and oh God, I want a taste. "That's two in only one minute."

Growling, I grip his neck and rip him up to me, pushing my tongue past his lips.

He hums against my mouth, and I know he's smiling. It's infuriating. "You like the taste of you on me. You taste good, baby, don't you? Sweet like a strawberry." He disappears, along with the toy, and flips me over, pressing me down to the mattress. "I'm gonna fucking devour you."

462

I push up to my knees and send my hips backwards, but his palm slides over my ass, up my spine, coming to rest between my shoulder blades. Gently, he pushes me down until my tummy is flat on the mattress. His hand slides underneath, fixing the toy back over my clit, and when it hits the right spot, a moan ripples through me, making my body quiver.

I feel his cock, heavy and long on my ass as he leans over me, his lips brushing my ear as he grips my hips, rolling them against the mattress, the toy. "How does that feel?"

"I can't...*oh God.*" The pressure is too much, but my hips start grinding on their own accord.

"That's my girl," he purrs. "Make yourself feel good."

I feel him drift down my back while I bite down hard on my lip, trying like hell to get a grip, to hold on just a little longer. His hands hook around my knees as he jerks them up my sides, and a second later I feel his breath, hot and damp, washing over the apex of my thighs.

"Please," I whimper. I'm desperate.

"Please what, baby?"

"Your tongue. Please, Avery."

"Mmm, 'kay. Anything for the woman my heart beats for." How he manages to say things that make my heart flutter at a time like this is beyond me.

I wish I could say I hold on longer the third time, but I don't. The second his tongue coats my center, slipping through my folds, the toy sucking at my clit, I come undone, ripping the fitted sheet off the corner of the mattress.

It feels like Niagara Falls between my legs.

And what does Avery do? He laughs. The fucking asshole *laughs.*

"Shit, Claire, we're gonna need to wash the sheets."

My chest rockets off the mattress, my head swiveling. "What? Why?"

"You've made a mess," he says simply, tone laced with amusement. His fingers swipe over my sopping core, spreading the wetness all over my ass, before his tongue covers the wet trail, licking it right up. "I could paint your entire body with all your cum."

With a deep belly groan, I bury my burning face in my hands and then stuff my whole head into the pillows where I can hopefully die a quick, painless death, face down. "I'm so embarrassed right now," I puff out on a squeaky whisper.

"Don't." His hand slides between my face and the pillow, lifting me to him. His lips meet mine for a tender, sweeping kiss. Pulling back, Avery rest his forehead against mine. "Don't do that. I fucking love you, and I love your body's reaction to all of this. Just let yourself feel good, Claire. Don't hide from me." His lips slide over my jaw, down my neck, finishing on my shoulder. "Okay?"

I can't stop looking at him. "I love you."

He flashes me a devilishly sexy wink. "I love you wild."

Avery disappears behind me while I rest my cheek on the cool pillowcase, taking deep, steadying breaths, trying to calm myself, which is pretty much impossible considering that thing between my legs. When his fingers dip inside me, my breath turns into a shudder, and when he draws a wet line from my pussy up the crack of my ass, smearing my arousal over my tight, puckered hole, I whimper.

And then he licks it off.

His tongue coats my hole, massaging it gently, two fingers plunging deep into my trembling walls, and my whimpers turn to full blown wails as I thrash wildly, not able to form any words at all, just sounds. My hips roll and thrust, grinding on the toy, riding Avery's fingers, pushing back into his tongue. I want it all, but I'm not sure I can handle it.

"Christ, Claire, I love every single inch of you. Every. Single. Inch." His teeth press gently into the flesh of my skin before the hot lash of his tongue returns and I come all over his fingers, not seeing a goddamn thing even though my eyes are wide open.

"F-f-four," I stutter out, spasming around his fingers. I try to claw my way up the pillows, for what, I'm not sure. I don't know what's going on. I don't even know if it's daylight. My senses are fucked, overloaded and overwhelmed. All I can feel, all I know, is Avery, and the way he makes every nerve ending in my body feel like it's on fire.

"I won't lie," Avery starts, his sizzling touch swiping over me, gathering my wetness and coating the tight ring of muscle that makes my hips jerk, makes me arch off the bed. He reaches under my belly, pressing on the toy, kicking it up another notch as I shudder and bury my face in the pillows. "The possessive animal in me loves the idea of having a part of you that nobody else ever has."

I get what he means, I really do. There are parts of me that hate the thought that I've shared this man with so many other women before me. That other women have gotten to experience his kisses, his tongue, his touch. That any woman has had his undivided attention for any amount of time, because that's a feeling I want to bathe in.

But what do I have that no one before me ever has? His heart. His love. His unwavering commitment and devotion. The gentleness in his soul that he doesn't let just anybody see. The words that leave his lips when he's overcome with a tired haze, right on the cusp of giving into sleep. Those sweet nothings where he tells me how much he loves me, how I make him feel, how he wouldn't change a single thing about his life because it led him to me.

I have that, and nobody else does.

So I understand what Avery's saying. But doesn't he know that he already has so much more of me than anybody ever has? Doesn't he know how completely and irrevocably *his* I am?

I'm brought back down to earth, to this incredibly erotic moment, when the pad of Avery's thumb moves methodically over that hole, stroking me tenderly, massaging. His generous lips, soft and supple, dance along the curve of my backside, the delicate skin on the inside of my thighs, while he murmurs how much he loves me, his words a gentle caress that makes my entire body tingle with a lust and desire so deep, like nothing I've ever known before.

The tip of one broad finger pushes lightly at my entrance and my body tenses at the pressure, fighting the intrusion.

"Relax, Claire," Avery orders lightly, running a soft, wide palm over the curve of my spine.

I take a deep breath. And then another. "I'm sorry. I'm trying. It-it…it feels good, I'm just so nervous." My head flops to the side and I throw a hand over my eyes when I find him peering up at me from beneath those ridiculously long and thick man lashes he's been blessed with.

Chuckling, he keeps stroking, tender and gentle. "So dramatic. Shoulda been an actress."

A small laughs bubbles up my throat, and he pushes forward as pain sears through me for a split second before my body starts stretching, trying to accommodate him, as if we've suddenly remembered we like him and decided he can come on in.

Still, I pin him with a seething glare. "You asshole!"

He flashes me that grin that roped me in nearly two months ago in that dark bar, the one that made me forget all my inhibitions, all my problems, and made me drop my walls, if only for a few minutes. "What? You were laughing, loose and relaxed. There wasn't going to be a better time."

I work hard not to roll my eyes at his shitty excuse. "Is it all in?" I wiggle my ass a little, enjoying the pressure but hissing at the slight sting of pain when I move.

Avery laughs. It's dark and ominous, and definitely not a good sign. "I'm up to the first knuckle."

466

The blood drains from my face, I'm sure of it. "First…first knuckle…like…the one right under your fingernail?" My voice gets higher with each word. No, that can't be right. Everything's so tight down there, full.

His tongue peeks out, touching the corner of his mouth like he's trying to keep himself from saying something that might get him kicked in the balls. It's probably the right choice, because I want to do that anyway just looking at that smirk threatening his face.

But now I'm frantic. My head whips around as I look for anything hard to grab onto, something stable. "Oh God, oh God, oh God."

Avery's finger just sits there, letting me adjust to the intrusion. With my cheek on the pillow, I watch him lean forward, his tongue gliding through my drenched folds, and when I moan, he pushes in a little bit more, drawing that cry right out of me.

He pulls his face back, licking at his gleaming lips. "You're doing so good, baby. Up to my second knuckle now."

"Only the second?" The high pitch of my voice does nothing to disguise my apprehension. How can I possibly take any more of this? There's nowhere left for him to go. "I can't. I-I-I can't."

He smiles at me. It's soft and sweet, oddly reassuring. I love that he gives me all sides of him. "You can."

With his free hand, Avery grips my left hip and starts rocking me slowly over the toy. The pressure of the sucking, hard and fast, is so drastically different from Avery's gentle touch, the sweep of his lips over my pussy as my juices flow freely. All of it, together, shakes my body until my eyes fall closed, teeth pressing into my lower lip in an attempt to still its quiver.

"Look at me, baby." It's a quiet command, but a command no less. When my gaze finds his, so intensely penetrating that I swear he can see right through me, he asks, "Are you ready?"

"I…I don't know."

"Relax, baby. 'Kay? Take a deep breath and let it out."

467

I search his eyes, warm and rich, like melted chocolate. When I nod, his chest expands with an inhale and I follow suit, trying to keep my breath steady and deep. We deflate at the same time, his finger filling me so completely. Pain slices through me for only a moment before it's quickly replaced by pleasure as he rocks my hips slowly and his mouth drops between my thighs. My clit cramps with need, the need to release, and when his tongue lashes over me, sucking me into his mouth, pushing inside, I know I won't be able to hold on much longer.

Avery owns every part of my body and I'm okay with that. There's nobody else I want to share it with.

When he raises his head and our gazes lock, he slowly withdraws his finger, and for a moment, I think that's it. It's over. I did it.

But then he pushes back in, plunging slowly, gently. My lips part with a breathy sigh, a whimper, a moan. It all comes out of me as my fingers tighten, clutching at the pillows, the sheets, my own freaking hair. I'm grabbing onto anything I can reach, holding on for dear life while Avery brings me higher than I've ever been before.

My body makes the unconscious decision to take over. My hips start moving with their own rhythm, rolling and pushing, grinding down against the small toy, my ass back into his hand. Every nerve ending is alive, vibrating, trembling with desire. I can't breathe, can't speak. All I can do is enjoy this moment, the way Avery gives me pleasure I never thought possible.

"Fucking Christ," Avery breathes out in a husky voice that tingles my spine. "You're fucking breathtaking, Claire. Wildly beautiful." I feel the bed shift when he moves, feel his warm breath tickle my neck. "How does it feel?"

"S-s-s-sooo…ohhh…"

He chuckles lowly in my ear as his finger keeps moving, stretching, taking, possessing every damn inch of me. He presses a lingering kiss to my shoulder. "I want you to come for me, baby. You're ready, I can feel it. Just hold on one more minute though, 'kay?"

One more minute? It seems impossible, but by now I know that I'll do anything for him, or at least try my damnedest. Still, as his pace quickens, as his finger plunges deeper, I know I'm walking a fine line, like a thread about to snap.

And then two fingers spear my other entrance, filling me in a way I've never been filled before, and I gasp, head snapping up off the pillows as he moves a steady, fast rhythm, in and out, in and out, claiming me as his with his fingers.

"I can't!" I scream out as I tighten around his fingers, bringing him deeper. "I can't-can't-caaan't! Can't...*ohhh*...wait!"

"Come," is all he says, and I do. I come so hard, my body thrashing violently as I try to get closer and further away all at once.

"Five!" I shriek, loud as hell. "That's five!"

Pulling out of me, Avery's fingers dig into my hips so roughly I think I'll have perfect handprints there in a few hours. He yanks me up to my knees and smashes me back against his chest as he sends the toy flying across the room.

"Let's go for six," he growls in my ear before lifting me up and slamming me down on his cock, and my vision goes black, save for the stars shooting across the dark sky of my vision.

Avery Beck sends me straight to the moon, and when I erupt around him, my climax rippling through my body like the tremors of an earthquake, we collapse together on the bed, sweaty and breathless, wrapped up in each other, just the way we're meant to be.

I turn in his arms—a near impossible feat as our skin sticks together—and take his face in my hands, gazing up at the man I love as I tell him how wrong he is.

"And you're wrong, by the way. You already own a piece of me that nobody else ever has." Confusion slashes his features and I climb onto his lap. "I thought I knew what love was. I thought I was in love with Aaron, and maybe I did love him in some way. But the truth is, I had no idea what real, genuine, true love felt like until you came into my life. I've never loved anyone the way I love you. My heart is yours, Avery. It belongs to you and only you."

The sweetest softness flickers in his eyes. He pushes my damp hair off my face, his thumb sweeping over my cheek, tracing the shape of my lips.

"You own my fucking heart, Claire Thompson. All of it. It's yours. I'm yours."

CHAPTER FIFTY

Claire

The old lady sitting across the room from me shoots me her third glare in the last two minutes, white brows furrowing before she huffs and shifts her gaze to the corner of the ceiling.

I get it: my knee is bouncing at the pace of a racehorse. If I had tap-dancing shoes, I might be carrying a sweet beat. Or I'd just be upping the annoyance factor by, like, a hundred and twenty percent.

I'm nervous. There's nothing I can do about. I grab a fistful of my hair like that'll help. It doesn't. Instead of twirling it, I grip it so hard my scalp burns.

Why am I like this?

My phone buzzes in my purse and I scramble to pull it out, desperate for the distraction.

Charlee: *You're fine. It's fine. You're such a hypochondriac.*

I know I'm freaking out over nothing, but I've always been like this. The second a thought like this enters my head, I run with it like a kite on a windy day.

Regardless, her words bring me no comfort, so I bury my head in my hands.

"Claire?"

I rip my face out of my grasp, gaze locking on the middle-aged doctor. She smiles at me as if I don't think I might be dying.

"Hi Claire." She gestures for me with her hand. "I'm ready for you. Why don't you come on back?"

Gulping, I manage a shaky smile, slinging my work bag over my shoulder while I follow her through the door and down the hall, where she ushers me into one of her exam rooms. Stark white and smelling a lot like bleach, this isn't where I want to be.

"Two visits in just over a month. To what do I owe the pleasure? You don't have strep throat again, do you?" I can see why she might think that, given that I haven't spoken a single word yet.

I shake my head, fumbling with my hands while I search for words. "No, I…well, I…" I squeeze my eyes shut. "I'm sorry. I'm being ridiculous. You're probably going to think I'm crazy. It's just that my parents…" I trail off, because I really don't know how to finish this sentence.

Dr. Tam offers me a patient and encouraging smile. "Take your time, Claire. I can tell you're feeling very anxious."

"My parents both had cancer," I finally breathe out.

She nods, scrolling through her tablet. "Leukemia for your dad, and ovarian for your mom."

"Right. I'm, uh…I'm worried I have ovarian cancer," I admit in a whisper.

Her bright eyes widen just a touch, and she shifts in her chair. "You may be at a higher risk of developing ovarian cancer, however, hereditary cases only account for about fifteen percent of all cases. Is there something particular that's got you concerned, or are you just interested in doing some genetic testing?"

I look down at my hands, the way they turn nervously in my lap. "I haven't been feeling right lately. It's just…it's a lot of the same symptoms my mom had that led to her diagnosis."

Dr. Tam crosses one leg over the other. "Alright. Go through your symptoms with me. What's going on with that body of yours?"

I take a deep breath, thinking about all the symptoms that started popping up about two weeks ago. "I'm having a lot of pain in my stomach." I rub a hand over my belly. "It just feels bloated and uncomfortable, crampy. I feel like I'm peeing more, but I'm also constipated." God, this is so uncomfortable. "I'm exhausted all the time, my back hurts, and I'm having trouble eating because of how much my stomach hurts."

She nods slowly, studying me, before she turns her attention to her tablet, fingers typing at the screen. "Okay, Claire. I'm glad you came. Certainly, those are all symptoms, as you know because of your mom—" and because of Google, "—and because of her, you are at a higher risk of contracting it." Spinning, she grabs a pad of paper off her desk and starts scribbling away.

"We'll start with a couple tests, and depending on those results, we'll discuss how to move forward. How does that sound?"

"Okay," I agree quietly. "What kind of tests?"

"Some blood work, a pelvic exam. We'll start with that, nice and easy."

"When can we do that?"

She checks her watch. "Our nurse is available for the next hour, so we can get them done right away, if you have the time today. I just want to get some more details from you before we proceed."

I nod, my throat working with a thick swallow.

Dr. Tam she rolls over on her chair, covers my hand with hers, and smiles. "It's okay, Claire. We don't know that it's anything right now. Those symptoms are very broad and could be numerous different things, many of them not serious. And if it is, well, you're getting in here nice and quick. We'll take care of it."

Out loud, I agree with her, but all I'm thinking about is how quickly my mom was diagnosed after her symptoms started. Four weeks. Four weeks and her entire life turned upside down. Eight more months and she was gone. Getting into the doctor quickly didn't help her beat cancer.

"Can you tell me what your cycles are like?"

"Uh, normal, I guess?" I shrug. "I'm not really sure."

"Are your periods irregular?"

I shake my head.

"How many days are your cycles?"

"Um…" I scratch at my scalp. "Twenty…seven? Ish? I think?" My cheeks heat. "I'm sorry. I don't really track my cycle."

473

"That's okay. I'm assuming that's because you're on birth control?" She answers her own question when she scrolls through her iPad, whispering the name of my birth control to herself. "And are you sexually active?"

"Yes. With my boyfriend."

She just smiles and nods, jotting it all down on her pad. "How long have you two been together?"

I hate this question. It feels like we've been together forever, but it's really not been long. It's only the end of the first week of August, and I don't count the three weeks I spent running from a relationship with him, so... "We've been together for two months."

"Ah. Still new. Isn't that some of the best fun you've had?"

I manage a giggle. It really has been the best time of my life. I've loved every minute of it, even the arguing. Because if we argue hard enough, I storm away from him and he chases after me. It always ends with Avery throwing me over his shoulder, telling me to stop being so hard-headed and stubborn, and that he loves me more than anything in this world. And then he shows me just how much that is.

Dr. Tam leads me into another exam room, where the same nurse who did my throat swab back at the end of June takes a couple vials of my blood while I look away, because I can't stand the sight of needles. Then she has me lie down on the exam table and prop my feet up in stirrups while she does a pelvic exam.

She barely says a word, though she smiles through every minute of it, until her smile falters and her eyes flicker. One hand presses on my belly while the other moves around inside of me and I hiss out in pain.

"I'm sorry, Claire. I know it's a bit painful." She pulls her hands back and takes off her gloves, moving to the sink to wash her hands.

I don't like the look on her face. It tells me she found something, something that isn't right.

474

Still, I pull my underwear on and straighten my skirt, meeting her out in the hallway.

"We'll give you a call and bring you in when we have the results, and then we'll go from there, okay?"

I don't say a word. I don't even nod. My eyes are burning, stinging with tears. I just know something's wrong. I can't shake the feeling in my stomach, like I drank sour milk. I want to vomit and then curl into a ball and pass out for six hours.

Instead, I plug my earbuds in, turn my music up, and walk home from the doctor's office in a fog, deciding to forgo the last three hours that I was supposed to return to work for.

When Avery comes through the door later that evening, I'm curled up under a blanket on his couch, the cat draped around my head, dog at my feet.

"You know," Avery starts, strolling over to me, "Sully was never allowed on the furniture before you came along."

I swing a protective leg over Sully, tucking him closer to me. "Dogs belong with their humans. Don't take him away from me."

Sully lifts his head and cocks it at Avery, as if he's backing me up. *Yeah, Dad. Don't take me away from her.* At least that's what I imagine.

Avery chuckles and crouches down in front of me, pressing his lips to mine, and then my forehead. "How are you feeling? You don't feel hot. It's not strep again, is it?"

I feel awful about it, but I wasn't fully honest with Avery about my reasoning for my trip to the doctor. He's aware of the symptoms, of course, but not about the diagnosis I've given myself in my head. I'm worried about scaring him, turning him anxious, making him more overprotective than he needs to be.

There's also a little part of me that's worried that he might...want out, if this goes down the wrong way. Charlee hoofed me in the shin and pinched my arm when I confided that in her last week after making the appointment. She's the only one who knows the real reason I was there today.

I know I need to tell him eventually, and I will. And Casey. And my dad. Fuck.

My dad's been doing so much better lately. We've been visiting him every other weekend and he's so happy and lively. He loves hanging out with the boys, and I love having my little family together. I don't want to bring everyone down. I think that's why I just want to hold off until I know more. It might be nothing, after all.

Or it might be something.

"Claire?"

"Hmm?" I lift my eyes to Avery's. They're dragging over my face, his brows pinched.

"You kinda zoned out there. What'd the doctor say? How are you feeling?"

I sit up, rubbing the sleep from my eyes. "I'm okay. Just tired. The doctor's just running a couple blood tests." I wave a hand around to distract from the fact that I'm about to lie. "Could be low iron or something like that."

"You've been working too much."

"No I haven't," I argue, folding my arms over my chest. The moment he says that, my walls start going up. He's brought it up a couple times recently. The truth is, I know he's right. I occasionally stay late and work at the bar downstairs, though that isn't my job, and I've even picked up a couple shifts there on the weekend. I need the money. Even though I'm hardly ever in it, I still have to pay for my apartment. With one income, it's not easy. Even with the absence of my grocery bill, because Avery's just taken to doubling his grocery haul every week.

He doesn't want to pick a fight with me, I know, because he just takes my hands in his, sweeping his lips across my knuckles. "I'm just worried about you, that's all. My heart hurts when you're sick."

My eyes soften at his admission, and I stroke the side of his face. "I'm sorry for getting upset. But I'm fine, okay? I promise." I'm just praying with everything I have that those words don't wind up a lie.

Avery heaves a quiet sigh before kissing my forehead. "Alright, sweetheart. You hungry?"

I grin up at him, head bobbing. Slipping off the couch and onto his lap, I throw my arms around his neck. "Chinese?"

"Well, it is Wednesday, so you know what that means…"

"Hump Day?" I wag my brows. Wednesday is always Chinese food, but I like to tease him.

Avery laughs, palm sliding over the curve of my neck as his tongue sweeps into my mouth. "I was gonna say Chinese night, but Hump Day works too." He slips me onto the couch cushions, laying me down as he covers my body with his. "In fact, why don't we do some humping *before* we get dinner."

"And again after?"

"Mmm. And again after that."

I sink my fingers into his silky waves. "I like the sound of that." Pushing up on my elbows, I kiss his perfect, soft lips. "I love you."

"I love you wild, baby."

I hurry into Charlee's office on Thursday morning, stumbling over my own two feet and crashing into her door.

She peers up at me from underneath the glasses she's wearing, arching a brow. "You okay there, Clarice?" She pulls the glasses off her face and sets them down on her desk, letting that smirk slip up her face. "Or did Avery give you noodle legs again?"

My hands flail wildly in front of my face as I wheeze, gasping for breath. I absolutely *ran* here from my office, and I am not a runner. "The doctor's office just called. They have my results."

"Already? You just went yesterday."

"I know." I swallow down the bile rising in my throat. I'm so damn nervous. "It's bad, right? It must be bad. They want me to come in today. It wouldn't be so important if…if…oh, God." I spin around, sinking down into Charlee's couch, clutching the neckline of my dress. Tears prickle my eyes and my vision blurs.

Before I know it, Charlee's arms come around me, holding me tight. "Deep breaths, Claire. It was just a few starter tests, right? They're just going to tell you what they want to do next."

I swipe at my wet cheeks, trying to agree with her. "I'm so scared, Charlee," I whisper.

She sighs softly, smoothing her hand down my hair as she hugs me closer. "I know, babe. When are you going?"

"I'm leaving in thirty minutes. The appointment's in an hour."

"Don't you guys have that big meeting with Avery and Wyatt today?"

Shit. Yes. I completely forgot in all of this. "I should be back in time for that. It's not 'til after lunch. Will you…will you come with me, Charlee?"

"Oh, Claire. Of course I will. I was planning on bullying my way into this as soon as you tripped your way in here."

I sigh into her hair, my shoulders dropping just a bit, some of that tension easing. "You're the very best best friend. I'm so lucky to have you."

"You are *incredibly* lucky to have me. I could have let you hang out with the cool kids in school by yourself, and then where would you be? Still cool, but Charlee-less."

I bark out a laugh. "I love you so much."

She gives me a squeeze. "I love you too, Claire Bear."

"And who did you bring with you today, Claire?" Dr. Tam smiles at the two of us as she closes the door behind her. I gotta hand it to her, for a woman who's about to dish out bad news, she still looks utterly positive.

"This is my best friend Charlee," I tell her, giving her a smile, as shaky as it is.

"Ah. Nice to meet you, Charlee. You two seem very close."

Charlee squeezes my hand. She's been my partner in crime for most of my life. I can't remember before her and I like it that way. We've been through everything together, which is why I want her by my side right now.

"We've known each other for almost twenty years. She's more than my best friend. She's my sister."

Charlee's bottom lip does a slight wobble. "Don't you dare," she whisper-yells at me, dabbing the corners of her eyes. "I spent two hours last night learning this smoky eye technique, and redid it three times this morning to get it to look this fabulous. If you make me cry, I will kill you."

Grinning, I lean forward, resting my forehead on hers. Charlee doesn't need an ounce of makeup, and doesn't normally wear much, but recently she's been watching all these tutorials and coming to work looking like a straight-up queen.

Waiting for your stupid brother to make a move, she muttered to me last week when I made a comment about her pretty makeup.

"It's lovely to have friends that are more like family," Dr. Tam comments, interrupting our lovefest. "Can I assume that means you're okay with Charlee hearing the news I have to share with you today?"

The news. So there is news. I knew it. Oh, shit. Crap. My stomach clenches like a fist when another wave of that damn nausea hits.

"Yes," I answer after a long pause. "I want Charlee here with me."

Dr. Tam nods. She sucks in a breath and leans back in her chair studying me quietly for a moment. "Well, Claire. Let's get right to it, shall we? Why don't I give you the first bit, which is I think what you're most anxious about. Hopefully, that'll help settle your nerves."

Okay, this sounds hopeful. Maybe I was freaking out about nothing.

"I reviewed your test results from your pelvic exam and your blood work, and there is absolutely nothing about it that rings any alarm bells in terms of ovarian cancer. I have no concerns whatsoever. That being said, you might consider genetic testing down the road. You can check if you have the BRCA1 or BRCA2 mutation, which would increase your likelihood of contracting ovarian cancer later in life. However, I'd hold off on that for now."

It takes a full minute for my brain to register what she's saying. And when it does, my entire body folds forward with relief, a whoosh of air bursting from my lips. "I don't have cancer? I don't have cancer!"

Charlee throws her arms around me. "I told you, you're such a hypochondriac!"

I wipe the tears that are streaming freely from my eyes. My cheeks hurt. I'm too happy to feel stupid about how freaked out I was. "Thank you," I say to Dr. Tam.

"I'm so glad I could deliver that news to you." She clears her throat and stacks her shoulders, expression turning serious. "Now, onto the next piece…" Pursing her lips to the side, she hums to herself while she scrolls through her tablet. I hear her murmur the name of a few medications, I think, before she finally looks up again. "When was your last cycle day one?"

I blink up at her. "Pardon?"

"The first day of your last period."

"Um…" My nose scrunches as I try to string the dates together. "It was…" My thought process derails when Charlee stiffens beside me. My gaze slides sideways, noting the way she's staring at my stomach. Oh, fuck. "It was a while ago," I whisper. "Longer than…longer than normal." Like, mid-June. And it's August 7th.

"I'm sorry, but I don't remember," I lie, for what purpose, I'm not sure.

"You were in here at the end of June with strep throat. We gave you rifampin because you have an allergy to penicillin, correct?"

My head goes up and down slowly.

The doctor studies me for what feels like ten entire minutes, like she's trying to read me, figure out what the hell's going on in my head. I'm not sure even I know what's going on in there. I feel a little lost.

"Rifampin has been known to lower the effectiveness of oral contraceptives."

"Oh my God," Charlee sputters beside me, her fingers tightening around mine. I turn to look at her, her wide brown eyes dragging over my body before landing on my face. "Claire…"

I twist back to the doctor. "I…I'm sorry…what's the…what are you…" I shake my head, trying to clear the fog. Clutching my stomach, I lick my lips. God, I feel awful. These nerves are rotting my stomach. "What are you saying?"

"You're pregnant, Claire."

Keeling over, I release the contents of my stomach all over the shiny linoleum floors.

CHAPTER FIFTY-ONE

Avery

"Fucking brutally hot, bud," Wyatt complains, jerking the knot of his tie down and popping the first three buttons on his shirt. "Why the fuck did we walk?"

"Because it's only a ten-minute walk from the restaurant," I remind him.

Fuck, he's not wrong though. It's scorching today. August is coming in hot, and at this point, I'm just counting down the hours to 4:00pm tomorrow, when Claire and I take off for the cottage like we've already done a handful of times this summer. She loves it up there, floating around in the water all day, staring up at the stars all night, and I love making her happy.

"I'm gonna drain at least three beers during this meeting." Wyatt polishes off his bottle of water and crushes it between his hands, tossing it in a nearby garbage can on the street. Shifting his sunglasses down his nose, he squints up at the sun before fixing them back in place. "We're calling Jacob. He's picking us up after this. I'm not fucking walking again." He adjusts his junk. "I'm sweating in places a man should never sweat unless he's balls deep in a beautiful woman."

Chuckling, I tug open the door of the brewery and watch as he pushes by me with a sigh of relief.

He smirks at me over his shoulder. "First one to see Claire gets the first kiss."

"I don't fucking think so," I say, but bark out a laugh when Wyatt tears up the stairs with me hot on his heels.

"Good afternoon, gentlemen," Julie, the receptionist, greets us with a smile. "You two are way too happy for ninety-three degree heat."

I flash her a grin. "I'm always happy here. There's free beer."

"And free office sex," Wyatt adds with a wink.

"Hey, fuck off, would you?" I flick his ear while Julie covers her laugh with a cough.

"I'll pretend I didn't hear that." She turns back to her computer, her voice low and teasing when she continues. "I'm getting good at pretending I don't hear some of the things that happen around here…"

"Oh, shit," Wyatt whispers over my shoulder as he follows me down the hall to Claire's office. "Julie's totally heard you two having sex." He shoulders me out of the way and bursts through her door. "Claire Bear, I get the first—hey, where is she?"

"Maybe she's not back from lunch yet," I say, but frown when I notice her messenger bag is gone.

We amble on down to the conference room and Wyatt makes a beeline for the drink station, cracking the top off a beer and forgoing a glass as he downs half of it with a smacking sigh.

"Hey Ave," Dex calls from behind me, clapping a hand on my back. "Wyatt," he murmurs, eyes twinkling with humor as he watches Wyatt polish off the rest of his beer. "Thirsty, buddy?"

"You have no idea. Avery made us walk here after lunch."

"Where'd you eat?"

"Ardo."

Dex dismisses Wyatt with the wave of his hand. "That's, like, ten minutes away, tops." His eyes land on me while he boots up his laptop. "How's Claire feeling?"

My beer stops its path to my lips, hanging there in midair with my hand. "What do you mean?"

Dex blinks up at me. "I mean, she took off like her ass was on fire this morning, saying she had to go back to the doctor's. Took Charlee with her. Charlee called an hour later and said they weren't coming back."

"What? She's not coming back?"

Dex shakes his head slowly. "Sorry, I thought you knew."

I didn't know, and now my pulse is racing. I dig my phone out of my pocket, ready to call her, stopping when I spy a message from her from before lunch.

Claire Bear: *I'm sorry Avery, but I'm going to miss the meeting today.*

I shoot her off a text.

Me: *Sorry I missed this, baby. Are you ok? Want me to come home?*

Claire Bear: *I'm fine, just not feeling well. You stay.*

Me: *You sure?*

Bear: *I'm sure. Cuddling with the zoo.*

Me: *Ok. Missing you here. I love you.*

It takes her way longer to respond than I'd like, and I watch those three dots jump around the screen and stop several times before I finally get a response ten minutes into the meeting.

Claire Bear: *I love you so much.*

Claire isn't at my place when I get home from work, and despite her message that insisted she was cuddling with animals, I can tell she wasn't. The bed is still perfectly made from this morning, and her blanket and book are still scattered on the couch where she left them last night. Sully's not begging to go out though, and his leash is on the counter, so I assume she's taken him out at some point today.

Using my key to her apartment, I push the door open, peeking my head into her space. I spy her hunched over a drawer in the kitchen, a t-shirt hanging off one shoulder, a pair of running shorts barely covering her ass. Her hair is a beautiful mess on top of her head, loose curls tumbling down her neck.

"Hey gorgeous," I murmur, moving toward her.

Her hand flies to her throat with a yelp and she jumps in her spot. "Oh," she breathes out with a sigh. "Avery. It's just you." She slams the drawer and leans against it.

"Just me." I slide my hands over her hips and pull her against me, noticing the red rim of her eyes, the tired purple circles underneath. "Were you expecting someone else?" I kiss her before she can answer, enjoying the way she opens for me, her body sinking against mine as her fingers find my hair.

"No," she replies when I pull away.

I wrap her in my arms, breathing her in while I slowly twist us back in forth. "How are you feeling? Dex said you went back to the doctor. I wish you'd told me."

Her soft sigh coats my collarbone. "I'm sorry. It was nothing, really. I'm just so tired."

I hum my agreement. She's been working way too much lately, and we've been going like crazy the rest of the time—cottaging with our friends, driving down to her dad's, dealing with my crazy mom, and having Vivi over for sleepovers at least once a week. It's rare that we get more than a night or two to ourselves. But she hates when I say she's working too much, and I don't wanna start that again tonight, so I don't bring it up.

"What'd the doctor say? Did she have your test results?"

"Hmm? Oh." She backs away from me, looping a hand through the air. "Yeah. Just low iron, adrenal fatigue, that kinda stuff."

"So you need—"

She cuts me off with a chaste kiss. "We'll talk about it later. I'm gonna grab a shower and I'll head upstairs when I'm done."

"Why don't you shower upstairs?"

She pins her arms across her chest. Uh oh. I've fucked up.

"What's wrong with my shower?"

"I didn't mean it like that, Claire. You can do whatever you want." I finger a curl, brushing it across her collarbone. "I just

485

know how much you love mine, and I just wanna throw you over my shoulder and cart you up there."

Her mouth twitches and her eyes roll with an amused huff. "I'm sorry. I'm on edge today. I know you didn't mean anything by it." *Whew.* Disaster averted. She squeezes my arm and smiles gently. "I'll be up in fifteen, okay? Promise."

I nod, kiss her cheek, and watch her disappear down the hallway. But when the water starts and I hear her pull back the shower curtain, my eyes land on the drawer she slammed shut. I'm not into secrets, and I trust Claire, but the tension tingling in my spine tells me that something's not right here. She's keeping something from me, and I don't know why.

I shift the drawer open, my heart sinking when I spy the labeled envelopes inside, the wad of cash that she threw in here in a hurry when I walked in.

Rent. Hydro. Wifi. Emergencies. There's a fifth envelope labeled *Groceries*, but it's ripped in half, presumably because she eats every meal at my place. There's a dollar amount written on each envelope, and I count every bill in the drawer, frowning when she comes up three-hundred-and-twenty dollars short.

No wonder she's been an anxious mess and working like crazy. What I don't understand is why she doesn't just ask me for help.

Actually, I do understand that, because I know Claire, and she'd rather get tossed out on her ass before asking me for money. Still, I pull the cash from my wallet and add it to the drawer, hoping she never finished counting it in the first place.

Claire joins me upstairs fifteen minutes later like clockwork and does her best to put on a happy face, but she's quiet and distant, distracted, and I don't like it. After dinner, I tug her down beside me on the couch, brushing her hair off her face and placing a kiss on the tip of her nose.

"There's something I want to talk to you about," I tell her quietly. If I'm being honest, I've been thinking about this for a while. The thought sprouted at the cottage, and I haven't been able to shake it. I would have asked her sooner, but Claire is tricky—see the three weeks I spent chasing her stubborn ass.

She doesn't respond, just hums as I stroke her face, pale green eyes fluttering closed. Her cheeks are rosy, her face a little bit warm, her long lashes laying against her silky skin. I sweep my thumb under her eyes, a silent plea to look at me.

"I want you to move in with me, Claire."

Her body tenses in my hold as soon as the words leave my lips. "What?"

"I want you to live here with me, Claire. I want my home to be your home. Our home."

She turns over in my arms, palms pressing into the cushions as she pushes up to sitting. "I...what...I mean...why?"

I snort a laugh, moving beside her. "What do you mean why? Because I love you. Because I don't want to be without you. Because I want you in my bed every night."

"I already am in your bed every night," she mumbles, looking down at her fists as they clench in her lap.

"Right. So let's make it official. Let's make my bed your bed. You have an apartment you never use. I think today was the first time you've showered there since we started dating. It's like we already live together. You can save so much mon—"

"I don't need your money!" she growls out, jumping to her feet. "I don't need it, Avery! I-I-I...I can do it on my own!" She buries her face in her hands, turning away from me as her cries pierce the air.

I launch off the couch, gripping her biceps. "Hey, hey. Claire, honey, I didn't mean it like that. Not at all, sweetheart." I rub her arms, her forehead hitting my chest while she trembles in my arms. My eyes squeeze shut, heart swelling. I hate when she cries; it feels like my heart is being ripped from my chest.

"You can't fix everything with money," she whimpers.

"What do you mean? I'm not trying to—"

"You are," she cuts me off. "You're only asking me to move in because you think I'm poor. You think I need you to take care of me."

My mouth opens, my eyes flickering at her words. Yes, I want to take care of her. Yes, I know she's hard up for money, but only because she's paying for an expensive condo by herself. She makes good money and she works hard. But her being short on rent is not why I want to live with her.

"I know you can do it all on your own. It hurts that you think that's the only reason I'd ask you to move in." I take her face in my hands, forcing her to look at me. "I love you. Plain and simple. This time with you has been the best time of my life, and I never want it to end."

Tears roll down her cheeks as her eyes squeeze shut, her fingers wrapping around my wrists. "You're going to change your mind."

My heart stops. "What?"

"You won't want me forever," she says on a shaky exhale.

"Claire, you're—"

Her eyes flip open, blazing. "Crazy?"

I shake my head furiously. "*Wrong*. You're fucking wrong."

She pushes away from me, disappearing down the hallway. I follow her, stopping short when she starts pulling clothes out of the dresser she uses, tossing them in her workbag.

"Claire." My arms circle her waist from behind, pulling her into my chest, and I nuzzle my face into her neck.

"*Stop*, Avery." She spins in my arms, getting right up in my face. "You can't solve every argument with sex!"

"I have no idea what we're even arguing about!" I shout, throwing my hands in the air. "I asked you to move in with me and you got your back up and started ripping my head off!"

"Because you're just trying to solve my money problems!" She struts out of the bedroom and down the hall, beelining for the door.

"You think you're in love with me and you're not! You're just caught up, being in a relationship for the first time. I give it six months before you're fed up with me." She shoves her feet in her Converse shoes, and her finger in my chest. "Two if I move in here with you!"

"Are you fucking serious right now?" I stalk toward her, backing her up against the door. She drops the attitude, apprehension creeping into her expression. "You're trying to tell me I don't love you? That I'm not fucking *crazy* about you? That I can't possibly know what love is because I've never felt it before?"

Those mossy eyes flicker as her head tips back to meet my gaze.

"I won't apologize for not loving anyone else before you, Claire, and I won't even entertain the idea that you think that I don't love you. Tell me, are you trying to convince yourself because you're worried about getting hurt, worried I'm going to leave? Or are you saying this because you don't love me? Because you're trying to let me down easy?" That's fucking bullshit. She knows it and I know it. She's as crazy about me as I am about her.

"I-I…" She looks away, stifling a cry, teeth pressing into her quivering bottom lip. "I love you, Avery."

Gripping her chin, I jerk her face up to mine, hating every single one of those tears that track a hot path down her pink cheeks. "Then what the hell are you doing?"

Her hands find my shoulders, pushing down as she presses up on her toes. My arms wind around her back, holding her to me while she kisses me. Her tears coat her lips and mine, and I hate the saltiness, because all it represents is her pain, all the pain her ex has caused, the distrust he's put in her head, the way he's fucked with her huge heart, made her believe herself unworthy of love and happiness.

"I love you," she whispers again when she pulls back. "I just need some time."

"What? Time? What do you mean?" I reach wildly for her as she backs away, opening the door. "Claire, what are you doing? Where are you going?" Shit, I'm frantic. Is she leaving me? She can't. I can't.

"I just need a minute to think," she says as she slips out the door, licking at her lips, swiping at her sopping cheeks. "Please don't come after me."

"Claire, no!" I follow her down the hallway, watching as she climbs into the elevator. "You can't—"

"I'm sorry," she chokes out through a sob.

Those bleary green eyes never leave mine as the doors close, swallowing up the woman I love more than anything in this world.

The cat wanders into the hallway, wrapping himself around my ankle as he meows up at me, tilting his head to the side, and tears slide down my face, because I have no idea what just happened, only that I just watched the love of my life walk out on me.

CHAPTER FIFTY-TWO

Claire

Disappointment is when your own brother can't even look at you.

He's just slamming around the pots and pans he's cleaning like it's his damn job while I'm sitting on the floor, braiding Vivi's hair before she goes to bed.

Casey and I fought a lot growing up, the way siblings do. Like, hair pulling, slapping, biting…All siblings do that, right? Or was it just us? I'm pretty sure it wasn't just us. Dex and Charlee were the same, and Avery and Harper still hair-pull and smack each other around all the time.

We bickered, but it was never real. He never stayed angry with me. We didn't go to bed without saying goodnight, and he was there with a hug for me every single day.

But tonight? Tonight he's angry.

"You sleepin' ova, Auntie Claire?" Vivi asks me, brushing her doll's hair.

"Uh huh," I murmur absently, wrapping a hair tie around the braid I've just finished. Gripping her head, I pull her backwards, pressing a kiss to her forehead. "That okay with you, princess?"

"I fink Uncle A'wy will miss you."

"He'll be okay." I hate the bitter, sour taste of the words, but hope for his sake it's not a lie.

A loud clanging has my head lifting, my gaze landing on Casey as he grips the countertop, hanging his head over the sink. He shakes his head, not knowing I'm watching him.

"Daddy mad," Vivi whispers to her doll. She's so damn observational. Twisting, she places her little hand on my knee. "Don't worry. Daddy still luh you." She holds her palms up in a shrug. "Sometimes we just get mad."

491

"I know, baby." I pull her into my lap and smother her in a hug, because I need some loving right now. My head hurts, my heart aches, and my stomach is in complete disarray. The first thing I did when I exited the condo building was promptly throw up in a street trashcan that already smelled suspiciously like vomit.

Dr. Tam guessed that I'm about seven weeks along based on the date of my last period. I feel like a total asshole. When she said seven weeks, I argued that that would have been before I even took the antibiotics, at which point she explained that pregnancy is measured based on the first day of your period, not the day you conceive. I don't know a thing about my own body and this whole thing feels like my fault for not being more aware.

So, seven weeks. It explains the pain in my stomach, the nausea I thought was due to my severe anxiety. It explains the exhaustion, the bloating, everything. And apparently, it's only going to get worse.

Dr. Tam wants me to go for an ultrasound next week to confirm the due date.

Due date. Two words that shouldn't be as absolutely gut-wrenchingly terrifying as they sound to me right now.

I sink back against the legs of the couch, cuddling Vivi to me while she sucks on her thumb, her attention leaving her doll as it settles on the movie on TV. She's trying something new today—*Moana*—and she seems to like it.

She kicks her legs out when she giggles. "Dat a silly chicken! He keep hurtin' his head!"

I watch Casey stalk off down the hallway, head buried in his phone as his fingers fly across the screen. "Where are you going?"

He doesn't even bother lifting his head to look at me. "Got a call to make."

Well, I'm not stupid. He's either calling Charlee or Avery. Charlee already knows I'm here, though. I called her in tears on my walk over, after she spent most of the afternoon with me. Avery, well…I'm sure he disregarded my request for him not to follow me and went down to my apartment. Which is why I never went home.

Home. My apartment doesn't even feel like home anymore. Home is with Avery. With Sully and Chester. Our little family, tucked together in bed. And yet I lost my damn mind when Avery suggested we make it official.

I don't know what's going on with me, other than the fact that I'm growing a baby with a man I've been with for just a few months who definitely didn't sign up for a lifelong commitment with me, and my hormones are fucking whacked, clearly.

I mean, did I seriously suggest that he doesn't really love me?

"Did you seriously tell Avery you think he doesn't love you?" Casey snarls out, storming back into the living room and speaking my own thoughts. He slams his phone down on the island. "Are you okay? Like, actually, what's going on in that head of yours?"

Okay, so I guess he called Avery.

Vivi's face snaps up to mine, her big eyes turning watery as she feels my forehead. "You got a headache, Auntie Claire? Uncle A'wy luh you."

"I told your *boyfriend* you're here and you're safe, because he about lost his damn mind when he went down to your apartment to find you missing, and you're not answering his calls."

"I turned my phone off," I whisper, averting my gaze, because my brother is scary right now, and I can't bear his disappointment. It's worse than when my mom found out I got my belly button pierced at thirteen after she explicitly told me *no fucking way*. "You didn't…tell him…did you?"

"No, because that's not my place nor my job. I'm not his girlfriend; you are. Lack of communication ends relationships, Claire. Get your shit together."

I glance down at Vivi, her wobbly lip, her round eyes bouncing back and forth between her dad and I. "I'm not having this conversation in front of your daughter."

"Great. It's bedtime anyway." He moves to take her from me, but I jump to my feet with her in my arms.

"I'll put her to bed."

Casey sighs, cupping Vivi's face. "I love you, sweetheart."

"Buttafwy kisses?" she asks on a heartbreaking whimper.

The corner of his mouth lifts as he leans forward, brushing his nose across hers. He kisses both eyelids before he kisses her pout. "Sleep tight, my beautiful girl."

"I luh you, Daddy."

The sweet interaction tugs my heart in a thousand different directions. Casey's such a good dad. What if I'm not a good mom? Avery would be an amazing dad. If he wants to be. But he's already given up his bachelorhood for me. Would he want to give up more? He won't recognize a single bit of his life anymore.

When Vivi's all tucked in, she twists the knife in my heart a little deeper. "We call Uncle A'wy and say goodnight? I blow him a kiss."

I blink back the tears, resisting the urge to bury my face in her pillow. "Not tonight, baby. It's too late."

Her sweet little face drops, laced with disappointment. "In da mornin'?"

I nod, because I can only say no to her so much, and really, how long am I going to last without talking to him? I crave his gravel of his voice as it moves against my neck, the warmth of his mouth on mine, the sweep of his touch, both gentle and rough. I crave him, and I know I can't and won't stay away. "Okay, sweetheart. In the morning."

Vivi wraps her arms around my neck, grunting as she squeezes me tight as she can. "I huggin' all my luh into you, Auntie Claire. You feel it?"

I close my eyes, smoothing my hand down her braids. "I feel it, baby."

When I make my way back out to the main room, Casey's sitting at the kitchen island with his head in his hands, a beer and a juice box in front of him. I slip onto the stool beside him, and he slides the juice over to me. I'd rather the beer, but I can't, for obvious reasons.

"I'm so disappointed in you, Claire," he says after a moment of silence that hangs way too heavily in the air between us. Those words slice right through me, leaving me to bleed out on the ground.

"I know. I'm sorry. I should have known better. I should have been tracking, taking extra precautions. I should have known about the antibiot—"

"No," he growls. He sighs, his eyes lifting to mine. "I'm not disappointed that you're pregnant. I'm happy for you. You and Avery will make great parents. I'm disappointed in the way you're handling this, running away from your problems, from your partner. You're not being fair to him. This is something you have to deal with together. You can't just walk away in the middle of an argument, slam the door, and not tell him where you're going. You're so much better than that, Claire. You and Avery have worked hard for this relationship."

My hand flies to my stomach on its own accord. "But what if he doesn't want this? What if he doesn't want...us? Three months ago, he was going out to clubs every weekend, taking home different girls."

"Things change, Claire. People change. He wanted to change, for you."

My head moves back and forth, tears prickling my eyes. My nose starts tingling and I know I'm close to ugly-sobbing. "This is too much, too big of a change."

"He likes the life you two have together," Casey insists.

I know he does, sure. Why wouldn't he? We're out and about every weekend, doing something, drinking something, seeing people. I've never had sex more in my entire life. I mean, it's constant. Our love is wild, untamable. Except that a baby will change all of that.

"We're talking about a whole new life here, Case," I argue weakly. "He might not be ready for that." Hell, I'm not.

Casey jumps to his feet, face twisting in anger as he points a threatening finger in my direction. "You don't get to make that decision for him, Claire! He does! You should know that better than anyone!"

His words hit me hard, like a punch to the gut, sucking all the air from my lungs. Casey almost didn't have a choice. Vivi almost lost her life before it even started. I may not be ready to be a mom, but I'll love this little thing growing inside of me more than anything. I already do. And I'm even *considering* that Avery might not want that, too?

It's not my decision to make; I know that. It's just...what if it's the decision Avery makes anyway? What if he *does* want out? I love him too much to imagine a future without him.

Casey groans, rubbing at his eyes. "Please don't cry, Claire. I can't. I can't handle the tears."

"I'm scared, Casey! I'm terrified!" I'm a snotty, blubbering mess, falling apart right here in my brother's kitchen. Casey yanks me into his chest, his arms a force field around me as I cry, soaking his shirt. "I'm not ready! I'm not ready to be a mom! We aren't ready to be parents! I don't want to lose him. Oh, God," I choke out. "It would kill me. But I never wanted to trap him, to make him feel like he couldn't leave."

This isn't supposed to be how it happens. We're supposed to move in together, decide on forever, and then have kids. At the very least, kids should be a conscious decision made together, marriage or no marriage. Not, *Hey, I know we've only been dating two months, but—surprise! I'm pregnant, and now you'll be in my life forever!*

496

Casey grips my shoulders, holding me at arm's length. "You're not trapping him, Claire. Not even close. It's a surprise, yes. Trapping is what Angela did, going off the pill and not telling me, and I'll tell you, as trapped as I felt at the time, I've never felt freer now. That little girl in there is the best damn thing that's ever happened to me." He points down the hall to where his daughter sleeps soundly, before taking my hands in his. "It doesn't matter if you're ready or not, because it's happening. You need to *get* ready. Do you think I was ready?" He laughs bitterly. "I was nowhere *near* ready to be a dad, let alone a single one. Shit, I still don't know what the hell I'm doing with Vivi ninety percent of the time."

"But you're an amazing dad!" I drag in a long sniffle, swiping at my cheeks. Those tears are on a warpath and they're taking no prisoners.

His head bobs in agreement. "I am. Because I love her. Unconditionally. She's mine, a part of me, the something good I finally did." He takes my face in his hands, his green eyes searching mine. "That's how I know you'll be a great mom. Look at how much you already love that little thing growing inside of you. You want to protect your baby already. The problem is you're protecting it from a fallout that hasn't even happened. You're just expecting the worst."

"But what if he leaves, Casey?" I sob harder, louder, and he pulls me into him again. He smells like home, like comfort. "People always leave. Sometimes they choose it, and sometimes it's chosen for them. I can't...we can't lose him."

His answering sigh is soft and quiet. "But you are, Claire, and it's nobody's fault but your own. You're pushing him away because you're scared. You aren't giving him the chance to be the partner you need in this. You can't dictate the way he reacts or the way he handles this."

Casey takes me by the hand, leading me over to the couch. "Is there a chance he might not feel ready? Absolutely. But maybe he'll *get ready*. Maybe he'll *choose* to get ready, like you are, right now. Maybe—and I think he will—he'll surprise the hell out of you and choose to stay, without a shadow of a doubt, because he fucking loves you. Have some faith and give him a chance to do the right thing."

Sniffling, I drag the heel of my palm over my nose, spreading something wet and slimy around.

Casey makes a face and hands me a Kleenex. "Ew."

I manage a giggle and settle into his side as he wraps an arm around me. "Do you really think I'll be a good mom?"

"Claire, I think you'll be an amazing mom. You're the best mom to Vivi, and she's your niece." He presses a kiss to the top of my head. "Shit, look at all the mistakes we made with Viv, and she still turned out to be the best kid in the world. We kinda know what we're doing now. We won't make so many mistakes this time around."

Casey sighs, hugging me tight. "I love you, Claire. Avery loves you. I don't want to see you give up on someone who makes you so unbelievably happy because you're scared and stubborn."

I sit up straight, glaring at him. "You wanna talk about stubborn? Charlee's been watching makeup tutorials because she thinks it'll get you to notice her."

Casey's cheeks flush and he scratches at the stubble on his jaw, chuckling. "Charlee doesn't need makeup. She's beautiful the way she is. And I already notice her," he adds with a sideways glance.

"I know that." I fold my arms over my chest. "So why aren't you making a move?"

"Should I?"

"Well, do you like her?"

He stands and walks back to the kitchen, returning with the drinks we left there. I'm still unimpressed with my juice box. "I thought we were talking about you and my new niece or nephew."

I level him with a look, making him laugh.

"Do I like her?" He runs a hand through his hair before he flashes me a grin. "Only for the last ten years or so."

It's after eleven when I finally tumble into bed, having watched Casey drink way too many beers while I crushed seven grape juices and ultimately felt like my bladder was going to explode.

I plug my phone into the charger and wait for it to power up, pulling at my lip.

I'm unsurprised to find six missed calls and seven texts from Avery.

Avery: *Claire, where are you?*

Avery: *I went to your apartment. You're not there.*

Avery: *Are you ok?*

Avery: *Please just let me know you're safe.*

Avery: *Casey called. I'm glad you're safe. You can call me anytime.*

Avery: *I can't take this. I hate being without you, and I hate fighting.*

Avery: *I love you.*

I just finish reading those texts when a new one rolls in, and those tears I tucked away a couple hours ago come streaming down my face again.

Avery: *I can't sleep without you. I miss you so much. My heart hurts without you.*

We haven't spent a single night apart since we started dating. Not a single one. He's wrapped around my body like a koala bear every night, and I feel empty and lost without him here.

So I start typing out a message back, telling him how much I love him, that I'm sorry for being stubborn and irrational, and that I can't wait to see him tomorrow, to kiss him, hug him. My thumb hovers over the *send* button while I reread my message, making sure it's perfect.

But before I can send it, the bedroom door whips open, and the slice of moonlight streaming through the window illuminates Casey's heaving chest.

"Claire. Get up. We need to go." He flips on the light switch, letting me see the tears soaking his cheeks, his frantic face.

"Dad's in the hospital."

CHAPTER FIFTY-THREE

Avery

She left me on goddamn *read* all night, those three little dots squirming around the screen, as if she'd passed out in the middle of responding. Had it seriously been that easy for her to sleep without me? Because I didn't sleep a fucking wink. I gave up at 3:38am and went down to the gym.

That's why I'm storming through the front door of the brewery at 8:30 this morning, hopped up on caffeine and hellbent on seeing Claire. I refuse to go a minute longer without talking to her, hearing her voice. We need to fix this, and I'll drag her out of here if I need to.

I take the stairs three at a time, thankful for my long legs, and jog right by Julie as she calls out to me. Claire's office is empty, again, but I don't believe for a second that she called in sick. She almost never takes time off. If she did today, this is way more serious than I thought, although, to be honest, it's always felt serious to me. Watching her pack her shit and haul ass away from me will do that, I guess.

"Avery," Julie calls after me as I move across the floor. "Claire's—"

I swing open Dex's door, his brows jumping when he spies me, and before I know what's happening, a tiny body wraps itself around my legs.

"Uncle A'wy! I miss you!"

I look down at my tiny strawberry girl, her bright smile, wide green eyes, and drag her into my arms. "Hey munchkin girl." She peppers my face with kisses before I can beat her to it. "What are you doing here?"

She points at Dex. "I go to Uncle Dex house at mint night!" I think she means midnight. "He take me to McDonald's for bweakfast." She presses her palms to my cheeks, whispering against my lips, "I got toy."

"Wow," I murmur, forcing a smile. Something's not right. "Lucky girl."

"I figured you'd be with Claire," Dex says, taking Vivi from my arms. "Go find Auntie Charlee. She's getting your bag ready. You remember where her room is?"

Vivi's head bobs before she twirls around me, sprinting down the hallway while she yells, "Auntie Cha-Chaaa, here I cooome!"

I watch to make sure she makes it to the right office before twisting back to Dex. "What's going on? Where's Claire and why did Vivi come over in the middle of the night?"

His brows pull together, like he's wondering why I don't know. I roll my eyes, not because I'm annoyed, but because I'm fucking exasperated.

"I asked Claire to move in with me last night and she lost her damn mind and ran out on me. I haven't talked to her since."

He looks a bit like he wants to smile, or laugh, but can't. Instead, he clears his throat. "Gavin was taken to the hospital late last night."

"What?"

He leans on the edge of his desk. "John—he owns the winery next door—hadn't been able to get a hold of him. He went over there late last night to check in on him and found him unconscious on the couch. Couldn't wake him up."

"Fuck." I raise a shaky hand to my mouth. "Is he...did he..." I can't even say the words.

Dex shakes his head. "He's alive, but not conscious last I heard. Nobody knows how long he was out for."

I don't know what to say. I just know I need to see Claire, hug her, be there for her, with her.

"Charlee's heading out to the house today. Taking Vivi."

"I'll go with them," I say without hesitation.

Dex offers me a small smile. "I figured."

I move to leave, but Dex's hand lands on my shoulder.

"Hey, Avery, listen." He plows a hand through his hair and sighs. "I know Claire can be stubborn, but it's because she's been through a lot of heartache in her life. She's constantly waiting for the other shoe to drop. Don't take it personally. You know she loves you." He squeezes my shoulder. "She might try and push you away, but she needs you right now."

Dex drops Charlee, Vivi, and I back at my place, where my dad meets us to take Sully and Chester back to his house. I pack Claire and I a bag, not knowing how long we'll be there for, but I'll stay as long as we need to. Then we load up my truck and hightail it to Jordan Valley. Traffic's moving the opposite direction, so we make it there in under an hour. Also, I'm driving twenty kilometers over the speed limit while Charlee grips the door handle with one hand and my forearm with the other, fingernails digging in. I'm honestly not sure if it's because I'm driving fast, or because she's on the verge of falling to pieces. If I had to guess, I'd say probably a bit of both.

We take Vivi to John's winery, and she's perfectly content to run around his large office with Turkey, particularly excited when John promises her pizza for lunch and a ride on his golf cart later. Then we head down to the hospital.

I glance at Charlee as I throw the truck in park. She's been silent since we left Toronto. Her big brown eyes are filled with tears as she looks up at the hospital, hands clasped tightly in her lap.

I reach over and cover her hands with mine. "Hey. It's gonna be okay."

The second her eyes meet mine, those tears overflow, tracking a path down her cheeks. "The last time I was here was the day

503

Claire's mom died. They-they…they can't go through this again, Avery. They don't deserve this." Her voice cracks on a sob and I pull her into my arms.

"Claire's my best friend," Charlee cries softly. "She's my sister. I'm so…I'm so damn tired of seeing her go through heartache after heartache." Her tears wet my neck, fingers clutching the back of my shirt. "And Casey, he…he's spent too many years being strong for everyone else. And Vivi, oh God. She loves her Gramps so much. She'll be crushed if he…if he…"

"Shhh." Gripping the back of her neck, I hold her tighter. "I know it's hard not to, but let's not jump to the worst possible scenario. Let's try to be positive for those Thompsons we love so much. They're going to need us. Okay?"

Charlee nods and pulls away, wiping at her cheeks with the back of her hands. "They're my family," she whispers, broken.

I press my lips to her forehead. "I know, Charlee. Mine, too. Let's go show them how much we care, and that they can always count on us."

As soon as we step off the elevator and onto the third floor, I can hear Claire. She's crying, that much is certain. And screaming. Charlee's fingers tighten around mine and I give her hand a gentle squeeze, trying my best to be reassuring.

"How could you do this?" Claire's frantic voice fills the hallway as we move toward the sound. "This isn't a decision you get to make on your own!"

A throat clears before a voice I don't recognize starts in. "Claire, I can understand why you're—"

"No!" she growls out. Her forest eyes, rimmed red as tears cover her pink face, flicker to us as we step into the room, quietly shutting the door behind us. The man she's yelling at appears to be the doctor. "I haven't even started on *you*. How could you lie to me? Right to my face? That's so unethical!"

"Claire, honey." Gavin's voice cracks from his spot in bed. He's propped up on a bunch of pillows, looking pale and absolutely depleted. "He did it because I asked him to. I didn't want you two to know." His eyes move over her and Casey, before sliding to Charlee and I. He gives us a weak smile. "My favorite significant others."

Claire grits her teeth so hard I can hear them clacking together from across the room. I go to move to her, but Charlee holds me back. When I glance down at her, she gives me the tiniest headshake.

"How could you not want us to know?" Claire steps toward him. Casey follows every one of her steps, like he's ready to restrain her if he needs to. He looks absolutely wrecked. "We're your *kids*! What if John hadn't come to check on you? What if Casey had come with Vivi tonight like he was supposed to, and found you there, passed out? Your granddaughter!"

"I'm sorry," Gavin pleads. "I knew you both would have tried to convince me otherwise."

"You're damn right we would have!" It's Casey this time. "We need you! Your grandkids need you!"

Charlee flinches at my side and Casey's eyes close as he inhales a deep breath through his nose. When he speaks next, it's a quiet whisper, his voice gravelly as he attempts to hold back the tears. "Claire's right, Dad. This decision should have been made together, the three of us. We're your family.'

Tears slide down Gavin's face as he looks up at the ceiling. "This doesn't change that. We'll always be a family, no matter what."

"But you won't be here!" Claire shouts. "You're leaving us! You're choosing it!" Her scream dies on her tongue as she buries her face in her hands, her small body wracking with sobs.

"Oh, sweetheart, come here," Gavin begs, reaching for her.

Claire twists away from him, pushes past her brother, but halts. She turns back to Casey, and with a sigh, he pulls out his truck keys and tucks them into her hand.

"Be careful," he whispers, squeezing her fingers.

Claire just nods and runs right out the door, leaving us all staring after her.

I'm two steps behind her, already halfway out the door when a deep sigh comes from the bed. "Just give her some time to calm down before you go after her, Avery."

Charlee asks the question that I'm afraid to. "What's going on?"

Casey opens his mouth to answer her but all that comes out is a choking sob. He shakes his head, tears streaming down his face, and Charlee rushes to his side. He envelops her in a hug so visibly crushing as he cries into her hair.

"Gavin came to me in March complaining of extreme fatigue and bouts of weakness," the doctor says softly, stepping up to the bed. I'd almost forgotten he was here. "We ran a few tests and determined that the cancer had returned a third time, more severe than before."

"I declined chemo," Gavin says quietly. I'm not sure he's even telling us, so to speak, or if he's really just coming to terms with his own decision, like he's saying it out loud for the first time, truly realizing the weight of his decision.

Charlee's cries strengthen in volume and intensity, and I can see the way her body is shaking from here while she falls apart in Casey's arms.

Me? Well, I'm having a hard time feeling anything, because it feels like I have a black hole in my chest where my heart should be. Something's cracked wide-open, and it hurts like hell. That's about the only thing I can focus on.

Gavin studies Casey and Charlee for a long moment before his gaze slides over to me.

"I'm dying."

506

CHAPTER FIFTY-FOUR

Claire

I'm not sure how I even made it here, in the kitchen of my childhood home, the only real home I've ever known. Blinded by the tears that slid relentlessly down my face, it's a miracle I was able to make the fifteen-minute drive from the hospital.

Entirely too reckless, I know. But all logic has flown out the window, and my brain has officially shut itself off.

I'm so damn angry. I'm angry at the doctor. I'm angry at my dad.

How could he do this? How could he decide this all on his own? How could he choose to leave us, to leave his family? How could he choose to *die*?

The doctor's words linger with a sharp sting, making my head spin along with the room.

Compromised bone marrow function. Unable to fight infections. Body is weak. Shutting down. Lucky to make it another week.

Another week. A week. A *week*? That's all the time I have left with my wonderful, hilarious, compassionate dad? Vivi's only grandparent?

No. I refuse to accept that. It's not enough. It'll *never* be enough.

Nausea chooses that moment to rear its ugly head, and I'm not sure if it's due to the hormones, or the fact that I'm overwhelmed with a grief so deep I can't see properly.

I just barely make it to the bathroom in time to empty the contents of my stomach—a whole lot of nothing—into the toilet. I'm empty, but it keeps coming, and I'm just dry heaving, fingers turning white as I grip the edge of the toilet and just beg myself to hang on.

Everything hurts, every bone in my body, every muscle.

But nothing hurts as much as that vital organ that's currently cracking wide open at the thought of never seeing my dad again, never jumping into his arms when I pull into the driveway, never having him call me *my girl* again.

The tears are merciless, rolling with no inclination to stop, and all I can do is rest my cheek on the cool toilet seat and sob.

Somewhere in the back of my mind, I register the sound of the front door clicking open, the soft whispers in the living room, the quiet but quick pad of footsteps through the hall. But I can't stop crying, can't lift my head, can't do *anything*. I don't feel anything at all except utter heartbreak and disappointment, rage with a god who deems it okay to take both of my parents way too young.

"Claire."

I hear Avery's quiet voice, that low baritone sinking into my bones, and while it washes over me with an eerie sense of calm, I can't do this right now. He can't see me like this, falling apart over a toilet bowl. I'm furious, I'm sad, I'm hurt, I'm…destroyed. I'm fucking destroyed. And I'm going to take it out on him like I always do, because that's my biggest fault—not knowing how the hell to communicate my feelings in my deepest, darkest moments. In the midst of my greatest struggles, when all I need is the love and support of my people, what I do best is push them all away.

"Oh, baby." I feel the warmth of his body as he sinks to the floor behind me, feel his gentle but firm touch as his fingers dust over my shoulder, wrapping around my neck. His other palm rests heavily on my back, a simple reminder that he's here, that I'm not alone.

Except that I want to be. Well, maybe I don't want to be, but I should be.

So maybe that's why I shrug away from his touch and spring to my feet. It's probably not the best decision, because saliva coats the inside of my cheeks and my head spins. I want to vomit again, but there's nothing left, and I refuse to do this in front of Avery.

"Don't," I grind out, pushing by him.

"Claire, I—"

"No!" I reel on him, trying to stay steady on my feet. "I didn't need you three months ago, I didn't need you last night, and I don't need you now!" The lie is blatant and bitter, but I keep going. "Just leave me alone!"

He doesn't even miss a beat. If my words hurt him, he doesn't show it. "No."

I blink up at him as my heart pounds in my ears and my throat tightens. "What?"

His arms fold over his broad chest as he looms over me, backing me into the hallway. "I said no. I'm not going anywhere, and I'm not leaving you alone. You *do* need me."

"No, I...No." I shake my head, hands at my throat. "I...Avery." Oh God, what am I even trying to say? I stumble backwards into the wall as he pushes forward. With my palms on his chest, I shove him as hard as I can. He doesn't even budge. "No! D-don't touch me! Don't, Avery! I don't need you!"

My head swivels to where Charlee and Casey stand in the living room, watching us. The broken look on my brother's face tells me I'm making an impossible situation all the more difficult, but I don't know how to be what he needs right now.

I don't even know how to be what *I* need.

I'm fractured, in pieces I'm not sure how to put back together. Will they ever fit again? How can someone love all the jagged pieces?

"I-I-I-I...Oh, God." I bury my face in my hands, sobbing. I can't do this. I'm falling apart. I can't even speak anymore. Nothing's working. A connection has been severed somewhere, I'm sure of it.

Avery's fingers wrap around my wrists, pulling me into his chest.

"No," I cry weakly. "I don't...I don't..."

"You do," he whispers, warm lips touching the crown of my head. "And it's okay. I need you too, you know. It's not one-sided. Charlee needs you. Casey needs you. Vivi needs you." He pauses. "Your dad needs you. Claire, we all need each other, and we're stronger together."

"I'm so angry," I weep, smashing my forehead off his chest as my body vibrates so violently I feel it all the way down to the tips of my toes.

"I know, sweetheart."

"He lied to us!"

"He did."

"He's dying!"

"He is."

I want Avery to deny it, all of it, any of it. I want him to tell me I have no reason to be angry. I want him to tell me my dad would never lie to me, that he's not dying, that it's not too late for him to start chemo.

But he doesn't. He hears my pain, sees it, feels it, and he just takes it all. And in that moment, I know—my pain is his pain.

I look up at Avery's smooth chocolate eyes, the tenderness they hold, the ones I've been denying myself of, and I break. My fingers crawl up his chest, gripping the collar of his shirt. "A week," I choke out. "The doctor said we'd be lucky to get one more week with him. I'm terrified, Avery. *Terrified.*"

His hand comes up to cup my cheek, the pad of his thumb wiping at my tears, fingers pushing back the hair that's plastered to my wet face. "I know, honey. I know." Hauling me forward, Avery tips my chin up, searching my eyes. "Don't spend it being angry with him. Spend it showing him how much you love him, how you're the strong, feisty, compassionate woman you are today because of the dad he is and the love he's always surrounded you with."

His soft lips meet both of my cheeks, kissing at the tears that won't stop falling. My arms wind around him as I bury my face in his chest and fall apart in the tight hold of the man who makes me feel nothing but so wildly loved.

"He's going, Claire, but that doesn't mean he's leaving. He'll never leave."

It's dinner by the time I have enough strength to creep back into my dad's room at the hospital, and even then, I'm dragging myself.

I peek my head through the door, holding up a tray of drinks and a greasy paper bag, because if he's only got a week left, he deserves to eat all the food he loves, not hospital slop.

Dad's chuckle is quiet but hearty, and it makes something in my chest flutter. "Is that your version of a white flag?"

"Yes," I squeak out, moving into the room. "And an apology."

His Adam's apple bobs with a thick swallow, and when he blinks, a single tear rolls down each cheek. "Come here, my beautiful girl."

Ditching the food, I crawl onto his bed, curling up at his side. The tears come immediately, soaking his neck while his fingers stroke my hair, my cheek, my shoulder.

"I'm so sorry, Dad. I'm so sorry I yelled at you and ran out of here."

"Don't you dare apologize," he whispers. "Don't you dare. You're allowed to feel every emotion you're feeling, and you're allowed to be angry with me. I wasn't honest with you."

"But why?"

He's quiet for a minute. "Because you would have convinced me to stay and fight."

"Why?" I beg quietly. "Why won't you? I don't want you to go, Daddy."

His sigh is heavy, and when I hear him sniffle, my heart breaks a little more. I look up at his cobalt blue eyes, weathered and tired.

511

"I'm tired, Claire. So damn tired of fighting. My body is exhausted."

I know. I know all that. I see it all. But I want to be selfish. I want him to do it for me, for Casey, for Vivi, for the grandbaby he'll never get to meet. I want him to fight.

But more than that, I don't want him to be in pain.

"I'm not ready to say goodbye."

His eyes fall shut, tears streaming down his cheeks, dribbling into this scruffy beard. "I know, sweetheart. And I'm not ready to say goodbye to you either." Pulling my face up to his, he kisses my cheeks, my nose, my forehead, and finishes softly on my lips.

"But that's the beautiful thing about death. It's not goodbye, Claire. Your mom has been with me every step of the way since she left this earth. And I know she's been with you too. With all of you, even Vivi." His mouth tilts with a small smile. "Hell, I think she knew Vivi before any of us did. She sent her to us, you know. To help us all."

His smile is gentle, filled with so many unspoken promises to walk beside me every day, even if I won't see him.

"So I'm not saying goodbye, sweetheart. This isn't the end. When one chapter ends, another begins. My story isn't done. There's no goodbye, not when it comes to us. I'll be with you. And I'll see you later."

With Vivi fast asleep in her bed and Turkey wrapped tightly around her body, Avery, Casey, Charlee and I curl up together around the firepit out back. It's been quiet, none of us saying a word, just sitting around, staring up at the stars.

But it's comfortable.

Despite the ache in my chest where it feels like I have a knife lodged in my heart, the corner of my mouth tugs up when I look at Charlee in Casey's lap, her head on his shoulder, his fingers trailing over her back.

Casey grins suddenly, a welcome laugh piercing the silent air. "Remember that time Dad took us fishing? With the frog?"

Charlee laughs, lifting her head off his shoulder and flashing me her brilliant smile. "Claire, I was so pissed at you."

"At *me*? You should have been pissed at them!" I gesture to my brother.

Avery's deep chuckle vibrates against my back, his breath tickling my neck. "I need to hear this story."

"Claire and Charlee were in a canoe, and me, Dex, and Dad took a break. We found a frog, and I was about to let it go in the water when Dad swiped it from my hands." The flames dance in Casey's eyes, permanent smile glued to his face as he remembers. I want to be mad, but I can't help smiling too. "He told the girls to paddle over to see the baby bunny."

"Bunny?" Avery questions. "I thought you said frog."

Casey's grin is pure evil. "I did." Charlee giggles again, settling back in his chest, Casey's arms coming around her. They look so cozy, like they're right where they're meant to be—together. "So they paddle over, excited to see the bunny Dad's holding. He tells them to stand up so they could lean over and see it from where we were on the edge of the shore."

Casey's head dips, his laughter booming around us. "And then my dad drops the frog on Claire's head," he wheezes. "Yells *boo!*" He swipes at tears and all I want to do is punch my brother right in the face. "Claire lost her damn mind, flailing all over the place. She lost her balance, latched onto Charlee, and—"

"And she fucking took me down!" Charlee finishes, pointing at me. "The canoe tipped and we went flying backwards!" She jabs her thumb back at Casey. "These assholes were laughing so hard it was five whole minutes before they finally helped us out."

"Hey now." His laughter makes his words shakes, and he grabs her hand, pinning it to her side. "It was my dad's fault. It was his idea. I was just a young, impressionable teenage boy."

513

Charlee and I roll our eyes with the same ferocity. Avery's still laughing like a jackass behind me, but as we spend the next hour reminiscing, laughing, and crying, I notice the weight crushing my chest lifts just slightly, letting me breathe again.

When I yawn for the seventh time, Avery clears his throat and stands, lifting me in his arms. "Alright. It's been a long day and there's a tiny redhead inside who's hellbent on seeing her Gramps at the ass crack of dawn tomorrow."

Casey and Charlee follow his lead, following us hand-in-hand into the house.

Outside my bedroom door, Charlee wraps me in a hug so big, so suffocating, I struggle to breathe. But I soak every second of it in, her warmth, her smell, her innate Charlee-ness. She's my best friend, my sister, and she's always by my side, showing me unrelenting love and support.

"I love you, Claire Bear," she whispers.

"I love you so much, Charlee. Thanks for being here."

"Where else would I be? You're my family." She kisses my nose, wraps her arms around Avery, and then heads down the hall to the kitchen, where Casey's making her a tea before bed.

In my bedroom, Avery strips off his shirt before heading to the bathroom. When he returns a few minutes later, I'm holding the soft cotton in my hands, feeling it against my skin. I'm debating putting it on, because I'm not mentally able to have sex tonight. If I put it on, Avery will get the hint. But for the first time in over two months, I missed a night with him. I missed his body against mine, the fire from his skin heating mine, his fingers pressing, caressing, skimming.

Avery steps in to me and takes his shirt from my hands. "No shirt. I know you're not there, Claire, and neither am I. Tonight is just about being together, holding you. And I need to feel you." His hands slide down my arms, fingers lacing with mine. "I missed you like fucking crazy. Please, just let me feel you."

When I nod, he lifts me in his arms, carting me over to the bed. It's small, and I miss his bed—our bed—but I like this. There's no room for empty spaces, just me and him and all our limbs, tangled together, just the way we should be.

When he slips in next to me, I turn in his arms, pressing into his chest, shoving my leg between his. "I'm so sorry," I murmur. "I'm sorry I yelled at you. I'm sorry I left."

"You scared me, Claire." His voice shakes. "I thought you were leaving me. I thought I was losing you."

My lips touch his shoulder. "I'll always be yours, Avery, as long as you want me."

"I want you forever," he whispers into the darkness.

My gaze searches his through the sliver of moonlight that sips through the crack in the blinds. "Forever is a long time, Avery."

His fingers press into my face as he holds my gaze. "Forever, Claire."

The fear that grips me, squeezes at my heart, loosens its hold just a bit. "I want you forever, too."

CHAPTER FIFTY-FIVE

Claire

I stare down at the black and white print in my shaking hands. If it hadn't truly hit me before, it's hitting me like a brick wall now.

It's real. This whole thing is real. I'm growing a baby inside of me, half me, half Avery.

And I'm utterly and undeniably petrified.

The ultrasound technician squeezes my hand, flashes me a reassuring smile, and then hands me a Kleenex for my tears, which pretty much haven't stopped since Thursday. My eyes burn and my nose is raw.

"What a wonderful way to start your Monday, isn't it?" she says with a happy sigh. "There's nothing like seeing the magic you've created for the first time."

I don't have the words to agree with her, though I do, as scared as I am. Everything's lost somewhere in my throat.

"I can schedule you in again for Friday morning, if you'd like. You can bring Daddy with you. We should be able to hear the heartbeat loud and clear."

My face lifts, meeting her kind eyes. "Hear it?"

Smiling, she nods. "Yup. I have a 9:30 slot, or a 10:15."

Friday. That makes eight days since the doctor told us one week. Dad will be gone by then, or, by some stroke of magic, he'll still be hanging on. Though I doubt it. By yesterday afternoon, he wasn't able to stay awake for more than an hour at a time.

But if he is, I'll bring him with me. With me and Avery. I'll tell them both by then, and then I'll show them.

"9:30 will be fine," I mumble, staring down at my picture, my baby.

A few minutes later, I stop outside Dad's room, staring through the small window in the door. Vivi's sitting on Avery's lap by the edge of the bed, and Dad is propped on way too many pillows. There's a table between them as they play cards, and Casey and Charlee are sitting off in the corner, talking quietly. Turkey is curled up at Dad's feet, his head resting over his legs. That was Avery's doing. He managed to convince the doctor. Don't ask me how; the man can talk anyone into anything.

Casey catches my eye and slips out of the room, closing the door quietly behind him. His eyelids are heavy, red and raw. "Hey. Where'd you disappear off to?"

I pull the ultrasound picture out of my purse and slide it into his hands. His smile is so big, warm, genuine. He wraps me up in his arms, rocking me back and forth.

"How far?"

"Eight weeks this Friday," I whisper.

"You still haven't told him." It's not a question.

I take a deep breath and let it go. It feels oddly cleansing, cathartic even. "I will, Casey. It's just, with everything…I'm so overwhelmed right now. There are so many different emotions in my head, and I can't sort through them." How do you find the right time to tell someone he's going to be a father, when your own father is wasting away on his deathbed?

Casey pulls me into him, kissing my forehead. "I know, Claire Bear. I know." He hesitates for a moment too long, and I know whatever he's going to says next isn't good.

"What?"

"The doctor came while you were gone."

Remember when I felt cleansed and cathartic a minute ago? Yeah, that's fucking gone. "And?"

"Today," he whispers.

"Today what?"

517

"Today," he repeats, his pale green eyes searching mine, waiting for me to understand the meaning of that one simple word, to fall apart right here in the hall.

"No." I shake my head furiously. "No. He said a week. On Friday, he said a week." My voice gets higher, louder with every word, and I see Avery's head lift from his spot in the room, his eyes meeting mine through the door. "Casey, it's only day four! No! He still has...he still has..."

I collapse in my brother's arms, both of us shaking, soaking each other's shirts.

"He's supposed to have more time," I cry.

"I know," Casey murmurs, because what more is there to say?

I drag myself through the door twenty minutes later, when I'm finally able to compose myself well enough to go inside and spend my dad's last day with him, with our family.

Dad's skin is paper thin and ashy. Deep purple bruises dot the delicate skin under his tired blue eyes, and when they meet mine, his gaze tells me he heard me out there, that he knows I know. That he's sorry.

"Hi Auntie Claire," Vivi singsongs as I sit on the edge of the bed, my dad resting one hand on top of mine, Avery's coming down on my back. "I beatin' Gamps."

"What are you playing?" My throat is raw, making the words crackle.

"We payin' go fish. Gamps said he wanted to take me fishin' one more time."

As if my heart isn't already broken enough.

"Who's winning?" I somehow manage, croaking my way through the two words.

Dad snorts weakly. "Who do you think?"

Vivi's grin is broad as she thumbs at herself. "I winnin'!"

"Okay, sweetheart, let's see..." Dad hums to himself, looking over his cards. "Do you have... any...sevens?"

Vivi glances at her cards for all of a split second. "Nope! Go fish, Gamps!"

Avery leans over her shoulder, tapping at a card.

"Dat a seben?"

He nods and kisses her temple. "Uh huh."

Her little brow furrows. "Oh." She looks at her grandpa. "Sorry, Gamps. I lie."

He chuckles lightly, taking her card. "Not to worry...pumpkin." His lips close around the straw in the cup of water Avery offers to him. "Charlee, when's that...brother of yours...coming?" His words are slow and lazy, quiet.

"Dex is on his way. Just left Toronto a few minutes ago."

He nods. "Good, good. Wanna...see him."

"Of course." Charlee looks down at her lap, hiding her tears. "I'll tell him to hurry up."

Turkey lifts his head suddenly, whining as he looks at Dad, his head cocked to the side. He crawls up his side, laying his head over Dad's chest.

"Somebody better take care of my damn dog," Dad growls out, making us laugh, even if it's weak as hell.

Casey curses under his breath, looking away. I know what he's thinking, because he's brought it up at least ten times this past weekend. Casey wants Turkey, but the person who owns his condo unit doesn't allow animals.

"We'll do it," Avery pipes up, glancing quickly in my direction. "Claire and I can take him. And Casey, when you get a new place, you can take him if you'd like."

Casey stares at Avery for a long moment before his mouth twitches. "Thanks, man. I appreciate that."

Dad chuckles. "You guys are gonna have a...damn zoo...in there. How many's...that?"

"Two dogs, a crazy cat, and a temperamental redhead," Avery says with a pointed smirk in my direction.

Dad barks out a laugh. "Too right."

Casey stands abruptly, pretending to stretch. He meets my gaze and gives it a deliberate flick in the direction of my purse, where I stowed my picture before we came in here. "Who wants to go get a donut?"

"*Me!*" Vivi shrieks, scattering her cards everywhere. She stands on Avery's lap, shaking her hips back and forth while she rubs her belly. "Donut queen, donut queen, I am da donut queen."

Casey scoops Vivi off Avery's lap and takes Charlee's hand. He looks back at Avery, who happens to be staring at me. "Come on, Avery."

"It's okay," I whisper, touching my lips to his.

His palm curves over the back of my head, his lips pressing to my forehead, lingering there. "I love you."

"I love you, too."

"That's one hell of a…man you got there…honey," Dad muses after the door shuts behind them. "Makes you wonder…what the hell you ever saw in…Adam."

My eyes narrow. "*Aaron.*"

His grin is devilish, because last day or not, he's still my dad, and he always will be. "Oh. Right. *Aaron.*" He winks. "Well, anyway…Avery blows Aaron out of the…water."

"You're just saying that because he's rich." I know that's not true. My dad loves Avery, and Avery *does* blow Aaron out of the water. He's a freaking cannonball.

"No. I'm saying that because…his love for you…is unyielding. He blew off work to be here…with you, with us. Loves the shit out of my granddaughter…Feeding me water through a straw…Never leaves your side, and in the just over two months you've been together…I've seen way more of him…than I ever saw of Aaron…in three years."

His fingers creep over mine, squeezing. "Whatever you're hiding from him…you can tell him. You can trust him with it."

My gaze snaps up to his. "How did you know?"

"Because you're shit at lying…not sneaky in the slightest…So what is it, Claire? What aren't you telling him? And why?"

I look down at our entwined fingers, bringing his to my lips. "I love him so much, Daddy."

"And he loves you."

"I'm terrified he's going to leave me when he…when he finds out."

"Claire." I can tell it takes all his effort, but his hands slip up my arms, gripping my shoulders. "That man isn't going anywhere…I promise you. He looks at you…the exact way I always looked at your mom."

"You think so?" My parents were always crazy for each other. I was one of those lucky kids, the ones who knew what true love looked like, who never had to worry about broken families.

Except my family did break, just in a way I never saw coming.

"I know so, honey. He's…crazy about you."

"Dad, I…I have to show you something." Moving off the bed, I dig my picture out of my purse, holding it to my stomach while I lay down next to my dad.

"Is this where you…disappeared off to?"

I nod, still clutching that picture to my stomach, terrified of so, so much.

"Well, let's see it. Come on."

I meet my dad's eyes, warm and patient like they've always been with me. And then I flip the picture over.

His hand flies to his mouth and the bed vibrates with his quiet cries as he takes the picture from my hands. "Oh, Claire. Baby…" He meets my gaze. "You're gonna be a momma."

I swipe at my tears. "It was an accident. Avery doesn't know yet. I'm so scared."

He takes my hand, holding it to his lips while he cries.

"And you'll never meet—"

"No." His head moves wildly. "No, Claire. I had a dream. While I was out. I remembered when I came to on Friday morning…as soon as I set my eyes on you…a little boy with dark brown hair…bright blue eyes. He called me Gramps. Said he had my…eyes." Taking my face in his hands, he drags me into him. "I'll always be with my babies. *Always.*"

"You promise?"

"I promise, my beautiful girl…I'll always be with you."

CHAPTER FIFTY-SIX

Avery

When we return later with enough donuts to feed the entire hospital wing, I know Gavin's hanging on by a thread. He doesn't have a day left, an hour. He has minutes. It's in his face, the heavy, droopy set of his tired eyes, the way he's leaning on Claire, like she's his lifeline.

The doctor and one of the nurses slip out the door, looking somber.

"It's time, son," the doctor speaks quietly to Casey, laying a hand on his shoulder. "We've administered an IV that will keep him free of pain until his body decides he's ready."

When Casey disappears through the door, Charlee whips out her phone, pacing up and down the hallway, frantically twirling and tugging at the tip of her ponytail.

"Dex!" she exclaims after a moment, the single syllable laced with endless panic. "Dex, you have to hurry...No, I can't tell him to wait! That's not how this works...Dex, please! Casey needs you. I need you." She keels over, clutching at her stomach while she sobs.

"Hey, hey," I urge softly, wrapping an arm around her. "Let me talk to him. Take a deep breath, Charlee." I pull the phone out of her grasp and her into my arms while she cries on my shoulder. "Dex?"

"Avery?" He's just as frantic as his sister. "Fuck, man, I'm, like, fifteen minutes away. Fifteen minutes."

"Okay, Dex. Just drive carefully, okay? Get here in one piece. We'll be here."

"I need to say goodbye to him. He's been a dad to me."

I pause, peering through the door. "Do you want me to put him on the phone?"

"You don't...you don't think he'll make it? You don't think I'll make it in time?"

I... "I don't know, Dex."

"Fuck!" he shouts. "Put him on. Please."

I've never experienced heartbreak like this before. Being in here, surrounded by all this perpetual love, where everybody is terrified it's all going to disappear when the person is physically gone, it's...earth-shattering. Claire refuses to leave her dad's side while he talks to Dex on the phone, Casey and Charlee are holding each other, and Vivi is just standing there, taking it all in, like she's suddenly getting it.

She looks up at me with those huge green eyes and her wobbly bottom lip. "Everyone sad, Uncle A'wy. Now I sad, too."

"Come here, sweetheart." I hoist her into my arms, cuddling her close. "We're just sad because we have so much love in our hearts. Sometimes it pours out as tears."

Charlee's sobs bring my attention to the bed, where she's wrapped her arms around Gavin while he whispers in her ear.

"Thank you for being my daughter's...very best friend. She's so lucky to have you, and so are...Casey and Viv." He wipes at her tears and smiles at her. "If you and Casey don't get...married...one day...I'll roll over...in my grave."

"Dad!" Claire swats at his shoulder. "You-you...you can't say things like that!"

"I'll say whatever I want. I'm dying. They've been...pussyfooting around this thing for...far too long now." His eyes twinkle as he looks at his son. "Isn't that right, Case?"

Casey runs his fingers through his hair, staring straight at the ground.

Gavin's weathered eyes settle on me and Vivi. "Son," he says to me, taking my hand. "Thank you for loving my Claire, my Vivi. Thank you for...coming into our lives."

"Yes sir," I whisper, nodding. My vision clouds with tears as I try my damnedest to blink them away.

"You're part of our...family. And in case you were wondering...I'd be so proud to call you my son-in-law...one day."

That does me in. I can't blink these tears away. I glance up at the ceiling, letting them slip down my face. Then I squeeze Gavin's hand. "Thank you, sir."

He looks at Claire, his eyes drifting down her body, lingering on her stomach. "I know I can trust you to look after my babies, Avery."

"Always. I promise." I'll always take care of Claire and Vivi. *Always*.

He smiles up at me. It's soft and small. "Good man."

Turning his attention on Vivi, he holds his arms out. "Come here, baby girl," he says while I set her gently in his lap.

Vivi presses her hands to his sopping cheeks. "You cwyin', Gamps. You need magic kiss?"

His head bobs, just barely. "Please."

She litters every inch of his face with sloppy kisses. "There," she whispers, tapping his nose. "You all betta now."

Claire moves to my side, slipping her arms around my waist and tucking her face into my side. I don't have a fucking clue what to say, what to do, so I just hold her.

Gavin brushes Vivi's loose curls off her face, tears sliding down his cheeks. "Beautiful girl," he murmurs. "I have to go, sweetheart."

"Where you goin', Gamps? I come?"

His head shakes and he offers Casey up a small smile when he joins them on the bed, laying a hand on his dad's arm. "I'm going to heaven to be with grandma."

Vivi's eyes start watering, that lip of hers trembling. She looks around the room, taking us all in, and finally looks back at her grandpa. "You goin' to heaben? But…but I can't come to heaben." She traces his cheek, his eyelids, his lips, as if she's memorizing how he looks, feels. "I won't see you anymore?"

Gavin blinks furiously, taking a second to peer up at the ceiling. He kisses his granddaughter's nose. "You'll see me. I promise. I'll come visit you…in your dreams…my sweet girl."

She places her palm over his heart. "And you be in my heart, like Gamma?"

"Always and forever."

She snuggles into him, nuzzling his neck. "I luh you, Gamps. I be good girl for you."

"You're always my good girl…I love you, sweet Vivi."

Vivi sits up and smiles. "You gib Gamma hug for me?"

Gavin grinds widely as he brushes away Vivi's tears. "Oh, honey. I can't…wait…to give Grandma…a hug. I'll tell you a…secret." He leans in close, cupping his hands around her ear. "Grandma gives the very best hugs."

His gaze moves between me and Charlee. He looks at Claire, at Casey, before settling back on Vivi. I know what he's trying to tell us, even before he gives Vivi one last kiss and she squeezes him as hard as she can. He wants to be alone with his children, and he doesn't want Vivi to see this.

I scoop up the tiny redhead and she wraps her legs around my hip, stuffing her thumb in her mouth when her cheek hits my shoulder. I kiss Claire, place a hand on Casey's back, and finally squeeze Gavin's hand. With Charlee's hand tucked into mine, we leave the three of them in peace.

Together, we amble around the hospital for fifteen minutes, rounding the corner back into Gavin's wing when we see the doctor leave his room, shutting the door quietly.

He doesn't see us, but we see him. We see the way he pinches his nose, scrubs his mouth, and then looks up at the ceiling, two hands on his hips while a tear slips out of his eye.

"No," Charlee whimpers. "Oh, God." She runs to the door after the doctor walks away, looking through the window, fingers pressing into the glass. "No."

"Cha-Cha," Vivi urges quietly, beckoning her with her hand. "Don't cwy. Gamps safe in heaben. He wif Gamma."

I peer through the window in the door. Vivi is right. Gavin's eyes are closed, his hands at his side while his dog rests his chin on his chest, staring up at him. Claire and Casey are wrapped in each other's arms, their cries piercing the air in the hallway.

Hauling Charlee into my chest, I wrap her and Vivi up in the tightest hug I can muster. It's not just for them, but for me too. My heart is broken for this family. *My* family.

"I'm here! I'm here. Fuck." Dex skids into the hallway, grabbing the edge of the wall while he wheezes. "There was no parking. I had to park…" He looks at us, at his sister, his best friend's daughter, the three of us tangled together. And his face breaks. "There was no parking," he whispers again, walking toward us while tears coat his face. "I was here, and there was no parking."

The door to Gavin's room creaks open, and Casey and Claire step out, faces soaked to the brim, eyes nearly swollen shut.

And I do the only thing I can think of. I open my arms, gesturing to Dex, and he steps forward, sweeping Casey and Claire in with Charlee, Vivi and I. The six of us stand there, one little family huddled together while we hold each other and cry.

527

CHAPTER FIFTY-SEVEN

Avery

I wake up Wednesday morning the way I hate to wake up—cold, and with my arms empty.

Rolling over, I swing my arm out, brushing it over Claire's empty side. It's warm, so she hasn't been up long.

"Claire?" I call out.

The bedroom door is cracked open, and I shoot up in bed when I hear somebody retching in the bathroom down the hall. I hear the toilet flush, the tap running while I scramble out of bed, pulling on a pair of shorts.

Trying to pull on a pair of shorts. I trip over my feet and face-plant on the cold hardwood.

Groaning, I flop over onto my back. The door creaks and I see Claire's bare feet, her cute sky-blue toes, as she pads into the room, closing the door behind her.

"Baby?" I moan, reaching for her. "You okay? I tried to come. I fell."

Her soft giggle is music to my ears, because I haven't heard it in a week. She spent the rest of Monday and most of Tuesday curled up in my lap, alternating between sleeping and crying. By last night, though, she managed a couple smiles. They were sad, but beautiful as hell, as they always are.

Claire steps over me, feet on either side of my waist, and offers me her hands. It's a nice gesture, but that's all it is, because there's no way in hell she can pull me up.

When I make it to my feet, I yank her into me, burying my head in her silky hair, all messy bedhead. Her cheeks are warm and flushed with heat, her eyes red and swollen from all the emotions she's been dealing with over the last few days.

528

"Avery," Claire whispers, kissing my shoulder. "I need to talk to you."

"Okay, baby." I pull her over to the bed, patting the spot next to me, but she just stares down at me.

"Um, could you maybe…get dressed?" She scratches her head and clears her throat, gesturing at my dick. He's slightly traitorous this morning, standing at full attention. "It's hard to focus with that, that…*thing*."

Chuckling, I peck her cheek as I walk by her. "He's just saying hello."

I manage to get dressed without issue this time, pulling on a full outfit. Scratching at my abdomen, I turn around to find Claire sitting at the edge of the bed, fumbling with something in her lap. A piece of paper, a picture, maybe. When I take a seat beside her, slipping my arm around her waist, she releases a heavy sigh, pressing whatever she's holding into her stomach.

"I've been hiding something from you." She's quiet and timid, sage eyes searching mine from beneath those thick lashes of hers.

Sweeping my thumb under her chin, I tip her up for a kiss, the inherent hint of mint on her lips. "I know."

Her mouth opens partway, eyes wide. "You-you…you know?"

"I don't *know*, I just know there's something you're not telling me. You're shit at hiding when there's something on your mind. You're not sneaky at all."

She huffs a tiny laugh. "That's what my dad said. I…I told him Monday."

"Well, whatever it is, I'm glad you shared it with him. I didn't want to push you."

"Because I tend to freak out when you push me?"

A smile tilts my mouth. "On occasion."

"*Every* occasion."

I tweak her nose. "But I just love you more with each freak out." Truth. If I wasn't already aware, watching Claire disappear into the elevator Thursday evening solidified that I have absolutely zero desire to ever be apart again.

"And I'm still not sure why," Claire says on a sigh. "I give you nothing but trouble."

"Are we seriously having this conversation right now? I love you, Claire, everything about you. Good and bad. But for the record, I don't think the bad is all that bad. It makes you human, and you got past my less than stellar history. Do you love me any less for it?"

Her head shakes. "No. Of course not."

"Then why would you think there would be any parts of you that I don't love?"

Her green eyes grow, flooding with tears as they flicker between mine. "I'm scared, Avery."

"Then tell me what you're scared of so I can help you."

"I just…I want you to know it was an accident. I didn't…I didn't know. I would never try to…try to…" She doesn't finish, just squeezes her eyes shut, letting one lone tear slip out. When I brush it away, she leans into my touch. Sucking in a deep breath, she looks down at the small paper in her hands. "Here," she whispers, holding it out to me.

I take the picture—that's what it is, I think. It's black and white, a large fan shape sweeping out over most of it. In the middle, is a small black oval, with a white-ish…blob?

I have no idea what I'm looking at here.

There's a ton of words littered across the picture, most of which mean absolutely nothing to me. The date and time, however, tells me that whatever this is, it's where Claire disappeared to Monday morning at the hospital.

My eyes focus on the simple details at the top, the words I *do* understand.

West Lincoln Memorial Hospital, Obstetrics and Gynecology
Patient: Thompson, Claire, 26 years

"Avery," Claire whispers. "Say something, please."

"What is this?" I'm mildly aware of her knees bouncing a mile a minute, the way her fingers are drumming away in her lap. I think she brings them to her mouth and starts chewing on her nails, but I'm too focused on the words I'm reading, the picture in front of me.

And my heart kicks it up until I feel like there's a horse galloping away in there.

"It's...it's my...it's our...Avery, it's—"

"Our baby," I finish quietly. "This is our baby." I trace over the shape I called a blob a minute ago. It's not a blob. It's my fucking baby. *Our* fucking baby. Half me, half the woman I love.

My head lifts, meeting her anxious gaze. Mine drifts down her body, settling on her belly, the way Gavin's did when he made me promise to take care of his babies. Because he knew.

"You're pregnant."

Claire averts her gaze, staring at her toes, her knees, a spot on the wall. It goes everywhere but my face. "I'm sorry, Avery."

"You're sorry?"

Her head moves up and down with a sniffle. "I didn't know...when I was sick, the antibiotics...I'm so sorry. I should have known better. I..." Her body falls forward with the gasp that bursts past her lips, and I watch as she wraps herself around her knees. "Please. Please don't leave me, Avery."

I blink at her. She's still not looking at me. Instead, she's falling apart right beside me.

"Leave you?"

In slow motion, I watch my hand drop to her back, rubbing down her spine, as if it's not connected to my body. I'm in a daze, I think, but what she's saying resonates somewhere in my brain, and it's not gonna fly.

Gently gripping the back of her neck, I haul her up. When she finally looks at me, I yank her into me, our lips a breath away.

"Leave you, Claire? Why the hell would I leave you?"

"I...I'm—"

"Pregnant. With my baby. With *our* baby. We made a fucking *baby*. Holy. Fucking. *Shit*." Before I know what's happening, my arms come around her in a suffocating hold as I crush her down to the mattress, peppering her face in kisses while my tears coat her creamy skin. "I fucking love you, Claire, and I'll love the hell out of this baby."

Sliding down her body, I push her shirt up, examining her belly. It's still as small as it's always been, with maybe just a touch more softness to it, but she's also been eating Taco Bell like it's her job for the last four days. A combination of all the different emotions coursing through her, I'm sure.

I wrap my arms around her middle and smoosh my face into her warm belly. "My baby," I murmur, touching my lips to her smooth skin. "I'll be the best daddy in the world. I promise." I'm gonna try my damnedest, at least.

Claire's fingers rake through my hair as her body quivers under my touch. "You're really not going to leave me?"

My head whips up. "I'm never leaving you, Claire. Baby or no baby, I'll never let you walk away from me again. You have to know that. You're my forever." I slide my hand over her stomach, watching the muscles there jump and clench. "Both of you. My family."

Claire buries her face behind her hands and weeps. "I thought...I thought you might...Oh my God," she cries. "I'm so happy right now."

I crawl up her body, pulling her hands away so I can see her beautiful face. Grinning, I tell her, "You know, tears normally mean the opposite of happy."

She just shakes her head furiously before crushing her mouth down on mine.

"How far along are you?" I ask, trailing a finger down the side of her face, her neck, across the tiny freckles on her shoulder. God, I want to pull this tank top right off her, but it's been less than forty-eight hours since her dad left us, and even though we haven't had sex in almost a week, I don't want to pressure her.

"I'll be eight weeks on Friday. I have another ultrasound..." She peers sheepishly up at me. "If you'd like to come."

"Hell yes I wanna come. I get to see my baby in person."

"And hear his heartbeat."

My ears perk up. "Heartbeat? He already has a heart?" She nods, biting back her smile while I double back around to that other word she said. "*His*? It's a boy?"

"Well, no. I mean, I don't know. It's too early to tell, but my dad...he said he had a dream. He was talking to a little boy with dark brown hair—" she fingers a wave on top of my head, "—and bright blue eyes. He called him Gramps, and said he had his eyes."

That muscle in my chest stutters while a strange warmth rushes over me. "He's with him, Claire. He'll keep him safe until he's ready to come into the world." I drop my forehead to her throat, pressing my lips to her collarbone. "I can't believe we made a baby."

Closing my eyes, I shake my head. "My mom is gonna absolutely lose her ever-loving mind. We'll need to restrain her." I make a mental note to maybe record her reaction. But right now, I don't care about that. "When did you find out?"

"Last Thursday," she replies on a timid whisper.

I pause my assault on the columns of her throat so I can look up at her. "Is that why you ran out on me?"

She nods. "I'm so sorry. I wasn't expecting that news at all. I was terrified. Terrified of everything. Not being ready, you maybe not wanting this, me not being a good mom—"

"You're going to be the best mom," I growl out, pinning her to the mattress beneath my body. "The fucking *best*, Claire."

"But is this really something you want, Avery? It's…it's so fast. So soon. We've only been together…I mean, three months ago, you were—"

"Miserable. Without you I was miserable, and I had no idea until you came along and showed me everything I was missing. I knew I wanted you the second I laid eyes on you, and every moment you denied me crushed a part of my soul, until you finally let me in. There's nowhere else I'd rather be than with you, at home, snuggled up with our crazy zoo on the couch.

Sweeping my thumbs over the freckles that dot her cheekbones like tiny stars, I take her face in my hands. "I promise you, Claire, as long as I'm with you, I am exactly where I want to be."

She throws her arms around my neck, kissing me with a fierceness that only fuels the fire burning in my belly. God, I want her. I want every inch of her. I want to kiss on every freckle, suck on her milky skin, mark her as mine. My best friend, my lover, my partner.

I rip my mouth off hers, trying to catch my breath. "Move in with me. I'm only asking you a second time as a courtesy. If you say no again, I'll fucking pack your shit myself."

Her mouth opens and those long lashes of hers flutter. "Avery, I—"

"Say yes." My teeth tug on her lower lip. "Give it up, Claire. Say yes."

She gets this mischievous little smirk on her face, the one that makes me wanna flip her over, slap her ass, grab a fistful of her hair, and ride her into next week. "I'll only say yes if you fuck me until I can't stand."

"Mmm…" I drag my nose along her collarbone, nipping at the dip in her shoulder. My lips trail over her jaw, up to her ear. "You want me to carry you everywhere?"

"I am pregnant, so…"

"Fuck yes you are." Now I do flip her over.

534

Tearing her sorry excuse for a shirt off her body, I lick up her spine, enjoying the goosebumps that dot her skin, the shiver that shakes her. I slide my hands into her pajama shorts, dragging them down her hips, over the swell of her ass. Gripping the base of my cock, I pull it out of my shorts, rubbing the tip through her soaking slit. Always ready for me.

Gripping her neck, I whisper, "With *my* baby," before I slam into her.

And once I've had my fill—which is actually entirely impossible, because we go three times and I still want her—Claire rolls out of bed, a sweaty, wobbly mess. I watch her stop in front of the full-length mirror, hands on her belly.

I step up behind her, covering her hands with mine, my chin on her shoulder. "Where is he? You're so tiny."

Giggling, she lifts my fingers to her mouth, kissing each one. "I won't show for a while, but I can't wait, even if I'll look like a beachball. Or a beached whale," she adds with the crinkle of her cute nose. She tips her head over my shoulder, beaming up at me. "I can't wait to see part of you growing in me."

Christ, I've never heard anything better.

I hug her so tight, hoping like hell she can feel how much I love her, how she owns every bit of my heart, how I'll never go anywhere without her by my side.

And ten minutes later, when we're finally decent enough to join everyone else out in the living room, including Harper and Wyatt, who drove down together Monday afternoon, I can't fucking help it.

I sweep my arms out, garnering every single bit of attention in that room while Claire drops her forehead to her hand and mutters out an *oh no*.

"I'm gonna be a fucking dad!"

CHAPTER FIFTY-EIGHT

Avery

I'm groggy when I wake up, the warm body I'm draped over squirming, vibrating in my hold. I'm marginally aware of the sweat coating her skin as she slides against my hold, which is kind of Claire's new normal. She's always hot. It's also the end of August now and I'm wrapped around her like a burrito because heaven forbid I give her any free space while we sleep.

Also, we stayed at her dad's last night, and her childhood bed is fucking tiny.

Still, Claire starts turning in my arms, whimpering, so I twist around her, watching her face, the deep furrow of her brows. Her lips part on a sigh, a small cry pushing past, puffing out against my face.

"Dad," she whispers, clutching at my shoulder.

My heart breaks for her in this moment, so I bury my fingers in her hair and press my lips to her forehead. She's been doing well, as well as can be expected. She misses her dad like crazy, of course, but she's managed to spend the last three weeks focusing on all the happy memories they shared. She smiles often and laughs, telling me stories every day, but there are days I catch her sitting on the balcony, just staring off into the distance, silent tears slipping down her cheeks.

The week after Gavin died, I sent Claire, Casey, and Vivi off to the cottage. My heart ached watching her go, but I knew they needed each other. They needed a break from the noise, this wild world. On the third day, Claire called in reinforcements.

And so we all went. Me, Charlee, Dex, Harper, Wyatt, and my parents. And the animals. God, the animals. There's far too many.

When we got there, and Vivi came running down the driveway, jumping into everyone's arms, all Claire and Casey could say was that they wanted their family there.

"Mom," Claire gasps suddenly. "Mom, wait. Please don't—" She rockets up in bed, right out of my arms, breathless and wheezing, her cheeks flushed pink. I watch her eyes move around the room like she's taking in her surroundings, coming down, remembering where she is.

Sometimes, waking up is the hardest part for Claire. Because it's when she realizes it was a dream, and now it's over. She never knows when she'll see her parents again, when they'll visit her. But they always come back.

Her emerald gaze locks with mine and tears start sliding furiously down her cheeks. She clutches at her chest, right where her heart is, right where it hurts, and reaches for me with her other hand. I take her into my arms, kissing up every cool trail on her warm cheeks.

"Tell me about it," I murmur against her hair.

She loves to talk about her dreams. They're new memories for her, memories they're making together, despite the distance, despite the fact that her parents aren't *here*, even though they'll always be with her.

She pulls back just a touch, wiping the back of her hands over her face. She sniffles and gives me a sweet smile, all crooked and bleary-eyed. "He was smiling. He said he was so happy, safe. He was with Mom." She swipes at more tears and looks up to the ceiling. "They looked so happy together. Mom said they're taking care of our baby until he's ready to meet us." The softest giggle puffs past her lips. "She said he was so handsome, like you, but stubborn, like me."

Claire reaches forward, stroking her fingers down the side of my face. "Mom said she's so happy we found each other, Avery."

I'm sure I've never smiled so hard in my life, and Claire's answering beam tells me she thinks so too, her eyes dipping down to my mouth, where my face has absolutely split in two.

The happiness searing through me right now is similar to when I saw Baby Beck on that little machine three weeks ago, when his— or her—heartbeat filled the air around us, like it was placing us in this protective bubble where nothing could hurt us anymore, because love would always mend our wounds. Love would always win. That's how I felt, anyway.

We had decided to wait to tell my parents until Claire was past the first trimester. It had been surprisingly easy to convince Harper to keep her mouth shut. All I had to say was, *Please, Harp. For Claire.*

Except that when the ultrasound tech showed us the teddy bears you could get where you put a recording of your baby's heartbeat into it, I had to have one. And then we went back to Gavin's, and my parents were there, where they'd been since Thursday for Gavin's celebration of life. I took one look at my mom, her eyes locked on the bear I was clutching in my hands, and I just couldn't help it.

I yelled it out. For the second time. Because, fuck me, I want the entire world to know. This woman is growing our damn *baby*.

And my mom literally *fell to the floor* in a fit of hysterics, before practically tackling Claire into the wall. Vivi was there, didn't have a clue what was going on, but wanted in on the action, so she just started jumping up and down, shrieking.

Harper had a feeling I would crack at the ultrasound, so she'd been standing in the hallway videotaping the entire thing. My mom's reaction video has over eight-hundred thousand views on YouTube, still climbing.

I'm busy cuddling the ever-loving shit out of my baby mama when the bedroom door creaks open and I hear the quiet pad of tiny

538

feet moving across the floor. A flash of red peeks over the edge of the bed before Vivi starts climbing up.

"Oh," she says, crossing her legs as she sits down before us. "You awake." She holds up two slices of bread, one in each hand. Just bread, nothing else. Not toasted, no peanut butter or jam. Just the bread. "I bwing you bweakfast in bed. Daddy say I toast it, but—" she shakes her head, "—I say no."

Vivi manages to haul our asses out of bed, and we meet Casey outside on the back porch, where he's got real breakfast set up on the patio table for us.

"Plain bread didn't do it for you?" he asks, amused eyes on his sister as she immediately starts digging in, forgoing a plate and any utensils whatsoever. Her appetite has been ravenous.

Casey reaches for a piece of bacon and Claire growls, slapping his hand away. "Mine."

He holds his hands up in surrender, giving me a wide-eyed look which I'm pretty sure says I should, quite frankly, fucking run while I still can.

"I can't believe this is our last weekend here," Casey murmurs, spinning his mug of coffee around on the table, pensive gaze drifting over the yard.

Claire pulls her knees up to her chest, resting her cheek on top. "Yeah." A fat tear sneaks down her face, dripping off her chin. "I'm gonna miss it so much. I don't want to say goodbye."

"Me neither." Casey sighs deeply. "What do you think the new owners will do with it? With the house? The property?"

"Whatever you want," I reply simply, lacing my fingers together behind my head, watching Vivi, Sully, Turkey, and Chester rolling around in the grass.

Casey's brows pull together. "What?"

Claire's nose scrunches in confusion, her forehead marred with a crease. I watch it smooth out as her mouth opens. "Avery," she says slowly. "What did you do?"

Grinning, I pull out the contract I stuffed into my back pocket before we came out here. I slap it down on the table.

Casey and Claire scramble for the papers, but Casey gets there first, elbow his sister's hand out of the way.

"It's the purchase of sale contract," Casey whispers. "For the house."

Claire dashes around the table, ripping the papers out of her brother's hand. I watch her lips move as she reads, and then her eyes meet mine. "Avery…why is…why are…me and Casey…"

"You're the new owners," I tell them, in case their names and mine on the deed weren't clear enough.

"You bought my dad's house?" Casey's stare is unwavering. "You bought it…for us?"

"Yeah." I smile, sitting up straighter, running a palm down my chest. It feels warm in there, like I'm proud of my decision. "I did."

"Why?"

"Because this is your home. It's where you grew up. It's where you come to find peace when everything else is too much. It's where so many of your memories were made with your parents, and even though they're always with you, I know this is where you two feel them the most."

My eyes settle on Vivi, making snow angels in the grass. Grass angels? I don't fucking know. "It's where Vivi remembers her Gramps, and she loves it here. You love it here. I love it here." I look at Claire, my favorite blubbering mess. "I want our child to love it here, to know they'll always have another place to call home."

Claire throws herself into my lap, soaking my neck as she whispers how much she loves me, over and over again.

"Now you can come back here whenever you need a break. When you want to see the stars that you can't see in the city. When you want to just sit out here and be in nature without all the noise, the lights, the bullshit. When you just need a reminder, you can come home, whenever you want. It'll always be yours."

I'm on the phone with my mom when I walk through the door on Monday evening, and Claire's not here. After today, though, we'll forever be coming home to each other, and that's something I can get behind, a forever I didn't want until her.

Though she hasn't spent a night there since we've officially been together, today is the day Claire finally says goodbye to her apartment.

"—and the cutest little suspenders. But I bought a dress, too. I know you think it's a boy, but just in case. I mean, you never know. Avery, you should just see the dress. It's adorable. And you can keep it, even if it's a boy, because then you can have a girl for your second. And, oh! Your dad's painting the baby's room, because of course we'll have a room here, and I'm thinking we should go with a nice pale bl—"

"Mom," I cut her off with a chuckle, dropping my bag by the door and tugging my tie over my head. I ruffle Sully's ears and spy the note Claire left on the counter, letting me know she's downstairs grabbing the last of her stuff. "For the love of God, woman, take a breath. You know Claire's not due 'til March, right?"

"March will be here before you know it, Avery." Her tone tells me she's unimpressed that I've momentarily dashed her dreams and has likely got her arms pinned across her chest.

I hope March *does* get here before I know it. I can't wait to meet our baby, to be a dad. I hope I'll do an okay enough job, but I don't half-ass things, so, I guess I'm feeling a little confident about the whole thing.

Which means I'll probably have my ass absolutely handed to me when the baby gets here.

"Any luck with a house?" Mom asks.

"No," I say with a sigh. "Claire says I'm too picky." I think she's not picky *enough*. "I just want it to be perfect."

Mom hums her agreement. "Well, don't worry. You have plenty of time. You'll find your perfect. Besides, as long as you're together, it'll always be perfect."

It's when she says things like that that remind me why I love her crazy, and why I went to her for advice about Claire all those months ago, *regardless* of her crazy.

Throwing my suit over a chair in the bedroom, I pull on a pair of jogging shorts and a t-shirt. "Alright, Mom. I gotta go find my girlfriend and tear her away from her old apartment."

One of my mom's famous, heavy sighs fills the phone. "Avery," she says, exasperated, even though I haven't done a damn thing to warrant said exasperation. "When are you going to ask that girl to marry you?"

"Soon enough."

"Soon enough? What the hell does that even mean? You better do it before she smartens up and ditches your ass on the side of the damn road. Don't be an idiot."

Keeling over with a laugh so deep it makes my cheeks hurt and belly clench, I shake my head. "Thanks, Mom. I love you, too."

After I hang up, I pull two canvases out of the closet in the spare bedroom. Harper took both pictures. One is Claire and I the morning after we started dating. I'm leaning my forehead against hers, smiling like a goof. The second picture is from Claire's birthday at the cottage. Gavin's got Vivi on his shoulders, Claire wrapped around one arm, and Casey by his side, their backs to the camera as they watch the sun sink low over the lake. Claire has no idea this picture even exists.

I prop both up on the walnut shelves that Casey and Gavin made, the ones I took down from Claire's wall yesterday and hung back up here in our living room.

And then I make my way downstairs to collect my girlfriend.

542

Claire is standing in the middle of the empty space, looking around, just soaking it all in, the very last box sitting at her feet. Stepping up beside her, I slip my arm around her waist and press my lips to her temple.

"How was your first day back at work?"

She turns to me with a smile. "It was good. I'm so happy to be back. The time off was nice, but I missed it." She snuggles into my side, a soft, happy sound leaving her throat. "Dex gave me a raise."

I snort a laugh. The brewery has had an insane summer with their patio expansion. The kitchen and restaurant only opened earlier this month, but business is absolutely booming. Weddings are fully booked for the fall, and after their first successful wedding last weekend, he drunkenly announced that he was giving everyone raises. "You deserve it, sweetheart."

"I haven't worked in three weeks. Four if you count my crappy attendance my last week there."

"Life happens," I remind her. "But you were integral in the expansion projects. You worked your ass off."

"Hmm." She spins into my chest, fingers dancing up my biceps, sweeping over my shoulders. "I did, didn't I? Is that what drew you to me?"

"Mmm..." I pretend to think, pulling my bottom lip into my mouth, squinting. "It was that color-coded binder of yours. So damn sexy," I whisper, brushing my lips across hers.

Her grin lights up her face before she rests her cheek on my chest, staring out the window.

"Will you miss it?" I ask her quietly.

"No," Claire says without hesitation. "I'm happy to be closing this chapter. But do you know what my favorite memory here is?" She turns back to me with a coy smile, teeth pressing into her lower lip. "When you came over and saved me from the monster spider."

I throw my head back, laughing. "It was tiny."

"It was on performance-enhancing drugs."

I scoop the box off the floor and tangle my fingers with hers, kissing her soft pout. "Come on, roomie. I hid a spider somewhere upstairs and I can't wait to see how long it takes you to find it. Your frying pan is waiting on the counter."

"I knew my spidey senses were tingling. Is that what's for dinner?"

"Only the best for the woman I never thought I'd find."

"This one's nice," I call over my shoulder, scrolling through the pictures on my laptop from my spot on the couch.

"You say that about all of them," Claire shouts back. She's been standing in front of the wall of pictures for nearly an hour. Some of that time has been spent rearranging photos, but for the most part, she's just staring at the two canvases I put up. "And then you hate every single one when we go see it."

"Well, they're not good enough," I grumble. They manage to hide all the imperfections in the photos when they list a house for sale. But I'm detail-oriented, so I don't miss a single thing once I'm inside. Our realtor hates me.

"Avery, you know I don't care. I'll be happy anywhere with you. I'm happy here."

"You won't be forever. We need a yard."

We have two dogs and a cat who likes to randomly take off at the speed of light across the entire length of the condo. Sure, they look cute right now—Sully, Turkey, and Chester all snuggled up on the giant dog bed together. But in the middle of the night, I swear the entrance to hell has been opened.

"I've been living here all of two hours and you're already looking for a new place to live."

"You've been living here since you accidentally told me you love me," I mumble around a handful of Sour Cherry Blasters. They're the only thing that keep Claire's nausea at bay, so I bought

544

twenty bags at the grocery store last week. It's not faring well for me so far. My tongue is raw, and we're already down five bags.

Claire sinks down to the cushion beside me, resting her head on my shoulder. "That one looks nice. Let's buy it."

"You've looked at one picture!"

"And it's a very nice powder room."

"You're infuriating."

"You're picky."

"Damn right I am. That's why you're mine."

Giggling, she touches her lips to mine. "I really don't care where we live, Avery. I want you to choose."

"You gotta give me something," I plead, shaking her. "Brick or siding? Two-car garage or three? Unfinished basement or finished? Pool or no pool?"

She thinks for a moment, tapping her chin. "Pool."

"Hell yeah!" I whoop, punching a fist through the air. Grabbing her, I tip her backwards over the couch, covering her body with mine as I drop my laptop to the ground. "We're fucking getting somewhere!"

"Does that one have a pool?"

"No." With my foot, I slam the lid down on the laptop. "We'll have to keep looking."

Claire lets out the longest, most dramatic groan I've ever heard. I consider timing it on my watch once we pass the ten-second mark.

"Are you done?" I ask with the arch of my brow and a smile I can't get rid of.

She smirks up at me. "Maybe. Can we go to bed?"

"Bed?" I slide my mouth across hers, then down her neck and across the expanse of her shoulder, yanking the collar of her tee to the side as I go. "It's only 7:30."

"I know. And I wanna spend the rest of the night in our bed. Naked," she adds on a whisper, nipping my earlobe.

545

She had me at *our bed,* but I'll take the naked part, too. In fact, I rip her clothes off and leave them right there on the couch before I toss her over my shoulder and cart her off to *our bed.*

She bounces with a yelp and a giggle when I drop her to the mattress, grinning up at me like a stunning, breathtaking fool while she watches me pull my clothes off, tripping over my shorts in all my eagerness to be naked, too.

"Come here," I whisper once I make it to the bed, sinking my fingers into her luscious ginger waves, hauling her to me.

The second our lips meet, it's explosive, just the way it always is, filled with unrelenting love and passion for the woman who owns my heart.

Claire pushes me back into the pillows and climbs on top of me, straddling my hips, her hot, wet mouth sliding down my neck until she pauses on my collarbone. "Our baby's going to be so stubborn and hard-headed."

"Just like you," I manage, her teeth nipping at my skin. "What the hell have I gotten myself into?"

Her face lifts as she sinks down onto my cock, tugging on my hair, pulling my head back. Her grin is pure evil as she starts moving, hips rocking. Dropping her lips to my ear, the tip of her tongue flicks out to taste my skin. "The best time of your life."

Fuck, she's not wrong. Life has been anything but ordinary with Claire, yet I wouldn't have it any other way. It hasn't always been easy, but it's always been worth it. Each day is better than the last, a promise for the future, for a life worth living to the fullest with her by my side.

"You are my life," I tell her honestly. My eyes float down her body, settling on the softness of her tiny, eleven-week belly. I place my hand over our baby before sliding my arm around her back, cupping her cheek when I bring Claire into me, kissing her softy. "Everything I'll ever need is right here in my arms."

And then I wrench her off of me, flipping her over and yanking her up to her hands and knees, where I slam into her with reckless abandon.

Because that's the way I love her, and the way I always will.

Wildly.

EPILOGUE

Claire

I let out a groan from where I'm sprawled out on the couch. Turkey's got his tongue in my ear while Sully cleans my toes, and Chester's dashing around the house chasing after a wayward feather that's escaped from one of these giant pillows on the couch.

And I'm fucking starving.

Snapping a selfie of my pouting face with Turkey's head on my shoulder, I send it to Avery with a quick message letting him know that mama's hungry.

His response rolls in a minute later, with a picture of a greasy bag of Wendy's in his front seat, and the world's largest Frosty in the console.

Avery: *Mama's beautiful. On my way.*

I swear I didn't send him out for food. He happened to be going out with my brother, and as he walked out the door, I gently suggested that a Frosty sounded nice. He reminded me that there was leftover dinner in the fridge for lunch, but kissed my cheek and promised to pick me up something anyway. Just one of the many reasons I love him.

Wrapping a fuzzy blanket around my shoulders, I pick my tea up off the counter and slip out the patio door and into our backyard.

The pool is closed—we never got to use I this year, because we've only been here for a week. Avery considered cranking the heater up to ninety, but I just think October's not really pool weather in Canada.

I smile as I take in the changing colors of the leaves, the candy apple reds, the rust oranges, the deep purples. It's all stunning back here in our little oasis.

Avery found this house two days after I officially moved into his condo. It hadn't even hit the market yet, but he bullied the realtor into an early showing. I say bullied, he says persuaded.

Still, I'm glad he did. It's one of those times I hate to admit I love how relentless and unwavering he is. I love every inch of this place, and it's only a ten-minute walk to his parents' house. Jess has been over every day, naturally. Austin ambles over an hour or so later, apologizing for letting her escape from the asylum again.

I don't mind, of course. Avery and his dad have been working on the baby's room already. Casey's building us a custom crib with a matching dresser. It's coming together so quickly, regardless of the fact that we've been here only seven days and I'm not due 'til mid-March.

And Lord help me, I cannot wait for this baby to come. I haven't been able to keep a single Crunchwrap Supreme down since week ten. I think it's my mom's doing. She always scrunched her nose up at me when I ate them, warning me that they were going to make me sick. Well, they finally did. So. Fucking. Sick.

"How's my gorgeous baby mama?"

I look over my shoulder, watching that handsome man of mine slip out the door. He scoops me up in his arms, sliding beneath me on the lounger, nuzzling his face into my neck.

Is it crazy to admit I actually love this term of endearment? It's constant, all the baby mamas flying from this man's mouth. Last week, we went to a black-tie dinner and dance fundraiser where he promptly introduced me as his baby mama to every single person we talked to, one protective hand laid across my belly at all times. I hid my red face in my hands, but an hour in, I tugged him off to a private bathroom, locked us in, and made him have me for dessert. I couldn't help it. He's so proud to be a daddy, and that just cranks my gears in a way I can't explain.

My tummy chooses this moment to growl like an angry bear. I grin up at Avery. "Hungry."

With a rumbly chuckle, he carts me off to the kitchen, setting me down on the edge of the counter, and unpacks my supersize french fries and equally large Frosty. He swipes a fry through the ice cream and pops it in his mouth, earning a swat on the shoulder from me. *My fries.*

My legs swing happily from my spot while I grab for my food. "Thank you, baby."

Avery's deep brown eyes travel down my body, taking in my lack of pants and his baggy t-shirt hanging off one shoulder. "You aren't dressed yet."

"No." I tear the lid off my Frosty, swirling my hot, salty fries around before shoving them past my lips, humming while I chew. Curling my legs around his waist, I pull him into me.

Avery's eyes crinkle with his smile. "Why not?"

I lift a shoulder and let it fall. Both our gazes fall to my little eighteen-week baby belly as a dollop of ice cream drips from my handful of fries, splattering on the white tee.

"Because I knew that was gonna happen."

His eyes squeeze shut with his laughter as he tips forward, leaning his forehead against mine. "I fucking love you." With a napkin, he cleans the ice cream off my shirt before he pushes the cotton up, dropping a kiss to my belly. "And I fucking love this belly."

"How was the shop?" I ask, feeding Avery a smothered fry.

"Good," he mumbles, swallowing. "It's coming along. On track to open mid-December, but we might push it to January. Casey's busting his balls."

"So are you," I remind him.

Avery and Casey have gone into business together. It's rather annoying at times, because my brother is over almost every night, nothing but shoptalk about wood and tools going on. But I'm happy for them, especially Casey. He's still teaching at the college, but this is his last semester.

After talking with Avery, I gave my half of the money from the sale of Dad's house to Casey. I don't need it, but he does. He put a chunk of it aside for Vivi, another handful aside for a down payment on a house, and the rest went into the shop they purchased a few weeks ago.

Casey's had a particularly tough go since Dad's passing, and this has brought him so much happiness. I'm glad to see him get what he wants, what he deserves.

When I'm all done with my five-star meal, Avery pulls me off the counter, claps a hand to my ass, and says, "Go get dressed before I bend you over the couch and fuck you so hard our baby feels how much I love its mama. We have company coming."

I'm bubbling with excitement an hour later, looking around our yard. Charlee and Harper have been outside for the last forty minutes, draping pink and blue balloons and decorations over every inch of greenspace.

Charlee wraps her arms around me from behind, the two of us swaying. "I can't wait to find out if my little munchkin godchild is going to be a girl or a boy."

"Boy," I answer without hesitation.

She spins around me, tapping my nose. "You never know. Wouldn't put it past your dad to screw with you."

I laugh, because she's not wrong. But I know he was right. I can feel it, feel our little boy inside of me. Still, there's a part of me that wonders…what if? Dad was so sure he'd met him in his dream, and I want that to be true. I want our baby to have known his Gramps. And his Gram.

Wyatt strolls through the patio door with Vivi on his shoulders and Casey at his side. Harper huffs, smashing down a sign she made on the table.

"Seriously," she mutters, turning to us, hands in the air. "Why does he have to carry Vivi around?"

"Because he adores her," I say. Everyone does; we know this already.

A sneaky smile lingers on Charlee's lips as she studies Harper. "You've got the hots for Wyatt."

"I do not!" Harper pins her arms across her chest, her gaze shifting sideways, cheeks turning pink as she catches Wyatt's eye. He winks at her, sliding Vivi down his front so she can terrorize the dogs.

"You do so," Charlee says. "You're into your brother's best friend!"

"Am not! He's a pig!"

"Are too! He's sexy as hell!"

"*You're* into your brother's best friend!" Harper whisper-yells, jabbing Charlee in the shoulder. "And your best friend's brother!"

Charlee just smiles and shrugs, plucking a cookie off the table and popping it in her mouth. "You're not wrong."

These girls of mine are crazy. I don't know why I let them talk me into having a gender reveal party.

Oh, wait. Yes I do. Because these girls are *crazy*.

"Auntie Claire!" Vivi yells. She holds her hands up in the air and spreads her legs. "I comin'!" I watch her tuck and roll, somersaulting across the grass to me. When she crashes into my legs, she jumps up, smooshing her face into my belly.

"Hi baby," Vivi whispers against my stomach. "It your big sister, Bibi." Big sister, because she's dead set on it. Bibi, because she can't pronounce her own name. Smiling up at me, she gives my belly a rub before smooching it. Then she dashes away, making a beeline for Avery's parents as they step into the yard.

"Oh," I say with a little gasp, rubbing a hand over my belly when something kicks inside me with a little more ferocity than the flutters only I've been able to feel from the inside out.

And then it happens again, this time with a even more intensity, just enough to knock the air right from my lungs.

"*Avery!*" I shriek.

His wild eyes tear my way as he shoves his drink into Wyatt's chest, dashing across the yard to me. "What? Are you okay? What's wrong?" His hands run down my arms, lifting them as he looks me over, checking to make sure I'm still fully intact.

I place his hand over my belly and wait. Sure enough, there it is, as if that tiny thing in there knows Daddy is right on the other side.

Avery's lips part, his lashes fluttering as his eyes lift to mine. "Is that…it's…"

"He's moving," I whisper.

A single tear rolls down his cheek as he presses both hands to my stomach, letting them roam as Baby Beck flits around in there. He bends his head, nose skimming my belly.

"Hi baby," Avery murmurs. "It's your daddy. I love you so much."

"Don't touch me," Harper sobs out. I glance up to find her camera in one hand, tears streaming down her face while she simultaneously tries to take our picture and swat away Wyatt.

"You're crying," Wyatt half laughs. "Harps, you're turning into your mom." He pulls her into his arms, hugging her, and she only struggles for a moment. His arm darts out, wrapping around Jess' trembling hand, and he tugs her into their hug, holding both overly emotional Beck women while they cry.

Ten minutes later, when all the tears have been tucked away— temporarily, I'm sure—Avery, Vivi, and I gather around one lone, oversize gray balloon.

Avery hands the string to Vivi. "You know the drill, munchkin?"

Her head bobs. "I hold da balloon. You pop it. Stuff spwinkle out."

"And if it's blue?" Avery asks.

"It a boy!" she screams. "I get a brudder!"

He chuckles, smoothing back her hair. "And if it's pink?"

Vivi's brows pinch together with her less than impressed pout. "It not be pink. It be blue."

Our friends and family count us down from ten, and when we hit zero, Vivi shrieks at Avery to *go, go, go!* With his eyes on me and a soft smile, he raises the pin to the balloon.

A loud pop fills the air.

Blue confetti rains down from the sky, decorating our hair, clinging to Avery's eyelashes as he swoops in for a kiss, murmuring how much he loves me into my mouth.

Fresh tears stream down my cheeks as my heart soars with joy.

Avery joins me in the living room later that night, one of his hoodies in his hands. He looks deliriously delicious in a pair of low-hanging sweatpants and a long-sleeve Henley that shows off every curve and dip of his outrageously glorious muscles.

"Want to watch the sunset?" he asks, fitting the neck of his sweater over my head.

Smiling up at him when he takes my hand, I let him haul me off the couch. "That sounds nice."

Curling up on the lounger, Avery retreats back into the house to retrieve a blanket. When he returns, I snuggle into his chest, enjoying the feel of being wrapped up in him while the sun glows orange and pink as it descends toward the horizon.

Avery's lips meet my neck, my cheek, my ear. "Are you happy, Claire?"

Twisting, I capture his mouth with mine. "So damn happy."

I feel his smile against my lips before he turns to gaze out at our yard. "Do you like it here? Do you like the house?"

He knows I do. I still secretly think the biggest reason he chose this particular house is because when we came for the viewing, he discovered that the Toronto Blue Jay's first baseman lives next door. He happened to be getting out of his truck with his gear when we were finishing up, and Avery fan-girled *hard*.

We made an offer on the house forty-five minutes later, and an hour after that it was accepted, even though the house hadn't officially been listed on the market yet. But because Avery's Avery, he doesn't do anything half-assed—he made a generous offer substantially over asking price. He says it's because my face lit up when we walked around, and it did, but, well…you know him.

"I love it here, Avery. I love our house. But you know I would've been happy with you anywhere."

"I know," he says softly. "You always say that."

"Because it's true. With you is my favorite place to be."

"Mine too." The sun dips just low enough at this moment to trigger the solar twinkly lights strung across the yard. Avery sucks in a deep, raspy breath. "Claire," he whispers, shifting beneath me.

He slips out of the chair, and I watch in slow motion as he sinks to the ground beside me on one knee.

My heart stops.

For a second.

And then it detonates.

Avery tucks his hand in his pocket, pulling out a small, blushing velvet box.

And I'm still not breathing. My jaw's just hanging there in midair while I watch his hands shake, watch him scrub an anxious hand over his jaw, his eyes.

"Fuck, I'm so nervous," he mutters, I think to himself. Those soulful, penetrating, chocolate brown eyes rise to meet mine. "Claire, I-I…fuck," he says with a sigh and a tiny chuckle. "I think you broke me, baby."

"Avery…" I cup his cheek, thumb sweeping under his eye. "What are you doing?"

"What does it look like?" His grin is wobbly, not the self-assured smirk that pissed me off so much when I first met him. I've never seen him like this before.

555

"You don't...you don't have to do this." For God's sake, why the hell am I talking?

His smile falters as he drops back to his butt on the concrete. The increase in distance is marginal, but I'm acutely aware of it. And I hate it.

"What do you mean?"

"I mean...you don't have to do this, if this is just what you think needs to happen. If this is what you think you're supposed to do." I look down. Down at my hands. Down at his hands, which are clutched tightly around that pretty box. "If you don't...want to."

Still talking, eh, Claire? Cool. Keep going. See where that gets you.

I'm not sure what I expect. Maybe for him to just sit there in silence, staring up at me. Maybe a fight. Maybe for him to just stand up and walk away, cool off on his own. Maybe even a breath of relief, an *oh thank God; I'm so not ready for this!*

Whatever I expected, it certainly wasn't this. Not Avery, sitting here in front of me, that goofy grin sliding onto his face, taking over.

"Luckily, I was prepared for this."

I've never been more confused. "You were?"

"Mhmm," he hums, head bobbing with a nod. "You wouldn't be you, the woman I love, if you didn't make my proposal so fucking difficult with your hard-headedness."

Avery pulls me off the chair and into his lap. His fingers dance over my face, twisting a loose wave before he tucks it behind my ear. When his arms encircle me, wrapping me up, all I feel is his warmth, his love, his utter devotion, to me, to our family, and I swear I could drown in it.

"Claire, from the moment I met you, you've made my life anything but easy. You're stubborn, infuriating, and extremely hotheaded at times. In fact, sometimes I piss you off just so I can bend you over my knee and slap your ass so hard, get you more riled up before I fuck you sideways."

I fall forward with a bubble of laughter, and he beams, tipping my chin up, his lips meeting mine for a soft, sweeping kiss.

"You've fought me every damn step of the way, but I'm a better man because of it. You taught me the value of being relentless in going after the things I want, and what I want, what I've always wanted...it's you, Claire. Your love. To share the space you're in. To share your time, your life. You're my best friend, my favorite sparring partner, and my family. The only place I want to spend the rest of my life is right next to you, wherever you are."

I'm grateful for the suburbs, for our oasis smackdab in the middle of a concrete jungle. Because here in our little bubble, I can hear the quiet, quick pitter-patter of my heart as it restarts, looking into the eyes of the man who showed me what true love is, what it looks like, how it feels.

Avery looks down between our chests and I follow his gaze to find him turning the box in his hands. He licks his lips, looking back up at me. "Can I finish what I was doing before you interrupted me?"

A giggle puffs past my lips. "Please."

"I love you, Claire. I think I knew that it would be you from the moment we met. I saw you, and something inside me just clicked, like I'd known you before. You strolled into my life and took over without even trying. I can't even..." He trails off, eyes falling shut as he shakes his head. I drop a tender kiss to his lips.

"I can't even remember what it was like before you came along. All I know is that my life was lonely and empty. It wasn't living. You brought me to life, Claire. You gave me a family I never knew I wanted. My heart exploded when I met you."

He looks back down at the box in his trembling hands. With careful fingers, he flips the lid, revealing the most breathtaking ring I've ever seen. The teardrop emerald shines up at me, the tiny

557

diamonds wrapping around it, decorating the delicate gold band, catching the twinkle from the lights above, the moon in the sky.

Avery takes my hand in his, bringing it to his lips, kissing each finger. "You're the love of my life, Claire. Spend forever with me. Dive in with me. Please...*marry me.*"

I meet his timid gaze, feel the gentle quiver of his hand as it holds mine, as if he's really not sure that my answer will be anything but—

"Yes."

"Yes?"

"Yes, Avery." A grin absolutely shatters my face as I throw myself at him, tackling him backwards to the ground as I shower him with kisses. "Yes, yes, yes, a thousand times yes!"

Avery's arms come around me, crushing me to him. He rolls us onto the grass, settling himself between my legs as he looms over me. "*Mine,*" is all he growls, before he shoves the ring onto my finger.

"You and me, Claire. It's you and me, forever."

It's the only forever I want, and the one I never expected, the one I never saw coming.

I never wanted to love him. I found excuse after excuse to deny what was right there in my heart, drawing me toward him like a magnet.

I drafted lies in my mind, placed another man's mistakes on his shoulders, replaced the love in my heart with a fear so deep I couldn't see straight.

But the truth is, and has always been, that Avery is the very thing that keeps me grounded. He evens me out, the calm to my storm, the rain to my fire, bringing me down to that perfect simmer where everything is just right. He's my comfort and my support system, my challenger and my biggest fan. My very best friend and the love of my life.

Avery is mine. That's all he'd ever been, and all I'd ever need him to be.

Letting him brush the hair from my eyes, tucking it behind my ear. I melt into his touch. With my face in his strong, capable hands, he pulls me into him for a tender kiss that soothes the aches that linger inside me and brews a love so strong and deep that shakes me right down to my core.

"I love you, Avery," I whisper against his soft, full lips.

"I love you wild, Claire. Always have, always will."

The End

Acknowledgements

Writing this right now is so utterly surreal.

I could have never imagined I'd be here, only dreaming to one day be able to create a world in which readers could escape, be swept away, and fall in love. And yet here I am. How did I get here?

I got here with the help of my people, the ones who believed in me and supported me every step of the way.

My husband, Richard, is the first person I need to thank. You heard my dream and didn't doubt it. You cheered me on from the beginning and didn't question the countless hours I spent buried behind my laptop, up all night writing and re-writing. You boasted about me everywhere you could, whenever you could, proud of every small milestone I hit along the way in my writing journey. Thank you for being my best friend and my partner.

To my friends and family, the ones who were eager to support me, to help me reach my dreams—thank you. Thank you for your unrelenting love and encouragement. Thank you for believing in me (and not judging me for the spicy scenes).

To Liz Tom, my first and best Wattpad friend. You are amazing and so utterly talented, and I can't wait to own all the books you're going to write and publish. Thank you for being my sounding board when I need one, my shoulder to lean on, and my voice of reason when things get hard. Having you in my corner during this journey is something I wouldn't trade for the world.

To my amazing Wattpad readers who go on every journey with me, no matter the destination—thank you. You guys deserve your own party, preferably with booze, Taco Bell, and exceptionally sexy, large men. Thank you for being the type of people who lift me up and cheer me on. Thank you for falling in love with Claire and Avery, for sticking with me since Day 1. Thank you for loving the smut and the kinks, enduring the rollercoaster ride, feeling all the feels, and making me smile with your incredible—and often

560

outrageously ridiculous/hilarious—comments. You're one hell of a group.

Thank you to Miss Bizzarro (your name will forever remain unchanged in my heart) for being the most incredible teacher ever, one I was lucky enough to have for two years in a row. Thank you for telling me all those years ago that I could do it, that you believed in me. The words of a compassionate teacher when you're just a kid who dreams will always stick with you.

To Jonathan, my editor, thank you for taking my first manuscript ever and helping me make it better. Thank you for all your hard work, and I hope I didn't scare you too much with Claire and Avery's experimentation chapter.

A ginormous thank you to Vanessa, my publisher. Thank you for seeing the potential in my writing, for falling in love with Claire and Avery's story. Thank you for taking the time to understand the characters, their past and present, the things that make them tick, and the things that make their story unique. Thank you for your unending support on this journey. You've taken my dream and made it come true. I can never thank you enough for that.

And lastly, to the person who left this earth way too soon, who reminded me that life is worth living and dreams are worth chasing…thank you. I would have never stepped outside of my comfort zone, would have never pursued my wildest dream, if it weren't for you. I miss you, and I love you.

Did you enjoy Love You Wild?

Leave 5 stars and a nice comment to share the love!

You didn't like it?

♠

Write to us to suggest the kind of novel you dream of reading!
https://cherry-publishing.com/en/contact/

Subscribe to our Newsletter to stay up to date with all of our upcoming releases and latest news!
You can subscribe according to the country you're from:

You are from...

US:
https://mailchi.mp/b78947827e5e/get-your-free-ebook

UK:
https://mailchi.mp/cherry-publishing/get-your-free-uk-copy